The RAM
and
The SYNDICATE
Part VI

by Mark Cunnington

*To Dave
Happy Fishing
Mark Cunnington*

Trio Publishing

Also by Trio Publishing

The Syndicate
The Syndicate 2nd Edition
The Syndicate (R.I.P.) Part II
Return of The Syndicate Part III
Running The Syndicate Part IV
Revenge of The Syndicate Part V

First published 2008

Published by Trio Publishing
50 Gillsman's Park
St. Leonards on Sea
East Sussex
TN38 0SW

ISBN 978 0 9537951 5 4

Copyright © Mark Cunnington 2008

All rights reserved. No part of this publication may be reproduced, stored or introduced into any type of retrieval system, or transmitted, in any form, or by any means without the prior written permission of the publisher.

This book is sold subject to the condition that it shall not, by way of trade or otherwise, be lent, re-sold, hired out or otherwise circulated without the publisher's prior consent in any form of binding or cover other than in which it is published and without a similar condition including this condition being imposed on the subsequent purchaser.

Printed and bound by Chandlers Printers Ltd
Heathfield, East Sussex

INTRODUCTION

As humans we all fear danger and unpredictability. If we manage to avoid them completely, and all traces of them completely, a different fear can emerge – the fear of stale conformity and of being in a rut. In old age this latter fear hardly matters, is desirable in fact, yet to the young and energetic, safe and boring is worse than danger and unpredictability. For those on the cusp of losing youth to middle age the notion can be equally distracting. Sometimes, however, you can get a little too much of what you wish for.

Our story starts from where we left it.

Chapter 1

The Eye was dead – sort of. Not in the traditional six foot under, shuffled off this mortal coil, pushing up the daisies definition, but dead in terms of seeing into the future regards the capture of large carp when under the influence of mind-altering, 'good stuff', Swiss, bootlegged absinthe. The Eye couldn't 'see' anymore. The shutter had slammed down on his window into the future and despite his desperate attempts to lever it upwards – much to his complete devastation – it wouldn't budge one measly millimetre. I had pondered on whether I should start calling him The Eye*patch*!

Whatever section the Dutch surgeon had cut out of his brain to rid him of his life-threatening tumour, the one I had so heroically warned him of – eventually – after spotting it during my brief sortie into his brain, had not only cancelled out his cancer, it had also cancelled out his curious capacity to cast his clairvoyant conscious unto his upcoming carping captures. The surgeon's scalpel had saved his life and in the process, although he would have been totally unaware of the fact, had cut a huge part out of it. As far as The Eye was concerned the surgeon had used a double-edged scalpel.

"*Man*! The Eye can't *see* no more!" he had raged in summary after imparting the latest chapter of his life story to me via mobile phone in his peculiar, truncated, chopped style of speech. "Fucked The Eye's brain!"

"Yeah… *but*, you've got to remember you're clear of the cancer. *And* the chemo's finished. You know, the big picture and all that." I had reminded him. It had been six months since his operation and all tests pointed to him being in the clear. "Think yourself lucky you don't live in the UK! You'd probably still be stuck on a bed in a corridor waiting for the bloody scan, or if by some chance you had managed to get the op, died from a flesh-eating superbug!" I had all the relevant incorrigible facts to hand – I do read the newspapers occasionally, when I can drag myself away from the latest informative PVA bag article in a glossy carp magazine.

"What made The Eye The *Eye*!" he had protested, ignoring my sage pronunciation on the current balance of his life.

Feeling The Eye's appraisal of his situation was something akin to a man who had won a luxury yacht quibbling over the colour of the seating upholstery, I had heaved a heavy sigh. "You're *alive*, The Eye. Alive and kicking… alive and *fishing*! Alive and fishing, I might add, armed with a certain exclusive, revolutionary, indented, dirty brown bottom bait boilie! Besides," I had said, "you can still knock back the absinthe whenever you feel like it."

"Don't want to sound ungrateful," The Eye had said ungratefully. "Not the same.

Drinking for the sake of it. The Eye's fishing blind, man."

The Eye's arguments were risible. I had felt like telling The Eye to stop his shameful griping. 'Drinking for the sake of it' – I ask you. A billion pound industry was propped up on *that* little actuality. An endemic binge drinking culture had seen a multitude of staggering drunks (including English cricketers) puking up in town centres and wobbling around on foreign pedalos. Ladettes lying paralysed by inebriation on main roads, swathes of inner city A&E departments swamped with the physical consequences of alcohol-fuelled violence and a mass of sexual conquests with all their attendant repercussions – STDs, unwanted pregnancies, lost virginities and sobering (only too late) experiments in sexuality – were all firmly camped on the doorstep of 'drinking for the sake of it'.

And as for fishing blind! There were thousands of anglers who fished blind all the time – it was hardly a radical concept. In fact all of us had done it to a greater or lesser degree throughout our fishing careers. A new water situation, a no clues, no shows day, no gen to go on after a month away, the night-time re-cast when proper provision for getting back on the spot had been forgotten, sheer laziness – all factors in the 'smack the baits out there and chance it' scenario. In any case, his absinthe success rate, or lack of it, meant he was fishing blind, or at least without the aid of foresight vision, for the bulk of the time.

Rather than getting his stiff rig hooklength in a knot over this occasional loss of foresight, he ought to be thankful he wasn't dead. Thankful the Grim Reaper hadn't nipped back from his heavy workload in Baghdad, Afghanistan, Dalfur – wherever – to fit him in and finish him off. Thankful chance had led us to meet and I had spotted his black smudge. The dark, brooding, deep black smudge of active cancer to which I had alerted him – an act which had undoubtedly contributed to saving his life as much as the skill of his consultant surgeon. In any case, as I had pointed out, now he was in possession of the exclusive, revolutionary, indented, dirty brown bottom bait boilie he wouldn't *need* to see. The awesome power of Pup's megaboilie would do the seeing for him!

I had previously sent The Eye his first instalment (ten fun-packed kilos) of revolutionary, indented, dirty brown bottom bait boilie prior to his life-saving operation. I must admit I had considered it to be a bit of a gamble sending it. What if he had died on the operating table? Ten kilos of *our* exclusive bait could have fallen into the wrong hands! In the end I had managed to quash such thoughts and had posted it anyway. He deserved the bait by way of rewarding him for his input into my fantastic run of revenge – the one seeing the complete and utter ruination of the ex-handsome Hollywood. If The Eye thought he was having it tough losing his special absinthe-aided power, then he ought to try looking into the mirror to see the face of another man every morning. One surgically imposed on the gory, gaping bloody mess constituting the remnants of a previous visage thanks to it clashing with a whirling dervish of flailing outboard motor propeller. (As fiendishly instigated by yours truly! Take that, Hollywood! You fucking Frankenstein freak!) A replacement face, I would like to point out, *considerably* less handsome than the one chance had genetically dealt him at birth.

Now, that *was* something to whinge about! Never mind being cured of brain cancer and losing an incidental, sporadic, absinthe-dependent vision of where your next big carp was coming from. What about having your chops ripped off and being subjected to a face transplant? How about having to deal with the fundamental emotions of what actually constituted you as an individual and your feelings of personal identity, specifically feeling as you originally were internally and yet looking distinctly unoriginal and like someone *else* externally? It was you, but it wasn't. Pretty soon, I would have imagined, alienation from the trauma of not looking as you had for thirty odd years would be so psychologically damaging you wouldn't be 'you' on the *inside*.

In short, it's feasible you would experience mega personality breakdown, total psychological destruction followed by physical self-loathing and manic depression. What would you do? What *could* you do? You know, objectively and dispassionately speaking. I reckoned Hollywood's options were: join a circus as its resident freak, hit the lithium or end it all shotgun in the mouth, brains and blood up the wall, gore-fest style.

Ha-ha! Ha-ha²! Maybe even Ha-ha³! As usual the thought of Hollywood's horrendous accident/dilemma had immediately amused and soothed me and had engaged the more caring part of my nature. The caring part of my nature always comes to the fore when I think happy thoughts.

"Welcome to our world," I had said.

"*Our* world. Pah!" The Eye had corrected. "Still got yours."

This may or may not have been true.

I had had no more moments of brilliant white light shafting its way through dark clouds to illuminate the future since my correct diagnosis of The Eye's organic bullet in the head. Whether my powers were gone for good or simply lying dormant, waiting to spring into action at some as yet undefined, uncontrollable, unknowable instant as they had in the past, remained to be seen. Mind you, it wasn't for lack of trying. I had attempted, with the aid of The Eye's absinthe, to mind-meld with Amy to see if she was, as The Eye had been so sure, the actual reincarnation of the ghost. To find out once and for all if the ghost had transmigrated into the baby that had been growing in Sophie's womb. Metempsychosis The Eye had called it and I had tried in vain to substantiate his theory. I had once again drunk the peculiar tasting green liquid as I had that fateful night with The Eye. The one where I had sat around a bivvy table with four grapefruit scented candles, two glasses, a strange spoon, some sugar cubes, some cold water and several bottles of absinthe. Although that evening had ended fairly ignominiously, what with me falling face first through the bivvy table and The Eye hanging himself out to dry as mozzie fodder over his Trakker Armo MKII bivvy, I had at least succeeded in achieving my goal. When the repeat performance took place at a kitchen table with Amy sitting on her mother's lap, despite me not damaging either my face or my furniture, I had failed dismally. Amy's mind had stayed a locked compartment. A secret. A no-go area. Although I had slipped straight into The Eye's head I couldn't do it with Amy. In a way it was as it should be – what daughter would ever want her father knowing her every thought and classified adventure?

Sophie, a shaking, tremulous wreck during the whole episode, had kept asking. "Are you in? Are you in? Are you in yet?"

"No," I had said – had kept on saying, consoling myself that at least she wasn't asking me during an act of sexual intercourse.

Despite me drinking nearly a whole bottle and straining my consciousness as hard as could against the little girl opposite me, the answer had stayed the same. I hadn't been able to do it. I hadn't opened her mind. The Eye's theory was doomed to be forever so.

In retrospect, even if I had been able to, I wasn't so certain I would have found anything other than Amy's mind. Why would there have been any small part of the ghost's old consciousness left for me to find? Surely if the transmigration was complete I wouldn't find it, otherwise, I had theorised, someone somewhere would remember a past life. Most likely many *had* made such a claim and most likely they had all been spurious. I had simply never read the right colour supplements to glean such implausible information. Still, at least I had tried with Amy even if it had been without any success. Once again I was left to reflect on how my psychic powers had refused to work to order. I suspected the main reason the one time they had, had been more down to The Eye's efforts to open his mind rather than my prising it open with the cold, hard steel blade of my mental machinations.

Sophie and I had decided to let the matter rest with the one failed experiment. Amy was Amy, whatever she may or may not have been subjected to in her mother's womb. It was another strange facet of our lives we would have to learn to live with, one of many proving beyond resolve. As Rambo had said before, what was the point in beating yourself up over something which was impossible to get your head around? Although, personally speaking, this had been a concept far easier to say than to implement, I could now see a true, complete explanation of all my weird and wonderful adventures was never a real possibility. Now, after ridding myself of the Hollywood monkey on my back, it felt – perhaps for first time in my life – as if I could go with the flow and take Rambo's advice.

"How are things going on Pup's bait?" I had enquired of The Eye, changing the subject.

"Awesome!"

For once The Eye's answer hadn't sounded shortened and staccato. There really was nothing else to be said about Pup's incredible bait. He was *the* boiliemeister! "Well, there you go then," I had said. "You've nothing to moan about. You've lost one thing and gained another and I bet I know what will catch you the most fish overall!"

"The Eye knows, man." The Eye had admitted. "What made The Eye special, though."

"Better to be a living legend than a dead one," I had informed him.

There had been no reply and the implication had been The Eye was beginning to come to terms with his lot, much as I was coming to terms with mine. I hoped he was, I liked The Eye and would forever be in his debt for his contribution to my revenge plan. Even, and this was a big even, if I ended up supplying him with a container full of exclusive, revolutionary, indented, dirty brown bottom bait boilies.

Perhaps the strangest facet of my life since my successful run of revenge on Hollywood was the concept of living it on a more level and mundane footing than in the past. I could now virtually accept my previous adventures for what they were without forever searching for answers I could never attain. It was a huge, momentous personal stride forward and a sign of my recent maturity. And there was more. *Conflict*! Or rather the *lack* of it.

You see, there was no hideous competition going on, no sexual temptation, no ghost harassing me, no murder to solve, no fish stealing to stop, no *charadee* fish-in to organise with even more sexual temptation, no relationship threatening revelations to cope with and no run of revenge to plan. There was only relatively ordinary life to cope with, once the past was successfully compartmentalised, and it came as a bit of a shock to my system. It was genuinely how I felt, even if it was rather an inverse and perverse reaction to the situation.

In the aftermath of calm Sophie and I had continued the re-building of our relationship with a great deal of success and we were united in offering the best to Amy and each other. It was almost serene. I could focus on putting my new start with Sophie into fruition without distraction and really enjoy the delights of owning Hamworthy Fisheries.

The straggling offshoot ramifications of my last adventure were now all neatly concluded. The Eye was sorted for all intents and purposes, Rambo was settled with Steffi (international porn star to domestic goddess via relationship with ex-army, ex-mercenary, ex-gunrunning, ex-camouflage-clad man mountain) and he was as close as I supposed he ever would be with accepting the demise of 24/7 camo clothing. Pup was painlessly ensconced in The Syndicate, Hollywood was done and dusted and although it grated that a lot of my fish were still swimming in his syndicate lake, I could live with it. I could live with it because he was annihilated, his life an absolute train wreck – he was ex-Hollywood. His handsome face no longer featured in my sex life, which was more than good enough for me. I could write the stolen carp off, I had more than enough swimming in Hamworthy. And they were bigger. And they were growing faster. *And* my Dad was better than Hollywood's Dad.

Shoehorning Pup into The Syndicate hadn't been as awkward as I had first thought when I had struck the exclusive deal on the exclusive, revolutionary, indented, dirty brown bottom bait boilie. As luck would have it one of the members, Noel, dropped out for personal reasons – I'm not sure what it was and to be honest

I wasn't interested, maybe his wife had run off with his daughter's boyfriend, or son's girlfriend – and Pup with his four grand's worth of induction waiver, fifteen hundred quid's worth of yearly membership waiver and around another four grand's worth of stylish new kit funded by my cash-in-hand stock pond carp sale slotted straight into his place. He signed his contract, didn't pay his money and he was in! In return Rambo and I got our sticky mitts on his killer bait – the one Wilton had mauled Pup's arm in a fury for not being able to lick out the last few atoms' worth of base mix from a bowl.

(Incidentally, as a point of note, I think it's fair to say, if you are on a syndicate waiting list, please don't be under any illusion as to the democratic process supposedly waiting to give you a place in a fair, unbiased, judicious and rational manner. Oh no! It can be far more arbitrary than you could ever imagine! Syndicates are often run as a dictatorship, they are autocratic and membership can be won on a subjective whim or need – sometimes one wholly irrelevant to the supposed requirements of entrance. In Pup's case he had a killer boilie, which I, as Beloved Syndicate Leader, had need of, and so, on the strength of this one ace in his hand, he shot to the top of the list. He not so much jumped the queue as quantum leaped it. What about the rest who had patiently waited? What about those whose names had been on the list for years? I'm afraid there's no word to describe the noise shrugging shoulders make. My paramount consideration was exclusive access to the boilie and all else flew out the window! Let those on a syndicate list be warned!)

Pup had had an autumn's worth of good fishing to acquaint himself with all his new gear before Hamworthy shut up shop for winter. (As I think I might have mentioned before, Hamworthy *isn't* a winter water.) It had been interesting to watch him slowly get to grips with session fishing, to see him take off from his first underarm rod tip wrapper of a cast in the *charadee* fish-in. To see him get back into some sort of 'fishing head on' mode after years of anorak bait introspection. In those few short autumn months I like to think I had taken him under my wing, given him a little helpful nudge and guided him in the right direction regards swim choice, location and tactics.

Of course, the real reason wasn't down to altruism on my part; it was down to me checking up on him! I had been making sure the cunning whelp wasn't using *our* bait! I had paid big time for the exclusive, revolutionary, indented, dirty brown bottom bait boilie and just because he was the man who had rolled it, had *invented* it, didn't mean the sod could fish with it! It was mine! We had a deal. Mine to be shared with Rambo, and The Eye, now it looked as if he wasn't going to die young.

I had felt a bit like Tom Watt clocking the 180 degree rotated signpost Tropicano when I had fine tuned Pup's rig, the express intent, *obviously*, to check out the round thing hanging on the end of his fractionally too long hair rig. I had pointed this out.

Pup had eyed me coolly. He hadn't been fooled. "Don't worry, Matt. This *isn't* your bait. Only a boilie novice could ever begin to think this is the same bait as the one you're on. For a start, look at the consistency of the mix, its mass, its density."

I had gone to open my mouth only for Pup to put a finger to his lips. "Please *don't* embarrass yourself any more by saying it's a different colour as well. The colour of a bait is mostly irrelevant, not always, some mixes don't take colour readily, but your brown bait could be pink if I wanted it to be, blue even." I was thinking blue would suit better, for purely scanning and alliterative purposes. Pup continued. " *My* bait is one of the other five crackers I was telling you about… all Wilton approved. I'm at the fine tuning stage."

"Is it as good as my one?" I had asked feeling slightly miffed at the prospect of my bait having five others equally as good.

Pup had tilted his head and pulled his bottom lip up into his top one. "No. Not yet. Maybe it never will be."

"So what's in my one that makes it so special?"

Pup's brow had furrowed. "Not even *Melloney* knows the *full* answer to that question! Shame on you for asking, I've *told* you before!"

"How is she?" I had said, diverting the tack of a conversation clearly going nowhere near where I wanted.

"Fine."

"Melissa?"

"We're divorced."

"Really? You kept that quiet."

Pup had scrunched his shoulders. "She wanted to marry the American guy and I wasn't bothered if I ever saw her again so we got a quickie divorce. She didn't want anything from me, her new bloke…"

"Brad."

"…Yeah, *millionaire* Brad could give her everything she ever wanted, so I'm a single man again."

"And they said it would never last," I had said smiling.

"*They*, were right! Now where should I cast this one?"

"You see the big tree on the far bank, now follow its shadow on to the water… you want to be twenty yards short of the end of the shadow."

"Why? What's there?"

"The boot's on the other foot now," I had said grinning. "You'll catch from there without knowing why."

Pup had thrust a short burst of mocking air through his lips. "I'm *gutted*, believe me!"

Pup had caught, not spectacularly, but for a new face much better than average. Rambo and I with our superior watercraft, experience and venue knowledge and, oh yeah, Pup's exclusive, revolutionary, indented, dirty brown bottom bait boilie had had a field day. Fish up to the low fifties had graced both our rods, two each in fact, although neither fish was a candidate for a sitting with Alan, our resident artist. All four were previously known forties and all four had packed on the best part of ten pounds in a little over a season and a half.

Rambo had let out a low whistle. "Think how big your sixty might be now."

I already had and was moving on to other areas. "You've never had a sixty have you?" I enquired innocently.

"Do you know, boy, there are times when I wish you hadn't saved my life, then I could beat you to a pulp without feeling guilty."

"Only you couldn't because you'd be dead."

Rambo had waved a hand. "You're splitting hairs again, bringing up these incidental points."

I had given Rambo half a pout. "Next time I won't bother, how's that sound?"

Rambo had returned my pout with an earnest stare. "Let's hope there's *never* a next time."

Rambo had meant it, certainly. I, however, was having some odd feelings over whether I was quite so sure.

I had thought, what with the momentum of this new super bait going in, the pair of us could overcome Hamworthy's winter inertia and keep on catching all year round. I had been wrong. The odd blank had started to crop up and by the middle of November we had both started to struggle. How strange. Rambo had kept plugging away longer than I had, but in the end he had cut back to four trips a month and had spent more time with Steffi than I imagined he had ever spent with another human being – apart from the person being a soldier or me!

Christmas passed and the start of March saw Rambo's first spring capture despite the weather being mild throughout most of the winter. The number of morning frosts I could remember safely fitted on to the digits of both hands and along with the furore in the press our new 'one size fits all' scapegoat became global warming. (Help Save The Planet by unplugging your TV and not leaving it on standby mode.) Too hot, too cold, too wet, too dry, too windy, too still, not catching, a dropped fish, a bad cast, a snapped catty elastic, the breakdown of the family unit, feral, gun-toting, knife wielding gangs, pathetic politicians, higher taxes – *all* down to global warming. (Help Save The Planet by only boiling a partially filled kettle for your tea.) The funny thing was, some of it was true, particularly the façade of 'green taxes'.

Everyone – in the media that is – was talking of the moral judgement constituted by the evidence of your own personal carbon footprint. Measure it and weep! Hide your head in shame and crawl under a rock you disgusting, energy using, energy wasting, convenience shopping, car driving, airline seat occupying, plastic bag filling, Planet Earth murdering monster! How dare you unlock all that carbon dioxide with your inefficient heating, lighting, travelling and purchasing, you non-recycling barbarian!

From many of The Syndicate members' viewpoints the most pertinent effect of whatever it was that was happening could be seen in Hamworthy's gin-clear depths. Something was changing, had changed, and its impact was of interest and concern to all those wetting a line in Hamworthy's water. It was only early in the year and the evidence was right before my eyes.

"Why the hell do you think all this weed has taken hold? It never used to be weedy. Look at what's survived through the winter." I waved an expressive arm. "If it carries on growing like it did last summer it'll be nigh impossible to fish in some areas," I stated.

"Global warming, boy."

"I *knew* you'd say that," I told Rambo.

"Not that *you* believe it," Rambo replied watching me from the corner of his eye.

"Mm," I mumbled with non-commitment.

"You think it's because the ghost's gone don't you? Because Rocky foul-hooked the murderous ballpane hammer and put an end to whatever fifth dimensional powers the ghost was using to nudge it to our world's attention?" This was true, there was no point denying it, so I remained silent. "Tough one to prove," Rambo said with a smile laced with a little more sarcasm than I cared for.

"*Prove* global warming," I said.

"Oh, they can do that easily enough, boy. Don't you worry! When they start caning you for extra taxes to waste on some hair-brained scheme, they'll have all the facts and statistics to hand. There's money to be made in global warming, boy, good money. Consultants, research experts, government, alternative energy firms, ordinary firms extolling their green credentials, they'll all have their noses in the trough. Then some expert will say, hold on, the energy cost of making, fitting and maintaining your own personal wind turbine is twice what the fucking thing produces. The main reason being the wind's broken due to global warming and the reason the wind's broken is due to the destabilisation of the weather caused by excessive energy consumption." Rambo guffawed, seemingly pleased with his nonsensical circle of contradictions. "Everyone will be frantically adding up this, that and the other to see what fucks up the atmosphere most and they'll all arrive at different answers. The average man on the street won't stand a chance of making an informed decision. The only thing certain is the government will tax you to the hilt and charge you by the hour for everything associated with living and call it 'climate tax'. Meanwhile, China will gobble up energy and chuck out carbon dioxide so fast the rest of the world would need to never turn on a light bulb again to compensate. I reckon it'll be a better scam than the Y2K conspiracy."

I lifted my eyebrows in concurrence with events of eight years ago. "My central heating programmer was unaffected, I have to admit *and* the toaster never went down." I looked out over Hamworthy. "Something *is* happening, though. Whether it's a natural cycle or whether it's man-made I don't know, but we don't get winters like we used to."

"Easy, grandad!" Rambo mocked.

I ignored the facetious comment. "You are right about my theory, though. The weed's nothing to do with milder winters. Its growth was all held in check by the power the ghost was exerting in trying to bring the murder weapon to light, I'm convinced of it. Once she had succeeded and we had released her to the afterlife, nature could get back to normal." I paused, my thoughts drifting on to other matters. "You know, I'm glad I'm out of the rat race. It's nice not having to work or do anything apart from running the finest carp fishery in the northern hemisphere," I said, a random thought from out of nowhere.

Rambo nodded, unconcerned with the tangential element to my mental meanderings and rogue theories on curtailed weed growth. "We definitely landed in the roses, boy. Maybe we'll have time to smell them now things have calmed down."

"I hope so," I said, considering if I really meant it. Now was not the time to broach the matter of my recent thoughts. "Shall we get the boat out and put the weedkiller in?"

"Might as well, boy, it's why we're here."

Chapter 2

The warm March morning was to be passed putting twenty-five, 15kg boxes of Casaron G into Hamworthy's water. Rambo rowed The Syndicate's new fibreglass boat with effortless ease, his huge, powerful arms bulging with writhing, toned muscle as he did so. Almost immediately, such was their effect on me, I had to make a conscious effort to stop myself from continuously ogling them. No wonder I used to be shit scared of him – even in a white tee shirt, jogging bottoms and trainers – he really did have a 'rip you limb from limb' physique. I dragged my eyes away from his contorting biceps and briefly pondered on the hold Steffi had over him to make him commit, not only to her and to her moving in with him, but to giving up camo clothing. A white tee shirt, jogging bottoms and brand name trainers spoke several thousand words – several thousand words boiling down to make one succinct expression; Steffi Rules!

As we glided along slickly to the first swim, a small sick part of my imagination briefly envisaged the pair of them having sex. I had seen Steffi in action with Frans on the dreaded DVD and every now and then the images of her sneaked into my mind's eye. Rambo in full sexual flight was, mercifully, still a closed shop. It had better stay that way, I decided, and slamming a mental door shut, scooped up a handful of gin-clear Hamworthy best and splashed it over the back of my neck. The sudden cold was a shock to my system and helped padlock the door before it swung violently open, forced by the crunching boot of my fascination.

"Sorry about all the rowing," I said. "I couldn't face buying an outboard motor. I had this awful fear some sort of delicious ironic accident might manifest itself upon me."

"Maybe it still will, boy."

"Sorry?"

Rambo gave me an evil glare. "You never know, I might slip out of a rowlock and slice your face off with the edge of an oar. That'd be even *more* ironic!"

I was going to come back with something pithy – only my pith chip let me down at the crucial moment. My motherboard groaned and mentioned upgrading, but it was too late, the moment of response was gone. Instead I settled for edging my arse a few surreptitious inches further back on the wooden seat on which I was sitting. Rambo pretended not to notice and I in turn pretended not to notice the fleeting smirk shooting across his face. I forced down notions of boating accidents and stupidly let my mind harp back to the DVD.

"How many times a week do you have sex with Steffi?" I asked before I could strangle the question at birth.

Despite rowing, Rambo's shoulders imperceptibly shrugged. "Fuck knows!"

"Well obviously," I interjected.

Rambo was amused. "I don't keep count!" he laughed. "Why would I count? *Why would I keep record?*"

"How many *thirties* have you had?" I countered.

"Ah, that's different. Different altogether," Rambo replied with a smidgen of irritation.

"Can you still wrap fifteen pound Big Game Line around your hands and snap it like cotton? You know, like you did during the TWTT?"

Rambo's face was now a picture of puzzlement. "Have you been sniffing the weedkiller, or are you having a mental breakdown?" Rambo stopped rowing and let both oars drag in the water. The boat slowed and turned slightly into the wind. "Huh! Why am I even asking? This is *you* I'm talking about! Mad Matt Williams with the washing machine mind" Rambo knew me too well. "What's troubling you, boy?" he asked coaxingly. "Or will it be quicker and easier to say what *isn't?*"

I wiped a self-conscious finger across my nose. "I was thinking, well, have been thinking over last month or so, if I'm honest." Now seemed as good a time as any to broach my recent thoughts.

"Mmm?" Rambo cajoled.

"What it was, you see, was," I mumbled incoherently. "I was wondering if this point in our lives would mark the end of the road." Rambo gave me a look as blank as a piece of paper in a broken inkjet printer connected to the PC of an author with writer's block the size of the Great Pyramid. "You know how we've spoken in the past," I tried to explain, hoping to alleviate the vacant expression on my human boat propulsion unit, "of our lives being like a story book? How we're the two main characters in an unlikely epic tale of carp angling?" Rambo nodded, his face still professional poker player devoid of clues. "I sort of thought, came to the conclusion, you know, that it might be all over. That we're at the story's end."

"In what way?" Rambo asked slowly.

"The adventures. All the stuff." Rambo remained silent. I stumbled on. "Look, don't get me wrong, I know a lot of it was horrendous, dangerous, life-threatening even, on *lots* of levels. It really was terrifying. It's just, looking back on it, now it seems it might have ended…"

"Yes?" prompted Rambo once again.

I was feeling very self-conscious now. "…Well, it *was* amazing, wasn't it?" I needed confirmation.

"Yeah! Of course! You know it was, boy," Rambo confirmed.

"Well, although it frightened me at the time, and it was horrendous, and it nearly, *totally*, derailed me," I stared into Rambo's eyes. This was a hard confession to admit and through it my ridicule index was likely to go stratospheric. "I'm also frightened it might have ended." I wrenched my gaze away from him and looked out over the water. "All this," I gestured with my head, "should be *more* than enough. People would die just to fish this place, let alone *own* it!"

"*Have* died," Rambo pointed out.

I held up a finger to register a point well made. "*Exactly!*" I clasped my hands together and started to wring them. "I'm back on track with Sophie and I have Amy. And I have memories. Memories of things I've seen and done that possibly no one else has ever seen or done." I was nearing the crux of my recent reflections. "When I was fighting the madness, I dreamt of the position I'm in today. A day of calm, of no stress and of an easy, uncomplicated life, and now the day's arrived, I can't stop thinking of yesterday and all its excitement!"

Rambo's face spread into a grin and he started to row again. "So now you're worried you're going to grow old and die ensnared in mundane ordinariness?" Rambo shook his head in mock admonishment. "Soldiers have a similar problem, boy, when they come back into society. Once the relief of having survived, of having safely been re-united with kith and kin subsides, there's often an itch. What you've got to keep on reminding yourself of is all the shit you've been through before and how bad it was before you start putting on the old rose tinted, boy."

"I know! It's what I keep *trying* to tell myself! I'm back with Sophie and Amy, I've got Hamworthy, I'm financially sound, we're all healthy and the demons are locked in a box. What *more* could I want? All the loose ends are tied up!" I fell silent,

"But?"

"But I'm closer to forty than thirty after this birthday."

Rambo gave a weary shake of his head. "Oh, for God's sake! Enjoy what you've got, boy! Can the mid-life crisis! You're in a different phase of your life now. Me too. Don't you think I haven't thought along similar lines? Things change and *I* think they've changed for the better." Rambo waged a serious face at me. "Believe me, boy, if we'd carried on like we had in the past, one of us would have died sooner or later. I thought you were going to die of *anorexia* at one stage! How unfashionable is that? For a carp angler!" Rambo's expression turned earnest. "We both know how close to pegging out I came!" Rambo pulled hard on the oars and the boat spurted forward. "We've sailed tight to the wind and got away with it. Been *fucking* lucky to get away with it! We're intact, all present and correct, arms, legs, fingers, toes and minds. Only *just* in your case!" Rambo unexpectedly swung one oar out of the water and slapped the paddle against the top part of my upper arm knocking me across the boat. My other arm quickly braced against the gunwale and stopped me taking an early bath. "Savour it, boy!" Rambo barked. "Retrospective regard and the survival of the horrific will always make good anecdotal material down the pub. It might not be so with the quiet life, admitted, but that doesn't make it any bloody better to have had to have gone through it in the first place!" Rambo waggled the still threatening oar to underline his statement before placing it back in the water. His voice mellowed. "You can't go making trouble, Matt, it'll find you if it wants to. If none does, and let's hope it doesn't, we'll grow old together and talk about past events while we're fishing. Look around, think what you've got. More importantly, think what you nearly lost. I'm not talking *just* about carp waters here," he emphasised. "This is just your stupid brain's way of keeping occupied now you've managed to come to terms with the past." Rambo's voice became chatty. "Personally speaking, I'm quite happy having sex twice a day with the most exciting woman imaginable *and* fishing for huge carp whenever I want."

"Well, when you put it like… *Here!*" I exploded as Rambo's trap locked its teeth around my shinbone.

Rambo's laughter cackled across the water. "Open the first box of the weedkiller, boy," he instructed glancing at his wristwatch. "I'm down on my average today and you frittering time away jabbering on about your life's change of pace won't help the cause!"

Duly put in my place I did as I was instructed. Rambo was right, of course, absolutely one hundred per cent right from any rational viewpoint you might care to take. After all the things I had said to The Eye I was still engaged in thinking ludicrous stuff like this!

Throughout the day we diligently applied the granular weedkiller to all the swims as we deemed it necessary. I was all too aware we were doing this a month late in an ideal situation. Unfortunately, I had been caught out with regards to getting the appropriate approval from the EA. Despite owning every blade of grass and every molecule of water on the Hamworthy estate, I still needed to get EA approval to put weedkiller into *my* water. This situation I had found galling, when informed, especially as it was one I could do little about. Consequently, despite the weed manifesting itself as an obvious problem in the making, it wasn't until now that we were able to do something about it. Bloody bureaucracy!

The decision to actively do something to halt the perceived march of the weed was taken on a couple of crucial angling points. One was to keep open as many swims as possible and to prevent areas becoming unfishable, therefore restricting members' options, and secondly, there was the compelling case for fish care. Dragging fish out of heavy weed wasn't going to do them any favours.

By four in the afternoon we had completed our task and once the human outboard motor named Timothy Eugene Ramsbottom, Rambo to his friend – me – had rowed the SS Sexwithapornstar safely and energetically ashore, it was time to prepare for a 48-hour session as ample reward for a hard day's graft. The rest of the membership had been told the water would be closed for the day, so, after we had upturned the boat and left it on its dry dock base, a leisurely set up ensued. We both elected to shower in the functional wooden clubhouse, cleansing the day's grime and chemicals from our respective skins, and donned fresh clothing. More nostalgia started to flood over me as Rambo emerged from the shower room in his combats and army boots.

"Where're you going to fish then, boy?" he asked. It was a loaded question.

Let's be fair, swim choice on an empty venue *can* be a traumatic choice. I know everyone dreams of turning up to an empty car park and equally empty lake, one completely devoid of anglers, but it does impose its own unique pressures. For a start, you can't really blame anyone else other than yourself if you choose the wrong swim. There's always the dreaded scenario of blanking for two days with someone else bagging up big style in a swim you had previously discarded. I would go as far to say this can be so traumatic it might force you to congratulate the hauling angler by way of a series of violent hacks to the cranium with any available heavy, blunt instrument. Maybe it was this inherent understanding of a perennial problem that prompted my response.

"Where do *you* fancy?" I replied cagily.

Rambo's eyes narrowed and a digit of composed wrath was levelled at me. His understanding was equally inherent. "You want *me* to say so *you* can try to get in there, don't you? Pulling the old Supreme Syndicate Leader stunt."

"Not at all. I want you to say," I responded, " so it merely proves to me how predictable your first swim choice is."

"Oh, I *see*," said Rambo with exaggerated comprehension. His voice quickly hardened. "Like I don't know where *you're* going to go."

"Why don't you choose where I want to go, *if* you're *so* sure."

Rambo's eyes widened. "You'd *love* me to do that, wouldn't you?"

"Meaning?"

"Meaning, letting me choose you the best swim and *then*, because I'm such a gentleman and because I feel so desperately sorry for you, allowing you to go in it."

"Are you intimating I'm incapable of choosing my own, preferred, definitive, absolutely first choice and that in some way I need the emotional and physical underlining of my choice via a decision provided by you?"

"I'm not intimating," said Rambo walking up and parking his barrel chest so close to me, should he have been wearing a set of medals on his camouflage jacket, they would have touched my sweatshirt, "I'm *saying!*"

I cocked my head at an angle so I could stare up at the rugged outcrop constituting Rambo's chin. He needed a shave. "I'll write it down."

"Eh?"

"My first choice and then your first choice."

"Go on, then."

I reversed away from the man mountain, found a scrap of paper and a pen and wrote out the two swims. I folded the paper in half and gave it to Rambo. "Mine's the one next to the 'M' and yours is the one next to the 'R'," I informed him facetiously.

Rambo carefully placed the piece of paper against the wall so the written side was hidden. "Pen!" he called, holding out a hand whilst the other pinned the offending scrap to the wall like a police suspect.

I gave him the pen and schoolboy-in-class style he wrote on it, hiding his efforts with a contrived body screening action. Once he had finished he screwed the piece of paper into a ball and plonked it into my hand. "My swim is the one with the 'R' alongside it, yours is the one with the 'B'."

"The 'B'?" I enquired.

"Boy!" Rambo revealed.

I unscrewed the piece of paper. Written in my hand it had 'South-east point swim – R; North-east island swim – M'. I flipped it over and saw what Rambo had written; 'North-east island swim – B; South-east point swim – R'. I gave Rambo the crumpled scrap of paper and he in turn read it and guffawed at its content.

"Creatures of habit," he offered. He put a large mitt on my shoulder. "Have a good session, Matt, but not *too* good, eh?"

We both laughed at our little unscripted act. It showed our knowledge of each other and how deep our friendship had become over the years. Only two very good friends could have acted out our little skit – one picking up so quickly on the other's lead and interpreting so accurately all its tiny nuances and inferences. I hoped my casting and bait application would be as cute.

Rambo and I drove off around the grass track in opposite directions, he anti-clockwise from the functional wooden clubhouse, myself clockwise. A myriad of memory flashbacks always accompanied me as I drove past the ancient wood to my left. It still looked bitter and twisted, yet time and familiarity had lessened its malice to a state in my mind of nothing more than idle curiosity. Parking alongside the swim entrance to the spot where I had fished Hamworthy for the very first time, I gave the wood one last cursory glance. Deep inside it laid the hidden pyre where we had burned Rambo's would-be assassin.

As I walked my bivvy bag down to the official bivvy-erecting site, here, I mused, was the official site where the ghost had visited me on my inaugural overnighter. I briefly pondered on the plausibility of erecting a couple of commemorative plaques to celebrate this rich past history.

As I started to shift the rest of my gear from van to swim I thought of a few others. Ones to commemorate the world's first pornographic carp fishing DVD; Rambo's secret (as far as Pup was concerned) knee trembler with Melloney; my doggy-style bivvy-bang with Melina; the place where I had unloaded the Glock 17 into the would-be assassin; the resting place of the ghost's bones; the spot, if only I knew it, where Michael had murdered her; Michael's suicide pitch and Rambo's subsequent capture of Swansong via a – break into a salty olde sea dog imitation – dead man's cast and the bush where Rambo and I had hidden in order to spy on the fish stealing campaign of Hollywood, Darren and Rocky. For the water-based locations perhaps a marker buoy could be utilised – something reserved and stylish that flashed neon red at night. These could mark where Rocky had foul-hooked Michael's murder weapon, the ballpane hammer, and there could be one for each of the teeth smashed from the charred skull of the failed assassin that I had catapulted out into Hamworthy's depths.

On second thoughts, maybe this was not such a grand idea. Someone was bound to trip over a plaque when heavily laden with gear and break a neck, or, get a line entangled around one of the buoys and become so befuddled by their collectively disorientating, strobe-like effect, they would have an epileptic fit, fall in and drown. Then I would have to put up another commemorative plaque for them, thus exasperating the whole problem!

My first night passed without any action, the only event of any note a news item on the local radio relating to the fire at the warehouse of Leviathan Boilies. Their business was based about twenty miles away and the fire was apparently being treated as 'suspicious' by the local police force. Leviathan Boilies was one of several fledgling bait companies who had immerged to prominence over the last couple of years. They had hit the ground running with large advertising campaigns and a host of big fish allegedly caught on their products by a list of high profile anglers. ('Allegedly' – cynic or realist? You decide.) They clearly had money behind them and, on the face of it, a descent product.

I smiled to myself, what did I care? Police, I assumed, were searching for a Leviathan Boilies user with a horrendous run of blanks to his credit and a denial complex over his lack of angling ability! Whatever the situation, I could sleep easily in my bivvy because I *knew* Leviathan Boilies' bait wasn't a patch on the three round things on the end of my hair rigs! All in all, I reckoned, in rather a callous fashion seeing as someone's entire livelihood might have been ruined, it served them right for having such a pretentious name.

As if to prove the point of having superior bait, at around eleven o'clock in the morning, I had my first take. My margin bait to the island had been snaffled and I was out of my bivvy and down to my right-hand rod as quick as a paedophile to a park's playground on a sunny Sunday. What a sick simile, I thought, as the rod hooped over – and me a father!

The fish didn't feel big, but it had been a while since I'd had a comparative experience, so I thought I had better do my best to land the beast and find out. After a relatively uncomplicated tussle I stared in mild disbelief at the fish safely enveloped in my landing net. I had caught a fish destined for the stock pond like on my very first visit to Hamworthy – only this time I had to stick to the rules! I double-checked to make certain and sure enough, at a few ounces over twenty, the fish fell well short of the 25lb return limit.

"Oh, well," I muttered to myself. "Pup's bound to need his gear replacing one day or another, so here's the first few hundred towards it!"

I phoned Rambo to tell him. "At least you've caught one, boy. That's more than what I've done," was his pragmatic response.

"Yeah, but you don't know what you're doing," I jibed.

Rambo chuckled down the phone. "It's not *my* fault! I'm blaming the bait!"

"You can't pull that one off! Not with the boilie you're using! Mind you, someone on a Leviathan Boilies product is!"

"What?" replied Rambo, "I haven't the faintest idea what the hell you're on about, boy."

"Leviathan Boilies? You must have heard of them, they're the dog's bollocks, if you believe the hype." There was silence. Anticipating a continuing non-response I carried on. "I heard on the local radio station their warehouse got torched. I would have thought they'd have realised petrol was a dangerous flavour carrier."

"I'd have thought *you'd* have realised listening to local radio rots your brain."

"Five Live goes a bit wonky on the AM at night," I explained somewhat sheepishly.

"Pathetic excuse." Rambo seemed uninterested in the fate of a million smoke-damaged boilies and struck out on another tack. "You make sure you put the fish in the stock pond as stipulated in the Fisheries' rules and don't forget to put it in the logbook."

"*My* rules," I reminded him in my capacity as Supreme Syndicate Leader.

"*Fisheries'* rules."

"I'll wind in straight away, sir."

"See that you do." Rambo hung up.

Bloody jumped up Hamworthy Fisheries First Lieutenant Rambo. *I'm* Supreme Syndicate Leader, I thought. I can do what I want. So I went and done it, which coincidently – *coincidently* – was exactly what Rambo had told me to do.

"You've taken around five minutes longer than it should have taken you to sack the fish, wind in and put it in the stock pond," Rambo informed me when I popped in to visit him having released my tiddler from its temporary black-meshed home. "*If* you'd stuck strictly to the fifteen minute sacking rule."

"Sorry, *boss*," I said caustically.

"That's all right. I'll let you off if you tell me what bait you caught it on," came the dry reply.

"Ask The Eye, he knows."

"Absinthe addict he used to be... Because the green stuff helped him see... But a tumour in his brain... Halted The Eye's future viewing, oh the pain... Now an exclusive, revolutionary, indented, dirty brown bottom bait boilie is his main weapon of attack... Just like Matt Williams, in fact... At last this boy has had a run... Only a scraper twenty? That's not much fun!" Rambo gave me two raised eyebrows and a grin.

"Well, it started off crap, got worse in the middle, only to end up being as upsetting as watching an England penalty shoot-out. Don't give up the day job, bankside Poet Laureate."

"I haven't got a day job," Rambo declared.

"You haven't, if you don't count harassing me over fisheries' rules."

"You wouldn't want the membership thinking there's one rule for you and one for the rest of us, would you? It'd set a bad example."

"Fair point," I conceded.

I left Rambo and started the return walk to my swim, going anti-clockwise, past the stock pond and up the east side of the pit. Carrying the empty sack on the return journey was miles better than lugging it laden with twenty pounds' worth of future slush-fund carp. I hoped it was a walk I wouldn't have to make again, although at a push, I would do it rather than having to make it to photograph a Rambo-caught sixty! My capture of Gut Bucket at the last knockings of the first ever Hamworthy Fisheries' Fish-In meant I held the whip hand in at least one solitary category when compared to Rambo. To be fair, it was a good category, a PB is always a good category to be best in, and I was loath to even consider losing it! Now, what that tells any resident psychoanalyst about me as an individual, I would rather not know. In defence I would ask how many of you would be happy to see your fishing partner catch a bigger PB than your own? See! The dark side! We all have a dark side. Ask Luke Skywalker, he'll tell you all about it!

Around halfway back I heard a car engine behind me and on turning recognised it as Pup's vehicle – the boiliemobile – as I liked to think of it. Pup slowed and beckoned to me through the windscreen, so I walked around to the driver's side. Pup furiously wound down the window. With the vague realisation he still drove a car boasting of 'handraulic' window activation, I greeted him.

"All right, Pup?"

"How's the boilie fishing?" he asked, his eyes gleaming as if to say it was a question that didn't need to be asked.

"Rambo's blanking and I've had a scraper twenty," I answered flatly.

"Oh. You must be fishing badly."

I couldn't stop myself laughing at Pup's inverted viewpoint. A lot of anglers blame their bait, especially pyromaniacs, or, at the very least, change it when they're having a poor run. Not the boiliemeister! If his baits weren't catching, there was only one person at fault and that was the poor sap at the opposite end to one of his children!

"How about we settle for blaming the fish," I said forging a middle way. "They're not feeding enough yet to get caught. It's always patchy this time of year and not even your baits can catch on here in the winter."

Reluctantly Pup conceded the point. "Yes. Odd that. What you need is a winter water to go with this one. It is Hamworthy *Fisheries*, plural, after all."

He had a point. I had never thought of why it was called Hamworthy Fisheries. Maybe Michael had had expansion plans. A nice little runs water, stuffed full of twenties and thirties, where a couple of takes a day during the winter days were the norm, would certainly be excellent entertainment.

"Good call," I concurred. "Do you know of any?"

Pup gave me an evil glare and with good reason. He was the person who had put us on to Hamworthy in the first place, when Michael had run it. The truth of the matter was, without Pup's input, I would never have got to own Hamworthy Fisheries. He had set the chain of events into action at the outset by putting us forward for membership.

"I'll ignore that question," he said with fake magnanimity, "and answer it with one of my own. Have you heard the news?"

"Leviathan Boilies?" I answered. Surely such bait related news could be the only subject he was concerned over.

Pup snorted his contempt. "Not those semolina schmucks. Their baits are crap! In the original bait definition terminology, I might add, despite the advertising telling you otherwise. No, I'm referring to Ivan Pulimov, the London based oligarch! His statement yesterday."

"Ivan who?"

Pup rolled his eyes as if I was a moron. "Ivan Pulimov? Ever heard of him?" I shook my head. "He's a Russian billionaire living over here and he's a bit of an Anglophile," Pup informed me. "Similar to Abramovich, the Chelsea guy, in that he made mega bucks on the back of the old Soviet Block's state-run power industry. He's made his home in London with his family and he's bought up several established British firms." Pup's face cracked a grin. "I suspect he'll buy a Premier League outfit soon to complete the set!" Pup waved a dismissive hand. "That's all by the by though."

"So, are we any nearer getting to the point?" I enquired. "I'm only on a 48-hour session, you know."

"Sorry. Pulimov is in the news because he, get this, wants to help rally the British people to celebrate 'British identity', with a series of financial rewards. To do this he's offering cash prizes to individuals, organisations, who achieve worthy results in traditionally 'British' fields. A *Russian* offering cash incentives to celebrate *Britishness*. Great!"

At least I understood this last bit. "So he's offering cash prizes for Olympic standard inept management, queuing, tea-drinking, weather discussion, bowler hat and umbrella usage, wearing hideous male summer attire, roast dinner/fish and chip eating, esteemed incompetence in foreign languages and having a stiff upper lip, is he?" I quipped.

"Not exactly. No."

"So he's gone the multicultural route rather than the traditional?" I said, warming to my flippant theme. "The so-called British diversity element inherent in eating curry, Chinese Takeaways, employing foreign construction workers and spawning Islamic terrorists!" (Politically incorrect joke: Woman in burka to husband. 'Does my bomb look big in this?')

Pup shook his head in irritation. "No! Whoever's advising him is more savvy than that! They haven't fallen for idle clichés of the traditional past, nor have they gone down the PC route. Look, I'm getting bogged down here. You don't *need* to know what other fields he's supporting, short of the fact he's offering *twenty-five* grand to the angler catching the first authentic, British, seventy-pound carp!"

"You're joking?" I said, genuinely taken aback.

"Nope. It's all in the papers. Look!"

Pup grabbed a copy of The Sun off his passenger seat and thrust it in my direction.

The paper had been folded back on itself at the appropriate page. I perused the list – the list of achievements with cash rewards. I noticed, along with the fact the paper had become impregnated with the bouquet from the house of a thousand rampaging flavours, how professional sport had no place on it. Recreational sport, however, and pastimes were heavily represented alongside a few more pursuits that could only be described as eccentric or esoteric. Therefore, the likes of fishing, gardening, walking, pub-life, village cricket, local football and rugby, featured along with oddities like Morris Dancing, May Pole design, jam making, steam engine restoration and cheese rolling. Various heritage activities such as maritime, architecture, countryside and religion – featuring both pagan and Christian versions – were also listed. There were awards for direct specific individual achievement, like the carp fishing one, and ones allotted to more general achievement and excellence to either individuals or groups. I could see it was a hornet's nest in terms of what had been included, and more pertinently what had been excluded, but overall it was a fair stab at an agenda to define Britishness – if indeed you ever could define it.

Whatever the true motivation for such a stunt, from my point of view and from all carp anglers' points of view, there were two huge pluses for inclusion. One was inclusion in itself – to be recognised as a distinctive part of what makes us what we are and our history – and the second being a genuine chance to bag a year's salary for catching one fish. No prizes for guessing which one was likely to feature most highly in the average carp angler's mind! The big reality check, for nearly all aspiring anglers, was having access to a water holding a seventy.

As I re-read the page, I wondered if there was a catch-by date tucked away in the small print at the bottom. Something like this was bound to have limited media mileage, although the initial splash would be as big as – I don't know – a seventy crashing out? More like a blue whale going in belly flop from a ten-metre diving platform. The angling press were going to have a field day! It was at this stage of realisation when an alarm bell started clanging in my head.

"There's a website dedicated to the claims procedure," said Pup. "As far as we're concerned you need photos, one witness and the set of scales for inspection. If a seventy remains uncaught in a calendar year from today, the prize money goes back into the kitty and is divided up between those who have achieved the required levels of excellence within the timescale." Pup, bless his little round baits – come to think of it he probably did, or baptise them – had unwittingly answered my question.

"Do you know of a venue where there happens to be a seventy?" I asked. It was a leading question.

Pup eyed me in disbelief. "*Here*, by any chance?"

"Most likely," I agreed. "Pity this is a strictly no publicity water!" Pup's mouth gaped. No words came out. "Give me a lift up to my swim and I'll remind you, I've got a copy of the rules in my rucksack."

A frowning Pup opened his passenger door, I hopped in and he drove me in silence to my swim where I got out, went in my bivvy and rummaged in my rucksack for my 'on site' copy of Hamworthy Fisheries' rules. I folded the copy, much like Pup's newspaper, to the second page, and showed it to him.

"Read it!"

Pup took this instruction literally and started in a faltering voice.

"The Hamworthy Fishery Syndicate. Hereinafter referred to as 'The Syndicate'. I, the undersigned, accept that my initiation cheque for the sum of £2500 shall be held by The Syndicate's bankers until such time I decide to withdraw from The Syndicate, when it will be refunded in full but with no interest having been accrued. This sum shall be known as the '1st deposit'. I, the undersigned, accept that should I breach any of the following points of contract written below I will forfeit my '1st deposit' and be immediately expelled from The Syndicate with no refund of the annual fee. Breach of such points of contract will be by the decision of Matt Williams alone and I accept his decision to be final and binding. Members will be granted one meeting with Matt Williams when under provisional expulsion where a definitive decision will be made with no further appeal. Points of contract are as follows: Anyone publicising fish catches in any form whatsoever will be in breach of contract. Anyone caught attempting to move fish or suspected of trying to move fish or in suspected negotiation with third parties to move fish will be..."

"That'll do," I told Pup. "You see?"

Pup stared down at the rules, the very ones he had signed only weeks earlier. He might not have paid for the privilege, but he was still bound by the rules like all the others.

"And you're going to hold me and the others to this and let us bomb out on a chance of winning twenty-five grand?"

"Got it in one."

"And this applies to Rambo?"

"Sure does."

"And *you* as well?"

"Naturally."

"Anyone would still be twenty-two thousand five hundred up on the deal," Pup pointed out.

"And not fishing Hamworthy Fisheries any more, *if* their claim was accepted."

"But come on! How many waters hold a seventy? What a chance to win twenty-five grand!" Pup exclaimed.

I ignored his plea and considered his question. "Unfortunately, with a prize like this, there might soon be a few more. Hamworthy will *not* be one of them, genuine or otherwise," I added.

Pup declined to argue with me over Hamworthy's status and only commented on the first part of my statement. "I see what you mean. Rent a seventy from abroad, stick it in a puddle over here, catch it and then give it back?" he suggested.

"Something like that, only change 'rent' to 'nick' and forget the bit about giving it back."

Pup nodded. "Could be the cause of a few strokes to be pulled, this one."

I laughed. "Someone's bound to try it on, even though I suspect the fishing world would know it was bogus if a seventy suddenly came out of nowhere."

"Hamworthy's nowhere," Pup insisted. "You've kept this place a secret as much as you can. People know it exists, the waiting list is proof, but who apart from the members and those few foreigners who came here for the fish-in knows it's produced a sixty? Has the potential to produce a seventy? How many people have past or present members told? Presumably you asked for confidentiality? Now whether you got it is another matter…"

"It's all irrelevant, Pup," I said interrupting him. "Nothing from here *ever* goes forward for publicity. From my point of view it's the natural way of things."

Pup gave me a look to suggest this policy was as natural as a piece of day-glow sweetcorn. "From my point of view a nice, fat cash injection would be great," he said wistfully. "I could buy loads of bait making machinery with twenty-five grand," he enthused. "I could step up production to a commercial level and make the jump to a proper working premises."

"Don't bother," I sneered. "It'll only catch fire. You'd be better off staying at home. Besides, your house is a temple to bait! It's unique! Come to think of it, you're the quintessential, garden shed rocket scientist. You ought to be on the list, well, not *you*, but the lone-inventor-working-from-home concept! Very British! No investment available, so you go it alone!"

"Catch fire?" queried Pup. "What do you mean 'catch fire'?"

"Leviathan Boilies went up in smoke," I said matter of factly. "I heard it on the radio last night. Their warehouse burnt down. If you get offered smoke damaged boilies on the cheap at a boot sale, they're probably theirs!"

Pup's eyes narrowed and his brain went into bait mode. "Maybe they were trying a new, faster method of air drying and it went wrong. Some kind of controlled, huh, *uncontrolled*, heated forced draught method. Interesting."

"Pup," I told him. "You're reading too much into it. Some fucker torched the place. Someone who'd been blanking for months on their bait. I very much doubt if it was a case of an industrial process going wrong."

Pup's face broke into a smile. "From what I've seen of their baits that's *exactly* what it was!"

Chapter 3

Rambo rubbed the grey stubble on his chin in what seemed like slow motion. The back of his huge hand was covered in liver spots, three or four of which seemed to have merged together in the apparent attempt to create the face of Jesus. He lifted his cane walking stick parallel to the ground, the effort showing on his tired, wrinkled face as he pointed to the far side of the pit. His large, once powerful body wobbled and struggled to hold itself without the wooden prop.

"Now, what was that swim called?" he said in a quiet croaking voice.

From my wheelchair I tried to make out where he was pointing. Unfortunately it was all a blur – and so was my memory. I stroked the tartan blanket covering my lap, much like the way you would stroke a fond family pet.

"I can't remember," I said in a hoary voice.

Rambo, now leaning on the cane, looked at me, his eyes watery and dull. An age elapsed. "That swim I was pointing at. What was it called?"

"What swim?" I asked.

Rambo's brow furrowed and his saggy face flickered with puzzlement. The puzzlement passed. Time passed. "That swim," he began slowly, pointing to the far side of the pit with a crooked index finger from the huge, gnarled hand bearing the face of Jesus in liver spots. "What was it called?"

Rambo's finger had started to gyrate so violently on the end of his arm, nearly a quarter of the far bank was covered by its wavering scope.

"Look at you, you daft old sod!" I gently chided him. "You used to be an Adonis. Now you can't even hold your hand still!"

Rambo wiped a bead of water away from a rheumy eye. His chest rose as he sucked in air, either in readiness for the upcoming effort of speech, or in pride to correct his bowed body. "At least I can still stand up, old man."

This rang a bell in my muffled conscious. A memory came back. "Do you remember how you always used to call me, 'boy'?" I asked.

Rambo considered this – for quite a while. "Boy? Boy. Yes, that's right," he eventually agreed. "I *did* used to call you, boy!" He stared at me wrapped in my blanket, wheels for legs. "You're not a boy now, old man. You're an old man, old man."

I laughed and this caused me to cough. Coughing hurt. "I know," I managed to say between hacks. "I feel it. Feel every year of it," I admitted. A melancholy mood of reflection descended upon me. "Mostly I feel for every lost function and all those things I used to do without giving them a second thought," I said sadly, caught in a haze of time long elapsed. "Everything seems to take such an effort now. I guess it's the way of life," I looked up at Rambo – at least some things hadn't changed. "Not that it makes it any better. Do you know, I couldn't even hold a rod now, let alone fish with it."

"Come on you two, time for your medication." It was Sophie – a Sophie aged around thirty.

"How is it *you've* never aged, darling?" I enquired.

"Because she is alvays having ser gudt night's sleep in a proper bed. Sleeping in ser bivvy makes you old very quickly. All of your fishing has finally caught up vitt you!" The distinctive voice was Steffi's – and she too looked the same as she had when I had first met her.

This was all *wrong*, I thought! And *that* thought, I suddenly realised, was a third party thought! Not a thought of the ancient Matt Williams sitting in a wheelchair with a tartan blanket wrapped over his skinny, muscle-depleted, useless legs, but of someone else! It belonged to someone remote, a voyeur regarding the scene. What *was* going on? The third party thought again and in a flash of cognisant awareness I knew it was another Matt Williams – it was *me*! The correctly aged me. I turned to the scene again. The women were *exactly* as they had been fifty years ago, yet Rambo and I were close to pushing up the daisies! The pair of us had one foot in the grave, the other on a banana skin placed on top of a diesel spill on sheet ice!

Steffi suddenly waved her hand violently under her nose. "Oh, my Godt! Vhat is zat terrible smell?"

"It's the smoke!" said Sophie. "Look at it!"

Smoke was drifting across the water, huge swathes of it, and it wafted over to us, driven by the wind, to create the impression of scurrying low-level clouds.

"Why, that's monster crab!" said Rambo, his timeworn voice laced with incredulity. "Someone's burning monster crab!"

"An *inferior* version of the Rod Hutchinson original," said Pup. A young Pup.

"How come you haven't aged, either?" I demanded, the epitome of a grumpy old man.

"I keep myself fresh by keeping myself frozen, like my baits," Pup replied, giving me a scallywag wink. "No preservatives are involved. If I have to go out of the freezer for a long time I air-dry myself. Feel." I felt Pup's hand. It was strong, young and supple. "Melloney rubs essential oils into my skin as well." Pup's voice dropped to a hushed whisper. He held a hand up to guard his mouth and stooped down to my level. "Especially around the genitalia. Works wonders!" he hissed. "Ooh oh! There goes the fire brigade! Hear the siren?"

I listened. I couldn't hear it to begin with, but gradually my failing ears picked up something. "That's a funny sounding siren," I remarked. "It sounds more like one of those bite alarms we used to use."

"You dumb bastard!" shouted Rambo, whose aged body rejuvenated – Doctor Who-style – before my very eyes to become the Rambo I had known in, if not my youth, then my mid-thirties. "That's your fucking buzzer!"

He whipped the tartan blanket off my legs and slapped me hard across my face. My ears rang with a tolling bell several decibel levels above the buzzer's screech. "You're not *old*!" he screamed, his spittle flecking my face like fine drizzle. "You're *dreaming*! Now get out there and deal with it! That fish could be worth twenty-five grand!"

Rambo hauled me up out of my wheelchair and flung me violently, in the style of a bouncer ejecting a troublemaker, down towards the water. Like a bungee jumper, I pinged right back.

I fell back on to my bedchair, disorientated, in the dark, with limbs akimbo, bivvy contents (telly, stereo system, cutlery, plates, hanging pictures, newspapers, china knick-knacks, Monopoly set, house plants) everywhere, my brain addled – *plus* the added distraction of an unseen Delkim howling out carp fishing's greatest message: FISH ON! As I gathered my thoughts I realised I must have awoken from my dream and attempted to barge my way through my bivvy's fully zipped, integral mosquito screen – and failed dismally. Like a Wimbledon tennis ball punched back from a loosely strung racket wielded by a volleying expert, I was now resolutely back on the base line. Finally rationalising my mind and body into some semblance of a response I, metaphorically speaking, cut the racket's strings (unzipped the door!) and did the old Linford Christie act – without the impressive lunch pack gyrations and, naturally, *sans* Lycra – down to the offending Delkim and rod combo.

'Over here, you stupid fucker!' The Delkim seemed to scream. 'The middle rod! The *middle* rod, you dopey bastard!'

I hit the middle rod.

'At *last*!' the Delkim said and finally shut up.

It felt a good fish.

Now, whether this was because it had already done four laps of the island and I was trying to pull it back around was hard to tell. I hoped not. Shortly, after feeling a couple of strong kicks, I realised I did have direct contact with the fish and with this uplifting comprehension causing a smile to crack on my face, some two seconds later, everything went solid. The fish was weeded, the smile gone, the uplift flat.

"How long does the bloody stuff take before it works? It should all be gone by now! Useless weedkiller!" I muttered under my breath.

Despite my deluded state, I had a backup plan, backup *plans*, in fact. The first one consisted of leaning back on my rod as hard as I dared – just short of the very point I felt disaster would come into play. Nothing budged. I looked up at the beginnings of a new day and mentally chastised myself for my slow response to the run. Now there was only one thing to do – it was time for plan 'C' and a slightly different version of the old waiting game. I put my reel back on to its free spool facility, made a tight line and placed the rod back on my middle buzzer.

"You let me know when that fish makes a break for it," I told the Delkim sternly and with my instruction relayed, I turned my back on the whole sorry affair of hitting a run too late and went and made myself a cuppa.

The fish, if it was still on, and I was pretty certain it was, had continued to sit tight even though I had made and then drunk half my mug of tea. I glanced at my watch – it was a good fifteen minutes since the carp had crash-landed in the weedbed. Although I was fully aware tardiness had cost me so far, I knew a knee jerk reaction of haste would do me no favours. I had played this trick before and I knew it would work – given time the fish would move from its perceived safe haven and when it did; cue time for me to haul it in!

The morning sun was sneaking over the eastern horizon as I contemplated my tea, the weeded fish, my weird dream and Pup's news of a twenty-five grand reward for a seventy. Strange how they had all worked themselves into my subconscious and had manifested themselves so vividly in my dream. I chuckled to myself, wondering how many unscrupulous anglers might chance their arm with some major league stroke pulling to have a crack at the marvellous jackpot. Equally, how many Hamworthy members would be tempted to blow their membership? In the end, adding up the pros and cons, I concluded the publicity and recognition would be a wonderful fillip for the carp fishing industry and shade the possible downside. I could see thousands of anglers cracking jokes about being 'after the seventy' on their local waters and Two Tone's capture, should she ever crack the barrier, was going to make somebody's *life*, let alone day. And if Gut Bucket or another one of my monsters came out over seventy? Well, I'd do everything I could to stop it being put forward. I really didn't need the publicity and the attendant microscopic, invasive press interest. Not with all the skeletons – literally – Hamworthy had in its cupboard!

'Excuse me,' interrupted the Delkim in a much more reserved tone than earlier, 'the carp is making a run for it.'

The fish was off and out of the weedbed – only without the previous right-fin-to-the-floor panic! I got to the rod, lifted it, my mind emptied of all previous considerations, and I waited for it to move a considerable distance before clicking off the free spool and leaning into it. The Ballista Slim arced over gracefully and I pumped the fish back towards me, giving it plenty of stick until I was sure it had cleared the original weedbed. Once I was happy the fish was in open water, I backed off the pressure and silently prayed there were no more weedbeds. Not for world peace did I bother God, nor for the end of world famine, only for a piece of clear water between my underwater opponent and myself. (Before you get all judgemental, you tell me what *you'd* consider most important at the time – provided, *obviously*, you weren't fishing in a war zone *and* had plenty of sandwiches with you.)

As it transpired the water this particular tussle was now taking place in turned out to be a weed-free zone. My prayers had been answered – although secretly I suspected the same situation would have existed if I had taken the standard beauty pageant spiel slant on 'things to be prayed for'! Mentally I clenched a fist in celebration. Excellent! Things were going my way – my quarry was now only yards from the bank and the final coup de grâce was in sight.

I think the fish had clearly realised it was pitched against an adversary armed with a hugely superior intellect and in deference it had let me pump it back to within a few yards of my rod tip with little fuss. Suits me, I thought. The heavy load plodded ever closer and as I managed to get the fish up in the clear water, I could see a huge ball of weed engulfing the fish. So large was the ball of weed, a mixture, as far as I could make out, of Canadian pondweed and potamogeton, the carp was almost completely hidden by it. The apparent calming affect of having a huge gob of weed around its head was making the fight a doddle! Come to Daddy, I thought, as I eased my net under the mass of weed. I lifted it up, there was an almighty splash and there, nestling in my landing net, was my prize.

It was only when I went to hoist the net out of the water I realised something was wrong – namely, a severe lack of carp! Like a complete dork I placed the net on the bank, downed my rod and parted the weed with both hands, desperately searching for the vanished carp. It wasn't there! In utter stupefaction I glanced around over my shoulder, dreading the notion someone had witnessed my shameful charade. Ten pounds' worth of weed! *That* was what was in my net! Not a beautiful carp, not a trophy of testament to my angling skills of problem solving in the wake of prior mishap, or of thinking on my feet. Bitterly I asked myself, who, by anyone's reckoning, had the superior intellect now?

With a face like thunder, I emptied the green straggly mass on to the bank. The fish must have slipped the hook at the last moment, avoided the net and gone back to the depths of Hamworthy, no doubt laughing as it did so. God knows how. But it had – after *all* that! I felt gutted. Okay, I had been a slug out of the sack – accepted – but everything else had been well thought out and had gone to plan, only for me to be kicked in the teeth at the death. What a piss off!

Rambo didn't sound pissed off when I told him via the mobile. Not if the sound of hysterical laughter cramming itself into my right ear was anything to go by.

"And you actually looked for it in the ball of weed? Pulling it apart with your fingers? Ha-ha! Global warming strikes again!" He dissolved into convulsive cackling. "Boy, I'd *love* to have seen the look on your face."

"You had anything?" I asked, interrupting his chuckling.

"A mid-thirty common this morning. Nothing during the night, though," Rambo informed me, sobering slightly from his high-octane attack of the giggles. "There's still a few fish moving down this end, so I'm hopeful of more action."

"How much bait are you putting out?" I asked.

"Not loads. Thirty or so freebies around each on two rods and I'm fishing singles on the one I'm casting the furthest. The fish came to one of the rods with free offerings," informed Rambo.

"I'm putting out something similar. It'll be interesting to see how results go compared to last year now we're on Pup's exclusive, revolutionary, indented, dirty brown bottom bait boilie."

"They'll be better, boy!" Rambo assured. "Funny isn't it? I'm not even thinking of fishing one of his pop-ups at the moment."

I laughed. "I know, and that's how he originally made his name. Mind you, Bbp doesn't roll off the tongue so good as Pup!" And it didn't. Bottom bait Pete, no matter how good the bottom bait, was not a runner in the moniker stakes. "By the way," I said glibly, "some Russian bloke's offering a twenty-five grand prize for the first seventy caught in this country."

"Run that by me again." I ran it by Rambo again, imparting all the info Pup had given to me. I also gave him my opinion on the matter regarding Hamworthy lunkers leading to a lucrative liaison with a large lump of legal tender. "Too right, boy," he agreed. "The last thing we need is any publicity and the press asking awkward questions. Hamworthy's past, and *ours* for that matter, doesn't bear too much inspection."

"What if someone *does* fluke out a seventy and decides to chance their arm?" I whinged.

"Don't worry unduly, boy," Rambo encouraged. "The chances of it even happening are slight, and if by chance it does, *I'll* keep a lid on it."

I love it when Rambo talks like that – a feeling of all being well and under control wafts over me.

I signed off from my chat with Rambo and wasted the next several hours of my life willing my buzzers to erupt into life. I was feeling desperate, there was no getting away from it, even if I knew Pup's boilie would give me another chance sooner rather than later. The truth was if I had landed the last fish I would have been cock-a-hoop, but the nature of my cock-*up*, had left me annoyed and on edge. Such is, and always will be, the fine line between success and failure in our marvellous sport. The difference between a blank and a fish under your belt can be, paradoxically, both small and massive at the same time.

As I waited and willed and then, for a change, willed and waited, I had to break off from this intense activity to field a couple of phone calls from Syndicate members concerning the twenty-five grand prize. Word was soon getting round. Was I, they enquired, going to budge on the publicity rule in this one-off special case? Even if, they pointed out, the pit, as a venue, was not to be revealed. No, I *wasn't*, I answered firmly, slamming their hopes into the dust. Anyone trying would be out on their ear pronto *and* have Rambo to deal with, I reminded them. Both Dean and Phil seemed to take my ruling with good grace, although I guessed the pair of them would be mightily miffed at missing out on the chance of such a massive amount of money, should fate decree they land a seventy. Too bad – I didn't want to be the one rueing their remuneration, regretting their reimbursement or repenting their reward due to the media spotlight unearthing an incriminating facet of either mine, Rambo's or Hamworthy's dark past!

At two in the afternoon I had a chance to redeem myself when my left-hand rod belted off. No sooner had the Delkim sounded than my mobile started to squawk, and I was left in slight consternation as I struck the run – on time, this time – that either Rambo had already landed a fish bigger than the one I was shortly hoping to land, or, that I would have to answer 'no' to another griping Syndicate member optimistically looking to top up their bank balance. As it turned out, one thirty-seven pound, ten ounce linear mirror later, the missed call was from Sophie.

Showing my true love for her by phoning her back before I had even photographed the fish – although, naturally, not before sacking it – her reasons for contact were a powerful antidote to my feelings of exuberance.

"Mr Furlington's phoned," she told me after we had exchanged the usual pleasantries.

"Oh, Christ! What the fuck did he want?" I exploded, my nerves instantly put through a cross cut shredder.

"Do you *have* to swear?"

"Sorry."

"He didn't say. He just asked me to get you to phone him as soon as possible."

Frantically my mind searched for reasons, the worse case scenario being some unforeseen challenge to my ownership of Hamworthy – say either Michael's long-lost twin brother turning up or a relative of the ghost contesting the Will.

I felt stressed. "Did it sound important?" I asked anxiously, rubbing a thumb and index finger into temple and brow as I performed a small circular walk.

I heard Sophie let out a sigh. "Of course it's important! That's why he asked *me* to get *you* to phone him *straight* away!"

"Good point," I conceded. "Shall I phone now?"

"I think so, Matthew, don't you? *If* you can spare the time."

"You know what they say about sarcasm, don't you?" I warned.

She obviously didn't because she ignored the question. "I'll text you his number, all right? Let me know what it's all about. I'm sure it's nothing to worry over. Love you."

"Love you, too."

Sophie hung up from the landline and the text winged its way over shortly. I rang the number for Farrington, Farrington and Furlington and after telling the receptionist whom I wanted to speak to, and then who I was, she put me through to Mr Furlington. It took ten or so seconds before he picked up and I could hear my heart banging as I waited, my breathing hard and heavy.

"Aah, Mr Williams. Thank you for phoning back so promptly," Justine Furlington enunciated in his Radio 4 tones.

I have to admit I felt uncomfortable hearing the voice of the solicitor and executor of Michael's Will once again. Alongside the worrying facet of him contacting me, I had no doubt he regarded me and all of Hamworthy's membership as a form of violent pond-life and as the type of members of society with which one would preferably rather not associate oneself. He had a point – the last time he had addressed the Hamworthy membership en bloc it had ended up in pandemonium, culminating in a punch up between Rambo and Rocky that would have cost you the best part of twenty notes to watch on satellite TV.

My own voice sounded unusually crude and uneducated to my ears as I spoke. "Hello, Mr Furlington. How are you doing?" Like I cared.

"Very well, thank you and I trust you are equally healthy. Now," Mr Furlington pushed on quickly, probably due to the need to save time in order to further procrastinate on a house conveyance and in the process bizarrely attempt, via an inflated hourly rate, to justify the grotesque cost of his bill. "I expect you are more than a little disconcerted at my out-of-the-blue communication with you."

"You could say that," I acknowledged.

"Fear not, Mr Williams, I am gladly *not* the harbinger of bad news. Quite the contrary, in fact."

"Oh?" I said, my grasp of the English tongue as succinct and lucid as ever.

"Indeed. Let me explain. By chance a client of mine, I was dealing with him on a separate issue of which I am not at liberty to discuss with you, client confidentiality you understand, happened to mention the matter of an estate lake he owned."

"Oh?" I said again. This was a different 'Oh' than the first one in terms of it being an octave higher and by definition registering even greater interest than its predecessor.

"When he further went on to transcribe how his intentions of disposing of this asset had rather oddly fallen to the wayside due to the apparent evanescence of his would-be vendee, as you can imagine, my interest was piqued."

"Oh." Which may or may not have come across as something akin to 'what the fuck are you on about?'

"You see, Mr Williams, when I requested the name of his will-o'-the-wisp purchaser he told me it was Michael Edward Brown!"

"Oh!" **Exclam.** *Brit. Informal* an expression of surprise.

Mr Furlington ignored my facile grunt. "To be sure of any ambiguity I described the late Mr Brown's physical appearance and my client assured me that, yes, it was the same person. As you can appreciate at first I considered my situation to be somewhat delicate, due to having worked for Mr Brown in the past and by way of currently representing my client. However, I quickly concluded there was no conflict of interest and told my client how I had acted for Mr Brown during his life and how ultimately, in his death, explaining at the same time the answer to the mystery of his tragic non-appearance, I had acted for him in terms of being the executor of his Will... which leads us to you."

"I see," I said, not really seeing at all.

"What this means, Mr Williams, in a nutshell, is the possibility of an opportunity for your good self."

I felt as if it was time to be more proactive. "Go on," I said. "I'm always up for a grab at opportunity."

"Indeed Mr Williams! Aren't we all!" joshed Mr Furlington.

Too right, I thought, the sly bastard was probably only doing all this because there was a chance of a pay cheque at the end of it. I couldn't see him bothering to contact me solely for *my* benefit – he was a fucking *solicitor* for God's sake!

Mr Furlington went on. "My client has at his disposal a four-acre estate lake, a four-acre estate lake that the late Michael Brown had been in negotiation to purchase several years ago. When Mr Brown passed away, negotiations were still at an early stage and with no formal documentation lodged on my client's part and none lodged on Mr Brown's, the link was broken and lost… until my fortuitous conversation yesterday. As you may well have realised, Mr Brown was extremely secretive in his business dealings and my client had been left with no contact details. Mr Brown had always been the one to instigate any communications and once these had ceased, my client had been left with nowhere to turn." Mr Furlington halted, in his own mind allowing the pea-brained recipient of this latest info a chance to grapple with its implications. There, that should be long enough. He continued. "The chain of communication can now be re-forged, albeit with a different person, *you*, Mr Williams, but a person, nevertheless, shall we say, with similar interests to the late Mr Brown." Mr Furlington paused yet again, waiting to gauge my response.

"You certainly could say that," I genuinely enthused. Excitement was mounting inside me – could this lake turn out to be the winter water I had so casually mentioned to Pup? Was this the answer to the recently realised riddle of why The Syndicate was called Hamworthy Fisheries rather than Hamworthy Fishery? Michael *had* been an expansionist!

Mr Furlington's voice became even more luxuriant at my eager response – 'cat', 'cream', 'humungous fee' were the buzzwords that sprang to mind. "At this moment in time you are not known to my client, I have not told him your name. Similarly, my client isn't known to you. He knows a person exists and I have explained your circumstances, much as I have explained his to you. At this stage, all I can say is my client is keen to instruct me to ask the obvious question."

"And the obvious question is?" I said. I like these sort of things spelled out, just in case I get the wrong end of the stick and look a right plonker.

"The obvious question is, Mr Williams, would you be interested in purchasing his lake?"

I gave the question some thought, less than half a second in fact – and although a little voice in the back of my brain was screaming out something to do with not sounding too keen and giving away my poker hand – I blurted out "Not half!" with indecent haste.

"Excellent!" purred Mr Furlington. The only association with 'cat' now was I had let the bloody thing out of the bag. "Perhaps I can give you his number and you can contact Mr Hattersley direct. His first name is Felix."

"Yeah, that'll be fine, no problem," I said, somewhat mentally knocked off balance by the forename.

"I'll forward it to you by text. We have caller display at the office, no need for your number," Mr Furlington oozed and then continued, his manner more business-like. "If things should work themselves to the position where a sale is possible, I think it best if I still represent Mr Hattersley. From your point of view, you too would need legal representation, clearly not from myself or from someone within our practice, but if you wish I could make a recommendation."

Galled at my previous naivety I tried to inject a little scepticism into my reply. "Someone like that firm, now what were they called? Underhand, Shyster and Judas?"

"I haven't heard of them. Are they local?" asked Mr Furlington apparently unperturbed by my attempted satire or not noticing of it. I didn't answer and Mr Furlington filled the void. "No. I was *actually* thinking of Honey, Honey, Splenda and Sucre. They're based in Maidstone. Highly recommendable. Shall I give them your number?"

"Sweet," I replied.

"Excellent! I'll send it forthwith. Good day, Mr Williams."

"Bye, Mr Furlington."

I hung up. The number for Mr Hattersley came through thirty seconds later, via a business card text, the one for the Maidstone Mafia, shortly after.

Chapter 4

"What do you think, gentlemen? I'm offering you the chance of ownership," wheezed Felix, theatrically flourishing his hand towards the tree-lined lake, which had finally appeared before our eyes after a ten-minute walk. The ten-minute walk had been preceded by a forty-minute drive from Rambo's house and once again I was left to reflect on how many waters there were tucked away in my near vicinity – ones I knew nothing about.

As I surveyed the scene comprising the bottom bay, I caught sight of a set of lily pads coming out in spring splendour. Immediately I was reminded of the old SS water and, to be honest, I was smitten and immediately became excited at the prospect of owning the water. Although a little overgrown for fishing purposes the lake was secluded, surrounded by mature broad-leaved trees, mainly birch with a few oaks and beeches, and was as pretty as a picture. Like many estate lakes, the damming of a natural stream had originally formed it. The stream entered at the opposite end of the lake to where we were now standing and, as I looked closer, I spotted the dammed end with overflow some fifty yards to my right. The overflow, a large concrete pipe, allowed water to cascade back into the original path of the stream, the course of which followed the route we had walked since parking our cars in a lower field.

We had been informed the lake contained a few carp of the wildie variety, numerous tench and a host of stunted silver fish. In the distant past a local angling club had leased the lake, but time, and anglers' needs in general, had marched on and the current fish stocks where clearly inadequate. Everyone present realised the lake would need to be completely restocked, the trees and bankside vegetation heavily managed and the introduction of on-site amenities to turn it into a first class fishery.

I was undeterred, the setting and the results of tests on the water quality undertaken by Felix last year, which he had shown us whilst we walked up through the field, were paramount. Clearing swims and restocking, although hard work and expensive, were aspects we could control – the setting, appearance and water quality weren't! Felix had offered the prospect of ownership by his willingness to sell – in return, all we needed to do was to come up with enough money. Simple as that!

As it turned out, the previous seven days had seen the start of several offers. Apart from the initial one from Mr Furlington to contact Felix Hattersley – a man who turned out to be so fat you could almost see his arteries simultaneously being constricted by crushing exterior blubber and a rampaging cholesterol count – I had offered Hamworthy's Lieutenant, Timothy Eugene Ramsbottom, the chance to accompany me to look at a possible prospective winter water. The final, and only unwanted offer, went to Pup, from an unknown self-styled bait baron. The offer on Pup's rolling table was the opportunity to sell his entire range of bait recipes lock, stock and boilie and to merge his vast knowledge with a new bait company in readiness for a comprehensive, mass market, commercial launch.

Pup, being Pup, had told the self-styled bait baron he could go shove a throwing stick up his arse – sideways. *Literally*, that is what he had said. No 'How much for?', 'What are you actually offering?', 'Tell me more' or 'Who exactly are you?'. Only the scathingly terse reply had been uttered, followed by the equally curt 'click' of disconnection. Maybe he had been right to do so. Perhaps it had been a wind-up. I had only questioned his attitude in the interest of wanting to find out a smidgen more if only for curiosity's sake.

"Weren't you even the slightest bit interested?" I had asked Pup when he had told me.

"No! Of course I wasn't interested! Why on earth would I be interested?" he had indignantly responded.

I suppose, if I were a bait anorak and an ace boiliemeister, owning a house reeking of the pungent pong of a thousand rampant flavours, I might have told him to sod off as well. Who knows? All I knew was, bearing in mind the current pleasing view in front of my eyes, I was glad I hadn't followed in a similar vein and been quite so rude and dismissive to Mr Furlington. In fact I had been told, *warned* in reality, to play it canny and keep any enthusiasm, should it rear its hearty head, well in check.

"Keep a fucking lid on it," Rambo had said in the van as we had arrived fashionably late for our appointment. "Or it could end up costing you big style."

I had said I would try and bear it in mind and play it cool.

"It's a lovely water, I'll give you that," I said answering Felix. "Although maybe a little small, ideally, for what we had in mind," I said playing out my part as told.

Rambo gave me the subtlest of approving head nods. The art of striking a deal, with all its nuances and suggestions, he had cautioned, started from the moment we arrived. This was all very well, but my enthusiasm meant my mindset from the very outset was, if the place was half decent, and now having seen it, it patently was, I would like to buy it. Hamworthy *Fisheries*! Plural. And I had never wondered why! I don't think anybody had, not until Pup had mentioned it. It *had* been Michael's long-term game plan, to own and then syndicate more than one venue. He evidently had been trying to negotiate a second water, until the pair of us had turned the screw on him over the ghost and he had finally discovered enough inner guilt to top himself.

I was utterly convinced, now I had seen the venue that I wanted to complete what he had started. A nice little winter syndicate was the order of the day! One to be made into a runs water with stacks of twenties and the odd thirty, or, even better, stacks of thirties with the odd forty – I really was getting carried away! The pair of waters would dovetail perfectly to give the ultimate all year entertainment. Carp fishing perfection for all four seasons! The opportunity was there for the taking, as

Mr Furlington had suggested, the question, of course, was cash.

Apart from Rambo's disapproval of a full on, buy, buy, buy mentality, there was the small matter of Sophie's practical objections.

"Why on earth do you need *another* water?" she had asked. "I thought the present one was the finest carp fishery in England?" she had said sarcastically. "So what's the point?"

"Britain," I had corrected. "Sometimes I say 'in the Northern Hemisphere', although that's a bit stupid because there isn't much I know of in the Southern Hemisphere, so I should say 'in the World'."

Unsurprisingly this hadn't dampened her line of attack. "How much will it cost? Do we really want to use a large amount of our nest egg on buying *another* carp fishery?"

"I'll only use money I inherited from The Syndicate," I had countered

"Will it be enough?"

"Yeah, plenty," I had lied. "If I go in with Rambo. The guy's desperate to sell."

She had given me an unconvinced look of mild disapproval and thankfully left it at that. At least we weren't arguing about each other's lovers and had settled for the old chestnut of money! Instinctively, I felt I was on a reasonable footing in both the financial and behavioural sense by proposing to use only Syndicate money. Time would tell if she felt the same, the time being if and when I put an offer in. I now knew, having seen the lake with my own two eyes, it was going to be a 'when'.

Unfortunately, regards my little white lie about being desperate to sell, the only thing Felix Hattersley looked desperate for was a sit down – and maybe a bacon sandwich or three. Sweat beaded on his large rotund face and the skin on his huge ham arms, showing below a voluminous, short-sleeved shirt glowed red behind a mass of freckles. It was hot for the time of the year, granted, (yeah, yeah, I know, global warming) yet I couldn't see him giving the place away no matter how uncomfortable he felt. Although a veritable fat bastard, Felix's demeanour was far from one of a man riddled with low esteem and poor body image. He came across as assured, confident and with the intelligent air of someone who had benefited from a prosperous upbringing. I had the feeling he had attended a public school. He wasn't going to be a negotiation pushover. What a shame!

I had the thick edge of 160k in Syndicate funds, built up over the years by Michael, and to a much lesser extent, myself. To add to this sum were all the 1st deposits held in a separate account. I had paid back one deposit to Noel when he had left, Pup was on a freebie as was Rambo, and as Supreme Syndicate Leader, I didn't pay one either, so there were sixteen £2500s making £40,000. It wasn't going to be anywhere near enough. Felix knew what his water was worth, although he obviously hadn't managed to sell it or seemingly get any other interest in it since Michael had disappeared off the scene. Or had he? There was another unknown in the mixing pot. Were we going to be used to gazump someone else? Was the sole reason Rambo and I had been duped into coming along simply to raise the bid? And would it in turn be raised once more by the competition, sending the price spiralling in a giddying rise of cut-throat inflation? We would have to wait and see how the game panned out.

The bottom line of my financial situation made me realise if Rambo and I had become a partnership in deeds over the years, we would have to become a legal one to buy Felix's water. I didn't have enough to fund it all on my own and I dare not ask Sophie for a sub from 'our' money. The thing was, did Rambo have the wedge or the inclination? Had Steffi spent it all and would she have a say? I hadn't asked as yet.

"Shall we walk round?" Rambo asked.

"Certainly," said Felix.

"How did you come to own this place?" I enquired as we set off.

"The estate as a whole has been in the family for over two hundred years," Felix answered. "I'm the last in line and with no possibility of having a heir, I'm selling it off."

On hearing this, I quickly thought how right I had been concerning his upbringing, yet how wrong about the lack of low esteem and poor body image. From his last statement the man palpably felt he had no chance of ever pulling a woman, let alone knocking her up!

Felix soon put me right on this score. "I'm homosexual, you see, and *shan't* be adopting!"

There was an uneasy silence from Rambo and I, although Felix didn't seem fazed by his bursting out of the closet like a rhino charging out of a swimming pool locker.

"Oh, right," I said politely.

Felix seemed affable enough with my response and continued with the background history. "The house was sold along with the grounds years ago, but the lake, with its separate access and surrounding boundary is still available. There's seven acres overall. I think the first field we walked up through, the one next to the road, would be well suited to converting into a hard standing car park. At the lake, with its surrounding land, there's ample room for some useful utilities. You could easily clear an area and put up some outbuildings. They'd have to be wooden structures, glorified sheds essentially," he pointed out. "I'm afraid the covenant would stop anything more intrusive and permanent. However, water and electricity wouldn't be a problem. They could be laid on without too much bother. If you went for the full monty and put in a sceptic tank, you could at least have a proper toilet and washing facilities. There's nothing to stop you doing that, or running the lake as a commercial venture."

Nice, I thought, another functional wooden clubhouse.

"The potential's there and so is the cost of doing it!" observed Rambo. "What with swim clearing, the re-stocking and all the other expenses, you'd be looking at over a hundred grand to get everything up and running. And that's on top of what you want for the place. It's a lot of money."

"I'm sure we can sort something out that's agreeable all round," said Felix wiping his brow with a hanky and stopping to lean against a tree, one affording him some shade. He took a deep breath. "Why don't you two circumnavigate the lake together and have a chat, talk things over and I'll wait here. I know you'll want to discuss things without me being in the way."

"Okay," agreed Rambo. "And just so we've something to discuss, what sort of ballpark figure have you got in mind?" he asked, cutting to the chase.

Felix straightened himself up from the tree, possibly so his weight didn't push it over and devalue the estate. "I'm looking, as estate agents so eloquently put it, in the region of three hundred and ninety-five thousand," said Felix.

"Mm, *are* you?" said Rambo in a voice making plain the exorbitant nature of the figure.

"The young boys, whose company I like to keep, tend to be rather expensive," Felix countered flatly.

If his last line was meant to throw the pair of us, it certainly worked. After exchanging mute glances and what seemed like an age, we managed to nod, turned are backs on Felix and set off round the lake. Once we were out of earshot I asked Rambo the 50k question – in terms of the show 'Are You Smarter Than a Ten Year Old?'

"What do you think?"

Rambo gave me a considered look. "I'm not particularly au fait with their hourly rates."

I rolled my eyes. "Not the fucking rent boys, the lake!"

Rambo snorted. "Just kidding. What's your first impression?"

"Felix *definitely* needs to go on a crash diet."

Rambo's face hardened to a diamond-like toughness. "Enough of the jokes, eh, boy?"

"I like it," I answered soberly, suitably chastised. "A lot."

"Me too! I like the results of the water test."

Excellent! At last we were coming from the same direction! I wondered if Felix had ever managed a similar trick with one of his young boys. Fortunately, Rambo was off to other more important matters and dragged me with him.

"The lake's got a good pH value, despite the trees. Look at the pads," he said pointing to a set coming up in the margin we were passing. "There are plenty of nutrients in the water, they wouldn't be growing otherwise. It's got potential, the setting's good and if the place is set up right from the start and looked after, it could be a cracking water. The thing is, do you want the hassle? And can you afford it?"

"The hassle?" I ventured.

"Yes. The *hassle*, Matt," said an earnest Rambo. "Setting it all up, sorting out contractors, sourcing the fish, sourcing the *members*!"

"We'll use Hamworthy fish, won't we?" I asked surprised.

Rambo stopped walking and turned to face me. "If this is going to be a winter runs water, do you want to be the one who decides to stock it with mature fish who have a track record of turning the lights off from December to February?"

"I never thought of that," I admitted. "Would they behave the same in a different water?"

"I don't know. My view is, why take the chance? The stock pond is pretty empty and you would need a lot of fish fast. This place needs to be slightly overstocked if it's to be a winter runs water and offer a different type of fishing to Hamworthy." Rambo's face turned sombre. "Just remember, Matt," he said gravely. "You'll still have to come here in the summer to keep an eye on it. Check on the fish, check on the members, you'll have to have members to get some money back, plus they'll be the eyes and ears with a vested interest to help look after the place, provided you can weed out the bad ones! You think of all what constitutes running The Syndicate, then times it by two. *Three* to begin with! Maybe even six! *Ten*!" I mentally boggled at Rambo's exponential ramblings and let him continue uninterrupted. "There's no short cut! You'll fish less to begin with and there'll be aggro and admin by the shed load. In a few years' time, if you're lucky and pay what he wants, you'll have a winter runs water, a dozen or so good members and only be out of pocket by four hundred grand. If things go badly…" Rambo pulled the face of a professional gurner.

Damning him and his pragmatism, I felt slightly crestfallen. In my heart I knew part of the real reason for my desire to carry on what Michael had started was the extra purpose it would give to my carp fishing life. If things had gone quiet on the adventure front, what more perfect an antidote than the setting up of a brand new carp fishery? I could boast a portfolio of waters if it came to fruition and, more to the point, have somewhere to fish in winter. Somewhere I *owned*, where I had a real chance of catching something decent! I didn't want to muck about fishing other people's waters, fishing with people I didn't know and hadn't vetted, especially for fish of an undisclosed origin. Sod that!

I wondered if I was in the early stages of megalomania and chronic carp snobbery.

"It's only money," I garbled. "What else am I going to spend it on? I've got enough from Sophie's Mum to cover the other stuff in my life, but, and it's a big but, I haven't got enough Syndicate money to do all that's required here." It was time to ask. "How do you feel about coming in as a fifty-fifty partner?" I leaned over towards Rambo and put my hand on his shoulder. "What was the point of you killing yourself off, ripping off all your customers when you were an arms dealer if it wasn't for the chance of blowing the lot on a project like this?"

Rambo glared at me for a few seconds. "Is this a definitive business offer?"

"Too right, mate!" I replied. "Like I said, I can't afford the fucking lot myself! I'm not even sure I can afford fifty-fifty, even *if* we knock fat boy down a few thou!"

"Oh, we'll knock him down, don't you worry! Come on."

"'*We*'?"

Rambo smiled. "I'm *in*! I've always wanted my own water!"

"Brilliant!" I exclaimed. "Nice one!"

The new prospective Williams/Ramsbottom venture 'carpitalists' set off and carried on walking up to the far end of the lake sucking in the ambience. As we lapped the lake I pictured myself tucked up in the middle of winter on a day trip, the trees bare of leaves, a crisp January day temperature of thirteen degrees centigrade, (you know why) getting three runs in a day from fish up to low thirties. It was a compelling vision – especially compared to blanking your bollocks off on Hamworthy!

Money and circumstance had changed me. I *was* a carp snob – there was no denying it. I wanted to fish in exceptional surroundings, for exceptional fish with decent, sensible anglers – the less in number the better. It was an aspiration undoubtedly shared by many and fate had given me the chance to realise such dreams. Although Felix's water wouldn't be as easy a ride as Michael's, I felt a burning desire to complete what he had started – to make a deal and subsequently create a winter water. With Rambo now onboard it was possible to make that deal happen. When we met back up with Felix we said we would make him an offer via our solicitor in the next couple of days.

Chapter 5

"Why the bloody hell did we let him talk us into doing this?" I moaned, slumping against one of the internal, Barley White-daubed stud walls belonging to *Chez Rambo*.

It was a fair question – it was only four in the morning and I was already in his utility room with a van full of 'one I prepared earlier' fishing kit parked on the herringbone-block driveway. Getting up early was never a favourite pastime of mine, even if it involved fishing, and a few years on Hamworthy with sensible flight times for the ensuing overnighter had only lessened my resolve for them.

Rambo chuckled. "Probably because you know we'll win and your carping ego couldn't resist! Add in the possibility it'll take your mind off your mid-life crisis and we're somewhere near the truth!"

"I don't know about that," I lied. "In any case, we don't know if we're casters or boaters yet."

Rambo looked up from the massive rucksack he was packing. "I don't think it's going to make much difference. I fished The Bowl years and years ago and it isn't a big water. It's not as if there's going to be a two-hundred-yard island margin cast to make. Actually, there's not even going to *be* an island cast to make. The Bowl by name, the bowl by nature! If you were looking for an ideal venue to give bland uniformity and a complete lack of features, then The Bowl's top of the list!" Rambo stopped to cram an obstinate item of tackle deeper into his voluminous bag and, satisfied all was completed on the packing front, stood up and placed the ever-present Glock into the top of his camo trousers. He probably had a written note from Steffi giving him permission – for the camo trousers that is, not the gun.

Memories tumbled back from the past – I erased them as best I could.

Rambo continued his appraisal of The Bowl. "Not much fun for proper carping, but for something like today, ideal. With its virtually identical, interchangeable swims and complete lack of features making the draw of little consequence, it's perfect. I can tell you, free of charge, boy, that it's a venue where bait and its application reign utterly supreme." Rambo gave me an inverted-coat-hanger-in-the-mouth smile. "Remember, boy, we have a certain exclusive, revolutionary, indented, dirty brown bottom bait boilie and we can pile it in either with or without a baitboat!" Rambo stood up. "What time are we meeting Pup?"

"Six. At the registration tent."

Pup! It was Pup's fault I was suffering from sleep deprivation because it had been his idea for us to fish the competition at The Bowl. Over a calendar month had passed since we had visited Felix's water and despite little progress on that particular front, carp fishing had catapulted into the news thanks to the 'Pulimov effect'. As I had predicted, the fishing press had milked it for all its worth – well, the weeklies had, the poor old monthlies would frantically catch up as soon as their scheduling allowed – so had the national press and so had some of the more fly commercial venue operators.

Seeing an opening for an increase in revenue many had set up 'No Seventies in Here, Mate!' matches. Mocking their fatal lack of pig-sized carp regards the chance of lifting 'Pulimov's Prize', as it was rapidly becoming known, they had sought to recompense anglers by way of smaller – but worthy – cash prizes for winning carp catching contests. The bigger venues were offering rewards up to a grand first prize plus staggered cash rewards for second and third places. By pitching the entry fee at a ton a pair to organise, run and provide food over 48-hour comps, they soon found they could pull in more money than by selling day tickets. The carping army, gripped as one due to the galvanising effect of suddenly being depicted as an integral part of the British way of life – and portrayed as an acceptable cult, rather than the previous perception of a sad set of fuckers festering on the bankside smelling of shit and fish slime – leapt at the chance to participate.

A wave of something akin to hysteria grabbed carp anglers everywhere and those who never had access to a water holding a seventy, i.e. ninety-nine point nine per cent of them, went for the next best thing. A plethora of matches sprung up, seemingly overnight, as those who earned their money through the commercial carp fishery industry frantically scrambled aboard the gravy train before the eyes of the world turned and the moment was lost. The Bowl's owners, shamelessly grabbing on to two coat-tails, had set up a 'No Seventies Match' with the added perceived attraction of dividing contestants into those who cast out and those who employed a baitboat – a format originally grounded, legend had it, by a group of carpers chatting on an Internet carp forum. The Bowl was where we were heading – thanks to Pup.

Almost inevitably some of the fishing press had fallen into the trap of hyperbole and I had read one article where the author, probably on drugs, had asked if fishing was going to be the new football. Well, 'no', was the short answer. The same question had been asked when the English rugby team had won the World Cup and when the cricket team had regained The Ashes in a thrilling five test series. True, the nation had momentarily become infatuated with Wilkinson and Flintoff and their respective sports, but as ever it had been short-lived. Like zombie moths to an excessive flame we had soon forgotten and naturally gravitated back to our true back page obsession. Gone was the egg-shaped ball, the quiet intricacies of leather on willow and assuming its rightful place at the top of the pile was the beautiful game – players on 100k a week, Sky pundits telling you every match was fantastic, masses of imported players, re-mortgage-the-house priced tickets, whining managers, scapegoat referees, £40 replica shirts (as changed from last season) and the so-called 'golden generation' national team incapable of achieving even the lower tiers of underwhelming mediocrity.

To be honest I was glad – I couldn't keep up with all the injuries in rugby or when it was supposed to be a ruck as opposed to a maul. Equally I wasn't too sure of the exact difference between a googly, a flipper and an arm ball, let alone fathoming out cricket's fielding positions. Carp fishing was never a threat to football and it had been absurd to suggest such a notion, yet the continuing publicity was greater than ever before and by any method of reckoning a massive fillip for all of angling.

It wasn't only the fishing press who were absorbed by the ramifications of Pulimov's Prize. Famous anglers were quoted in broadsheets, they appeared on terrestrial TV rather than minority satellite productions and serious journalists rigorously explored the whole cult of carp fishing. Amazingly it was not ridiculed. Deep, meaningful pieces were written concerning the nature of angling, man the hunter, and shockingly to some, man the exponent of catch and release. The most fundamental rule of our little world almost seemed a revelation to the uninitiated and many a seasoned journalist marvelled at the effort, financial, physical and mental involved in pulling out a huge carp, weighing it, photographing it and quietly putting it back to allow someone else to aspire to his dreams.

All the positives of angling were described in detail and any less savoury aspects ignored. More publicity, more praise and more appreciation of the noble art of angling was heaped upon it than at any other time in its history. Sales of all carp fishing books, all *fishing* books rocketed – even old Izaak enjoyed a revival – and any voice raised against us from the antis was swept away by the towering wave of favourable publicity. As some crusty old politician said years ago, although admittedly not about carp fishing: 'You've never had it so good'.

On the back of all the interest trade flourished. Ex-anglers took up their rods again, saw they were crap compared to the modern ones, and bought new ones. Ditto reels and bite alarms. Large item sales went up. End tackle bits and bobs sold by the lorry load. Bait sales blossomed. Rod licence sales went through the stratosphere. Venues became jammed packed. A positive exuberance gripped British anglers and shook them so violently they became punch drunk with delight – and all because of a Russian oligarch.

Me? Much like the journalists I watched and marvelled and then, true to type, quietly turned to worry as Hamworthy became busier than ever. Alan, our resident artist, who I was pretty sure was now the longest standing member, told me he had never seen the pit so active. To reiterate my viewpoint, I wrote to all the members warning them of the publicity ban and how anyone publishing captures would be expelled. I hoped it would do the trick, but on my last visit the place had seemed like Oxford Street on a Saturday afternoon by normal standards. Of the twenty swims sixteen were occupied where usual occupancy levels would have been four or five at most, typically three. I prayed Gut Bucket would keep its head low and not offer one of the members the ultimate in temptation. From bitter personal experience I was an expert on the subject of temptation and just how difficult it was to ignore!

Today, my grumpy morning manner was not entirely caused by departing my bed in the dark. Apart from having to get up at stupid o'clock to fish in the match the chance of knocking down the price of Felix's water in the current climate was slim. We had instructed Mr Honey to tell Mr Furlington to tell Mr Hattersley that an offer of a 300k had been made by Messieurs Ramsbottom and Williams. Unfortunately Mr Hattersley had told Mr Furlington to tell Mr Honey to tell Messieurs Ramsbottom and Williams to poke it up their arse. Of course, Mr Honey hadn't said it exactly in those stark tones, but given the sexuality of the lake's owner it seemed an apt interpretation of the formal negative reply we had received. With the ball now firmly in our court we had promptly popped it into a tubular tin, sat on some chairs and reached for the Robinson's barley water. It was time to play the waiting game.

The Warp Factor 8 carp market was one reason for our procrastination, the attempt to flush out anyone else in the bidding, another. Many markets thrive on confidence; housing, investment etc. and we were willing to wager Felix felt it applied to carp waters as well – doubly so if another bidder was involved. At Rambo's say we held fire, trying to squeeze Felix into revealing the strength of his hand. It was a policy I felt to be high risk, one where we could lose our chance by misconceived disinterest, but Rambo had insisted. I had little option but to go along with it. As Rambo had pointed out, if we paid too high initially we would never – certainly *I* would never – be able to finance all the work to be undertaken afterwards. It was all very frustrating – I had Michael's dream to realise!

Why Pup was so keen for the pair of us to fish this particular match seemed unclear. He had repeatedly glossed over the details as he had continuously begged Rambo and I to enter. In an effort to persuade us, he had promised us the lot – to be our Team Manager, to oversee our efforts on the bank, to cater for our every whim and to treat us as if we were a pair of pampered divas. He had promised to roll us fresh bait for the match, to be our devoted gopher, to pay our entrance fees and let us keep the cash prize when we had won. Not 'if', 'when'. In short, nothing would be too much effort for him. Of course, it was blatantly obvious something was up – the rat we had smelt was big, fat, had died a week ago and was lying on a silver platter held half an inch from our noses – yet we had eventually succumbed to his constant chivvying. We had said yes due to *our* egos, I'm sure – not only mine – as Rambo had said. On finally relenting and asking why he so desperately wanted us to participate Pup had said he would tell us on the day.

"That's not good enough!" I had protested wondering what the boiliemeister was up to. "It's not anything *horrendous*, is it?" I had further enquired.

"No. Nothing at all," he had replied energetically flapping his hands as if to waft away my concerns.

"Nothing?" I had pushed further.

"I need more time to find out," he had vaguely proffered. "All I can say is the bait grapevine is buzzing and I *need* your help. That's *it* at this point in time." Pup had pulled a soppy puppy-dog-on-a-greetings-card face. "Remember, if it wasn't for me, you wouldn't own…"

Rambo had let out a weary sigh. "He knows, Pup, put another record on."

"Grapevine?" I had said distractedly, my train of thought in a different station to Rambo's. "What a *great* name for a boilie! Word of mouth rumour, the hint of a flavour, pretty apt I reckon."

Pup's head had swivelled and his eyes had hooked on to mine. "Grapevine! I like that too! Can I use it?"

"Feel free, I don't exactly have a patent on the word. But remember, if it turns out better than our exclusive, revolutionary, indented, dirty brown bottom bait boilie, *I'll* be asking the same question!"

Pup had given me a patronising grin that soon disappeared. "Don't be late. Six at the registration tent," he had cautioned.

As it happened we arrived at a quarter to, our journey from Rambo's house uneventful apart from me getting a brief glimpse of Steffi in her bathrobe when he had kissed her goodbye. Despite myself, I had imagined her going straight into a porn scene and peeling her kit off. Those days were over for her, and the sooner I could get to grips with it the better, I quickly reminded myself! Disturbingly, I had wondered, I have to admit, what it would be like to sleep with her. Those days were over for *me* as well! And, *definitely*, the sooner I could get to grips with it the better, I *very* quickly reminded myself!

Pup was already there and waiting. "All right, lads?" he asked.

"Apart from having to get up at four o'clock and *still* not knowing why you were so keen to have us fish here," came my sharp reply.

Rambo in full-on camo-mode towered over Pup and gave him one of his legendary index finger pokes to the chest, causing the baitmeister to stagger back on his heels. "Yeah! Come on, boy, let's have the word! You said you were going to find out more."

Pup looked conspiratorially to his left and right and motioned for us to move away from the tent's opening and around to the side. Once we were away from the bustle of anglers checking in and chatting to each other, boasting of their latest captures, the latest killer rigs, Pulimov's Prize and which women on telly they'd rather like to have sex with, Pup started talking in a hushed voice. "The bait world's in a state of high excitement," he declared.

"*All* carp fishing's in a state of high excitement, thanks to Mr Pulimov, so what?" I stated with a touch of irritability. God knows what was happening at Hamworthy while I, and more pertinently, Rambo, weren't there.

"But *not* because of that!" Pup countered. "The high excitement is over a new player trying to muscle in. Word on the rolling benches is someone is trying to make a big push into the market and is trying to monopolise and control a large section of the bait industry! There's never been anything like it before!" Pup keenly regarded our reaction to this bombshell. He was probably disappointed.

"New bait companies crop up all the time, boy, they don't last long, but they keep trying. It's the old make-money-from-your-passion scenario a lot of the time," was

Rambo's unruffled reply.

"But it's the method!" Pup retorted. "He's not starting up his own company, he's trying to muscle in on *existing* ones!"

"Who is it?" I asked.

"This is the strange part, no one really knows," Pup answered, his eyes wide and excitable. "The style is always one of anonymous menacing harassment. The offer is usually a combination of money, intimidation and threatening behaviour. It's not a normal business approach at all!" Pup sneered. "Many of the smaller, less prominent outfits have already sold out. They've had to sign a contract agreeing not to start up another bait business for five years. Apparently this has been backed up by suggestions of violence should they even think about it. For those who *don't* sell, well, his business methods are unorthodox to say the least."

"What do you mean?" I asked.

"You remember the radio news item from four weeks ago?"

"Leviathan boilies?" I remarked remembering Pup's piece of news.

"Exactly! Burnt out! *Arson*! Production halted for months if not for good. This bloke doesn't muck about, he offers his money, but if you turn him down it looks like you might get a little visit from his henchmen! I've heard of several other firms where the owner's been given a kicking or their car's mysteriously been vandalised!"

"Oh, come on! People can't go round operating like that!" I sneered, unimpressed by Pup's Jackanory-like fairy tale. "I expect everyone's putting two and two together and coming up with five!" I gave an unimpressed shake of the head. "I expect the fire was an accident and there's someone out there with a bit of financial clout looking to make legit acquisitions and the rest is rumour and bullshit!"

"Do you think it's the same bloke or gang who phoned you up?" said Rambo apparently more inclined to take Pup at face value.

Pup's eyes lowered. "Yeah. I think so, although I haven't been threatened physically. Those who have can't prove anything regards the nasty stuff. He's very professional in that area! I don't think the police have got a lead on anyone as yet." A look of disgust crept across Pup's face. "Word is those who have taken the money are keeping their mouths fully zipped and are not saying anything."

I listened to Pup rant on encapsulated in a personal bubble of sardonicism. What a load of old bollocks! How typical of the bait industry to go completely and utterly over the top. Whether they were bragging about the catching power of their latest wonder bait, supersonic particle preparation, killer pop-up or the financial implications of a few firms getting bought out, it was always the same old slant – overblown, overstated, excessively enlarged embellishment! The tossers! Not that Pup could be told anything to the contrary – his mind was made up.

"So, this nasty new player is definitely the bloke who phoned you up?" I asked.

"Yeah. It *is* him who's been pestering me, I'm almost certain… and that's why I asked you here today."

"Oh, great!" I exclaimed. "Here we go! 'Nothing to worry about' you said! Not bloody much by the sounds of it!"

Pup glowered at me. "I thought *you* thought it was all rubbish," he said coldly. "*You* don't know what he said to me." I shut up and shrugged my shoulders to show I was receptive to what was coming next, even if I wasn't. Pup's voice tone resumed normality. "He started phoning up lots of times, about a week after I had first cut him off. He said he'd heard I had an excellent reputation and wanted to make me an offer I couldn't refuse, which naturally I did, although not as brusquely as last time. He sucked me in to talking you see," Pup added his voice laced with guilt. "He said I might regret not listening fully to what he had to say. He said he'd be very generous in buying up my business and would allow me to stay on to oversee mass production. He wanted me to be the head of what would be, as he put it, 'the country's biggest and best bait company'. I told *him* I ran an individual outfit personally making unique baits and I was *not* someone who associated himself with any old mass produced shite! I told him my baits were better than anyone else's. Better than any factory could produce, no matter how much their R and D budget and no matter how many so-called superstars they had back-filling their targeted circuit water. I told him my baits would win through every time."

"I bet that upset him!" grinned Rambo. "*And* the consultancy carpers!

I slapped an open palm on my forehead. "You fucking idiot!" I moaned seeing where this was leading. "And then he said 'prove it' and you, like the complete and utter gormless muppet you are, agreed!"

"Now, just a minute," Pup started. "He began dismissing my bait, saying his products were better, saying there was no way I could compete with him and that I was too small!"

"So?" I said infuriated at how I had been dragged into the bait world's boilie wars. "Why didn't you put the phone down like last time? Blank him out."

"He'd been phoning up loads," Pup whined, "even before I spoke to him. The phone was ringing every hour, they weren't proper orders coming in, most of the calls were made by him! Mel was getting well freaked out by it." Pup stopped and spoke very softly. "You see, he said if I could prove my baits were better he'd leave me alone."

I gawped at Rambo, saying nothing. My incredulity Geiger Counter clicked faster than an amphetamine powered Jazz singer's fingers during an up-tempo song.

"And you believed him?" Rambo enquired with a cool air.

Pup's eyes hit the deck, his head bowed. "Yes," he mumbled self-consciously.

"With him allegedly beating people up and burning down their factories?" Rambo continued with the amused air of a parent interrogating a small child over a minor misdemeanour. Pup nodded. Rambo put a huge paw on one of his shoulders and patted him with it. I half expected to see Pup starting to get knocked into the ground like a bivvy peg. "Boy, you are a wonderful bait maker and my carp fishing has been vastly more successful thanks to it, even, if I say so myself, my original red bait wasn't half bad." Rambo shot me an enquiring glance and I nodded enthusiastically.

We *had* won the TWTT on it! "Unfortunately you are a bit of a dick when it comes to matters *not* appertaining to bait!" Rambo shook his head in a sorry manner. "Let's hope this doesn't spiral out of control in the next couple of days and leave me with the unhappy ordeal of having to crunch a few noses to put it right."

Rambo didn't sound exactly unhappy at the prospect of crunching a few noses – rather the opposite. I decided to keep this observation to myself and concentrated on being annoyed at Pup for dragging the pair of us into this ridiculous mess.

"So what was the exact low-down?" I said gruffly.

"This so-called bait baron reckons everyone else today will be on baits supplied by his firm. Not that he has any idea what's in them!" Pup remarked haughtily. "And I said you two would kick everyone's arses whether you were casters or a boaters."

"No pressure!" I mocked whilst secretly warming to the vision of me and Rambo wiping the floor with a mop dunked in the flavour of exclusive, revolutionary, indented, dirty brown bottom bait boilie – the flavour known to kill off ninety-nine point nine per cent of all Noddies in 48-hours flat!

In spite of my outburst of protestation I still didn't think someone was using violence and arson to help force through a few business deals. It was all too over the top and far fetched. Admittedly it did seem there was a person or company new to the scene bent on getting in, one throwing a bit of money around coupled with an aggressive not-taking-no-for-an-answer attitude. As to anything more sinister than that? No way! The bait world's grapevine (available in 10, 14, 18 and 22mm sizes) and its usual hysterical claims accounted for the rest!

Despite this I decided not to let Pup off the hook so easy. "You know, we ought to pull out. Just for not telling us the truth!" I chastised.

"Sorry," said Pup. "I thought it would end once you won. Maybe it will."

"You should have said," Rambo told Pup sternly. "Talked over the matter with us earlier." Rambo scratched the stubble on a jutting jaw Desperate Dan would have killed for. "Still, we're here now, we might as well stay and enjoy the fun. Let's go and sign in and find out if we have to cast or use a baitboat."

As always, we did as Rambo suggested and the three of us went back to the first tent's entrance – there were two tents side by side – and joined the queue of anglers who were registering. The back of the line was outside the tent and as the minutes passed we gradually edged forward until, after a quarter of an hour, we were nearing the front. It was then that I first saw him, sitting behind the trestle table doubling up as a desk. Time had aged him – badly – the once handsome face was drawn and lined, the hair grey and thinner, his eyes markedly duller and housed in sallow sockets behind thick-lens glasses. For all the temporal degradation it was undoubtedly him. I mentally chuckled at how my two greatest enemies had both become seriously downgraded in the appearance stakes due to their unhealthy involvement with myself. My sleight of hand had ruined Hollywood's looks and I was convinced the haggard soul before me had degraded far quicker than normal due to his past involvement with myself.

The person I was soon to encounter had been my original nemesis all those years ago – he had been Moriarty, myself, Holmes. In reality it had been more Tom and Jerry, given the cartoon-like ending of our final encounter! There, behind the trestle table, officially registering all the competing anglers, sat Tom Watt. Tom Watt, the arrogant, cheating fraudster from the original Southern Specimens syndicate. Realistically it wasn't such a big coincidence our paths were shortly to cross after all these years of avoidance, but the prospect still made me feel uncomfortable. I realised it was going to be socially awkward – as awkward as unhooking a gorged deadbait from a large, angry pike with a pair of eyebrow tweezers.

"Look who it is," I murmured to Rambo. "At the table."

Rambo, who was towering above everyone else present, clocked the figure at the table. A broad smile spread across his face. "Well, well. If it isn't Mr Wherethefucksmybivvygone! This should be comical."

I wasn't convinced and ushered Pup in front of the pair of us, employing him as a human shield, whilst quickly giving him a whispered potted history of our involvement with the seated bureaucrat. Ideally, I should have handed him a draft of my prison memoirs and he could have speed-read them – Data-style from Star Trek the Next Generation – thus fully briefing himself on the whole grisly tale. Sadly, seeing as no such tome was present and Pup's reading ability was probably limited to the narrow confines of bait literature and Hamworthy Fisheries' rules at a plodding thirty words a minute, Pup was rendered ill-equipped to understand the Byzantine features of the Watt/Williams relationship.

Who was I kidding? It had boiled down to one thing – he had fucking hated me and I had fucking hated him. Fucking hated him enough to lob a couple of Rambo's handy hand grenades into his bivvy and blow the lot to kingdom come – and get eighteen months in the slammer for doing so! Ah, nostalgia! I wondered if the passing of time had eroded his ire. To be honest, I had no strong feelings towards the sad, old, washed-up carper who was now a menial administrator wielding a wanked-out biro as he perched his saggy, arthritic arse on a pathetic, wonky plastic chair – apart from contempt, obviously.

Watt had hardly looked up from his paperwork, only for the briefest cursory glance at each angler, and so still hadn't noticed his least favoured carp anglers in the whole galaxy were about to burst back into his life. When it was our turn it was Pup as our official gopher who became the mouthpiece.

"Williams and Ramsbottom, anglers, under the management of Pup Enterprises," he stated.

The affect was instant. Watt's ballpoint ground to a sickening halt and I noticed the tips of the fingers holding it whiten as a sudden extra pressure was exerted on the pen. Watt looked up, peered over the top of his bottle-bottom specs and forced a smiled that fooled no one. "Why, Matthew, Rambo, how nice to see you again. What a surprise. How are you?" And he stood up and offered Rambo his hand to shake.

"Hello, Watt," Rambo said coldly ignoring the outstretched paw. "Got a new bivvy yet? Got a new *wife*, come to that?"

Watt pulled his now ridiculous unshaken hand away sharply. His lips pulled tight and colour drained from his face. "Yes, thank you. Rather a nice one actually," he blustered.

"Are we talking tents or tarts here?" Rambo asked drolly.

Watt went to answer back, but something checked him. "I think it best we just proceed with what's required," he said sitting back down. "I've tried to be civil and forget your wrongdoings of the past, but clearly you still…"

Rambo placed both of his huge hands flat on the desk, scrunching up some of Watt's paperwork in the process – he would have to iron it later – and lent into Watt's personal space. "*Our* wrongdoings?" he said menacingly, his eyes boring into Watt's. "I *don't* think so."

Watt's upper lip had beaded with sweat and his complexion resembled the colour of Rambo's utility wall, the one I had lent against and probably scuffed earlier in the day.

"One hundred pounds entrance fee and I need a credit card left as security for the baitboat," Watt stated, trying to put some semblance of authority into his voice and ignore the silverback gorilla stance of the camouflaged man-mountain eighteen inches from his nose.

Rambo lifted his weight off the table, eased backwards and Pup tossed a thin wad of tenners on the table followed by his MasterCard. Watt made a play of counting the money, even holding one of the tenners up to the light to check it. Once satisfied there were ten, and all were genuine, he placed the cash and card in a security box and issued Pup with a receipt for his card. He then gave us a green card with a number on it and an orange card with a number on it.

Watt's voice was brusque and his face had reddened a little. "The green card has your swim number nine on it. Take the orange card to the next tent and pick up your baitboat. Fishing starts at ten. I would say good luck, but I wouldn't mean it." Watt pulled off his spectacles in the well-rehearsed manner of a pompous prig. "Try not to ruin the event for everyone else. You know how over competitive you two become in a competition."

"Huh!" I huffed, slightly taken aback by how quickly the old git had recovered his composure.

Watt stood up and leant over to me, invading *my* personal space. I was sure I could see his body shaking, which was at least something – he was less self-possessed than I had first surmised. "You cocky little bastard," he whispered venomously. "You should think twice before ever crossing me again. I'm a very influential man, you know. I know people. I've got power. The power to crush you and your muscleman like a bug."

"Wow! Sorry, *Tommy*. I'm really scared," I said caustically. I gave Watt one of my most generous fake smiles, turned to Rambo and Pup and said, "Let's go, guys." We walked out the tent and while admitting it a cliché, I really did feel Watt's eyes burning into the middle of my back. Once outside I said to the other two, "Taking all things into account, I thought that went pretty well."

"What did he say to you at the end," asked Rambo. I told him. "Empty rhetoric," Rambo scoffed. "The man's a busted flush, washed up on a deserted beach like a piece of driftwood!"

"Yeah! And we were the tidal wave that put him there!" The pair of us laughed.

Pup looked slightly bemused. "He was your *old* syndicate leader?"

"Don't ask," I said, flicking a hand at Pup. "I wrote it all down once. If I can find the manuscript I'll give it to you one day and you can peruse it at your leisure. For the moment, take it as read we're the worst of enemies, as we once were, as we'll always be, certainly from his point of view. From mine he hardly seems worth the effort. He's like the old schoolteacher you were once afraid of, the one who's aged into frailty where you've matured into a young man in his prime. Tom Watt has no hold over me."

Having put all present straight on my relationship with Watt we entered the second tent and found no queue. I surmised everyone who had been in front of us in the previous tent must have been a caster. Heading up the second tent's official reception committee, all on his own, was another old geezer. A man in his sixties with a ruddy, well-weathered countenance framed by wavy grey hair and an expression hinting at vacancy sat behind a trestle desk similar to Watt's. 'Not quite there' was the phrase springing to mind as I weighed him up and approached the table.

Ben, as he introduced himself when Pup handed over our orange card, was The Bowl's 'Head Bailiff' and only temporarily held the position of official baitboat distributor for the 48-hour competition.

"Hello, lads," he said enthusiastically in a slow drawl as we reciprocated and told him our names. "Nice to meet you. Don't expect me to remember names, though," Ben warned in a speech suggesting 45rpm played at 33. (If you're too young to understand this last sentence please ask someone with experience in vinyl records – they'll explain.) "Names aren't me strong point. I forgets them. See too many people when I'm doing me bailiffing. Hundreds of blokes. Can't remembers all of them."

"No worries," I replied. "I don't think I could," I said giving the old boy a bit of support.

Ben screwed his nose up in appreciation of my understanding of his dilemma and proceeded to go through his entrant's speech with all the zip of treacle running down the side of a cup. A cup in a fridge; a cup in a fridge with the thermostat set on five; a cup in a fridge with the thermostat set on five in an unheated flat in Siberia; a cup in a fridge with the thermostat set on five in an unheated flat in Siberia during January.

In other words, *really, really* slow! In all honesty he was the *complete* verbal antithesis to The Eye.

"I hope you's going to have a good time this weekend, but we do needs to go through all them necessaries before you can crack on. So, if you's could all just come over with me." Ben beckoned us over to the side wall of the tent where half-a-dozen or so Angling Technics baitboat bags were lying on the ground. We shuffled over the few yards to where he had moved and waited for him to decipher the hieroglyphic on the orange card Pup had given him. "Let's see… number… number… number… number sixteen," he eventually declared to himself.

Ben turned his attention to the carry bags on the deck and he bent down and searched, very meticulously and very slowly, for the right one. He checked each individual one for what seemed like an age, and, utterly bafflingly, kept looking back at the orange card as he did so. Presumably, this could only have been to see if the number on the card had morphed into another one in a gremlin-like attempt to catch him out, or, his short-term memory was worse than that of a cannabis-addled goldfish. By the time – seven minutes and eight seconds, I was running my Casio digital on him – he got to the last but one boat, and knowing as sure as the sun was going to set tonight that our boat was absolutely, definitely, one hundred per cent dead certain to be the last one he looked at, I was willing Rambo to crack his neck in two with a rabbit punch so we could just take the fucking thing before one of us died – or at least needed a haircut.

The last boat Ben checked was ours.

"Here we are!" Ben said triumphantly. "Number," he checked the orange cue card one more time, "sixteen. Unlucky for some! But not yous lads, eh?"

I caught Rambo's smothered smirk and choked back a laugh myself. In an instant the whole scenario had turned to high entertainment. I realised anecdotal accounts of various formal situations – weddings, funerals, job interviews, having sex with someone for the first time – turning into chaos due to uncontrollable laughter were true. Now, whether picking up a hired baitboat to use in a 48-hour 'No Seventies in Here, Mate!' comp qualified, strictly speaking, as a 'formal situation' was a moot point. What wasn't in debate was the tension created by the painfully plodding, ponderous, process of finding our boat, coupled with Ben's eccentricity and the mix-up regards the demonic properties of the number sixteen had cracked me like a walnut. Ditto Rambo. Pup, meanwhile, just stood there doing nothing – apart from counting boilies in his head.

Ben didn't notice us fighting to keep a lid on our laughter and pushed on at a snail's pace. "She's one of them there Microcats," he said of our boat. "There's two of them there fully charged boat batteries in the bag and the transmitter's inside. Back here, every boat will have a spare pair of them there boat batteries and a spare transmitter battery. As long as you's not silly enough to flatten them there batteries when you's using your boat and yous keep bringing them back to be charged up and then yous use the spare ones, yous be fine." I was fighting a tide of laughter now – arse, bladder and mouth clenched tight. "If yous reckon on an hour's use, yous be fine." Ben paused to make sure we had grasped the gist of this and look us all in the eye.

Tears of mirth were welling up in mine and I quickly wiped them, defying the desperate urge to look at Rambo. I knew utter madness lay that way because, on the very edge of my peripheral vision, the peripheral vision I was telling my brain to ignore, I glimpsed Rambo's huge shoulders wobbling with barely contained hysterics. Pup on the other hand still seemed unaffected, and he listened intently to Ben's slow rustic speech without so much as the bat of an eyelid.

"Good," said Ben. "Do yous lads know how to use them there Microcats?"

We all nodded, although I was more concerned with sucking in my cheeks to keep my laughter internal. I saw Pup nod and it did cross my mind as to why. I doubted if he had even seen a baitboat, let alone mistakenly grounded one on a shallow margin in the middle of the night and had to do a bit of night-time skinny-dipping to get it back!

"Good!" said Ben. "There's them there instruction manuals in the bag if you needs to know. Beware them there left-hand joysticks that's whats I always say! Yous don't want to go dumping yous bait in the wrong place!"

Ben cackled with laughter and Rambo and I, taking the chance to vent our pent up delirium, disintegrated into howling laughter with him. Ben appreciated the response, unaware we weren't laughing at his joke – one he had probably cracked to every team this morning – but at the fantastically idiosyncratic performance to which we were bearing witness.

Finally, when Rambo and I were spent and when I was at the point of convincing myself laughter can cause asthma and kill you, and so wasn't really a laughing matter, we calmed down enough for Ben to finish.

"Two more things. Firstly all them there boats have been specially doctored to have different frequencies so yous don't have to fret there be any of that there interference from them there other boaters' transmitters."

"Good idea," I said. "Could have been a right old carve-up if everybody started driving everybody else's boat!"

Ben gave me a single nod as if to say I was a bright spark. "The last thing, is the worst thing," he conceded gravely. "Them there boats costs a lot of money, sos I have to get yous to sign this here form agreeing to the state of the boats as yous received it. I checks them for any new damage when yous bring it back at the finish. Any damage, I's afraid, will be paid for out of that there credit card you's given to Tom. Okay?"

"Fine," I said in tandem with Rambo.

"Now, where's that there form for your boat," said Ben walking back to his little desk. He rummaged through a folder in slow motion. "Number… number… number sixteen," he said to himself once he had stared at the orange card again.

After an excruciating time Ben found the form and laid it flat on the table. It was like a baitboat version of a hire car form with a little drawing of the boat and space to write down scratches, chips and other signs of damage. Ben went back to get our baitboat to check it through, clearly couldn't remember which one it was, and came back for the orange card. It was at this juncture Rambo decided he couldn't take any more. He went and picked up our boat, throwing the carry bag's strap over his shoulder, returned to the table and quickly signed the form.

"I'm sure everything will be fine. We can go and get set up, now," he explained jerking a thumb over his shoulder.

Ben looked down at Rambo's signature for some time, and then up at his face. "You's sure?"

"Positive."

"Right you is. I'll see yous later when I'm out and about with Hector."

Rambo's brow creased. "Hector?"

"My dog."

"I don't get on with dogs," said Rambo. "Especially when I'm fishing."

"Yous get on with Hector," said Ben scrunching his eyes and nodding slowly. "He's a Boxer."

"In a way, so was the last one," remarked Rambo. Ben looked blanker than he had earlier. "It's a long, long story, one I won't tell you one day!"

Chapter 6

"Casters to the left of me, casters to the right. Here I am, stuck in the middle with you!" I sang – somewhat randomly.

"What?" said Pup.

"It's an old song," I explained. "One I remember from my Mum's collection."

Pup gave me a look he probably reserved for readymade boilies and on discovering dog shit caked to his best shoes. "Why did you and Rambo laugh at Ben? He's a nice old boy," he said, obviously not wanting to discuss further the lyrical content of ancient pop songs.

"I know he is." There was little point denying the old boy's quaint mannerisms which were fine as far as it went – if you had a couple of years to spare.

"So why did you laugh at him?"

"Der?" I said sarcastically. "The speech, the slow-mo action, the number of times he had to look at the number on the orange card, the time he took to pick out our number sixteen boat, I just *knew* it would be the last one, the 'unlucky for some' joke that wasn't…"

"And that was funny, was it?"

I was getting a bit miffed by Pup's self-righteous line of questioning. "No, I'll tell you what *is* funny," I replied stridently. "What *is* funny is a certain knob-head thinking that if he can dupe his best mates into winning a competition, the arsehole who wants to buy up his bait business will quietly go away like he promised!" Pup could only pull the corners of his mouth down in minimal defiance – he knew the truth when he heard it. "Put the kettle on and make me a cuppa," I said with a flick of my head. "Before I tell Rambo to wedge that baitboat up your jacksey."

I wasn't really as cross with Pup and his naivety times ten to the power of the number of baits he had rolled in his lifetime as I had made out, but he *was* going to be a 'gopher' with a very large capital 'G' in a *very* impressive looking font!

I glanced at my watch. We had managed to get set up in good time and there were still over thirty minutes to the off. Whether the poor bastards who had to get their baitboats after us had managed the same trick, I doubted. Ben was a human time wasting machine and any interaction with him whatsoever saw minutes and then hours pass by as easily as a neutrino going through fag paper.

Ignoring the Ben dilemma, I scanned the panoramic view in front of me and was instantly reminded of Hamworthy – because The Bowl was nothing like it. The Bowl was similar to a big bowl – one owned by a person with a liberal line in terminology. It was similar to a big bowl made by a potter whose sense of geometrical proportion had been ruined by the ill-judged initial off-centre placement of a large dollop of clay upon his wheel. The resulting bowl's rim had wobbled into a topologically altered version whilst its depth and curvature had remained reasonably sound. Rambo's marker rod had revealed a gently curving bottom, one deepening by a foot for every twenty yards further out from the bank. The maximum depth turned out to be a smidgen over five feet. It wouldn't have mattered if Rambo had cast from the south bank, the east bank, the west bank or from the north bank, where we were fishing – and for once it was based on fact and not on urban myth – The Bowl was indeed a bland, featureless hole in the ground.

It wasn't a lot better above it. Despite its misshapen rim The Bowl didn't have a lot going for it in the 'pleasing aesthetics' department. There were no weedbeds, no margin cover, apart from a puny intermittent border of sedge grass, and absolutely no trees. Every angler was visible from every swim, and every swim was as obvious as a tattoo on a pole dancer's arse, due to the twenty by twenty mud patch depicting it. There was no shade to be had anywhere and what with global warming (Save The Planet by turning off your car's air conditioning. You could save up to 5% on fuel costs and only be slightly sweaty as a result of it!) I reckoned The Bowl was a sun cream Factor 20 water. Without it, a hard day's toil under a broiling sun on The Bowl meant a frying trip to Lobster City and a severe dunking in Calamine lotion that evening.

One thing was certain, if you were catching fish, everybody would know about it – unless you were doing it under the cover of night, with gagged bite alarms and without illumination. If this were the case, perhaps the Pup Enterprises team should have tried to develop night vision to keep tabs on the opposition and stuck to a strict regime of eating enough carrots to make Bugs Bunny look as if he was on permanent Ramadan.

Not necessary! *We* would be the ones doing the bulk of the catching! There's confidence for you!

Away from the water, some ten yards behind us, was the venue's one laughable 'feature', it being a four-yard high grass bank constructed from the original excavation's piled spoil – an excavation which had taken place originally in a farmer's field. In short, The Bowl was pretty much the worst type of commercial fishery in terms of its physical appeal. On the plus side, an average of over two hundred yards diameter made crossover casting from the opposite bank an unlikely worry in normal circumstances. Thankfully, and perhaps more importantly, there was at least thirty yards distance from mud patch to mud patch. You couldn't exactly wander down the margin and place baits, or blast them out at forty-five degrees, but as long as the two adjacent anglers weren't idiots there was sufficient room to prevent chronic casting claustrophobia. Water boundaries from every swim were pretty much obvious, the lack of ninety-degree corners to negotiate in the game of mentally marking no-cast zones being of great help.

The Bowl's true redeeming feature was the head of carp lurking in its chocolate coloured water. Overstocked, hungry, bait-orientated carp up to mid-thirties were there in considerable numbers and provided anglers with the agreeable benefits of being on a 'runs' water capable of turning up rakes of twenties plus the snifter of bagging a real lump. As importantly, the carp, with no features to follow, got caught with regularity from every swim – the local joke theory being they had all signed up to a contract on stocking, one forbidding them to favour any part of The Bowl's bottom and to totally disregard the direction of the wind!

In the modern carp world The Bowl's attributes were more than enough for most. Forget the looks, the blandness, the crowds, the mud, the lack of privacy – every fuck up was on display to mass ridicule – and feel the bend in your rod! To most carpers the size and number of carp in The Bowl more than compensated for its other shortcomings – by most standards, you understand – not including those used to fishing the mighty Hamworthy Fisheries, the most… you know the drill.

I warned myself I had better stop thinking about Hamworthy and start thinking about catching a few of The Bowl's residents, not unless I wanted a bollocking from Rambo. The camo-man rebirthed didn't do coming second, even if seeing him again in full British Army fatigues was a bit like the second coming! As I stood pondering all this I did feel extremely confident, purely because of our bait, despite my nerves having earlier been put on edge by meeting up with Watt. What had he meant when he had said he had power and could crush both of us like a bug? Rambo was most likely right in that it was all a hollow threat, yet his face was a stark reminder how competitions, apart from the inaugural Hamworthy *charadee* bash, inevitably brought out the worst in everyone.

And here I was fishing another one – one with a cash prize and the added spice of attempting to put a mysterious bait baron's nose out of joint! It was bound to end in tears. When I had mentioned this to Rambo as we had bumped our gear round, he had pointed out that The Bowl was the perfect place to hold a Pulimov's Prize competition. Its layout meant the only thing anybody trying to pull a scam really feared – getting caught – was a sure-fire certainty. The self-interest of sixty pairs of beady eyes and an unimpeded panoramic vision the reason! As usual he had a good point.

For now I turned my back on all the pairs of anglers preparing for the start and clumped across the hard-baked, bare mud towards the three bivvies we had previously erected – base camp Pup Enterprises – and the grass wall behind them. The grass wall looked like a huge green wave on the verge of breaking, one that would smash our three temporary homes into a 6oz/420 Denier pancake. Pup was kneeling near to my small stove making the tea and Rambo was checking out the baitboat. Outside Pup's bivvy were the six large plastic sacks full of our bait. As the Baitmeister he had rolled them and, subsequently, as the Bait Mule, he had humped them to our pitch. The bags were black, clandestine and secret, as they should be with such a deadly content.

I spoke to Rambo. "Does it work all right?" I asked. "We're up effluent creek without a pump/flexible antenna/charged battery/decent signal if it doesn't!"

"Fine, boy," Rambo confirmed as he performed a dry run on both the transmitter and boat's functions.

Pup handed each of us a tea. Baitmeister, Bait Mule, Tea Boy – by the end of this two-day stint he would truly understand the concept of service industry multi-tasking. "What are the tactics going to be, then?" he asked.

"I don't know about Rambo, but I'm planning to fish both rods at the bottom of the far drop-off," I said, nodding towards the spoil wall.

"This is no time for stupidity," scowled Pup once he realised the drop-off wasn't in the water – he knew nothing of The Bowl's boringly bland bottom. "My reputation's at stake."

"Your reputation has already slipped a few million notches as far as I'm concerned, mate," I replied.

"Don't be so hard on him, boy," said Rambo taking a huge swig of tea. How could he drink it so hot, I thought? He must have a cast iron gut and an asbestos-lined oesophagus!

I ruffled Pup's hair in an avuncular fashion. "I know," I said. "I'm only joking… although they do say many a true word said in jest."

"Tactics?" insisted Pup, trying not to smile whilst smoothing his hair.

"What size baits have we got?" I asked nodding at the black sacks.

"You've got tens, twelves, fourteens and eighteens in standard rounds, indented because I didn't know if you were going to be casting, and you've got exactly the same in dumb-bells. They're *not* indented. I've also got pop-ups, glugged bottom baits and neutral buoyancies in both round and dumb-bell hookbaits... in each size." Pup gave me a smug look saying 'What do you think of that, then?'

"Have we got any glugged, neutral buoyancy hookbaits?" I asked facetiously.

"Of course."

"In…"

"All sizes," confirmed Pup.

I was impressed and let out a low whistle. Rambo and Pup had sorted out the bait without any input from myself. Rambo, I suspected, had told him what to make and Pup had made it. I could see his reasoning. The Bowl's fish were driven by hunger and competition, yet the tendency to use standard baits could well produce standard results. The exclusive, revolutionary, indented, dirty brown bottom bait boilie was far from standard and to have it to hand in such a staggering array of sizes, shapes and densities meant we were surely the favourites! In fact I was now so cocksure I would have bet anyone running a book, having had a quick peek in the black sacks, would have shortened us to odds-on winners in a nanosecond.

"It's what I asked Pup to make," confirmed Rambo. "I'm thinking along the lines of going for a complete mix of sizes and shapes and to fish a mix of hook baits, a different one on each rod to begin with. If a pattern starts to emerge we home in on it and exploit it. What do you think, boy?"

Even though, even *though*, I had caught a sixty and Rambo hadn't, the cockles of my heart swelled with pride at being asked what I thought. "Sounds good to me," I responded.

Not a massive input, seeing as we were on the bank and the bait had already been made, but hey, it hadn't always been like this, not when I had first mixed up Rambo's red bait in his flat many moons ago! On that occasion I had been glad to stagger out knackered but alive!

"Are baitboats usually allowed on here?" I asked.

It was Rambo who answered. "No. Word is this place is still a spodder's wet dream, like it used to be when I fished it. It's all about getting enough bait out there to try and pull some fish into your swim, mostly particles like hemp, corn, maize and maggot, I should imagine, to keep costs down… although the method must be a popular line of attack." Rambo gave Pup a couple of raised eyebrows. "Makes me wonder about your bait baron, though. What did he say? That everyone else would be on his baits?"

"On baits made by companies he now owns. By baits I presumed he meant boilies. In the *loosest* sense of the word. I mean just because it's round, smells okay and is in a one kilo plastic bag with 'boilies' written on the side doesn't mean *anything*!"

"Hmm," said Rambo running a huge hand up and down the nape of his neck. "If we can, we'll try and rake the coals over our mysterious bait baron."

"All right?" came a new voice.

"You said that without moving your lips," I told Pup.

The body responsible for the gruff voice materialised around from the side of Rambo's bivvy. First inspections revealed it to be large, tall, muscular and with a fully shaved head on top of it – a fully shaved head with one pierced eyebrow and two studded earrings.

"Carl," said the head, as two powerful arms propped ring-laden hands on hips in a stance of defiance. "I'm the marshal for this zone, right! Basically, no fucking about! Obey the fishery rules, which I'll give you in a mo and we all enjoy ourselves and have a bit of fun, right! If you catch a fish, sack it up, gimme a ring, right, and basically I'll come and weigh it." A pair of eyes, open slightly too wide apart to be decreed 'normal', glared at the three of us. "My mobile number and the rules, right!" He handed Rambo a card and an A4 sheet of paper attached to a clipboard – presumably on the grounds Rambo was the biggest and therefore must be in charge. "Don't lose it, right, or basically, you won't be able to weigh in any fish."

After wondering if Rambo was going to give him a pasting for being so brusque – anything up to 'Quick call an ambulance!' severity rating – I mentally scoffed at Carl's brain-dead assumption of the biggest always being in charge. Inwardly I sneered at the so predictable physical slant the Carls of this world put on to everything. Okay, so he *was* right, and he had arrived at being right by using the muscle principal he so evidently based everything on – but that wasn't the point. In an instant I decided Carl was a bit of a tosser – most likely a violent tosser – and I didn't like him. And I had only just met him.

"Good luck for the comp," Carl's face turned into an ugly sneer, a simple trick considering from where he was starting. "But to be honest, mates, you got no fucking chance with one of those fucking things!" he laughed pointing towards the baitboat.

Now, whether the Microcat was upset by this disparaging remark was hard to tell. I, on the other hand, was. "So why's that, then?" I asked, a tad more aggressively than I meant to.

Carl gave a lopsided smile along with a sharp upwards bob of his head. "Mate. These fish want a nice spread of bait, right! You fished here before?" I shook my head. "You wouldn't know, see. Me, I've taken this fucking place apart, right! Spodding, right! Much better presentation than a load dumped on a fucking dustbin lid! It's not as if you've gotta cast miles, right!" And Carl gave me a buddy slap on the shoulder to empathise with my tragic plight of being a bloody, bleedin', bastard baitboater on a sure-fire, super smug spodder's spot.

"We'll be okay. We've got a good bait," I told Carl in a voice I hoped came across as a powerful understatement.

Carl stuck his ugly mug right up to mine. His breath smelt of alcohol – this morning's or last night's, I wasn't sure. "So have the others," he stated and on that revelation he disappeared the way he came and walked up to the next swim.

Once he was safely out of earshot I started to slag him off. "What an arsehole!" I said to no one in particular. "Hardly a friendly welcome was it! Bloody hell!" No one answered and this lack of encouragement shut me up – although my brain kept on working. I suddenly had a more constructive thought. "Hey, Pup! If he knows the baits the others are on and he's bumming them up, he could be the first link, more like the *missing* link, the Cro-Magnon muppet, to your bait baron."

Pup nodded vigorously in agreement. "Good call, he might be."

I carried on my act of spleen venting against Carl. "He's probably one of the boss's henchmen, a disposable one, one who gets wasted in the first half-hour of the film!"

"If he talks to me like that again, he won't last *fifteen* minutes, let alone half an hour," confirmed Rambo.

Pup puffed his cheeks, his eyes clouded by doubt. "I don't know, he looks as if he could handle himself."

A wry smile spread to Rambo's face and he ruffled Pup's hair exactly as I had. "One arm behind my back, blindfolded *and* hopping!"

Pup roughly pushed Rambo's massive mitt away from his head. "I'll be bald soon, you two'll wear my bloody hair away!"

"Break out the baits, boy," Rambo told Pup dismissing his protestations. "It's time to put the cargo aboard the good ship Spodspoiler!"

My stomach did a quick tumble and a welcome slug of adrenalin whizzed around my body, rubbing its hands together in glee. It was going to start soon! Pup might have been economical with the truth to get us here, might have been naïve in falling for his would-be prospective buyer's blatant bullshit, I might have been better placed keeping an eye on Hamworthy in case a member fluked out a potential Pulimov's Prize seventy and in doing so avoided meeting the odious Tom Watt – all true enough – but there *was* a meaty counterpoint. This wasn't sliding into the tedious torpor of a mid-life crisis, this wasn't languishing in the listless lethargy of sloth-like, sluggish somnolence, *this* was another adventure! I could *feel* it! Feel it in my mainline! For good or ill we were in it and for once it didn't revolve around either Rambo or myself. Pup! Pup was at the hub of it. It was all rather exciting in a way – in a worrying kind of way!

Several air horns foghorned the start of the comp. Either side of us a couple of marker floats plopped out thirty yards and immediately – the other angler in the pair getting into the act – underwent an intense spod bombardment. It was the RAF and Dresden all over again. If a spod hitting the surface of the chocolate coloured water was the carp's equivalent of a dinner gong then The Bowl's underwater residents were getting a multiple 'Grub's up!' ringtone in Dolby 5.1 surround sound. The anglers' pent up excitement had been released by the air horns and the frenetic response mirrored the current state of carp fishing fever. All over the venue, in every other swim, a phallic shape was arcing through the sky. In a moment of surreal thought, I imagined it to be similar to an explosion in a sex shop, one where lurid dildos wanged their hard, stiff way through the air.

For the baitboaters it was more 'toys for the boys' rather than the ones I had visualised for the girls.

Our Microcat was still moored in the margins, loaded to the hilt with a mixture of exclusive, revolutionary, indented, dirty brown bottom bait boilies. Sitting in the right-hand hopper was Rambo's rig and a glugged, neutral buoyancy hookbait. I carefully tilted the boat and held down the rear 'on' button to prime the pumps. Within seconds two powerful jets of water were thrusting out the back and I released the button. I let go of the boat and its stern sat down even further in the water due to the extra weight of water now sitting in the pumps. I picked up Rambo's rod and opened the bail arm.

"All ready, Captain."

Rambo pushed his thumb on the right-hand joystick and the Microcat scuttled off across the water, its two rear blue neons shining brightly.

"How far are you going with this one?" I asked as I saw Rambo's Big Game Line (clear, 15lb breaking strain) loop off his spool.

"I'll make this one the closest-in and take it out a bit to the right," Rambo answered. "We'll go straighter on my left-hand and your right-hand rod and make them the two longest. Your left-hand rod can be shorter if you want, but I think we want to try four staggered distances to begin with."

"Aye-aye, Captain," I said pushing the nautical allusion a little bit too far. "Both hoppers at once?" Rambo grunted the affirmative.

The Microcat had already covered the distance Rambo required and I saw the blue neons go out, indicating the release of the hoppers. Rambo turned the boat and the white neons of the bow showed towards us as he brought her back to shore. Busily I made a tight line and folded a small piece of electrical tape over the main line a few inches from the reel so we could repeat the exact distance should we need to. By the time I had trimmed it to a neat slither, set the hanger and cranked the red Delkim to a LAP setting, ('loud as possible' – feel free to use this acronym in future text messages) Rambo had virtually loaded the boat for his second rod.

The procedure was duly repeated three more times without the dreaded involuntary twitch of the left thumb on the left-hand joystick dumping our boilie bullion three foot from the edge as Ben had joked. That Rambo – nerves of steel. It was why he had been at the helm all four times and I had been the BAB ('bail arm boy' – use that one as well, although I'm not sure where).

Once this was done, and the boat was gently placed on a spare unhooking mat within my bivvy, all that remained was to place our sitting-outside-the-bivvy-in-the-sun chairs alongside each other a few yards to the rear of our rod butts – and wait. That's to say my sitting-outside-the-bivvy-in-the-sun chair and Rambo's sitting-outside-the-bivvy-in-the-sun chair. Pup was too on edge to sit, so he spent his time pacing up and down, and for variation pacing to and fro, across our twenty by twenty mud patch.

As he nervously walked he muttered strange incantations and oaths under his breath. For the first ten minutes or so it was quite amusing watching him beat himself up over the fact we hadn't yet had a take. The trouble was, by the time half an hour had passed, he had taken to marching back and forth across the section of rock hard mud between our rods and us, the resulting amusement turning rapidly to irritation.

"For fuck's sake sit down!" Rambo barked. "There's forty-seven hours to go! If you keep on like this for the duration it'll kill you! Trust me. I'll make sure of it!"

Pup looked in disbelief at his watch either choosing to ignore or not notice Rambo's threat. I reckoned it was the latter – Pup's brain was thinking bait! "Damn! Is that all?" he answered. "An hour's gone *already!*" he declared. "You should have had a run by now! If there's as many fish in here as they say there are, you *should* have had a run by now. Are you sure you're in the right spot and your rigs are any good?"

"There probably isn't a right spot," I calmly informed Pup. "They come out all over. We're just hedging our bets by going out different distances. As for the rigs, they're well proven." I got up from my chair and put my arm around, as they might say in an ad for a certain lager, probably the world's leading boilie maker. "Look, why don't you make us all another cup of tea. It'll give you something to occupy yourself." Remarkably Pup agreed and he sloped off to the tea-making zone without protest – maybe he was thirsty from all his walking about. "I know how he feels," I said laughing to Rambo as I re-parked my arse on my chair. "Everyone will be feeling similar, the intense need to get that first fish under their belt."

Rambo nodded and looked out at the other anglers. Many of the casters were still spodding their guts out – not literally, that would patently be ridiculous – and still weren't actually fishing. "I'm not too worried. We both know what a potent weapon we've got. It's only a matter of time, boy. No fish can resist the exclusive, revolutionary, indented, dirty brown bottom bait boilie." Rambo inclined his huge body towards me. "In fact I'll lay a wager one of us has a take before he's brought our three mugs of tea over!"

I tin-tanned my head to suggest this was possible, even if, in my opinion, a little unlikely. "Do you think this mysterious bait baron is here, watching to see how good Pup's product is?"

"Nah! Not in person, but definitely one of his goons! You never know, you might have hit the nail on the head with Carl… or Watt!"

"Oh, *don't*!" I said shaking my head. "Not him all over again, that would be *too* much!" I spent a few seconds watching my rod tips for any sign of pre-audible take action. "You know we're in one, don't you?"

"What, a carp catching comp? Yep, I'd got that one figured, boy."

"No. An adventure. Another escapade."

"You think that bloke's back writing again?" said Rambo giving me an old fashioned look and resurrecting our little joke, the one how our lives read like a series of novels.

I gave out a laugh. "I do! This is the tale of Sir Pup!"

Rambo gave a loud sniff. "We'll always be the two main characters, boy."

"Until one of us dies."

"Until one of us dies," agreed Rambo.

"There you go, M…"

I'm fairly sure Pup had managed to get out the first consonant of my name before his voice was drowned out by the spectacular howling of my right-hand rod's Delkim.

"That alarm, always was an attention-seeker!" I said to Pup as I exploded from my sitting-outside-the-bivvy-in-the-sun chair, leaving him to offer a piping hot mug of tea to a few trillion air molecules. I pounced on my rod and lifted into a carp.

Rambo was soon at my side with the net at his. "You can pay me later."

"I don't think we ever got round to shaking on it."

"Hookbait?" Rambo asked out the corner of his mouth.

"Neutral buoyancy, twelve-millimetre dumb-bell."

"Not glugged?"

"Nope."

"Interesting."

We fell silent and I slipped into a familiar routine, one designed at getting us on the scoreboard. Five minutes later I had succeeded.

"Upper double," Rambo remarked on placing the net and fish on to my unhooking mat.

"No idea, mate," I told him. "It's *such* a long time since I caught one *this* small!"

Rambo rolled his eyes and put the net handle down. "Get it in a sack and I'll phone up cod's mouth Carl. Let's see what *he's* got to say about it."

Not a lot as it happened. Looking as happy as a bloke with a barbed size two through his foreskin, Carl took a minimalist's viewpoint regards conversation. In fact the only words he uttered were 'eighteen pound, six', which was fine by me. It was all we needed to know. I made a point of writing it down in front of him on a spiral wire notepad, so I had a duplicate copy of the catches on the A4 official sheet. This seemed to aggravate him further, especially when I asked him to confirm both the weight and the time of capture. What with me taking notes and Pup constantly traipsing around the swim clenching his fist going 'Yes!' to himself, Carl couldn't get out of our company quick enough.

"Thanks awfully, Carl, most kind," Rambo had called in a pseudo-posh voice as he had stomped off.

By delicious chance, a matter of seconds later, Rambo's left-hand rod chose to rumble off.

"Carl!" I called. "You might want to hang on for a second! Save you a journey back!"

It was a statement that could have backfired. Pup Enterprises could have ended up with egg on its collective chops had Rambo lost the fish. It goes without saying, he didn't – Rambo rarely lost fish. I had always put this down to the fact they were too scared of upsetting him. In all the years I've fished alongside him there hasn't been a reason to make me want to change my mind!

As luck would have it the carp turned out to be a lump – but not by Hamworthy standards (sorry I'm such a carp snob) – it weighing in at a big three-O threatening twenty-nine pound eleven ounces. I wrote down the details on the pad adding a little 'R' next to the weight to signify the camouflaged one had opened his account. Instead of putting the time I cheerfully scrawled 'Ten minutes after my one!'. Gleefully I thought how great the feeling is when you're catching fish and how the pleasure multiplies when others aren't. Not a pleasant human emotion, as I think I had noted before, nevertheless a very real one. I had been constantly checking the rest of the field and although it was possible I had missed a capture, I very much doubted any team had caught two so quickly.

As he went to return his near thirty, Rambo decided to lighten Carl's mood and purely for the benefit of casual conversation to ask if he still thought The Bowl was a spodder's water.

Carl's face turned to thunder and his shaven head turned a hue somewhere between bright red and crimson – I didn't have a Dulux colour chart to hand, so it was a bit difficult to say. "Plenty of time yet," he said barely containing his wrath. "Early doors, right!"

Rambo's face was the epitome of understanding. "Right!"

"Right!" I chipped in.

I was just thinking how lippy I could be when Rambo was around – I wouldn't have said 'Boo!' to a goose on my own, let alone say 'Right!' to body-pierced, Carl – when he suddenly swung to face me and gave me an evil 'what you looking at?' midnight-at-the-taxi-rank stare, completely ignoring Rambo even though he had committed a similar crime. I suddenly felt acutely aware of the 'survival of the fittest' Darwinian principle, the one where the predator always picks off the sick, the young or the weak and eats them alive.

I held Carl's stare until I cracked and swallowed with what sounded to me like an audible 'gulp' – the well-known and well-documented audible gulp indicative of the definitive embodiment of someone shitting himself. Carl's lip curled the faintest of smiles and in that instant I knew I was scared of him and, even worse, I knew *he* knew I was scared of him. With this minor triumph safely stored on his hard man hard drive, he swivelled through one eighty degrees and left. I watched his back as he followed the line of the grassy spoil wall up to a bivvy I hadn't noticed before. One pitched well back and a quarter of the way around The Bowl's rim from where we were. Carl was sleeping on the job – so long as he didn't sneak back in the dark and slit my throat.

"Come on, boy!" hailed Rambo. "Time is of the essence! We're about to launch Stingray!"

"Anything can happen in the next half-hour!" said Pup surprisingly.

"How do you know that line?" I asked as I went to my bivvy to get out the Microcat.

"You get to watch a lot of repeat shit on the telly when you've rolled as many baits at home as I have," he said earnestly.

I was in my mid-thirties, a similar age to Rambo. What was our excuse for knowing the lines from a sixties' puppet show?

Chapter 7

By the middle of the afternoon the sun had broken out and it was hot. Damn hot. Global warming was on the march with a vengeance! (To Save The Planet stop going on holiday by aeroplane. It's equally important to remember to re-cycle all the holiday brochures collected whilst deciding where you're not going to go.) In response I had slapped on my sun cream, donned shorts, cap and polarised glasses. Not that the polarised lens was of any benefit in trying to glean what was happening in The Bowl's highly coloured waters. You could stare all you liked and be none the wiser. Perhaps the best route to achieve understanding would have been to wander to the twenty by twenty rock hard mud patch – the one designated as number nine, which was also the berthing spot for baitboat number sixteen (Don't come in number sixteen your time isn't up!) – and once there, stand and observe. Observe the boilie made by the rather obsessive looking young man, whose name was an acronym for pop-up Pete, getting severely eaten by The Bowl's huge head of carp.

That was what was happening.

The process for arriving at this conclusion was the simple method of deduction. Because Pup's revolutionary, indented, dirty brown bottom bait boilie was getting so severely scoffed, the slackers using it, the *only* slackers using it due to an exclusive arrangement with the aforementioned obsessive looking young man – yours truly and Timothy Eugene – when observed for a reasonable time, a very *short* time in carp fishing terms, would soon catch a carp. And then another one. And shortly after, another one.

Carp fishing can be a funny business – I had done enough of it to know. When it was panning out as it was for us it was ridiculously easy. Put the bait out there, the fish get on it, decent rigs, sharp hooks, good tackle, you hook them and you land them. Piece of cake! When it was panning out the other way, then no matter how hard you tried or whatever you did, nothing worked. Rambo and I were under no illusion as to the reason why it was so ridiculously easy – it was why we had forked out for four grand's worth of tackle from our stock-pond-raided carp slush fund!

Although conditions were great for getting a slap of the pink emulsion brush across the shoulders – a dollop of Bowl Burn – they weren't so good for fishing. It was bright, hot and there was no wind, and yet we had caught five in as many hours. As if to prove the truism 'one man's meat is another man's poison', Carl hated the fact we were hauling. Having nailed his colours so firmly to the spodder's mast on the back of his supposed experience on the water, he had consigned himself to looking a right numpty. On the other hand, Pup, Rambo and myself, but especially Pup, were absolutely ecstatic and not numpties at all! For someone whose entire life barometer was gauged by the success of the boilies he made, the results so far had pushed Pup into a state of rapture. To reiterate, Rambo and I were realists regarding what exactly was driving us to what seemed a certain win, but our eulogizing of his bait served to swell Pup's sense of pride even further.

"It must be the best bait ever!" I had exalted, after landing my third fish. I had spun and faced Pup, an outrageous grin splashed all over my face. "So what's the killer ingredient, oh, mighty boiliemeister?"

I had received the proverbial short shrift. "Piss off, Williams!"

Bursting with pride he might be, but a brilliant boiliemeister always holds his aces close to his chest – superglued face down, in fact. It's a well-known saying in the bait business.

Personally speaking, the one downside to proceedings so far was trying to conceal my fear of Carl when he had weighed-in fish three, four and five. I had attempted to act as confidently as I had before our little staring altercation, only to little avail. The truth was, and there was little point trying to fool myself, it was too late – I had already let the cat out of the bag by letting the gulp out of my throat – even though I had continued to fill in my notepad. An act of defiance, I considered, bordering on heroic and one surely meritorious of being mentioned in dispatches – a VC was probably a little over the top.

Unfortunately, trying to wing it had cut little ice. Carl's condescension towards myself was self-evident, although amazingly this wasn't his blanket approach to the three of us comprising Pup Enterprises. Firstly, I wasn't even sure if he knew Pup existed because he totally blanked him every time he was in our swim, even if this was at odds with the theory of him being one of the bait baron's henchmen. If you didn't have a rod in your hand you didn't count, seemed Carl's philosophy. With Rambo, as ever, Carl's approach was different. I'm not saying he liked him, or, moving down the scale of appreciation, didn't despise him as much as myself, he simply treated him differently. In the same manner he had assumed he was the leader of our team there existed the subtle body language of 'hard man respect' – for want of a better phrase. Perhaps Rambo's boast to Pup about how easily he could take Carl – I had envisaged Carl looking like two hundred and twenty pounds of mince dropped from a ten-metre diving platform on to the middle carriageway of the M25 – had somehow assimilated itself into Carl's walnut-sized brain. The top and bottom of it all, I concluded, hoping I was not prone to wishful thinking, was so long as Rambo was holding my hand I was as safe as houses.

Rambo – ever my guardian angel, where would I be without him? Most likely flat on my back and bleeding in the number nine, twenty by twenty rock hard mud patch having been the recipient of a thudding crunch from Carl's shaven head – a 'Glasgow Handshake' executed with such exquisite timing and power it would have made an old street fighter's eyes well up in nostalgic reminiscence had he seen it.

In my opinion, Carl was a cunt. There, I've said it – just don't tell him I did – and his presence was the one negative factor in what was turning out to be an enjoyable romp. Watt, despite his claims otherwise, seemed a spent force and it appeared as if his duties didn't involve contact with us. I doubted he could have stomached being a marshal in our zone – coming around taking note of our spectacular success would have probably killed the old git off!

On the whole it probably suited the pair of us to have no further contact. They say time is a great healer, although I was sure even if the pair of us happened to be cryogenically frozen for a couple of millennium he would never forgive me for blowing up his bivvy – the small-minded bastard – and I would never forgive him for being an odious, cheating twat!

In amongst all the excitement of finding out how utterly awesomely the exclusive, revolutionary, indented, dirty brown bottom bait boilie performed on a runs water, it was easy to forget Rambo's hopes of getting info on the person really responsible for us being here. It wasn't really clear to me how we were likely to get any gen on the supposed bait baron. It might not be necessary – if he carried out his promise to Pup to leave him alone if we won – but, from a personal viewpoint, I would like to have known how much of the rumour and myth were true. As for Pup not being hounded any more, pragmatism dictated this to be unlikely – if the bait baron wanted in on Pup's bait before, he most definitely would once he had heard how brilliant it was! The irony being, even if Pup did sell out, today's bait wasn't on the inventory! It was ours all ours – and Rambo would fight anyone who argued differently! And I would stand and watch him and cheer him on!

I surmised that maybe an opportunity might present itself at a later date, and to be honest I was happy enough to wait. In the space between runs and rebaiting I had comically imagined the bait baron to be spying on us with a remote surveillance device, one beaming back our every move to his evil bait baron's lair. Rambo had laughed when I had told him. To me, the whole rumour of this allegedly tyrannical man becoming the owner of a bait empire by illicit means still seemed slightly ludicrous.

As we sweltered in the sun, runless for the last half-hour and with four rods out, Rambo tactically exploited the lull and despatched Pup for a change of boat and transmitter batteries.

"Don't start gassing with Ben," I called after him. "There's bound to be an evening feeding spell... *today!*" Pup nodded to signify he had heard my warning and we both watched him make his way around the back of the other swims. "Bit of a legend, that guy," I said to Rambo.

"He sure is." Rambo fingered the stubble on his chin. "You know, boy, I'd *really* like to know what's in our bait that makes it so good."

"You and everyone else."

"The bait baron, you think?"

I chuckled. "There's an *outside* chance he might be interested! Mind you, I still don't believe in all this rubbish doing the rounds, do you?"

Rambo cocked his head. "Maybe it's true," he said a little to my surprise. "It's a lucrative industry, even more so now with all this Pulimov inspired action. You never know, boy, perhaps this bait baron had insider knowledge and knew the prize was coming along," he theorised. "Who would hazard a guess at the UK bait industry's turnover? It must be millions, but not so big you couldn't muscle in on it. A few big players and lots of smaller ones… I've got an open mind. If a company could mop up the smaller boys, stop the direct buying of baits between angler and bait company and make all the trade go through retail outlets, real money's there to be made."

"If you had Pup's bait you wouldn't need the others," I pointed out. "What would be the point in trying to corner the whole market?"

Rambo wagged a finger. "It doesn't work like that. If you look at other industries there's often a common ownership behind supposed leading brands in competition. It's all to do with the clever commercial manipulation of the customer. Brand loyalty to a perceived company all going into the same coffers keeps the leading brands strong, rich, able to advertise, profitable *and* stops any other newcomers breaking into the market."

"It's a fucking boilie, for God's sake!" I protested.

"It's a fucking food product costing up to ten notes a kilo. What else costs as much as that? And that includes food for human consumption!"

I fell into silence still unconvinced. In my mind the mini-adventure we were on didn't take into account the facts exposed by Rambo's sixty-second bait industry seminar. I could appreciate if a person or company was desperate to break into the market, it would be a better option to buy up established names rather than starting up from fresh. Christ, how many bait companies had gone pop over the last ten years? Loads – was the short answer. Setting up a range of baits involving all the paraphernalia of making, selling, distributing and most importantly publicising them was a huge amount of admin. Buying and bullying into established ranges did make a kind of perverted sense. Maybe the alleged bait baron was a violent venture capitalist with an unhealthy fascination for carp fishing baits!

"We'll see," I said without commitment and decided to take in the shimmering view across The Bowl. The heat haze rippled the distant anglers, none of whom seemed to be engaged in anything more strenuous than being slumped in their chairs. I glanced down to my left – no spod action to be seen – and up to my right where I saw two anglers firmly fixed and sweltering in their chairs. Two spod rods lay propped slightly off perpendicular against bivvies, their spods hanging straight and still from heavy main line. How different from the earlier mayhem. No alarms sounded in the hot air. The Bowl's carp were having a rest – if their reputation were to remain untarnished I knew it wouldn't last long.

"Have you seen anyone else catching?" I asked Rambo.

"I think nearly everyone has caught something," came the reply. "Not that I've been looking that closely."

"But we're still winning?"

"I reckon so, boy."

"Do you really think everyone else is on a bait baron bait? I mean, how the hell would you know? How could you organise it without going to ridiculous lengths? I'd have thought lots of the spodders were using particles." Rambo lethargically shrugged his huge shoulders. Behind his sunglasses I suspected his eyes were closed. "What do you think Watt meant by having powerful friends? Do you think he's somehow tied in with this bait baron?"

The reply was disinterested. "No idea."

I changed tack. "What about, Carl? How come he doesn't respect me like he does you?"

Rambo let out a soft exhalation of air. "Because he *knows* I could batter him. One arm tied behind…"

"I heard," I said grumpily. "And hopping at the same time."

"Don't take it personally, boy. It's the level people like Carl operate on. You could have won a Nobel Prize, an Oscar or the Booker Prize for your prison memoirs and it wouldn't make an iota of difference. He knows I could beat the shit out of him, whereas with you, he knows he could put you flat on your back in," Rambo slowly took off his sunglasses, lent forward in his chair and eyed me up and down, "five seconds."

"Thanks," I said without the trace of any in my voice.

Rambo reinstated his sunglasses and sunk back in his chair. "No worries, boy." A few seconds passed. Unexpectedly Rambo inched the sunglasses down to the bridge of his nose, his eyes glimmering as they peered over the top of them. "I would have said *two* seconds, but I wanted to let you down gently because you once saved my life."

"I wish I fucking hadn't."

"You don't mean that," Rambo observed, his face cracked in a huge smile.

I turned from Rambo, looking towards the east and away from the sun's bright afternoon glare. Strangely, I suddenly wondered what Steffi was up to.

Pup returned an hour later with fresh batteries and a fresh worry. "Ben gave me this, *before* he started talking to me." Pup waved a white envelope addressed to 'Pup Enterprises' in front of my nose. "He said someone had left it on his trestle desk, didn't know who. I thought I'd leave it until I got back before reading it."

"Did you hear that?" I shouted to Rambo who had nipped into his bivvy.

Rambo re-emerged from his tent. "Yeah. Open it up. I expect it's a writ from Watt!"

Pup opened the envelope. He unfolded an A4 piece of paper and started to read aloud with increasing disbelief. "It says, 'Nice start. I'm very impressed; you clearly have some good products at your disposal. It's a shame you don't want to do business. That is your choice. I will respect it. If you win I shan't bother you again. A shame it has to be this way. Yours sincerely, The Bait Baron.'"

I pulled a face. "Eww! He actually called himself 'The Bait Baron'?"

Pup nodded and thrust the letter towards me. I snatched it from his hand finding myself annoyed at the ego behind it. My eyes flicked across the brief computer generated note and landed at the nauseating sign off. If I had been Superman the words 'The Bait Baron' would have started to burn.

"What a jerk! The *Bait Baron*! Is he for real?" I smacked the A4 sheet with the back of my hand and went off on one. "Jesus Christ! He must have read too many bait company profiles! It's all very well us referring to him like that as a shadowy unknown figure, but to have the front to actually, *actually*, call yourself 'The Bait Baron', well, it's obscene!"

Rambo held out his hand for a look, so I passed the offensive note to him. He read it and gave a miniscule shake of his head. "Oh, dear me. Rampant ego alert! A dangerous character." Rambo screwed the ball of paper into a tight ball, slung it into his bivvy and issued Pup with a warning. "He's *not* going to go away like he's said. You *do* realise that, don't you?"

Pup blinked vacantly. "I kind of thought it meant he definitely would, now he's written it down."

Rambo's mouth opened, intent on imparting the saddening news to our gifted, if deluded, boiliemeister that life away from the rolling table was infinitely more double dealing, devious, deceitful, dishonest, calculating and crooked than his innocent mind could imagine. The intent was halted by a rampaging Delkim giving it the firm's guitar solo theme tune – not much fretwork, blistering plucking speed, amp set on six, which is kind of eleven, if you see what I mean. Rambo ran to his rod while I mused on the number of times a take had conveniently punctuated life's action and shifted its focus.

Our sixth fish of the comp was a lively fellah, one who managed to cross the other three lines already left in the water. I was made to go over and under with them to leave Rambo an uncluttered attachment to the kiting monster, sweat running from my brow as I did. Fortunately, the pair of us had called the over and unders correctly meaning Rambo could happily play the fish to the left of my left-hand rod in clear water. A window of opportunity to relax presented itself until my next input, so I collected the tool for said input and then stood at Rambo's side soaking up the ambience. Poised to wield the net, I observed the other contestants as I waited for Rambo to do his stuff and noticed many of them looking our way – I was watching the watchers. The Bowl had become a goldfish bowl, the pair of us the only two inside its glass walls. Even at such a long distance I could make out the jealousy in their eyes and afforded myself a superior smile – eat your hearts out, suckers, we're on a bait to die for!

To my right the strain began to tell and unsurprisingly not on Rambo's forearms. Morphing into my alter ego, Netboy, the superhero with the forty-two inch appendage, I assumed the classic lowered body position – Crouching Carper, Hidden Lumbago – of the expectant sidekick. I was not to be disappointed, with a little left hand guidance above the butt and a couple of steps back Rambo hauled, in both senses of the word, another carp over the aluminium spreader block. Simultaneously,

Pup Enterprises clasped one hand firmly on the corner of the first place cheque.

With our sixth capture safely placed on the unhooking mat, Rambo called up Carl as I indulged in a mathematically incorrect high-five with Pup. Carl must have been lurking close by as he appeared within seconds, striding into our swim before I had even unhooked Rambo's fish. Once I had, I took Rambo's rod out of the way and quietly disappeared to the periphery of the three bivvies. Carl had given me another one of his looks. It had made me mindful of the probability I would come up short on lasting *two* seconds, let alone five, if Rambo was out of the equation – and minus some teeth plus multiple injuries. It all added up – Carl's average deed was mean.

As I waited gutlessly in the wings – not even wanting to carry out my previous doughty spiral notepad jottings – an inhabitant of Spod Central West, the next pair up to our right, wandered down for a chat. The reason? Despite trying to conceal it, it would materialise as an attempt to pump me over the subject of what bait we were using. Let's be fair, we've all had it at one time or another, when it's been our day. You just have to accept it! Some carpers can't resist, they see someone hauling like a good'un and a little cog grinds around in their brain and they think, 'I'll go and try and find out what bait he's on'. Like you would *ever* tell them! Next thing, they would be asking to have a look at your secret rig as well! Bloody cheek!

Of course, information is much more openly displayed than it used to be years ago when everything, and I mean *everything*, was secret squirrel. However, watching the tall gangly figure with the large ten-to-two splayed feet and stupid grin on his face coming towards me, I knew he would go back to Spod Central West with nothing. Rien! Nada! Zilch! Nicht! Fuck all!

"You're doing all right!" he said as an opener. "How many's that?"

"Six. How about you?"

No point in being rude, I decided. This bloke didn't have much going for him and I didn't feel inclined to rub it in. Not only was SCW carper too tall, too thin with Sideshow Bob-sized feet grafted on at incorrect angles to the end of impossibly long legs, he was also the unfortunate possessor of an overbite a Freddy Mercury impersonator would die of AIDS for. His terrible skin was firmly in the anti-acne cream advert 'before' stable. Large, raised pus-filled pimples were dotted across his forehead, his cheeks, his chin – forget it – *all over* his face. Peppered by pock-marks bearing witness to previously picked pimples, here, if ever there was one, was a face not conducive to kissing. As far as I could reckon, this young man must be struggling for female company period! I cruelly and quickly checked out his right hand for any signs of self-abuse cramping.

"We've had a couple… It's a bit hot," he added by way of an excuse for lagging four fish behind us.

"Yeah, conditions aren't great," I concurred.

My new buddy pulled a top lip over his inclined incisors, the blond bum-fluff on it spreading wider as he did so. "I never thought a boater would win on here," he observed. "But it looks like you're going to. You must be on a good bait."

And there you have it! Within four short sentences he had broached *the* subject. "We are," I confirmed, waiting for his next one, the big one, the 'what is it?' one. Not that it would do him any good now, not in the comp, his question would be asked in hope – for Ron. Later on, as the crummy old joke goes.

"Have you ever fished here before?"

"Um, no… never," I answered, a bit thrown by my non-reception of *the* question.

"Fair play to you, that makes it even more impressive!" He held out a hand. "My name's Paul, I'll catch you later."

I met his hand with mine and received a firm grip, one with a groove in it, confirming my earlier fears. Not really, although I did feel a bit squeamish wondering where it had been when we shook. I think my grip weakened because of it.

"Sure," I said to Pimply Paul.

Pimply Paul seemed happy with this and turned himself and the mini-skis he had on the end of his legs about face and Coco the Clowned it back to Spod City West. Seconds after he left Carl walked by giving me his best hard man stare. Something, possibly shame, most likely suicidal, stirred within.

"How big?" I enquired with as much force as I could muster.

"Rambo's fish was twenty-three, six," Carl informed me.

"Oh," I responded with a hint of ingratiation, one born out of Carl not deciding to smash me in the face. I regretted it as soon as it left my body. Carl was gone, though, uninterested in my reply, strutting back up to his bivvy to await his next weighing-in job.

Muttering an oath under my breath I went back to Pup and Rambo. "On first name terms now, are we?" I asked sarcastically. "'*Rambo's* fish was twenty-three, six'," I repeated childishly.

"I'm only looking for an edge to get some gen on The Bait Baron," Rambo remarked, immediately making me feel both petty and stupid. "Carl might be the person we can get it from. If anyone's working for him, he is."

My short-term memory quickly dissolved. "Jesus! Are we really going to call him, The Bait Baron? With proper capital letters?" I asked in a petty and stupid voice.

Rambo raised his eyelids, flicked a look at Pup and changed the subject. "Who was that long streak of piss?"

"Pimply Paul," I answered. "He's been spodding his guts out, not that there's much of them, for two fish in the next swim up. He seems all right. I thought he was going to give me the third degree over our bait, but he didn't."

Rambo briefly nodded, his mind on other things. "Get the boat out then, boy. I want to get this rod back on the spot."

I retrieved the boat from its dry dock – my bivvy – and carried it to Rambo's side of the swim and put it in the margins. I could tell Pup had already put the fresh batteries in by its weight, so I set about loading her up with our assortment of boilies.

Rambo meticulously checked his hook and hooklength and put on a neutral buoyancy hookbait – if anything was emerging it was that the neutrals had the most positive feedback. Glugged or unglugged, at the moment, seemed to make no difference. Once all was shipshape and Microcat fashion, Rambo drove the boat out. It had hardly gone more than a few yards when his mobile started to ring.

"Answer it for me, boy. Thigh pocket."

Self-consciously I stuck my hand in the pocket, ignored the Glock that was nestling in there and pulled out Rambo's mobile. The display showed 'Home' – Steffi! I pressed the phone button and clamped the mobile to my ear turning my back on its occupied owner. "Hello, big boy. You know I have nozzing on, don't you?" said the heavily inflected, sultry voice.

"It's Matt, here," I said quickly, a thousand images spinning into my head. "Rambo's busy driving."

"Oh. Hi, Matt. I still have nozzing on!" Steffi said easily, totally unembarrassed. "Vott's he doing driving? I sought ser competition vas now."

"Not a car, a baitboat," I explained.

"Okay. Tell him I love him and I vill phone later. Are you vinning?"

"Yeah. We're winning."

"Gudt!" There was the briefest of pauses. "Have you had any of zose psychic revelations lately, anysing strange come into your head?"

Remembering how Rambo had told me Steffi found me a fascinating – if not fancied – person due to my previous future seeing/mind-melding/ghost chatting adventures, I found myself vaguely disappointed in answering negatively. "No. I'm afraid I can't control it... it comes when it comes. I don't even know if it will ever come again," I said wistfully. "I've only ever done it once to order."

"Vitt Ser Eye?"

"Yeah."

"Okay. You vould tell me if you had anozzer vision, ja?"

"Sure," I confirmed

"Zat's gudt. I vould like very much to know. Zo, bye for now, Matt."

"Bye, Steffi."

I hung up. "Steffi," I said to Rambo. "She said to say she loves you and she'll phone back later. She didn't have any... well, she'll phone back later anyway and explain."

Rambo theatrically dumped both hoppers with a swish of his left thumb. "She's never phoned to say that before, boy," he commented. "I expect she's gone mad with the credit card and she's on a guilt trip."

Chapter 8

I awoke in the dark with a start – one not induced by a rampaging buzzer. For some reason my heart was thumping and not solely down to the rather lurid dream I was having about Steffi. I say dream, more a recollection of *that* DVD – with certain self-imposed alterations – the one I had once so furtively viewed at home. Craning my head, I peered out into the gloom through my ever-present-at-night mozzie defence shield. (I had become paranoid about the whining bastards feeding on me ever since I had crash dived through The Eye's bivvy table and they had gorged upon my bare arms.) I could barely make out our four rods and beyond them the sheen of water. I sat up, pushing my sleeping bag down to my waist. My ears strained at the silence. Why had I awoken?

I removed my legs from the bag, swung them over the edge of my bedchair and slipped on my previously prepared loosely laced trainers. I unzipped the mozzie screen and stepped outside, stooping through the bivvy's opening. The night was cool without being cold even though I was still wearing my shorts – a welcome respite from the earlier heat of the day. I checked my digital watch, a basic Casio rather than an ex-SAS soldier's endorsed timepiece and saw it was turned two a.m. I arched my head back and gazed at the glittering array of stars in the moonless sky above. It was a familiar routine, but one in which the impact of the celestial spectacle never diminished. On shifting my thoughts to a more mundane and earth-bound matter I became acquainted with the fact my bladder wasn't full and didn't need emptying. No run, no noise, no need for a piss. The initial question still remained.

I walked slowly and softly around to the side of my bivvy and surveyed the night-time scene. The odd static light showed in a few swims, the visual aid forming the centrepiece for a couple of anglers having a beer and chewing the cud on important topics like world peace, world famine, global warming, (To Save The Planet install solar panels, wind turbines, heat pump technology combined with a condensing boiler, band 'A' rating, and low energy usage electrical appliances. Financial and energy consumption payback – sometime after you're dead.) the abolition of racial and sexual discrimination and the hooking properties of the Withy Pool Rig.

Further than that nothing stirred, which was exactly what you would expect at two in the morning. Any thoughts of skulduggery and mischief seemed misplaced. Despite the seemingly reassuring scene I still felt uneasy and, not wanting to go back to sleep, I turned and walked to the foot of the grassy spoil wall. After much slipping and sliding, I climbed to its surprisingly lush top and sat down facing The Bowl. Elbows on knees, hands cupping my face, feeling the stubble on either cheek, I settled on my perch and mentally drifted. The night was breathless, perfect and still, one ideally suited for passive contemplation.

When it comes to passive contemplation I rarely need a second invitation, so I mused on the reasons for my awakening, a subject that gradually shifted its focus to the meaning of my life. I soon came to the conclusion I had been wrong to assume all its ends were neatly tied. There would always be some small part of it unravelling, posing new questions, like Pup's present predicament. There would be new events, even if they were likely to be less bizarre than they had been in the past. If I lived my life to an average knock, to use cricketing parlance, I had another forty odd runs – years – to go. I was barely half way! Decisions I made now would continue to affect my time to come and would shape my destiny. Purchasing Felix's water, if it came off, would be huge new avenue of adventure. Added into the bargain there would be my old friend fate, interacting with my decisions and forcing circumstance. As another crusty, old, lying bastard – sorry – as another crusty, old, politician had once said, 'Events, dear boy. Events'."

Looking back on old times it was true to say fate had spectacularly guided me, especially after coming out of prison and on the trip to France. The trip to France! I laughed to myself. What I would give to be able to watch Rambo and Spunker have *that* fight again! Come to think of it, I still had the Cowboy coming out to draw on 8mm tape somewhere. *Somewhere*! How remarkable I didn't know the exact whereabouts of such a precious carp fishing heritage heirloom! Those had been heady days all right, a marvellous start to a new life after the drudgery of prison, even if the foundations for future disasters had been laid when I had laid Rebecca.

My bum started to ache so I lay down on the relatively comfy grass, clasped my hands behind my head and started to become mesmerised by the night's splendour. My thinking gradually shifted to short-term memories rather than events of years ago. The unease that had somewhat dissipated in my nostalgic reminiscing returned and began to nag. It was the cause of my wakening and I still had no inkling what it was. Looking into the night sky I soon spotted The Plough constellation and for no real reason counted its stars, starting at the arm end. At star number six, without any prior warning, the reason why I had awoken with a start thudded into my head like a silent arrow hitting its target. Not so much a psychic phenomenon, more a case of reading between the lines. A good detective would have called it the combination of analytical observation and the sudden spark of inspiration merging to make complete understanding. It was much more than a hunch – I *knew*. I had been thinking of what had happened, read the subtext of what had been said, had put two and two together and made the magic jump to four. Now I could explain it all.

I knew – *knew* – what Steffi had done, and because of it, the motivation for her phone call. The one I had fielded because Rambo had been otherwise engaged with the important task of driving the baitboat. There was no doubt, no ambiguity and no uncertainty. I had rationalised the events of the past with the things she had said yesterday afternoon to me on Rambo's mobile and in combination they had told me what she had done. If she hadn't done what I knew she had, she wouldn't have said what she had said. The two were mutually exclusive and indelibly entwined – and now, because I was cognisant of the situation, I was faced with a dilemma. I was shocked, sure I was shocked, yet somehow, I wasn't surprised.

Knowledge can be a dangerous thing. For once in my will-I-won't-I shall-I-shan't-I forever-going-over-the-same-ground-endlessly existence, I resolved it quickly. I decided I would confront her, tell her I knew what she had done and give her the chance to resolve it. I would not, however, under any circumstances, tell Rambo. Not telling him was the least of my worries – manufacturing an opportunity to meet Steffi alone in order to tell her what I knew, might not be so easy. If Rambo were to get wind of any contrived manoeuvring he could easily get hold of the wrong end of the stick – not a scenario in which I wanted to be involved seeing as the man always had a Glock in his trousers!

Shit! Fancy her doing that! I thought to myself, my face stretching to a grin.

I was mentally juggling some sordid images when I heard a voice and for the second time in a matter of minutes I was thrown back into the past. My déjà-vu moment was when we had prebaited the old SS syndicate at night. Watt's voice was as familiar now, despite the years, as it had been then and the fact I had spoken to him yesterday was irrelevant. While I had been lying on my back, fathoming out Steffi's deed, he and someone else had stopped at the bottom of the grassy spoil wall – on the side away from The Bowl. This fact alone indicated they were up to no good, having effectively 'sneaked around the back' for a clandestine meeting. Staying stock-still and holding my breath, I listened intently.

"… *Lots* more fish than anyone else! I know them of old and they are not nice people, I can assure you. Do you know one of them actually tried to kill me? All because I was catching more fish than them! He took two hand grenades, not the camouflaged gorilla, the other one, *hand grenades* I tell you, and threw them in my bivvy and blew it up! He went to prison for it, a paltry year and a half for attempted murder! I ask you! Where is the justice in this world! I just thank God I wasn't inside!"

It's difficult to lie down on lush grass in the middle of a cool night wearing shorts and simmer. I managed it, as I silently fumed, listening to Watt's skewed tale of half-truths.

"I hadn't seen either of them for years until yesterday. I assumed they had burnt up and disappeared off the carp scene altogether, neither of them were particularly accomplished anglers, you see. That's why I couldn't figure out how they were doing so well, not until he told me about the other one, the one who makes the bait. If ever there was a 'Brains' in an outfit, he's the one. Only *then* did it make any sense! It simply goes to show how, given a good bait on an overstocked, featureless water requiring no watercraft *and* a blessed baitboat to put it out, even a poor angler can have good results. I'm only thankful I'm not the marshal for this side! I couldn't stomach it! Seeing those two winning at a canter all because they've hitched a ride on a bait expert's back would make me physically sick!"

"Right," said Carl.

"Heaven knows what two-bit water they've been fishing since they were banned from my old syndicate." Watt paused as he sought to clarify and distance himself from what might have been construed in his earlier comment. "They joined long before my involvement otherwise I would have seen to it they never became members in the first place! I can't imagine many other syndicates would let them in! They're both highly objectionable types, rotten apples to the core…"

Watt's voice began to fade as he and Carl moved off and I took the chance to do likewise, quickly sliding down the opposite side of the grassy wall on my arse. I had a major league wedgie by the time I reached the bottom and had to extricate my pants and shorts from my arse crack in the style of a manic Rafael Nadal. Once comfortable in the lower garment region I legged it to my bivvy, made a glorious entrance, swanned through the bivvy's lobby, entered the sleeping quarters whereupon I flopped melodramatically on to my bedchair.

What a result, I thought exultantly – fate was pulling the strings in my favour again! It was obvious from what I had overheard Watt and Carl were hooked up with The Bait Baron in some shape or form – probably a simple snowman on a basic hair rig. No prizes for guessing who was the pompous, pretentious, pontificating, puffed up pop-up out of the two, whilst Carl was perfectly suited for being the deadweight, dour, delinquent muscle pinning it to the deck.

I wondered whether to wake Rambo up and tell him the news and not tell him the news. Tell him the news about Watt and not tell him the news about Steffi. "Sod it!" I said to myself. "I'll wait for a buzzer to wake him!"

I tried to get myself to go to sleep.

It's funny knowing a secret concerning a person much closer to another person than you are yourself. When it concerns another person who's your best fishing mate and said person is built like the non-proverbial camouflaged brick outhouse with the added punch of a Glock 17 tucked in his pocket it's even… less funny. Much less funny – and I was having little difficulty not laughing.

Watching Rambo play another fish during the sunrise of a new day, it dawned on me, quite literally, this wasn't going to be the breeze I had imagined. Not telling him wasn't so easy. A big part of me wanted to tell him and another part, the rational part, didn't. His reaction was what I most wanted to see, if I'm honest, and I was aware that if my game plan came to fruition I would confront Steffi at some as yet unspecified point in the future, she would hopefully resolve it, and I would never get to see the look on Rambo's face.

Sometimes you have to deny yourself these little pleasures for the sake of friendship.

"You'll never guess what happened last night?" I chirped, as Rambo turned what we both had marked down as a scrapping mid-double.

Rambo took his eyes off the boil of chocolate coloured water ten yards out and locked them on to mine for what felt like a longer period than was normal for the given situation. Pushing down on the rising panic caused by the possibility of Rambo using a hidden mind probe to lay bare my innermost thoughts, I lifted a couple of eyebrows and gave what I hoped would pass as a cheeky grin.

"You're right, I won't," said Rambo returning his mind probe to the fish.

Silence.

"So *are* you going to tell me, then, boy?"

I jolted from my screensaver mode. "Right! Sorry! Yes, last night! Let me tell Pup as well. Pup!" I shouted back towards the mini estate of bivvies. "Get your bait rolling arse out here now!"

Pup, who'd had a hard night reading classic bait pamphlets by fading torchlight, or at least he looked as if he'd had a hard night reading classic bait pamphlets by fading torchlight, emerged from his bivvy. "What?" he groaned. "What d'you want?"

I gestured to the most non-lark-like person of our trio to come and stand next to me, which, after a lot of sleepy-dust excavation from dark rimmed eyes, he duly did.

"I was just saying to Rambo, you'll never guess what happened last night," I told Pup once he pulled up alongside my hip.

Pup yawned prolifically and eventually thrust out a lower lip. "Don't suppose I will, given all the things that might have…"

"Just tell us!" Rambo barked in a voice resonant of a sergeant major bollocking a set of new recruits.

I told them.

"Interesting," remarked Rambo easing the – spotter's badge for the size – mid-double into my net. "Nice of Watt to paint the pair us in such a fair and reasonable manner."

Rambo dropped his rod to near horizontal, the battle now over, as Pup put his slant on events. "*I* came out of it rather well, don't you think?" he gloated. "I'm glad to see there's someone out there who appreciates the input of my work. You two don't realise how lucky you are to have an exclusive…" Pup was stopped in his tracks by Rambo's huge clamping paw flying out and fastening itself over his mouth, its thumb and fingers squeezing nostrils together.

"Is he with you?" Rambo asked me, his powerful arm now cutting right across my chin.

I eased my head back and looked at the asphyxiating boiliemeister out the corner of cold eyes. "No," I replied frostily.

Rambo hung on for a few more seconds before releasing Pup, who thankfully dragged in a deep lungful of air, and went on to ask a pertinent question. "The one thing *really* bothering me is what the hell you were doing on top of the grassy wall at two in the morning."

"Waiting to shoot the president!" I answered, hoping to deflect further questioning with a quip.

Rambo disregarded the Kennedy moment. "The revisitation of a few old nightmares?" he suggested with *almost* a smidgen of concern in his voice.

"Something like that," I answered matter-of-factly. "I couldn't sleep and it seemed a good place to go… you know, at the time."

"And so it was, boy!" Rambo declared. "Mighty fortuitous! Now, let's get this fish on the mat and we'll see what Carl has to say. See if we can wring any info out of him now we know the score."

When Carl came he was different, although I didn't twig it at first. "Right, boys?" he asked and he looked at Pup and myself when he did so. It wasn't the 'what you looking at?' look, either. "Got another?"

'No, Carl, we haven't caught one. We thought we'd give you a ring to see how you were doing, find out if either your shaven head or your eight Argos medallion rings needed a polish!' I didn't say. "Rambo has," was what I did say.

Carl greeted his superior hard man, fussed with the sling and put the fish in it. "Little bird was telling me about you three last night. Little story from your dark past."

"Oh yeah. Who was that?" I enquired thinking Carl sounded like The Eye what with the 'dark past/dark soled wellingtons' references.

"Someone you didn't like and who didn't like you," he answered enigmatically. *Thought* he answered enigmatically – little did he know, I had heard the whole episode.

"That narrows it down to a few hundred!" Rambo joked.

"Basically, I was right impressed," Carl continued, pulling up the drawstrings of the sling. He paused and looked over his shoulder at me from his squatting position. "This person told me you tried to kill him by blowing up his bivvy with a couple of hand grenades and did some bird for it."

"I did some bird in a bivvy once," I tastelessly bragged, recalling my epic doggy-style bivvy-bang with Melina. (The, admittedly, poor defence for my crassness rests in the realisation hard nut Carl was actually impressed by all of this and, subsequently, I had allowed myself to get a little carried away. Much like I had with Melina, come to think of it!) "It caned my knees because I knocked over a box of Pedigree Mixer and I kept kneeling on the bloody stuff!"

Carl cackled with laughter, although his interest quickly returned to his first theme. "But is it true, right?" he asked eagerly. "Did you really, basically, blow up the old cunt's bivvy?" I nodded. "And did you get put inside?"

I nodded again. "Eighteen months," I admitted, now feeling compelled to redress the truth to more acceptable levels because of Rambo's withering gaze. "Watt's exaggerating as usual. In truth, I didn't really try to *kill* him. He was outside the bivvy all the time. Outside chasing after me because I'd told him his wife had been playing away with his best mate."

"Substitute 'wife' for 'girlfriend' and 'Watt' for 'me' and you've got the bivvy-bang incident in a nutshell!" interjected Rambo indicating my culpability with a wry smile.

Carl's eyes fogged with the confusion of information overload concerning the intricate, interlocking tendrils of our sex lives at the time. I only hoped Rambo didn't get too loose with his tongue and let slip his contemporary knee-trembler with Melloney (You remember Melloney; the youngest sister of the Three Witches of Eastwick. There was Melina in the middle (see bivvy-bang) and Melissa; the eldest one who originally married Pup and who left him for Brad. You remember Brad; the toothpaste ad smile American millionaire from the inaugural Hamworthy Fisheries, the finest carp fishery etc. *charadee* Fish-In. You remember Hamworthy Fisheries' inaugural *charadee* Fish-In; the one with Horst and Helmut… I'll shut up now.) – Pup's current live-in lady – or we might, out of necessity, be digging our old sausage guns and rolling tables from the dumping ground commonly known as the attic. Life without Pup's bait was a tragic, sobering thought.

"*Meanwhile*," I continued, "Rambo was beating up God knows how many other syndicate members because of a disagreement over the legitimacy of a recently hooked twenty. It was quite an event," I calmly understated. "You should have been there, you'd have probably died of laughter."

Carl was like a bookish youngster having his favourite story read to him. "Sounds a crack," he enthused before slipping back into his usual aggressive self. "Watt's full of shit, right? I knew it wouldn't have happened like he said. Fucking liar!" Carl's eyes widened making him look even fiercer. "Where d'you get the fireworks?" he asked me.

"Rambo always kept a couple in his rucksack, which was convenient," I purred.

"Got any more?"

"Nah," Rambo replied. "Discontinued line. I couldn't take the chance! I never knew what he might want to blow up next!" Carl was shaking his head in a well-I'll-be-buggered-with-the-rough-end-of-a-pineapple smile on his face. "How long have *you* known Watt?" Rambo inquired. "Apart from it being long enough to suss out he's an odious creep… that's usually within thirty seconds of meeting him!"

Carl held up his set of scales, Rambo's latest capture suspended below them. "Sixteen-four," he said reading them. "You're *miles* in front!" He put the sling back on the mat and faced Rambo. "Not that long. He's got in with the bloke who owns this water and several others. One's a real pretty place, right. Basically, he wants to try and get it as a syndicate water, wants to persuade him to stop the day ticket crack. That's why he's working the comp, trying to weasel his way in. Fucking brown nose!"

"Do you work for this owner bloke as well?"

"I work for lots of different people, Rambo," Carl answered tapping his nose with a ringed index finger. "A little bit here, a little bit there. I'm a car mechanic by trade."

"Who's the person that told Watt about Pup," Rambo asked.

I felt a wave of excitement run over me. It was The Bait Baron, it must have been, but *who* was The Bait Baron? And would the newly found common ground between Carl and ourselves be a strong enough reason for him to tell us?

A buzzer sounded and instinctively Rambo and myself flinched – only it wasn't a buzzer. It was a buzzer ringtone. The moment for an answer was gone. Carl snickered at our reaction, like I suspected he had many times. "There's the phone! Someone else has got one!" Carl answered the nagging mobile, confirming the swim number he had to go to. "Better trot, right! You can put that one back now. I'll see you soon," he said as soon as he hung up. The bite alarm phone went back in his pocket. "I was way out with you lot," he remarked, strafing us with the nose-tapping digit. "Nice baits, pal!" he said to Pup.

As Carl headed off he suddenly pulled himself back, as if deliberating an internal struggle, and he flicked his head, gesturing me to one side. Dimly I put a finger up to my chest to check and once Carl had nodded affirmatively I moved over and stood next to him. For the second time Carl put his head close to mine, only it wasn't threatening and I could sense his awkwardness. "When you were inside," he asked softly. "Basically, what was it like?"

I wrinkled my nose. "*Not* very nice," I answered truthfully. "Your mind's free, that's the one thing to hang on to, but when that door shuts…" I gave a shudder of horror. "He pulled a few strings to make it easier with the blokes inside. I didn't have any aggro apart from doing the time."

"Rambo?"

"Yeah." I self-consciously scratched the back of my head, loosely laced trainers gazing. I lifted my head and held Carl's eye. "You know how I got through it, Carl? The one thing that really helped and held me together?" Carl was hanging on my every word like a torpedoed mariner to a life belt. "I forced myself to write down the story that ended with me blowing up Watt's bivvy, just to make sure of the existence of the truth. Watt was writing articles for Carpworld about the same water and they were *pure* propaganda." I paused and reflected on a sobering thought. "Mind you, no one's ever read the story! The handwritten draught is still shoved in a draw at home!" Rendering it pointless, I inwardly noted with some dissatisfaction. I continued. "I did used to think about what I was going to catch when I got out, although when I did, getting back into carping proved very difficult at first. Rambo and I had a good bait in those days, our red one. It was the one we used to take the water and Watt apart, despite whatever other bullshit he might care to tell you."

"But now you've got a better one, right?" said Carl flicking his eyes at Pup.

"Much better," I conceded. "The spodder's can't deal with it!"

Carl rolled his eyes and grinned, nodding his head quickly in tiny movements. "I know… *Now!*"

I decided to strike while the iron was hot and the boilie hadn't blown. "Who was it who told Watt about Pup and his baits? You didn't answer because your phone rang."

Carl answered readily without so much as a batted eyelid. Good baits don't *ever* blow! "He said it was some angler over the other side. Basically he mentioned it when Watt weighed in one of his fish. They'd seen you were hauling and mentioned

Pup. They knew he was a good bait roller, well known for his pop-ups. They'd used his baits in the past."

I grimaced internally with the arrival of yet another disappointment. "Just an angler, then?" It figured. There were bound to be guys in the comp who had used Pup's stuff in the past. It was probably how The Bait Baron had got wind of him in the first place and why he wanted to buy him out. You couldn't keep someone with Pup's reputation a secret.

"Right."

"Have you ever heard of anyone called The Bait Baron?"

Our old style relationship returned in a flash, catching me unaware and seriously underprepared. Carl's face turned mean and menacing. The medallion-ringed index finger was thrust under my nose. "Don't ask me about him!" he raged.

"Why?" I began before Carl grabbed me by the throat with one hand and made a zipping action across my mouth with another.

"Don't!" he whispered threateningly.

He let go of my neck, warning me again with a pointed finger. I rubbed the sore spots where his strong digits had dug in and returned to the earlier part of our dialogue. "Why do you want to know about the gulag?" I asked.

Carl's tongue appeared furtively between his lips. "If I get done, that's where *I'm* going! And that's *why* I don't want to talk about The Bait Baron!" And on that revelation Carl slapped me on the shoulder and abruptly left. I barely moved. Rambo could have him one arm behind his back, blindfolded *and* hopping!

"What was that all about?" Rambo asked as I walked back. "I was ready to wade in there when he got hold of you." I explained what had happened and how confusing it was.

"Who'd have thought detention at Her Majesty's Pleasure could have given me credibility points with a shaven-headed Spods v Baitboats weight marshal so many years later!" I joked. "His attitude towards me definitely changed for the better until I mentioned The Bait Baron, then he flipped back to how he'd been before. I don't know what to make of it."

"Me neither, boy," admitted Rambo. "All I will say is there must be something going on! The rumour must have an element of truth in it. Maybe Carl's got into trouble doing The Bait Baron's dirty deeds. He might be on an arson rap for torching Leviathan Boilies! Maybe the police have dug something up at last."

I puffed out my cheeks and shrugged. "Maybe."

"Let's hope we can find out before the comp's over."

I nodded at Rambo and mentally pictured my version of what Steffi had done.

The runs came thick and fast throughout the rest of the day – and not only to us. The heat of yesterday had been replaced by a front coming in from the Atlantic on a brisk south-westerly with accompanying cloud cover. As the cloud increased, rain began to fall and The Bowl's carp responded by going on the feed – I responded by replacing my shorts with tracksuit bottoms and waterproofs. Soon everyone was starting to catch. In between our fish catching activity and the Matt Williams' looped video artist's impression of what Steffi had been up to, I kept a sly eye on the two sets of spodders either side of us, Pimply Paul plus one and the unknown pair to our left. I also looked over to the far side of The Bowl to see if I could guess who Watt's informer could be. It was a hopeless task and one I soon gave up.

Whilst the identity of the informer remained a mystery the pairs either side were a good indication of our catching rate. As a rough guideline it appeared we were out-catching them by three fish to one despite all their efforts to decrease turn around times. For them, both anglers were able to contribute to the task of getting a hookbait and free offerings back out as quickly as possible after a run. Team Pimply Paul's method was for one to recast while the other started to spod out the bait to the spot. As soon as the baited rod was set the angler who cast it would also start spodding. Paul's team used the clipping up method, the other pair added a marker float into the beginning of the cycle.

For us using the boat, it was more of a one-man operation apart from the initial loading of it. However, keeping the boat in the water with two anglers fishing full-time proved the necessity of having a third man who was able to deal with the battery recharging situation. I spotted several 'runners', 'gophers', 'third men', whatever you wanted to call them, frantically legging it around to Ben's tent for battery reinforcements. The excellent spare battery arrangement kept the competition fair and the only real concern was the chance of the boat 'dying at sea'. At one point this had seemed a real possibility, seeing as Rambo was determined to push to the very edge of durability. He had continued to use the boat for a couple of 'last runs' after two quick takes despite its LEDs flashing a low battery level warning. A dead baitboat drifting aimlessly out of our reach would have been a true nautical disaster – especially as it was time to make hay whilst The Bowl's carp army were going barmy and having it big style!

In the end I needn't have worried because Rambo played his hand to perfection and the boat kept going. We kept our baits and freebies going in during the optimum time and when Pup was finally dispatched to Ben's tent he arrived back just in time to witness another take. A quick pit stop put the boat back in action and not a single second was lost. Ferrari and McLaren would have been proud!

The most tangible effect of the continued feeding spell on 'The Mystery of The Bait Baron', as I was stylising it in my brain, was Carl's heavy workload. He was in our swim and gone in a flash as he strove to cope with all the weigh-in requests coming through on his mobile. As a direct result of this we were unable to discuss his problems concerning The Bait Baron any further – well, Rambo was – I was keeping well out of it and so was Pup! Continuing speculation in the periods between takes asked whether Carl worked for, had worked for or was an adversary of The Bait Baron. Had his possible prison sentence offence been in the name of, or against The Bait Baron? It was intriguing stuff – almost as intriguing as why Steffi had done what I knew she had done!

Chapter 9

The occluded front passed over The Bowl by late afternoon and the weather brightened. The rain slowed, gradually stopped and the grey cloud began to disperse. Shafts of sunlight broke through the gaps as if enormous laser beams were burning through great swathes of dirty cotton wool. Like a herd of binge drinkers who had either run out of money or collapsed into a mass coma in the gutter, The Bowl's carp stopped 'aving it large. A state of affairs somewhat less than normal ensued and runs dried up quicker than a Saharan puddle. Everyone, anglers, gophers, marshals and officials breathed a collective sigh of relief. The effort of trying to maximise the last nine hours had left everyone drained and exalted in equal measures.

When it had become clear there was a lull in fish catching proceedings Pimply Paul had quickly nipped down from Spod Central West to ask how many fish we had now caught.

"I've lost count! I don't honestly know!" I replied. "But I can soon tell you," I quickly added, before he mistook my inability to put a figure on our success as a show of arrogance and contempt. I consulted the note pad and totted up the list. Even I was surprised. "Thirty-six!" I exclaimed. "How are you doing?"

Pimply Paul let out a low iffy whistle, the sound hissing out through his protruding teeth as much as his lips. "Wow! That's some going! We're on twenty-two! You're taking the place apart… with a *boat!*"

"They said that it could not be done… but we've gone and bloody done it!" I said in a pseudo movie trailer voiceover for the first part of the sentence before breaking into an overexcited Youth TV presenter for the second.

The spots on Paul's forehead merged into waves of heaving acne as he noted my immaturity. I felt myself step back instinctively – some of those pimples were going to blow at any minute and I didn't want to be in the way of the discharge!

"Apparently no one else with a boat is anywhere near your score," he informed me. "There are a couple of spodders on the far side who've caught a few more than us, they're regulars, but that's it!" I made what I hoped came across as humble yet knowing shrug of the shoulders. "Is your bait a special prototype?" he asked.

I laughed. It always came back to bait. When you were catching, any conversation with any carper eventually came back to the subject of bait, even if he had managed to avoid the subject during our first little chat. "It was until Pup's cat ate it!" I answered.

"What?" Paul's acne scrunched inward.

I waved vaguely at the air. "His cat likes boilies, some more than others," I told him, dismissing the subject. "In answer to your question, no, it's not a prototype, but it *is* a bait made exclusively for us," I said. "We paid a lot of money for the deal."

"And it looks like you'll be recouping some of it when you win first prize."

"Yeah," I conceded. "Looks like we will."

Paul concluded he wasn't going to wring anything else out of me or be given five kilos of our bait to try so he wound things up. "Well, I'd better get back in case I get a run,"

"Sure. Catch you later."

"With your bait I expect you could," cracked Paul.

As Paul returned to his swim I thought of a new verb to describe his gait. Gangle: To walk in the manner of a long streak of piss with feet angled between quarter to three and ten to two. Bless him. Maybe I would have a whip round later on and try and raise enough money to buy him a night out with a lady of ill repute. That or something potent to get rid of those spots, like a flame-thrower, to try and dry them out!

I poked my head into Rambo's bivvy to see what was occurring his end and saw my team-mate recuperating from The Bowl's frenzy by lying on his bedchair chatting on his mobile to Steffi. I discretely pulled away, visions of what I knew she had done dancing in my head. I went to see what Pup was up to – the answer being not much because he was dozing. All the exercise and fresh air had taken its toll on the boiliemeister and further investigation revealed him to be making little snoring sounds.

Pathetically, I stayed and listened to him for a few minutes on the off chance he started talking in his sleep, hoping he might disclose a few secret ingredients. I was worse than Paul! I wanted to know what was in our bait and I was one of only three anglers using it! After five minutes listening to him sawing wood I became bored and decided, short of Pup dying and his exclusive, revolutionary, indented, dirty brown bottom bait boilie recipe going with him – I'm sure he once told me he never committed a bait recipe to paper, only to memory – to take a chance on not knowing.

When I pulled up and out of Pup's porch a dog was standing in our swim, slap in the middle of the now, by virtue of the earlier rain, not so rock hard twenty by twenty mud patch. Dog breeds not being my forte, I consulted my Pocket Book of Rabies Carriers – HarperCollins Publishers Ltd, Book IV in the series of Things That Bite You and Make You Die Horribly – and deduced it was a Boxer.

I looked at the dog and it looked benignly at me. For the moment this was as far as things seemed likely to go as neither of us showed any inclination to move. My reasons for not budging were, if I'm honest, based purely on fear. My experience of dealing with Spunker had made me wary of any dog when fishing and, despite the one in front of me bearing no apparent resemblance in shape or attitude to the ex-Rottweiler, I wasn't going to chance it and move anywhere. If anything can provoke a dog it is movement and I wasn't blind to the possibility the Boxer could be faking its present reasonable demeanour. The game plan, such as it stood, was that if the dog did attack, I could reverse spectacularly quickly into Pup's bivvy where there was a fifty-fifty chance of getting mauled. As things stood, as *I* stood, out in the big wide open, there was only *one* person going to get savaged! Aren't I the perfect gentleman?

Keeping perfectly still I studied the dog intensely for any signs of an impending leap, one pre-empting my throat being ripped out by four-tenths of a second. Nothing happened. Nothing happened again ten seconds later and with it some hint of rationality replaced my fear. This dog is *old*, I pointed out to myself. Despite being in possession of the classic, aggressive-looking, deceleration-from-sixty-to-standstill-by-face-into-reinforced-concrete-wall features – my grandad would have said it looked as if it had been hit in the face with a stocking full of hot shit – the aged Boxer's fighting days looked long gone. The dog's muzzle was virtually grey, the individual hairs showing vividly around its charcoal-black mouth. The eyes, a deep brown colour, looked slightly less than fully open, as if a heavy burden lay upon them – the heavy burden clearly the passing of time. They too were surrounded by grey hairs, which gradually merged into mottled charcoal-black and tan-brown coloured fur higher up on the dog's head. The tan-brown predominated on most of the Boxer's body apart from the ears – charcoal-black – and a splodge of still pure white fur on the chest. One other observation was clear – the Boxer was a male.

The dog was now no longer looking at me. It was looking at the ground in a non-focused manner and I felt myself totally relax. My initial lack of movement had been due to fear and now I'd had time to run my eye over the pension-drawing hound in front of me, I was pretty sure why it had remained motionless. The dog was knackered. It was that simple. Wherever it had come from, whether far or near, or whatever speed it had travelled at – the smart money was on slow – had worn it out. It was shot. Tired. Dog-tired, done in, drained, droopy and drowsy. Now I could finally see – this mutt wasn't a throat ripper, it was a coffin-dodger!

I moved quietly over to the Boxer and the aged pooch lifted his head in greeting. I obliged him and stroked it. His fur was short, dense and still had a velvet quality. His tail started to wag.

"Hello, boy," I said, noting this was the expression Rambo used to greet me most of the time. The Boxer enthusiastically accepted my rubbing his super-soft, silky ears. "Where did you come from?" And then I remembered. "You're Ben's dog aren't you? Hector, isn't it? Hello, Hector." The dog's ears twitched in recognition of his name and I looked up to try and spot his encased-in-treacle, rurally rustic owner. Sure enough there he was, still over a hundred yards from our swim, making his way very slowly in the paw steps of his dog.

Ben's progress was painful, particularly for the young man in his mid-twenties walking along side him. I could see the more youthful of the two men struggling to hold his normal walking pace in check, so he could accompany Ben and converse with him. The younger man didn't look as if he was an angler. He was dressed in smart trousers, a long-sleeved, collared shirt with a loosely knotted tie and was armed with what looked like a notepad very similar to the one I was using to keep a tally of by how much we were thrashing everybody else.

"I wonder who that is?" I said, as much to the dog as to myself. "Give it another hour and I expect we'll find out!"

I exaggerated. Ten minutes. Ben used his two-stroke skateboard. Sue me.

"I see you's found, Hector!" Ben said as he made his way into our swim. He slowly ambled up towards the dog who reciprocated his master's movement, only fractionally faster, and met him a tad past halfway. The unknown young man hovered on the edge of the reunion, playing the role of outsider so patently his part. Ben arthritically eased his body over and firmly patted the dog's flank. In response Hector raised his head, an anthropomorphic look of pleasure on the mutt's chops and he wagged his tail, evidently relishing his owner's attention.

It was quite touching, and in the moment I could picture the thousands of hours the two of them, man and beast, had spent in each other's company whether at home or patrolling The Bowl's bland bankside.

"The other way round," I answered. "I think he found me!"

Ben stood upright with a grimace and a grunt, an invisible anvil on his shoulders, gravity pulling hard on him. "This young man's from them there newspapers," he eventually proclaimed, by way of an introduction to the smartest dressed person currently residing on The Bowl.

The young man, feeling his inclusion had been rubber-stamped, strode over and offered a hand. "Hi, Grant Gibbs," he informed me in a plum voice bordering upper class. "I'm a junior reporter for the Weekend Telegraph. *The* Telegraph," he stressed, presumably on the grounds he had me marked down as a Daily Sport reader/photograph perusing dullard, or, at a push, if I had been hard at it on a Nintendo DS playing Brain Training, The Sun.

I shook his hand. "How you doing?" It came out as flat as I felt.

Grant, being the unflappable type, was unfazed and his voice kept its keen edge. "I'm here to do a piece on the current cult of carp fishing and seeing as I've been reliably informed by Ben here, that you guys are going to be the winners, you're going to be central to the article."

"Oh!" I said by way of a downer response. My use of this favourite phrase really does know no limits.

"It won't be any hassle," assured Grant negating my negative nuances – his public school education had assured him a minus times a minus equals a plus. "If I can stay around with you for an hour or so," Grant made a placating gesture with his hand, "you carry on doing your fishing, I'll fire a few questions, pick up a few quotes and the whole thing's put to bed. We'll get a photographer over in time for the winner's presentation tomorrow, combine it with a few scenic shots and it should make a good piece." Grant saved his best for last. "National fame at last! Ya?" The 'ya' giving away more detail of his education and upbringing in a solitary uttering than everything else he had said earlier.

I nodded indifferently. Unfortunately, in terms of my willingness to participate, fifteen minutes of fame wasn't on my wish list – quite the opposite. 'National fame'! He could poke it! The last thing I needed was publicity. Between the two of us, Rambo and I had more skeletons in the cupboard than the average serial murderer had under his patio and in his back garden. And if you considered Hamworthy Fisheries, the finest carp fishery etc. as *my* back garden, I had one in there as well! I felt a prickly heat creep over my body. Keep calm, boy! I told myself, in the style of a Rambo order. All I had to do was keep my cards close to my chest and tell him as little as possible – much like Pup and his bait ingredients – and tell Rambo and the hopefully-still-reticent boiliemeister to do the same.

When I came out of my thoughts Grant was still wittering on in his too-posh-for-The-Bowl accent. "The Weekend Telegraph has a Food, Drink, Family and Great Outdoors section," he explained, oblivious to the fact I didn't care. "And with all the topical interest in the definition of Britishness and Pulimov's cash giveaways," Grant curled his top lip, "*there's* a publicity stunt to help achieve a political means if ever there was one, you guys are quite the flavour of the month."

I gave a bob of my head combined with a weak smile and caught Grant's eyes for the first time. They were nestling underneath a foppish quiff of dark, well managed hair – I imagined he thought he looked a little like Hugh Grant when he stared into the mirror. I also imagined he stared in the mirror an awful lot. His eyes were blue-green, bright, intelligent and *dangerous*. Disconcertion crept up my spine and hit me across the back of the head with a rolled up broadsheet newspaper – one masking hidden lead piping. (Mr Grant the journalist kills Matt the carp angler at The Bowl.) Talk about wearing the rose tinted glasses of nostalgia – I had chopped mine in for the dark mirrored shades of rampant paranoia!

"Sure, no worries. I'll tell the others," I bluffed.

I turned, left Grant, Ben and Hector and blundered straight into Rambo's bivvy without even knocking. He was *still* on his mobile. Good job he wasn't on pay as you go, he would have needed to top-up twice already! Images of what I knew Steffi had done clashed with a little man stomping around my head holding a lollipop placard bearing the words 'Silence the press!' He spun the placard like a manually operated Stop/Go sign at a set of road works. 'Matt Williams is a murderer! No one needs to know!' My prickly heat rash worsened.

"There's a reporter here from The fucking Telegraph!" I blurted, uncaring of cutting across Rambo's conversation with his well-read, East German, ex-porn star partner. "He wants to do a fucking article on us because we're going to be the winning pair and we're suddenly fashionable amongst the fucking chattering classes!"

Rambo whipped his head to confront me, a frown forming on his face – his military breeding allowing him to grasp the situation in an instant. "Got to go Steff, something's cropped up!" he said brusquely into the phone.

Pleased that Rambo was onboard, online and on-message, I shifted my attention to the boiliemeister. "I'll tell Pup," I told him and nipped out of one bivvy and quickly into the other in the fashion of a West End comedy farce.

I awoke Pup roughly by shaking his shoulder. As I did I tried to remember exactly what Pup knew about our shady past. He knew a bit about Watt because my big mouth had told him yesterday; he knew Michael had died in unusual circumstances; he knew I had been gifted Hamworthy; he knew Rambo was ex-military and he knew the recipe for our old red bait; but was blissfully unaware – *I* was blissful because *he* was unaware – of all the nasty stuff. The nasty stuff where individuals had died or had faked dying, where dead body parts had been moved or hidden, where a person had had their face ripped off and the small matter of Rambo's knee-trembler with Melloney, which when compared to all the other dark deeds *seemed* like small beer – until I remembered it might mean the loss of Pup's exclusive, revolutionary, indented, dirty brown bottom bait boilie!

However, I reassured myself, Pup had never told anyone the recipe for our old red bait, despite Rambo not threatening to break his legs and Pup did have a decent track record of keeping his trap shut. He had never buckled when I had pushed him on bait recipes, so, in theory, if I asked him to do the same again, all should be fine.

And then weirdly I remembered something else, something else that didn't add up. Something I had never thought of before.

"Wake up!" I hissed aggressively. "And keep your mouth *shut* until you listen to what I have to say!" Jerked from the land of nod in such a peremptory manner, Pup appeared momentarily disorientated as his two eyeballs searched separate areas of the inside of his bivvy. Dutifully he did as he was told. "There's a reporter here from The fucking Telegraph! He wants to do a fucking article on us because we're going to be the winning pair. This is all *your* fault! *You're* the reason we're here so leave all the talking to me and Rambo, okay?" Pup blinked vacantly – at least his eyes were now in sync. "I don't want *any* publicity about Hamworthy to get out," I warned. "I don't want every fucking seventy-seeking fuckwit carper in the whole fucking country coming down to poach the fucking place... And don't tell him *anything* about Watt or Michael, all right?"

"Yeah. All right, all right. I get it," whinged Pup just about fully rebooted from his shutdown.

"Good. Just keep calm like me!"

"I am calm," Pup assured. "*You're* the one who's having the nervous breakdown."

I chose to overlook Pup's ridiculous observation. "I've just remembered something," I said. "You once told me, on the very first time you rolled our old red bait, how you were embarrassed because you used a cat to test your baits, how unscientific it was and how you had moved on to be a master-craftsman."

Pup nodded very slowly. "Yes."

"You told me the cat had died, choked on its own vomit from gorging a brilliant mix. I joked it was called Hendrix and you said, no, it was called Tiddles. Do you remember?"

"Vaguely."

"Well?"

Pup looked at me as if I was mental. "So, I lied! Big deal! I probably thought I had ventured too much information and had to quickly cover my tracks. So what! I wasn't going to tell you two newcomers about Wilton, now was I? When we struck the deal to get me into Hamworthy, I told you the truth."

"Oh!" I said. It's a little conversational gem of mine, one I like to frequently employ.

"What made you think of it?" Pup demanded.

I suddenly knew what had made me think of it and that I might have made an ironic mistake, considering what I was asking Pup to do. I tried to convince myself the chance of it being a mistake was still slim. I mentally shook my head – it was too late to do anything now.

"No reason," I lied. "It came to me out of the blue. Too much time to think when you're fishing, it can be a killer." Pup's body language hinted he accepted my explanation. "Now, remember what I told you. Tell this young gun as little as possible if he asks you anything."

"Sure," said Pup easing himself off his bedchair. "I don't want any of my recipes appearing in print."

"Yeah," I said sarcastically. "There is a Food section in his paper, you want to be careful! You might get sucked into starring in an episode of Celebrity Boilie Making!"

"As the celebrity or as the resident expert?"

"Mouth zipped," I answered and re-entered the great outdoors.

Over the next hour Grant, his bum parked in my sitting-outside-the-bivvy-in-the-sun chair, fired away his set of journalistic questions. He had an annoying habit of running his hand through his long, foppish quiff every few minutes and in the end it aggravated me so much I felt like getting out my braid scissors and giving him a quick trim up. On the notion that an even better solution would have been to attack him with a petrol engine strimmer, I realised I must be a little on edge.

Ben sat listening in Rambo's sitting-outside-the-bivvy-in-the-sun chair with Hector lying at his feet until the pair of them succumbed to the need for sleep. Rambo and I stood throughout the affair, partly to be ready to leap into action should one of our Delkims squawk into life, and partly to dissipate the nervous energy generated by trying to not come across as someone – in my case – who had pumped seventeen bullets into an assassin, helped burn, then bury the body and catapulted its teeth across a fishery. In Rambo's case it was to avoid mentioning his odious mercenary/gun running/murdering arms dealing past and the small matter of his multi-alias, faked death, life insurance scam. To be frank, I wasn't too keen on my intermittent psychic abilities, our excavation of the ghost's bones, Michael's 'accident' and my inheritance being front page headlines either! I'm a bit touchy over things like that.

Meanwhile, Pup kept himself to himself for fear of revealing, in a moment of unrestrained madness, the boiling time to one of his mixes.

Grant asked us about the basic concepts involved in carp fishing – you go, you catch them, you put them back – and the equipment involved in making this happen. I could tell he was as sharp as a Gardner Talon Tip because he picked up the whole process very quickly and asked insightful questions highlighting his smart grasp on matters. He had an intense ebullient manner coupled with a polite well-mannered line of questioning and for forty-five minutes, apart from the hair thing, his nuts and bolts type questions were almost a pleasure to answer. Almost.

"This Pulimov guy," he said, his tone changing. "You know he's got links to the old Soviet state system?" Rambo and I shook our heads. We were but simple fishermen and had no need of information outside the confines of data enabling us to catch more carp. "Very wealthy individual. Some have hinted at his links to organised crime. Of course, and it goes without saying, it's unproven. His biggest asset is his controlling stake within Gaznost, the company which by 2020 will provide the UK with twenty-five per cent of its natural gas. It's why our current government are courting him and allowing him to promote himself in such an outrageous way."

"Your paper doesn't approve?" Rambo asked.

"Editorially, no. A Russian laying down a diktat to define Britishness is *not* what The Telegraph readers want to see in print." Grant gave us a measuring stare, one we failed. "Anyway, the big picture is not what we're hear to discuss... what I'm wondering is if you *personally* find it uncomfortable that somebody, a foreigner, has injected a cash prize into what is ostensibly a non-competitive, altruistic sport? You are, essentially, fishing here today as a direct consequence of his cash prize, albeit in a spin-off competition. Regards the original prize, I know, through my research, there are very few venues where a seventy-pound carp can be caught. I also know, as a consequence of reporting human nature, as is the case in any walk of life, large sums of money can lead to problems. You have told me, both of you, how much carp fishing is a part of your life, what a personal experience it is to you and on what level those experiences run. Isn't prize money a contradiction to those views?"

I gave Rambo a fleeting glance. We had dug a hole, sure enough, by waxing lyrical on the gentile manner of our pursuit, its sound environmental attributes and how, in its participation we felt at one with the Great Outdoors, and how we fished on our own terms, unaffected by others' influences. It wasn't bullshit as such, but of course we had emphasised the positives and excluded the negatives. Neither of us answered.

"By your very participation today, you start to take the Russian rouble, so to speak."

"Copping out to take the kopeks," I offered.

Grant laughed. "I like it!" He waited for his laugh to die. "I guess so," he added without humour.

"Carp matches aren't new," Rambo answered. "Relatively new, but they were around well before the rash of Pulimov's Prize spin-offs like this one. They're a change from what we do normally. It's a different type of angling and a bit of fun with, yes, a small financial incentive. Don't confuse our participation with our endorsement of Mr Pulimov, boy."

I caught Grant's face tighten imperceptibly at the use of the word 'boy'. "So you think *all* the publicity is positive?"

"Those with a financial stake within carp fishing certainly do. I'm well aware of human nature as well. I've seen the bad side of it, believe me," Rambo stated.

"Were you a soldier?" Grant asked, my heart pulsing as he did.

Rambo looked down at his camo ensemble and I wished Steffi had banned it altogether. This was not a line of questioning I wanted Grant to go down. What if he had spotted the bulge of the Glock? Rambo laughed easily. "What makes you say that? There are plenty of other 'soldiers' dressed like me hanging around this puddle," he answered.

"They might be dressed in the garb, *you* look the part," Grant retorted.

"Once," Rambo admitted.

"Where did you serve?"

Rambo shook his head. "It's not something I talk about. Not when I'm carp fishing anyway."

Grant nodded vigorously. "Sure. Point taken."

"And you, Matt, what do you do for a living?"

"I'm an electrician," I fibbed. "Self-employed."

"And you, Pup."

"I make boilies. Very good ones," declared Pup.

"Just that? You can earn a living making carp bait?"

"I can and I do."

"Have you a small industrial…"

"My house," Pup cut in. "A room for each boilie size."

"And you live there alone?" It was another one of Grant's astute questions. Singular pursuit anorak, sad bastard, therefore no female company – I could see the line of his reasoned thinking and he was right. It had been Pup's life until Melissa had popped up out of the hat – some magic trick it was too, some might say black magic – and brought her sister as first reserve for when she had absconded over the Atlantic with meal ticket Brad.

"With my girlfriend. She's the sister of my recently divorced wife," Pup boasted. I understood why he had told him, he hadn't been blind to Grant's supposition.

"Really?" exclaimed Grant.

At this precise juncture, as is the nature of carp fishing, my right-hand rod, feeling a bit left out and being the shy retiring type, got my right-hand Delkim to tell me it needed some TLC.

"A take!" said Grant checking out his carp talk vernacular.

The alarm's noise made Ben and Hector wake up with a start. By the time the pair of them had sauntered to my rod butts the fight was all but over. The kamikaze carp had bolted straight towards me, its sole intention to show Grant what a lousy fighter the carp was despite all we had told him earlier. A nicely scaled scraper twenty was soon on the mat and equally quickly a recently under-employed Carl was soon on the scene to do his bit.

Carl gave Grant a look similar to the one he had given me when we had first met. It was a form of intimidatory introduction – one designed to put the fear of Christ into the recipient and to dump them firmly on the back foot.

"Who the fuck are you?" he asked as he lofted my carp above the ground.

Grant ran his hand through his luxuriant hair. "I'm Grant Gibbs, reporter for The Telegraph, writing a piece on the cult of carp fishing. Matt and Rambo are my subjects, as winners designate."

"Right. Basically, writing a story on them, right?"

"Absolutely!" Grant gushed. If he was thinking Carl was a cretin, he was hiding it well.

"Why don't you ask him," Carl said, practising his head butt towards me. "How he blew up some bloke's bivvy with a couple of Rambo's hand grenades?"

"Yes, ask him," said another voice. "And when you've finished, come and ask me what it felt like."

I spun round to see a smug Tom Watt, beaming brightly like a magnesium flare, my heart turning simultaneously to black ash and coke.

Chapter 10

Sunday morning. Sunday bloody Sunday – and that was before two in the morning! Let me explain.

To say I hadn't slept well was on a par with saying the promotion of Steve McClaren to England manager, thus allowing him to pick Scott 'Frozen with Fear' Carson as goalkeeper against Croatia in a crucial Euro 2008 qualifier, hadn't been such a bright idea. My perception after Carl and Watt's revelatory intervention (and the 3-2 defeat coincidentally) was things had gone tits up big time – to put it in professional business terminology. What Grant would make of it all, what Grant would *do* with it all, only time would tell.

I had tried to play down the incident once Carl and Watt had buggered off and I had begged Grant not to write anything concerning the matter. I had told him it was a part of my life I wanted to leave buried in the past, how I was still rebuilding and how, if it was resurrected, the knock-on effect could seriously damage my livelihood. I had pointed out potential customers wouldn't like me doing work for them if they knew I had been inside, whatever the crime or motive.

I felt it had been a struggle to convince him and I had felt like someone trying to stuff their cock in a hole in the Hoover Dam – a hole with ominously jagged cracks radiating from it to every point on the compass. Grant had run his hand through his hair numerous times and had made light of my worries, insisting the article would go as planned before Carl's revelation. He had left at six in the evening, his return with photographer booked for nine today, provided we didn't 'blow ourselves up' by the morning.

"That's not funny, boy!" Rambo had warned.

"Only joshing, Rambs! See you tomorrow." I swear Rambo's hand had twitched towards his pocketful of Glock.

When Grant and eventually the bemused Ben and Hector had gone, the recriminations within Pup Enterprises had started. With justification I had taken the brunt of them. Pup had dressed me down on my double standards (triple standards if he knew the other potential slip-up I had already made) and the stunning hypocrisy of my laying down the law to him when I had already blabbed a big secret to Carl.

"He already knew!" I had protested. "Watt had already told him!"

"*You* confirmed it," Pup had retorted. "When you should have *denied* it!"

I had looked to Rambo for support. Needless to say I didn't get it. "He's right, boy. You should have kept your big mouth shut."

Discussing things further, we had collectively wondered whether Watt and Carl were in cahoots with The Bait Baron – the mysterious individual about whom we had still not uncovered one extra snippet of information. Even poor old Ben, and by definition Hector, hadn't been put beyond suspicion, although the notion did seem on the very fringes of plausibility. If any of this was the case, then the plot had well and truly thickened.

The stupidity of my actions were magnified by what I had overheard Carl and Watt discuss. Their clandestine meeting should have made my mouth clam up rather than loosen it and I had been told so in no uncertain manner. The next stage of reasoning had been to postulate on Carl's supposed dislike of Watt, his spiel on his upcoming trial and his change of attitude towards me all being an elaborate scam.

"We'll find out when we catch our next fish," Rambo had muttered darkly.

And we had. Once Carl had finished weighing a one in the morning upper twenty of mine – nice fish by the way – Rambo had grabbed him by the throat, lifted him off his feet and thrown him across our twenty by twenty mud patch.

"I've got a few questions I want answered, boy," Rambo had malevolently snarled. "The easy way or the hard, it's up to you."

Carl had swiftly picked himself up, his shaved head outlined against the backdrop of The Bowl's night-time sheen, and had charged at Rambo. Game on! Rambo sidestepped Carl's charging bull impersonation, adroitly slipped behind him and in one slick movement put him in a stranglehold with one arm. With the other, he yanked one of Carl's arms violently up his back. Smashing his leg around into Carl's shins and by lifting him off his feet for a second time, Rambo had dumped Carl face first into swim nine's topsoil and compounded it by landing on top of him. Air whooshed out of Carl's lungs. Rambo released his stranglehold so he could jam Carl's other arm up his back. Out of air, out of arms and outmuscled it was game over in less than fifteen seconds from game on.

I had contemplated pointing out that Rambo had used both his arms, there had been little hopping and absolutely no sign of a blindfold, but decided it unwise seeing as I was in enough trouble already.

"Now, boy," Rambo had hissed, his mouth no less than an inch from Carl's ear. "These questions I want to ask, are you going to tell me the answers or am I going to bust you up so bad you'll have to leave bungee strapped to a carp barrow pushed by an ambulance crew?"

It had been, in every sense, a rhetorical question.

I had turned my headtorch on and shone its light into Carl's face. Blood was seeping down both his nostrils and his eyes were wide open with panic. A strange guttural noise emanated from his gaping mouth as he fought to get some air back into his lungs – a process not exactly aided by Rambo lying on top of him.

"Yes," he managed to gasp. "Can't breathe, right!" Rambo had shifted his weight a fraction, although not his grip on Carl's arms, and gave him a minute to recover. "Okay," Carl panted. "Better."

"What the fuck's going on, boy? Did you set up Matt together with Watt? He's very sensitive about his past you know, especially when there's a journalist around."

It was true, I was.

Carl had denied the accusation. "No! I just said it! Basically off the top of my head! I didn't know Watt was there. Didn't think it was a problem, right!"

Rambo had seemed satisfied this was true and I had thought Carl was telling the truth. "So. This Bait Baron. What do you know?" Carl turned into a mute swan. "Well?" No response. Rambo, who was obviously a fully paid up member of the Guild of Obtaining Useful information by Gory Extraction (GOUGE), rammed his huge, gorilla-sized fist into Carl's kidney. The sound had been like someone hitting a high-class unhooking mat with a throwing stick sized for gobstopper boilies – even I had winced. Not as much as Carl though.

"Aaarghh!"

"Stop moaning, boy and answer the question. Remember, you'll have a bit of trouble carrying a dialysis machine *and* all your gear if you want to go fishing... on crutches!"

"But..."

Rambo had cranked the menace factor up. "Listen, boy, I'm losing my patience. Whatever shit you might get in with him won't be as bad as what I'll do to you."

Amazingly Carl had still been unconvinced and so the throwing stick sounded twice and, as a resplendent finish, Rambo had arced his arm around to piledrive his sledgehammer fist into Carl's face. Interestingly this had made a different noise, a smaller throwing stick on a cheap mat combined with the synchronised breaking of a dry stick.

Carl's nose was a goner and blood poured from it.

"All right! Enough! Enough!" Carl had cried, the blood bubbling from his mouth and lips. "I got a phone call, right! Months ago, some bloke saying he was setting up a bait company and needed a handyman, right!" Carl stopped to spit out some blood. "Basically, cash-in-hand, I'm on invalidity benefit, so all my moonlighting's cash-in-hand. I fix cars for cash, right! Basically I thought it would fit in nicely with what I already had going."

"Go on. You're going the right way to *genuinely* not needing invalidity benefit," Rambo had sensitively cajoled. "What did you have to do?"

"Turned out The Bait Baron wanted muscle for dirty work."

At this juncture Rambo had looked up at me and grinned. I too had felt a slug of adrenaline – it was just like the old days! We were on to something! The rumour was true!

"And?" Rambo had nudged.

"Basically threaten a few locals who weren't playing ball. Went okay, then I got a big call."

"Okay."

"Had to burn down a bait factory."

"Leviathan Boilies!" I had exclaimed.

Carl grunted a short, humourless laugh. "You heard right."

"On the radio."

"Went a bit wrong. Someone clocked me and had the guts to say so. We tried to get to him, me and the other local muscle, right! But he stuck to his guns. The police are investigating, right! The Bait Baron, the bastard, told me I was on my own if I got charged. Said I'd fucked up and some *professional* heavies would see to me if I blabbed and didn't take the rap. Basically told me to fuck off."

"Aah! Looks like you've got it coming to you every way, boy!" Rambo had said with fake sympathy.

"Tell me about it."

"So, boy. Who is he?"

Carl had tried to shake his head, but seeing as he was still flat on his stomach, his left cheek jammed into the ground with a pool of blood around his head, he couldn't. "Don't know."

"Come on, boy. Don't make me work you over again."

"Basically don't, right! I've met some of his blokes, not him. *They* don't know."

"Any of them here?"

"Don't recognise any."

"Watt?"

"No. He's got his head too far up The Bowl's owner's arse."

"Ben?"

Carl had snorted, blood shooting out of his nose. "*Nice* heavy!"

Rambo had then eased off his grip. "This Bait Baron's been hassling Pup," he told Carl. "He wants to buy him out, but understandably Pup doesn't *want* to be bought out. This is the reason why we're here. Some time ago The Baron started phoning him up, pestering, making life uncomfortable for him and his missus. Eventually, for reasons that are still beyond me, me and Matt agreed for us to fish here against all the other competitors who, The Bait Baron told him, would be on his bait. The reason? If we won, he'd leave Pup alone."

Carl wasn't stupid. "Like hell!"

"*Exactly*!" Rambo growled signifying Pup's brain had turned to a paste mix when he had bought that one. "But his people *are* here. Someone even left Pup a note from The Bait Baron in Ben's tent… Get up." Rambo had removed himself from Carl and let him go. Groggily the shaven headed, ex-Bait Baron goon had struggled to his feet. Blood had smothered his front and face and his nose, twice its usual size, had an undignified dog-leg in it.

"Show him the note, Pup."

Pup had shown him by the light of my headtorch and Carl, if he was able to, had read it. I still wasn't too sure, one way or the other, how dumb he was – Christ, the bloke couldn't even pull off a simple arson without somebody seeing him!

"How he operates, right!" Carl had given a weak shake of his lowered head, blood droplets falling from his nose. "Pulling the strings from out of sight."

"And there's nobody here in this comp who you can connect to him?" I had questioned.

Carl looked too dishevelled and downbeat to lie. "Nah."

"And none of these other blokes you came across who worked for him mentioned anything that might be of use to us in tracing him?"

Carl had wiped his nose gingerly with his sleeve. "Basically the only other person they mentioned was his best mate. Well, you know, it sounded like it was his best mate, right!"

"Name, boy?"

Carl had looked up at Rambo with hangdog eyes and a dog-leg nose. "His name's... The Carper."

"Oh, for fuck's sake!" I had exploded. "The Bait Baron, The Carper! What's with all this, 'The Something' shit, Carl?"

"He's fishing a huge, secret gravel pit for an unknown seventy," Carl had added softly.

"In his fucking dreams!" I had ranted. "Does he even *exist*? Is he for real? *Eh*, Carl?" I had thrown up my hands in exasperation. "Are you fucking having us on?"

Carl had assured us he wasn't and in the end we had believed him. Rambo had had a little private word, what he had said he wouldn't reveal, and at nearly three in the morning, Carl had sloped off into the dark to go and lick his wounds in his bivvy – and get blood all over his sleeping bag.

At first light I had tried to clear up his blood as best I could, being only partially successful. If anyone cared to look the ground had clearly been interfered with.

"Quite a night last night," I said casually to Rambo. "Nice to see you haven't lost your touch and the violence is still there on tap!"

"You never lose it," Rambo responded affably. "I keep myself fit. Mind you, if I'd have got into any trouble I had my mate as backup."

"What? Me, you mean?"

The withering look soon put paid to my rising hopes. "Don't be *stupid*, boy! You'd be about as much help as using sun-degraded, five-pound breaking strain Maxima to land a bonefish. I meant the Glock!" Rambo must have noted the flicker of dejection on my face. "Nothing personal, boy. You're just shit at fighting... Look out, here comes the national press!"

I followed Rambo's gaze and saw Grant had returned an hour before the competition was due to end with his pet photographer in tow. I wasn't too sure how to pitch things with Grant. Obviously I was desperate for closure on the final act of TWTT retribution, not so much for the deed itself – I had paid my dues to society for it – more for where it could lead Grant if he started sniffing around my life story. Rambo's as well. Blowing up Watt's bivvy all those years ago was small beer compared to what both of us had done since.

As it happened Grant broke the ice. "Hi, chaps. This is Oliver our staff photographer." We all shook hands and greeted each other. "He'll take a few shots of you to accompany the piece… one with a fish would be nice." Grant's expression asked the question.

"We're in with a shout, there's still the best part of an hour to go," Rambo answered. "No guarantees, mind, fishing's mainly unscripted as you can appreciate."

Grant nodded. "Where's Pup?" he asked.

"Still asleep," I told him. "We didn't get to bed until late last night."

"Catching fish?"

"Something like that," I said, painting quickly with a two inch sable brush from a tin marked 'Gloss'.

Grant ran his hand through his hair. (I could tell it had been washed and conditioned before he had left his house.) It was his way of steadying himself in readiness for broaching the delicate subject he was about to bring up. "I have to admit, Matt, I did have a little chat with this Tom Watt chap yesterday."

"Full of bile and bitterness was he?" I said with a sneer, my stomach tightening with fear.

"Oh, ya. Absolutely. He came across as a rather petulant individual. I can almost see why you did it!"

"Really?" I said surprised yet pleased with Grant's take on things. Quickly I pushed home the advantage. "You know, he seems to have become even more bitter over the years. He's a proper grumpy old man now. In his pomp he used to be able to hide his massive ego and deviousness behind a veneer of decency. Events have stripped it all away now and what you see is very much what you get." I shook a weary head for emphasis. "During the time we're talking about he was cheating, ripping us all off financially *and* getting paid to write articles full of lies, wasn't he Rambo?"

"He certainly was."

"It was a horrid time. We all got pushed too far." I wiped my nose self-consciously. "I admit it was an obsessive phase of my life. I wavered on the brink of complete ruin and only just pulled back in time. That might sound odd given the bivvy blowing up ending, but it's true."

"Yes," said Grant slowly. "An unusual story given its subject matter." You don't even *begin* to know how unusual I thought and long may the situation continue! "Right," Grant continued. "Shall we get Oliver to earn his corn?"

For the next twenty minutes Oliver wielded his camera, a Canon Eos 5D digital SLR, with speed and dexterity, showing us his perfectly framed results on the display screen. At half nine the cherry on the cake plopped in front of Oliver's 24-70mm F2.8 L USM lens when Rambo's left-hand rod rattled off with the slow power of the Eurostar leaving St Pancras. The camo-clad man mountain's full fish playing glory was expertly captured in God knows how many million pixel's worth of resolution – and so was the fin-perfect carp we collectively estimated at thirty pounds. You had to hand it to The Bowl's management/owner, for all its shortcomings in aesthetics, it did have some cracking fish in its unappealing chocolate coloured water. Not in the same league as Hamworthy Fisheries, the finest carp fishery this side of the moon, *obviously*, but nevertheless, still very good.

Grant was very pleased with all this useful material and so was Oliver. I was very happy they were getting everything laid on a plate, so was Rambo, and if Pup had been awake he would have been too. Happy that is, until Carl turned up to weigh in the carp. Trudging in, stooped over, arms cuddling his own stomach at a pace nearly as slow as Hector – not Ben, he wasn't *that* bad – the kidney-pummelled Carl was in a sorry state. Covered in dry blood, nose swollen to twice its normal size beneath two massive black eyes, he looked as if he had been hit on a zebra crossing by a JCB driven by a pack of baboons on crystal meth. Although his state was admittedly somewhat jauntier than the two hundred and twenty pounds of mince dropped from a ten-metre diving platform on to the middle carriageway of the M25 that I had imagined, the overall effect of his appearance was still shocking.

"Fuck!" exclaimed Oliver. "What the hell happened to him?" And Oliver, being Oliver, did the only thing he could to help Carl. He documented his suffering and took a picture of him.

I kept it zipped while I detected Rambo trying to look more casual than usual.

Grant, the more caring type, no, the more *inquisitive* type, spoke first. "Jesus, Carl! What in heaven's name happened to you?"

Carl lifted his eyes up to meet Grant's. It hurt, you could tell. "Basically sleepwalked up the grassy wall and fell down the other side, right!" he groaned.

What a trouper he was! Ten points to Slytherin! (Come on! Carl wouldn't be in *Gryffindor*, would he?)

Inwardly I might have been pumped by Carl's stoicism, externally only silence boomed. Grant looked at me and I, unable to face him, looked at Oliver and then down at my loosely laced trainers. Rambo eyed Carl without emotion, blanking the two journalists and probably wondering if he could have got away with hitting Carl a little bit harder, you know, just to be on the safe side. Everyone present knew full well Carl was lying, except maybe Carl himself, who may have convinced himself the sleepwalking charade really had happened in order to deny his current zero status machismo.

"I'll lift the sling up on the scales for you, boy. You just read off the weight," offered Rambo as helpful and practical as ever. "I can see you're struggling a bit this morning. Must have been a nasty fall."

I yanked the corners of my mouth down and out to signify a cringe to Grant. God knows what he was thinking. That's bollocks – it was *evident* what he was thinking because I could read the thought bubble hovering over his head. He was thinking that either Rambo or I – okay, not me, ridiculous – *Rambo*, had given Carl a right pasting for telling Grant about the hand grenade incident. It was a patently absurd idea – Rambo had worked him over to find out information concerning The Bait Baron!

Regardless of the fine print the fact still remained, the fact being Carl, the beaten up version, had turned up to weigh in a fish. Shit! Things were going seriously pear-shaped! Watt's bitter demeanour looked as if it had done us a favour until selfish Carl and his car crash appearance had made us look bad all over again. You would have thought, after Rambo had let him off so lightly, he would have had the decency to develop superhuman powers of self-healing overnight. Mind you, I thought cynically, if he had the capacity he would hardly be claiming invalidity benefit, now would he?

As Rambo and Carl went through the charade of weighing the fish, I noticed Grant looking at the spot where I had attempted to disguise the blatant forensic evidence of last night's assault. The hurriedly scuffed up discoloured ground screamed out in physical graffiti: *Carl woz beaten up here!* All I could dare to hope was Grant being as inept as the Portuguese police had been in the Madeleine McCann case. Realistically I knew this was as likely as Elvis turning up alive and singing in a chip shop in Blackpool whilst frying medium cod he was selling at two quid a pop. An implausible notion – mainly due to the bloody chips costing two quid alone, and whatever fish they're passing off as 'cod', double the price!

"Morning all." It was Pup. Awake at the crack of nine-fifty. "Caught another one? Pup Enterprises rolls on!" he said, clenching a fist. "We must be *way* out in front. Like I've always said, a good bait, a *really* good bait…" Pup's words dried up quicker than a kilo mix left out in the midday Luxor sun as he caught his first glimpse of Carl.

"Carl had a rough night," I said in a measured tone before Pup could put his foot in it. "Only sleepwalked up the grassy wall and fell down the other side!"

"Somnambulistic tendencies apparently," said Grant, indicating he may have breakfasted on a dictionary with a glass of mild sarcasm to drink.

Pup gave a distracted laugh, one I originally took to be caused by his lack of crossword solving participation or ownership of a thesaurus. I was wrong. His attention had been caught by something else. "What's that doing there? It's not ours is it?" he asked pointing out into The Bowl's Willy-Wonka-Factory's-river coloured water.

Everyone turned their heads to see a Microcat chugging up the margin heading from Pimply Paul's swim to ours. Once Rambo saw it he immediately looked the other way, I, however, only had eyes for the boat. The boat was in 'lights on' mode, some thirty yards distance from us, and running parallel with the bank approximately fifteen yards out.

"It must have gone haywire," I said. "It's way off course. The next baitboat users are the other side of those two spodders." I indicated to Pimply Paul's swim.

Rambo spoke next. "What's that in one of the hoppers?"

All of us moved towards the water's edge, Rambo still carrying the thirty in the sling. The fast moving boat was nearly level with us when it changed direction and ran straight towards the bank. The boat had looked empty apart from something brown in the far hopper, which, now it was coming straight towards us, could be seen edge-on in the left-hand hopper. It looked like a piece of cardboard. At the last moment the boat veered to its left and grounded in the margins in front of six pairs of feet. It was a piece of brown box cardboard – a piece of brown box cardboard with writing on it. I picked it up from where it had been lodged in the boat and perused the strange cargo, holding it like a hymn sheet so all the others could see. It wasn't any old non-descript section of writing – it was a message. A message written in the traditional style of a ransom note, one comprised individual letters cut out from newspaper headlines and then glued to a surface. It read: WE HAVE HIM! WAIT 4 INSTRUCTIONS

"What the hell's this all about?" I asked, fanning the cardboard in the air. Three blank faces indicated their complete lack of an answer – Carl, Grant and Oliver were totally nonplussed – although Oliver did steady my hand to take a photo of the cardboard tablet. Rambo seemed wholly uninterested in it and was busy putting his thirty back, whereas Pup seemed to have fathomed some semblance of understanding.

Pup's face drained of colour as I watched – it was like watching a bottle of Ribena with a hole in the bottom. "Oh my God!" he cried. Pup unexpectedly turned tail and ran back to his bivvy, re-emerging with his mobile. He jabbed frenetically at the phone's buttons. "Come on! Come on!" he shouted impatiently. "Mel! Mel!" he animatedly barked. "Is he there? Is he in his basket? …Just *look*!" Silence held sway as Pup waited, his face the absolute depiction of catastrophic concern. Over my shoulder I heard a camera shutter click again. Like a popped balloon Pup's intensity was gone in an instant. "He's not…" he said weakly, although the urgency was still apparent. "Okay… Double-check the garden. Ring me back." Pup's whole body sagged and he dropped slowly to his knees, giving the overall impression of a melting solid – like a clock in a Salvador Dali painting. "Wilton's not there," he wailed, looking up at the rest of us, his voice riddled with despair and desperation. "I think The Bait Baron's snatched Wilton."

Chapter 11

Guilt didn't creep up on me, instead it poured two pints of brine down my throat, upended me, gave me a good cocktail-mixing shake and set me on my feet. Sickness pervaded my very soul. I had to come clean and throw it all up.

"Pimply Paul!" I hurled. "I told him you had a cat who likes some boilies more than others! It was what made me think of the Hendrix/Tiddles thing!" I clasped both hands over the top of my head. "Oh, bollocks! *Sorry*, Pup!" I said with genuine feeling. "Please God, let's hope I've got this wrong and he's in the back garden!" It was my turn to sound desperate. I could always tell when I was on the edge – I started praying to the man I didn't believe in.

Pup's mobile rang and as a group we stared at it. (At that moment I dreaded to think what Grant and Oliver were making of all this – probably an award winning article. Oliver was certainly getting pictorial evidence – he had already snapped the baitboat note along with a close-up of Pup and if Grant wasn't actually making physical notes on a pad, I knew he was making mental ones.) Behind my back I childishly crossed my fingers hoping Wilton would turn up alive and well, sunning himself in some remote retreat in a corner of Pup's garden by a relieved Melloney. In a daze Pup fielded the call. Not one word was uttered as he clamped the phone to his ear. Within seconds his right thumb disconnected and his arm slid to his side. "Not there," he whispered. "He's gone."

In his shock, I don't think Pup had fully taken on board my confession. Rambo had and he asked me to explain fully what had happened. I gave him the truncated version.

"You and your *big* mouth! *Again*!" he chastised. His voice dropped a notch and he turned to face The Bowl. Like all good second in command right-hand men, I copied him. "Don't look now," he confided, "but whoever controlled the boat is behind the grassy wall. As soon as Pup spotted it I had a quick recce. I saw the transmitter aerial and a head poking above it. He's more or less directly behind us."

"Was the face covered in acne?" I sneered.

Rambo gave me a piercing look. I felt like a virgin earlobe on a ten-year-old girl's birthday. "There's only one way to find out, boy! When I say go, *run*! You go straight back towards the wall, I'll angle my run up towards his swim." Rambo answered the question I was thinking before I had chance to ask it. "He'll never suspect I've seen him. He'll still be there thinking he's safe and sound."

Rambo was right. No one would expect to have to deal with a mind as sharp as his battle-hardened one. Who else's first reaction would have been to look for the pilot?

"What about Grant and Oliver?" I ventured.

Rambo was dismissive. "Fuck them. It's too late to worry. We've got to get to the bottom of this and help Pup out, especially as some of it's of your making."

"Fair enough," I agreed, realising my hopes of a publicity-free life appeared to be hanging in tatters and the time for worrying was effectively over. I was feeling at least partially responsible for the abduction of Wilton, even if we were hardly bosom buddies – the little, boilie-mix-bolting bastard had clawed me the last time we had met!

Rambo crunched out the word signifying get-your-skates-on time. "*Go*!"

We both turned and sprinted towards the grassy wall and I caught a fleeting glimpse of puzzlement cloud Grant and Oliver's faces. Pup remained oblivious, cocooned in his world of anxiety, and Carl could only watch and wince, dreaming of his next ibuprofen fix. As we ran I soon discovered loosely laced ready-for-a-run-in-the-middle-of-the-night trainers were, apparently, more of a hindrance to sprinting than army boots. By the time I began to scramble up the wall I was breathing heavily from the sudden exertion. It also occurred to me what the hell was I going to do should I get to Pimply Paul first. Attack him and his blackheads with a hairgrip? Offer him a half-hour dermatological consultation? I pushed the thought to the back of my head. I would have to cross that bridge when I came to it.

When I reached three-quarters of the way up, I glanced over at Rambo to see he was already at the top despite having covered more ground due to his angled run. The man could move despite his huge frame! Within a few more strides, Rambo was doing what all soldiers had to do at one stage or the other. He was going over the top! Once I had conquered the south face of the grassy wall the view that presented itself over the other side was pure pantomime. Rambo was haring down the slope with the reckless abandon of a demented, kamikaze downhill skier, ready to parallel turn at the mobile piste-pole-with-acne moving along the foot of the valley.

If Pimply Paul had ever had to run to save his bacon before he certainly wasn't showing any signs of it. His lanky, puny, painfully thin body 'ran' – I use the word in the very loosest sense, even looser than the laces in my trainers – along the bottom of the spoil wall towards his swim and, with optimism so misplaced he would never find it in a century's worth of looking, possible escape. The guilt proving transmitter in his right hand – apparently weighing the equivalent to a lorry battery – dragged his whole body way out of kilter and made him list to starboard like a stricken cargo ship. This coupled with his implausibly large, quarter-to-three feet, flat-footedly flip-flopping to a beat more funeral march than drum roll meant his pace was less Bugatti Veyron and more steam-driven tractor. Pimply Paul was a muscle-deficient individual and his long levers, so distant from their fulcrums, answered the call of his brain like an ungainly Heath Robinson-designed biped disaster area. In truth, I had rarely viewed anything quite as comic – and I had seen some funny things during my fishing adventures.

From my superb vantage point, it was like watching a nature documentary of a possessed falcon swooping on to an ancient, arthritic, asthmatic mouse with poor skin – until that is, Pimply Paul had a brainwave and ditched the transmitter. With this huge load and drag factor now discarded, Paul's body could pull itself upright. Suddenly his body re-aligned and its stature became more purposeful as his arms and legs enmeshed into a state nearing synchronisation. He no longer looked like a careening craft and I thought I saw a flicker of hope flash across his spotty visage. I can do this, it seemed to say; I can make it to safety if I put on a spurt.

Paul spurted – and started to 'run' 0.1 of a mile per hour quicker.

Despite his efforts the relativity of Paul's improvement with regard to Rambo catching him or not catching him, made a practical difference somewhere between fuck all and none whatsoever. Two seconds after Paul put on his 'spurt', Rambo hit him like a prop forward smashing into a bulimic teenage ballerina. As Rambo's bulk hit Paul's midriff, shoulder first, Paul's limbs and body seemed to wrap themselves around him in a manner similar to how I imagined hanging spaghetti might when hit by a bowling ball. Paul's crumple zone was vividly seen to comprise Paul – it was like a container lorry hitting a twenty-year-old, rust-ridden Fiat Cinquecento.

With the chase over and the 'kill' made, I scampered down the slope to where Rambo was dusting himself off and where Paul was lying, limbs askew and awfully angled. Paul resembled, with alarming accuracy, a marionette recently accosted and then discarded by a scrapyard dog. A scrapyard dog fresh from twenty-four hours detention in a locked shed with only a black and white television showing ancient reruns of The Woodentops for entertainment.

"Nice tackle, mate!" I enthused.

"Thanks," the man mountain responded

"Have you snapped him in half?"

Rambo regarded the prostrate body looking like the chalk outline of a murder victim as drawn by Lowry and scratched the side of his stubbly cheek. A few sparks flew off from his hard-as-nails nails. "It's hard to say," he answered. "He's so lightweight, I barely felt anything when I hit him. There's fuck all to him. He's built like a rasher of wind!"

I squatted down alongside the stricken figure. Paul's eyes were closed but I could hear the sound of breath rasping into his battered lungs. From this I deduced, donning my Dr Williams MD hat, that he wasn't dead.

"What's with the message, Paul?" I asked in a strictly business tone. "We need to know what's going on… and I'm afraid you're going to have to be the one who tells us." Paul didn't respond and tried to play the tree-dwelling, Australian mammal card. I was too fly to fall for it. "It's no good you playing possum, either," I warned. "I can see your eyelids flickering. You see, Paul…"

"Oh, for God's sake!" said Rambo intervening. "We haven't got time for all this fucking about!" And with that statement of intent Rambo put the rugged sole of his size 13 (unlucky for some – or is it size 16? I would have to consult Ben) boot on to Paul's ribcage and pressed down. Hard. Paul let out a yelp of pain. "Now, *I* think you've got a couple of cracked ribs there, boy. If you don't want them converted into a punctured lung... *co-operate*!"

I caught the expression on Rambo's face. If he was putting it on, he was making a darn good job of it. Personally, I felt he meant it and his threat was totally solid and as far from hollow as possible. This was Rambo in his 'war' mode – frightening, ruthless and impervious to suffering – other people's suffering, that is. He was still the 'Terminator with Tackle' I had dubbed him all those years ago. His boot eased down on Paul's skinny torso like a powerful hydraulic press.

"The Bait Baron told me to do it!" Paul screamed, quickly finding his voice. "I was given the message and told to boat it down to you!"

"What's it mean?" Rambo demanded.

"The Bait Baron's boys kidnapped Pup's cat because he wouldn't join the business," Paul replied, his face crimson with pain and wet from cold sweat. Unattractively, his acne now had a grotesque sheen, like it had been lacquered, and the yellow, pus-filled spots were more prominent against his new mauve facial hue. "I only passed on the information *he* told me," Paul's welling-with-tears eyes latched on to mine, causing a pang of guilt to run through me. "I'm nothing!"

Rambo's interrogation continued. "Who did you pass the information on to?"

"The two blokes on the far side, Rick and Rob."

"The ones you mentioned who were closest to us in the comp," I asked. Paul nodded.

"We'll see *them* on the podium," Rambo said as an aside before grilling Paul further. "Who *is* The Bait Baron?" he asked menacingly.

"Don't know," Paul responded.

This wasn't the answer Rambo wanted to hear so he eased his weight forward to an accompanying groan from the human stick insect trapped underneath it. "Sure?"

"Aaarghh! Yes!" Paul gasped. "Even Rick and Rob don't know! No one seems to know! We're kept in the dark! We only get to hear the rumours about his best mate."

"Go on," Rambo encouraged.

"The Carper," Paul gulped. "He's fishing a huge, secret gravel pit for an unknown seventy."

I joined in to make it a stereo affair from the word 'huge'. "Tell us something we don't know! Carl told us the same shit!" I stated. "You know Carl was working for him before he fucked up on an arson job, don't you?" Paul shook his head. I puffed out my cheeks in disbelief – didn't anyone in this organisation know anybody else! "I said the same thing to Carl. What's with all this 'The Something', crap, Paul? Someone *somewhere* must know more and know some proper names."

"I've told you one someone *and* the somewhere!" Paul pleaded. "It's *true*! The others keep on mentioning him. He's the only person everyone seems to know of. He's legend! Find *him*! He must know who The Bait Baron is!" Paul paused, an air of terror flooding across his face. "*Please* get off! I'm gonna die! I'm in *agony*! I don't know any more, *honestly*! Please! *Please*! I'm already in enough trouble if he finds out what I've said." And on that note of begging for mercy, Paul started to blubber like a five-year-old over a broken toy.

Rambo looked at me and I shrugged. "Okay," he said indicating the near completion of his interrogation. "You don't tell anyone what you've told us and neither will we… Now, one last question, why take the cat?"

"The word was The Bait Baron thinks it's a brilliant bait tester. He thinks Pup will do anything to get him back, even work for him. It's a ransom situation."

"And he assumed all this because of you reporting back what Matt had said?"

"I think so," Paul whispered tearfully.

Rambo motioned with his head for me to come closer. I stepped over a pipe cleaner leg to do so. "If he did, he's a shrewd bastard to pick up on it so quickly," he whispered. "His chain of command's efficient, too. It's hierarchical, based on fear, ignorance and the ultimate protection of the top rank. No one appears to know anything or anyone above the next level up. The chain of command delegates everything down from the top, including violence to ensure loyalty and as retribution for mistakes!"

Rambo turned his attention back to Paul. "One more last question, Paul. Why get involved? What do *you* get out of it for helping run his sordid little business."

Paul looked up with his glassy, tear-reddened eyes. "Bait," he said simply. "The Bait Baron promised me free, pukka, top quality bait. It's ever so expensive," he added, as if to trying to justify himself.

"Bait!" I muttered to myself, thinking who would ever get involved with this type of chicanery solely for free bait. Ridiculous! Then, unfortunately, I remembered what *I* had done to secure a deal on the exclusive, revolutionary, indented, dirty brown bottom bait boilie! I had let Pup jump The Syndicate waiting list, given him free membership for life, waived the initial 1st deposit and then kitted him out with brand new tasteful tackle funded by carp sold via an illegal cash transaction, one resourcefully evading the clawing clutches of both Her Majesty's Custom and Excise VAT and Income Tax departments! Free top quality bait, I ruefully admitted, was a mightily powerful incentive if you were a mad keen carper! Even more so now Mr Pulimov had dangled his twenty-five grand incentive in front of the carping hordes! If Paul and Carl were to be believed The Carper was sitting it out on a 'one run a season' secret venue hoping for his big payday.

It occurred to me there was a certain core of logic running through the bizarre mysticism concerning The Carper should the rumour prove true. "It might make sense," I explained to Rambo in a whisper. "All this stuff about The Carper. What better way to advertise a new bait conglomerate than by catching the first ever UK seventy, an *unknown* seventy and with it Pulimov's Prize, on one of its baits?"

Rambo's reply was heavy with sarcasm. "Do you mean a bait company would *actually* fund a carp angler to fish full-time? Just so it could publicise his catches and hope boilie sales generated by a mass flock-of-sheep mentality, one based on emulation and basking in second-hand reflected glory, would be of ample financial reward?"

"It has been known."

"Well I never," Rambo sighed in mock astonishment. "And are those trainers the same make as David Beckham's football boots?"

"It works on lots of levels," I confirmed.

The 'Tackling of Pimply Paul by the Terminator with Tackle(s)' episode was over – we had gleaned as much as we were ever likely to from the horizontal beanpole. Rambo and I left him to his own devices as we theorised he could probably muster enough energy to dial 999 and order an ambulance or get one of his mates to pop him in a rod holdall and carry him home. There was even a chance he might recuperate adequately enough to move under his own steam. If he couldn't the carrion crows would make short work of him – as it was he already looked virtually pecked to the bone.

We left the grisly, scraggy, skeletal, scrawny, skinny scene and returned to our swim.

"What are we going to do next?" I asked as we climbed up the grassy wall once again.

"Have a word with Rick and Rob and see if we can't work our way up to another level. Hopefully Paul will be too scared for his own neck to warn them about what we now know and it may help us catch them off guard," Rambo answered grimly. "Other than that we wait for The Bait Baron's demands on how Pup can get Wilton back." Rambo gave me an earnest glare. "We're in it up to our necks now, boy! Pretty soon word'll get back to him we've been hassling his blokes and then the shit'll hit the wind turbine! There's only one way out and that's to sort it!"

Rambo was right. I too had a feeling this story was only going to be resolved when we had got to the bitter end. I fleetingly wondered if it would be any harder than my confronting Steffi on the quiet. Probably. Why *had* she done it? I put it on the back burner because I was male and couldn't multitask. To think only a short time ago I had considered our adventures as dried up as a menopausal spinster!

When we arrived at swim nine Grant and Oliver were still waiting alongside the pained Pup and the crushed Carl. With hindsight I had been a little surprised they hadn't raced after us to see what the commotion was all about. Naturally, I was relieved they hadn't, watching Rambo torture Paul for information after having brutally scythed him down wasn't exactly good for our image – what was left of it. On the other hand, I had no doubt they had attempted to prise info from an emotionally vulnerable Pup.

Grant was on us immediately like a journalistic bloodhound on the scent of a scoop. "Who was it?" he asked eagerly. "One of The Bait Baron's men?"

"One of The Bait Baron's long streaks of piss," Rambo answered Grant before bearing the bad news to the world's greatest working-from-home boiliemeister. "I'm afraid they *have* got Wilton, Pup," he gravely informed the inventor of the indented boilie. "But don't you worry, we'll get him back for you. Sit tight and don't panic," Rambo advised. "If he contacts you, you tell me and don't do anything or agree to anything until you have. Understand?"

Pup gave a wimpy nod of the head and mouthed the word 'thanks' and gave a very half-hearted smile. When Rambo spoke in this manner you had no reason to question the fact things would come out all right, such was his presence and formidable reputation. I, however, wasn't so awed as to not notice the use of the royal 'we'.

Grant motioned to speak, preceding it with his hair grooming habit. "Let me get this right. This Bait Baron has taken your cat, ya?" he confirmed to Pup in his public school voice before turning to Oliver for an aside. "Huh! It's a good job were not a red top or we'd have a field day with 'catnapping' puns." Oliver gave his associate a knowing grin although Grant quickly apologised. "Sorry, Pup, going off-message there. Okay, recap. The reason he's taken the cat is to try to intimidate and coerce you into, from your point of view, an unpalatable business deal. Is that correct?" Pup nodded. "And Wilton, your cat, is an integral part of your bait making business in terms of it being a reliable, shortcut predictor to the potency of any given mix you make?"

As he once more asked Pup if his interpretation of events and information was correct, I inwardly cursed Grant just for being here. This was rapidly turning into my worst nightmare – now I could see his journalistic mind getting to grips with what he had seen with his own eyes and heard with his own ears. Bollocks and double bollocks! You know, to transcribe it in a technical fashion. Bloody global warming! (To Save The Planet stop using your car, or at the very least buy an electric one – one like all the celebrities and politicians have so they can be photographed standing alongside it before they jump into their private jets and helicopters to go and have their hair done.)

"Originally he promised me he'd leave me alone if Matt and Rambo won," Pup said, his voice and gaze away with the fairies. "And we did win. Fair and square. And now *this* has happened."

Grant pulled in a sharp lungful of air. "Yes. Well. I think you were being a *little* overly optimistic and naively trusting if you thought that were the case."

"That's what *we* said!" I remarked.

"If anything you've only served to prove your worth, you see," Grant explained, doing his best to impart upon Pup what was once dubbed 'the bleedin' obvious'. "A good thing if you were interested in a commercial tie-up, not so good if you wanted to avoid this chap's overtures." Grant tweaked his head and ran his manicured fingers through his long hair – if I'd had a pound for every time he had done it this morning, I would have had about fourteen quid. "Who would have thought something so passive as angling could have such energy, dynamism, deviousness and depth coursing under its surface!" A smile flickered momentarily over Grant's face. "Actually that's rather a suitable analogy! What do you say, Oliver?" Oliver agreed and for reasons best known only to himself, took a close-up of Rambo. Grant gave a disbelieving shake of the head. "This has certainly opened up my eyes to the not so gentile word of angling!"

"*Don't* keep doing that!" Rambo warned Oliver as the photographer continued snapping, the adrenaline of poleaxing Paul evidently still whooshing through his veins.

"The thing is, Grant," I said quickly before Rambo decided to insert Oliver's camera into an area where the photos taken would only be of interest to a bowel consultant. "You can't write anything concerning these latest developments."

Grant looked unimpressed. "Fortunately, we have a thing in this country called 'the free press'… and I *can*," Grant insisted, "should I wish."

His statement was Rambo's cue to park his huge body right into the bay marked 'Grant's personal space', place a massive mitt on his highly educated shoulder and put him straight on one or two matters.

"*No*. You *can't*," Rambo gainsaid. "You've come here to write an article on us, this competition and the Pulimov effect… and that's where it's got to end," Rambo informed him. "Matt doesn't need the Watt incident regurgitated and we need to have a window of opportunity to get Wilton back before you splash the story all over your broadsheet and make our life more difficult." Grant's eyes seemed to flare in delight at the possibility, but Rambo carried on in his negative vein. "Nothing antagonises lowlife scumbags more than reading their latest 'business' propositions in the newspapers. When things are resolved I promise we'll give you an exclusive lowdown on it all, anonymously of course. *If* you're still interested, the public being well known for its short attention span."

Grant went to answer, caught sight of the busted Carl out the corner of his eye, possibly thought twice and cracked a smile. "Ya! Sure. I understand completely. I'll keep the recent matters under wraps and the article will be as was."

Rambo hydraulic crushing claw momentarily squeezed Grant's shoulder and I noticed his knees unlock in tandem with a split second wince. "*Don't* let me down!" warned Rambo.

To me we were sailing tight to the wind, on thin ice and treading on eggshells trying to force this issue with Grant and although I doubted if Grant was used to physical intimidation, I got the impression he was made of sterner stuff than his publicly educated demeanour might at first imply.

"You can trust me!" he assured. "In fact it might not be a bad idea for me to sit on The Bait Baron angle for the moment. You see, here's the thing, I have a feeling there's more to this than we all know. When you were gone Carl told me how he used to work for this Bait Baron guy and how he was asked to set fire to a rival company's warehouse."

"S'right," grunted Carl.

"Carl was so intimidated he actually carried out his job, although he did make sure he was seen, to bring it to everyone's attention. His intention is to tell the truth when police question him, and in doing so, show the world the shadowy, criminal hand of The Bait Baron. This is, not wanting to sound overly melodramatic, reliant on him remaining alive until his appearance in court!" Grant rested a supportive hand on Carl's shoulder. I don't suppose he appreciated it due to his battered, bruised and banged about body aching as much as a ten-pints-in-a-night piss head's bladder heading home on a toilet-free, bumpy, four-hour coach journey. "Carl's making a brave stand, especially as no one really knows who or what he's up against. At one end of the scale it might be a petty criminal chancing it, at the other it could be a serious organised crime outfit looking for new areas to infiltrate."

"Yeah. He told us The Bait Baron was leaning on him big time to take the rap," I concurred, repaying Carl's lie on how he had arrived in such a battered state by backing up his rather skewed version of the truth.

Grant nodded vigorously. "Let me do some digging. You do your digging," he said fervently. "We'll pool our information and if the jigsaw puzzle gets completed, we'll nail the sucker together. This could make the front page of the Daily Telegraph, let alone the weekend section!" Grant, greatly galvanised by the prospective grandeur of going global with his graphic, gritty, gumshoe-gained knowledge, turned his gushing prose on to me. "I'm not interested in your ancient misdemeanours, Matt, I've got bigger fish to fry!"

Time would tell how sincere he was being, but for the moment we had to go with it. I hoped a Grant fixated on The Bait Baron and his illegal operations was a Grant less likely to poke his nose into my affairs or Rambo's. "Sounds good to me," I said hastily.

Grant lifted his arm off the gallant, poacher turned gamekeeper, mob-defying Carl, or as I preferred, Carl the fuck-up arsonist and continued speaking to me. "One more thing, Matt. Carl said you wrote a book whilst you were in prison, one detailing the events ending with the blowing up of Watt's bivvy. Is that true?"

Carl's mouth was almost as big as mine. "Yeah," I admitted.

"What did you do with it?"

"Nothing. The manuscript's still indoors, stuffed in a draw."

Grant thrust a lower lip over his top one. "I'd like to read it one day."

"You help us out with finding what sort of organisation The Bait Baron is running and I'll let you," I told him.

Grant thrust out a hand with long slender fingers for me to shake. I shook it. "Deal!" he said in a voice hinting he had secured something of benefit. I wasn't fooled – flattering my ego wouldn't get him anywhere – I still didn't trust him.

Chapter 12

With the reporting of events so far resolved to everyone's satisfaction and the comp over, we left the shattered Pup to start packing up whilst the rest of us, the two journos, Rambo, Carl and myself made our way back around to the two tents for the prize-giving ceremony. Rambo said, and so I agreed, that Pup needed time and space to confront his loss, to reflect on the self-induced error of entering Pup Enterprises into the comp and to fester on my loose-tongued moment opening up a window of opportunity for The Bait Baron to snatch his ace bait tester.

The last bit was my slant on things. I wasn't expecting my gear to get packed away with a great deal of TLC. On honest reflection who could blame Pup if he did put my Delkims into their respective pouches with the aid of Thor's bivvy mallet. I had harangued him to keep his gob shut when Grant had turned up and had singularly failed to follow my own advice. In my one careless sentence to Pimply Paul, I realised that even if we managed to get Wilton back unmolested, Pup might never look on me in the same light as he had before I had opened my mouth. My worst fears had materialised over my slip-up and it wasn't a pleasant feeling to have let him down.

On the way, Carl offered his services to help find Wilton. Rambo accepted without hesitation, taking the viewpoint Carl could act as a valuable feed of information. We didn't have anything much to go on and it was a cert The Bait Baron would be leaning on Carl as the possibility of him being involved in a trial increased. Any insight into what he/his organisation/his cronies were all about could be useful. Feeling determined to make good my mistake, I imagined The Bait Baron to be quaking in his trainers, brogues, wellies, open-toed court shoes, whatever it was he shod himself with, at the fellowship we had assembled to track him down and smash his empire! And so he should! Rambo on a war footing, the might of the free press, shaven-headed, beringed, turncoat Carl and a vengeful Matt Williams were not to be trifled with! Okay, the list weakened considerably towards the end, but at least we were up for it.

Rambo carried the baitboat back, all safely packed away with its accessories in the carry bag in a condition exactly as we had received it bar a load more capture 'assists' on the clock. Once he had checked it in, where an unknown Bowl clerk had duly noted its fine condition and redeemed our deposit, we were left with nothing to do but to wait for the organisers to sort out the presentation. With little enthusiasm I kept a look out for Watt, dreading the prospect of him turning his hand to playing The Bowl's first 'No Seventies in Here, Mate!' presentation MC. As it transpired, Watt clearly quailed at the prospect of naming us as winners more than I did him doing so. Word amongst the other participants suggested Ben was going to present the cheques and trophies.

"You haven't got another appointment today, have you?" I asked Oliver when I found out. He was standing next to Grant, the pair of them looking so out of place amongst the seething sea of unwashed carpers in assorted outlandish, slimed-up fishing garb, they might well have just stepped out of a flying saucer and asked to be taken to our leader.

"No," Oliver confirmed.

"Good," I said dryly. "Because if Ben's doing the presentation you'll need your flash ready!"

If Oliver hadn't been able to deduce the not very subtle translation of my humour prior to Ben commencing his duties, he would have minutes into it. Ben's rambling opening speech – even Hector, lying at his master's feet, seemed to have settled down for a long haul (the supply of tinned dog food and ten gallon water bowl being a dead giveaway) – was not so much around the sun to meet the moon as around the sun, pop off to Saturn to get the shopping, come back, realise you've left the washing powder at the checkout, go back and get it, come back via Neptune to visit a favourite aunt before finishing, in true schoolboy style, up Uranus – and then realising, half an hour later, you shouldn't have been up Uranus, you should have been over the moon.

Luckily, in terms of not starting a riot, Ben was well known enough to be treated like a favourite uncle, one whose recent slippage into early Alzheimer's was still at the stage of novelty rather than infuriation. Consequently his horrendously slow, faltering, rustic style of speech was not subjected to vicious ridicule, only to gentle heckling and friendly banter, all of which the old boy took in his stride with good humour. Throughout his rambling monologue I had stopped looking for Watt and started looking for Pimply Paul – providing he hadn't died from an attack of hungry robins on the far side of the grassy spoil wall – and the unknown Rob and Rick. I was hoping to fathom out who the latter were by using a complicated assessment of body language – one indicating a pair of anglers who were good enough to come second, but not good enough to win. Alternatively I hoped to see Pimply Paul limp up to someone, flick a robin who had vulture-like aspirations off his bony shoulder, and surreptitiously point out Rambo and I saying 'Those are the two that beat you, and the big one is the one who beat me… up'.

"That's them," Rambo whispered, carefully avoiding attracting Grant's attention. (For the record Grant, diametrically opposed to his early state of conviction, was looking as bored as a father watching an infant school's nativity play whose only child *wasn't* starring due to last-minute sickness.)

"Who?" I whispered back.

"Rob and Rick."

"How do you know that?"

"I asked Carl to find out. He asked around and found out they came second. He said he still didn't recognise them as being Bait Baron boys. He hadn't come across them before."

"Which two?" I hissed out the corner of my mouth.

"The one with the chequered flag bandana next to the bloke with the straggly goatee. We'll have a quiet word after the presentation, once the Old Harrovians have gone," Rambo murmured. "They'll know about us, what they don't know is *we* know they work for The Bait Baron."

"*If* the pimpled one sticks to his word," I pointed out.

"… Brings me to the time to presents them there prizes for the first three pairs of anglers!"

Ben had finished!

There were ironic cheers, calls of 'Thank God!', 'I've got to be at work tomorrow!' and 'Bring on the strippers!' to the end of Ben's interminable opening speech. Ben smiled and held up a hand as at his feet, an unfed and hungry Hector – the dog had forgotten to pack his tin opener – settled for lapping up a drink of water. "Now yous all knows the next man I's going to introduce, he don't need one of them there introductions…"

"Why are you giving him one, then?" yelled a Realtree carper to my right to a decent ripple of laughter. There's always *one* in the crowd who thinks they're Oscar Wilde.

Ben soldiered on. He was slow, painfully slow, but the old boy was bulletproof when it came to riding out mild barracking. "… He's the man who's given yous lads some great fishing, he's the man who's responsible for this here great venue, he's Mr Bowl himself…" Ben paused in an attempt to heighten the effect of his build-up – and failed miserably. Ben's speech time frame was so slow-mo with his idea of an impact pause being so protracted it merely gave the impression he'd had a stroke. During the intermission several of the carpers in the throng dozed off, some nipped off to have a full English at the nearest greasy spoon *and* came back, whilst others merely slipped into that mental twilight zone us carpers refer to as 'between takes'.

Me? I lent over to speak to Grant. "This is *great*, isn't it?"

"Bizarre! Bizarre *and* boring! But above all else, definitely boring," Grant replied, running both hands through his hair at the same time, his slender fingers massaging his temples as he did so. Grant wrinkled his nose. "To be fair, *all* award ceremonies are boring." He looked me square in the eye. "*Promise* me you won't make a long acceptance speech thanking *every* tackle manufacturing company?"

"Don't worry," I sneered. "*I'm* not a corporate sponsored angler!"

"… Michael Kane!" Ben had delivered his punchline in the style of any self-respecting, fully paid up, union-card-holding service engineer – profoundly late.

"Michael Kane is The Bowl's owner! Not a lot of people know that," I originally and wittily informed Rambo.

"You're only supposed to blow the bloody doors off!" chirped the Realtree carper, ad-libbing one he had obviously rehearsed earlier.

"Stop throwing those bloody spears at me!" called another.

A cacophony of poor Michael Caine impressions filled the air until a man in serious need of a deed poll quelled the noise.

"Thank you, gentlemen and thank you, Ben," said the unflustered, bald-headed, moon-faced man in-his-late-fifties used to a lifetime of hearing the same jokes over and over with a genial disposition. (I concluded, ultimately, he could always ban them *sine die* if he did tire of it and having that sanction was enough to temper an indignant response.) "An excellent competition with some exceptional catches… as usual! I hope you'll all agree The Bowl has once again come up with the goods!" Mr Kane waited for applause and wasn't disappointed. "And I very much hope many of you will return to fish it again in a more leisurely manner than the last two days." Mr Kane went on to thank all the helpers, much to Grant's disappointment, with a thoroughness so great even the portable toilet cleaner got a mention. Satisfied he had plugged his business adequately with a clever 'man of the people touch', Mr Kane cracked on. "With no more ado!" he exalted, lifting both hands heavenward in the manner of a Roman Emperor letting the games begin. "In third place! With a cash prize of two hundred pounds… Paul Simpson and Craig Watkins!"

A ripple of applause rang out from all the anglers as Paul and Craig edged sideways through the crowd. Well, Craig did. Paul didn't have to bother on account of him being so thin he had to walk around in a shower to get wet. To all present it was patently clear Paul was physically the worse for wear. The exaggerated limp, dragging right foot and paralytic arm were quite a giveaway as would have been the swathe of black/blue bruising slowly forming on Paul's ribcage – should he have taken his shirt off to reveal a body impersonating a Belsen inmate.

"Fuck me!" The Realtree carper commented. "He looks as if he's had a row with a crane's demolition ball! What you been doing to him, Craig?" he shouted. "Using him as a spod rod to whack out cast iron anvils?"

Craig smiled and shrugged. Others laughed, even Paul tried to grin and make light of the fact he was creeping about like a ninety-year-old geriatric who had just crashed his Zimmer frame into a 4x4 fitted with bull bars. I made sure I laughed and kept looking straight ahead in order to avoid Grant's accusing stare.

Grant was having none of it and nudged my arm, gesturing with a frown towards Paul.

I shrugged. "Probably fell down the grassy wall," I postulated. "Happens quite a bit, so I'm led to believe."

Once Craig and Paul had shook hands with Mr Bowl and picked up their cheque they edged to one side to let the next pair meet the man who had taken a punt on shifting thousands of tons of soil out of a field and filling it with water and carp. Carp of a good strain, I mentally noted. I wondered where he had sourced them and whether it might not be a bad idea to ask him should our second syndicate water ever come to fruition.

"In second place with a cash prize of five hundred pounds… Rob Myles and Rick Watt!"

As Carl had predicted the bandana and goatee enhanced pair stepped up for the collection of their prize monkey.

"The son of your historic nemesis? Watt the younger?" asked Grant. "Watt the never had his bivvy blown up?" he added, hoicking his eyebrows up his forehead.

I snapped my neck around to face Grant, my head spinning as I became a different kind of prize monkey to the one Rob and Rick were receiving. My CPU usage had all been diverted into disassociating myself – via glibness – with Pimply Paul's half-hour sixty-year aging process and on sourcing an ideal strain of hungry-gutted, all-year-round, bait eating carp! Watt's *son*! Could it be?

"I honestly don't know," I admitted, feeling flushed, flummoxed and flabbergasted.

Events were moving too fast for my brain to cope with and as I grappled with the prospect of Watt's son carrying his father's hatred of myself across the generations, we were announced as winners.

"And the winners!" exclaimed Michael Kane. "And *what* winners! With over *twice* the weight of their nearest competitors, The Bowl's first Baitboat versus Casting, 'No Seventies in Here, Mate!', competition victors… Matt Williams and Tim Ramsbottom!" A generous round of applause greeted us, one founded in respect for what we/Pup's exclusive, revolutionary, indented, dirty brown bottom bait boilie had achieved.

Watt's son? Watt's son! *Timothy Eugene* Ramsbottom, if you don't mind! Watt's *son*? Not so elementary, my dear Watson. Jumbled patterns of disjointed thoughts blundered around my head as I blindly followed Rambo amongst the assembled rank of clapping carp anglers and emerged, heartedly back slapped, blinking into the open space reserved for the podium finishers.

"Well done, lads," Mr Kane said shaking our hands. "Stay put and I'll get The Telegraph's reporter to say a few words. Then we'll have some photos of you getting your cheque and the trophy." Mr Kane's large sundial face cracked into a massive smile. "What great publicity! Wait till I show my neighbours I'm in The Telegraph!" I think he was talking to me, but it could as easily have been to himself.

Rambo and I stood uneasily alongside Rob and Rick and Craig and Paul as Grant and Oliver were introduced. Tellingly they received the poorest reception. I doubted if there was a single Telegraph reader amongst the lot of us, although circulation was bound to rise for the following weekend – Mr Bowl and the prize winners' vanity would see to that!

Grant wisely made a very brief speech telling everyone about his upcoming article. Astutely he had sensed the anglers' apathy towards him and wanted to move things on to a successful conclusion as quickly as possible before he blacked out from boredom. With Grant's words over he took a back seat to let Oliver take formal pictorial evidence of us receiving our cheque and the tasteful piece of silverware inscribed with the legend, 'The Bowl Baitboat v Casting Challenge Cup Trophy'. It was like old times. I sneaked a look at Rick and wondered if he had ever sat on his daddy's lap and been told a bedtime story about the wicked Brothers Grimm, Matt and Rambo and the battle of the TWTT! I also sneaked a look at the cheque. One thousand quid! Not bad for a weekend's work!

With the prize ceremony over the other competitors drifted off to finish their packing up, contemplate the journey home and the prospect of work tomorrow. How glad I was to have left all that work nonsense behind!

However, work of a different nature needed to be done and it needed to be done now.

"Are you related to Tom Watt?" I innocently asked Rick having said my goodbyes to Grant and Oliver a few minutes earlier. Now was a good time because Rob was engaged in conversation with Mr Bowl.

I scanned Rick's face for telltale clues. A tiny flash of disconcertion washed over his face as he realised one of his boss's adversaries was talking to him. But did he know any more? Did he have an inkling into my SS syndicate past?

"He's my uncle," he answered. "My Dad's his brother. How do you know him?"

Rick's last question seemed genuine. Maybe he had no idea at all. "From a long time ago," I replied. "I remember reading his articles in Carpworld years ago, some were based on a fairly local syndicate I think." The competition might have been over, but I was still fishing!

Rick stroked his goatee beard. "I've never read them. I haven't got a lot of time for him to be honest. He was always putting my old man down, saying he wasn't as good an angler as he was. All that sort of shit! Arrogant bastard... until he changed."

"Changed?" This was getting interesting! I certainly hadn't expected Rick to be so chatty! "In what way?" I asked, feeling the presence of Rambo close to my shoulder, listening in on the conversation.

Rick laughed. "For a start his wife left him for a mate of his and at the same time some fucker blew up his gear, bivvy, rods, alarms, the lot, with a couple of hand grenades! Knocked the stuffing right out of him. Now the old fool's reduced to sucking up to," Rick had a quick look to see if Mr Bowl was in earshot, "Michael Kane. Trying to convince him to make The Bowl or another one of his waters into a syndicate. One in which he can be the acting head." Rick pulled at his goatee again. At this rate he was going to turn out to be even more of an obsessive-compulsive with his beard than bloody Grant was with his hair! "Me and Dad used to laugh about it! All his gear going up in smoke! Pity he wasn't *inside* the bivvy when it happened! That's what me and Dad used to say!"

"So, you don't *exactly* like him, then?" I said, feeling I was on to an out of the blue winner.

"Hate the bastard! For all the years he talked down to Dad." Rick gave me a smirk. "I'd love to know who atomised his gear. Pretty cool guy! He must have hated Tom as much as I do!"

Sometimes in life you have to play your big cards when the gut feeling is good. "I did!"

Rick looked at me incredulously and then at Rob for guidance. Rob couldn't give any because he was still engaged with Mr Bowl. Rick stretched his beard an inch and tried to speak only for the words to stall in his mouth. Five seconds later he bump-started them. "What? *You* did?"

"I *did* hate him as much! *And* I blew up your uncle's bivvy!" I jerked a thumb over my shoulder. "With *his* hand grenades!" I let this golden nugget sink into Rick's brain before pressing on with the irrefutable evidence of my deed. "Mike, who was one of Tom's fishing cronies, was knocking off Jennifer way before all that. I followed him home from fishing one day and saw the pair of them at it through the patio door's hastily drawn curtains! She even took it up the arse!"

"*Too* much information!" complained Rick, but he was lapping it up quicker than a thirsty dog on a summer's day – certainly quicker than Hector had a bit earlier.

I pressed on attempting to sate his thirst for dirt on his despised uncle. "It all went pear-shaped in the Southern Specimen syndicate when a competition introduced by Lord God Almighty, Tom Watt turned everyone into warring cliques. A war ended by my final destructive act and us winning the comp, although your sad uncle would never concede we had." I nodded slowly, bigging the pair of us up. "Tom Watt II's personality is almost solely down to us. We beat him fair and square! I blew up his bivvy *and* told him about Jennifer!"

Rick's goatee beard moved closer to his Wychwood boots, courtesy of a sagging jaw. "Neat!" he exclaimed smiling. "Dad'll love hearing all of this! Nice one!"

I pursed my lips, lifting my eyes from the ground to his. "We know you work for The Bait Baron, Rick."

The smile was gone from Rick's face in an instant. "Only temporarily," he replied defensively. "Only until I get a job sorted and can buy my own bait." I stared at him in silence whilst Rambo, as quick as ever on the uptake, applied subtle pressure by shaking his head in a 'you-ought-to-be-ashamed' manner. Rick looked at the floor. "I know it's not pretty, Rob persuaded…"

"We need a favour," Rambo told him. "No one will ever know. You know what's happened to Pup's cat?" Rick nodded. "The Carper. True?" Rick nodded again, flicking his eyes towards the fortuitously engaged Rob. "Fishing a huge, secret gravel pit for an unknown seventy?" Again, amazingly, Rick nodded. "Find him, squeeze him and find the whereabouts of The Bait Baron?"

"So they say. The Bait Baron's pinning his hopes on him bagging the seventy! It'll be lift off if he does!"

"Where?"

An internal battle seemed to be raging within Rick's soul. Clearly the decency gene so evidently missing from his uncle was present within him. "Come on," I cajoled seductively. "I fucked up your loathed uncle's life! You must owe me something!"

Rick gave his beard a tug and, joy of joys, went for it! "The MoD range near Lydd," he said in hushed tones. "Be careful. There are bigger bangs there than hand grenades." Rick went to walk but stopped. "Don't tell *anyone*, or I might never hold a rod again!" he warned gravely.

Chapter 13

The day after the three of us had got back from The Bowl the first thing Rambo and I had done was to buy an Ordnance Survey map. Before this, in the van going home, Rambo had explained how the MoD had various ranges dotted all over the countryside for the use of live ammunition firing practise. Rick had been correct in his warning because apparently we weren't talking exclusively about bullets! Tanks, artillery, bazooka, grenade launchers and small arms fire were all deployed on these type of ranges even if Rambo had been unsure if the Lydd range could accommodate all of these weapons.

Typically, he went on to explain, the ranges were situated in remote regions of the country away from densely populated areas, although he added, given the propensity for any government department to fuck up big time, you might have been forgiven for thinking a couple of them might have ended up being slap bang in the middle of London, Manchester or Birmingham!

Despite all this, the most interesting facet by some mile, a couple of billion or so, was The Carper fishing a gravel pit situated on said MoD range for an unknown seventy. The insight this gave me into the mindset of The Carper ranged from somewhere starting at extreme hardcore to the upper reaches of raving, psychotic, utterly-fucking-mental obsessive. In comparison it made my TWTT-fuelled obsession look like I was a fair weather angler who made it on to the bank for one sunny afternoon in August!

It was all very well being hit by a sudden downpour when fishing, but what about getting hit by a sudden shower of artillery shells? What about re-enacting mini-versions of WWI's western front and WWII's Normandy landings every time you needed to cast out? What about the possibility of being *targeted*? 'Okay, men. Forget the ancient tank this time, aim for the little green dome!' I logically concluded The Carper had to be dug in, (in a 'Fox' hole, gettit?) more for camouflage than for withstanding a direct hit – not even an Armadillo claimed to be *that* strong!

The mind boggled at the effort, ingenuity and shear willpower required to fish full-time, clandestinely, on a one-run-in-a-season-if you're-lucky, huge gravel pit situated on a MoD live artillery range. Even the aspect of getting to the stage of wanting to fish the venue in the first place hinted at a mentality of monumental focus. For a start, you had to presume The Carper wasn't fishing at such pains on mere hearsay and rumour. No way! This meant The Carper must have spotted the unknown seventy with his own eyes, which also meant he must have spent hours and hours and hours watching the water. Watching the water on a huge gravel pit situated on a MoD live artillery range! To be *that* driven to even go and look at the water in the first instance! Let alone go and look for long enough to eventually spot, what are we talking, here? The one fish in it? The one *big* fish in it? And then to decide to *fish* for it! To fish for it on a huge gravel pit situated on a MoD live artillery range!!

The entire concept beggared belief. M'lud, ladies and gentlemen of the jury, I rest my case.

Even Rambo, even indestructible, Terminator with Tackle, walk-through-eleven-inch-cavity-walls-with-full-insulation, *Rambo*, had puffed out his cheeks and shaken his head in disbelief claiming it was all a part of global warming madness. (Save The Planet by having extensive energy saving work done to your home. For example, if you live on a housing estate, were you aware fitting glass in your windows could save you up to fifty per cent of your gas bill if you haven't already been cut off for non-payment? And, if you're a fat cat, overpaid, city banker/Premiership footballer/government-funded quango chief executive, were you aware that turning down your external, Olympic-sized swimming pool's temperature by just one degree centigrade is hardly worth bothering about?)

I stared at the 1:50,000 Ordnance Survey map for Ashford and Romney Marsh that was spread on my dining room table, the bottom half of which was of greatest interest. "So close!" I said "What? Thirty? Forty miles from us?" Rambo grunted his concurrence. "An unknown seventy swimming around virtually under our noses! Who'd have thought it in these supposedly 'no-secrets-left' times in which we fish?"

"*If* it's true."

"If it's true," I agreed.

It *was* true. I was convinced of it.

My eyes followed the dominant feature of the map, namely the coastline of the outcrop of land poking out into The Channel, the extreme point of which was marked with Dungeness Power Station – Dungeness *Nuclear* Power Station. I laughed to myself. Perhaps the seventy had three eyes like Blinky in The Simpsons and glowed two-tone in the dark, plutonium pink and urgent uranium. A joke, of course, and outlandishly unlikely true enough, but what we were trying to get our heads around seemed nearly as unlikely.

I concentrated back on the map. Half a dozen large, blue splodges were splattered on it within a mile inland from the power station, one of which resided within the boundary of an area marked 'DANGER AREA' in red lettering. North of the pit lay the small town of Lydd and north of that, New Romney, another small linear development along the tiny 'B' road running through it. Spreading my gaze wider I could see the entire triangular section of land was bordered by water. Obviously there was the sea, but inland from the ancient Cinque Port town of Rye to the tiny coastal town of Hythe, the whole of the flat marshland was bordered by a river and a canal. The River Rother to the east ran from Rye into the sea, flanked either side by even more gravel pits. It linked into the Royal Military Canal to the north-west of Rye, which then ran in a vague arc all the way to Hythe. The canal marked the edge of the marshland and within it The Walland Marsh and Romney Marsh were crisscrossed with hundreds of thin, blue veins depicting miles and miles of tiny drainage ditches. If my school history lessons serve me correctly, I knew the Royal Military Canal had been dug by hand back in 1804 in anticipation of Napoleonic invasion, was 28 miles long (including its link to the natural waterways of the River Rother and River Brede), claimed title to the third longest defence monument in the British Isles behind Hadrian's Wall and Offa's Dyke (whoever she was) and cost £234,310.

Okay, so I Googled it! The only thing I could really remember from my history lessons was 1066 and all that.

"There she blows, Captain," I said, underlining the depiction of a large pit with my index finger. "It exists."

I looked up from the map at Rambo who was starring at the blue splodge of ink. I knew he was translating the splodge in his head into images, picturing the bleak, windswept, exposed pit it represented and the seemingly insurmountable problems needing to be overcome to fish it.

"How often do you think they use it for firing practise? If I was fishing there I'd be constantly worrying about the next practise session."

"I'm not sure. Once might be enough," Rambo remarked. "I reckon one 120mm Hirtenberger mortar round landing smack bang in the middle of your bivvy table would stop you fretting about the next one."

"How the hell did he get in there, fish spot for hours, if not days, get set up with all his gear, food, water, bait and fish it full-time without being noticed?" I demanded.

"And without being accidentally blown up," Rambo added. "I'm not too sure about that either." Rambo ran his huge mitt across his stubbled chin and mused on The Carper's venue of choice. "Having seen the map, maybe it's not quite as heroic as we're imagining, boy. It's too small for tanks and for large artillery, more a place for mortar, grenade and small arms fire." Rambo scrunched up his face. "Frequency of use may not be exceptionally high. He might only have to sit out live fire a couple of times a week."

"That's all! Fuck me! I might phone up the Army and get my name on the waiting list!" I replied with sarcasm. "They're so strapped for cash I expect they're running it as a syndicate! Trying to raise money for adequate body armour for the boys in Iraq! I can see the pitch in Carpworld now! 'Huge, bleak, windswept gravel pit with one massive, twenty-five grand winning fish. (Subject to verification.) Quiet, secluded location – except for intermittent live mortar bombing twice weekly! Annual fee includes free second-hand Kevlar helmet'."

"*Second*-hand?" Rambo was forced to ask

"Donated by the troops *without* adequate body armour," I answered grimly.

Rambo ignored my remarkably satirical skit on the state of the armed forces' plight in the Middle East. "You know there's only one way to find out, don't you, boy?"

My grim mood prevailed. "Yeah," I paused and changed the subject, prolonging the agony. "What's the latest word from Pup?" Pup wasn't talking to me at the moment because of my big mouth, therefore all conversations regards The Bait Baron's demands went directly to Rambo.

"I've got him stalling for time. Luckily The Bait Baron's not leaning on him too hard. He's giving him a bit of time to mull things over and he's assured him Wilton is being well treated."

"I expect he's got the bloody cat testing his own baits!"

"Wouldn't surprise me, boy… I wouldn't mention it to Pup, though," Rambo quickly added. "He's stressed enough as it is."

I huffed out a burst of air between my lips. "Fat chance! He's still not speaking to me."

"He'll come round. Once we get Wilton back." Rambo gave me the look, the look pulling us back to business. "When's it to be then?"

Rather oddly, and with the superb timing similar to that of my buzzers, the phone rang. I screened the call through the answerphone until I knew it was Mr Honey when I picked up as fast as a Wild West gunslinger. " Hello, Matt Williams speaking."

"Mr Williams, you *are* there. Good news! Good news!" Things went deathly silent for a few seconds. "As I say, I have some good news."

"Oh, I thought you meant it was good news I was in," I said, no doubt confirming to Mr Honey I had more money than brain cells.

"That was the *first* good news I indicated, Mr Williams. The second good news is the *main* good news," Honey oozed.

"The government have introduced a simple DIY house conveyance scheme?" I asked caustically. "Or has some geek invented online divorce software?"

Mr Honey chuckled. "Very drool, Mr Williams." What did he care if I was taking the piss, hinting at a world where solicitors were obsolete? He was probably charging me fifty quid every ten minutes just for listening to it. "No, it's our good friend Mr Felix Hattersley. Apparently circumstances have changed, any offer within five thousand pounds of three hundred and fifty thousand gets you your lake."

"Hold on," I snapped. I clasped my sweaty paw over the mouthpiece of the phone, my heart banging like a kettledrum played by an enthusiastic octopus with a natural disposition towards percussion instruments. "It's Honey! The solicitor from Honey, Honey, Splenda and Sucre!" I told Rambo. "Felix has run out of rent boys, lubricant, whatever, but the bottom line is he needs cash fast!" I gabbled. "Our squeeze has worked! There's no one else bidding! If we up it to three, four, five thousand it's ours! What do you think?"

"How quick can he sort out the paperwork and make it ours?" Rambo asked urgently.

"If we go for it, how quick can you sort out the legal paperwork side of things," I said to the phone.

I could hear Honey ease back in his highly padded, black leather chair, prop his expensive Italian shoes on to his large, oak desk and blow smoke-shaped '£' signs from a Cuban cigar the size of a cricket stump. "A week to ten days should suffice Mr Williams. It's a very straightforward transaction. One search and one deed of ownership subject to one contract of half ownership between you and Mr Ramsbottom."

I put my hand back over the phone. "The dickhead's got five hours' work," I rolled my eyes deep up into my head. "So seven to ten days," I translated.

"Can you afford the extra on your half? And the money to stock and sort it?"

It didn't really matter if I could or couldn't, I wanted Michael's dream realised. Hamworthy *Fisheries*. "I'll rustle it up somehow," I pledged.

Rambo gave an expressive movement with his hands, his face cracked in two and fairly radiated with glee. A Rambo rainbow smile. "Tell him, 'yes', boy. Tell him '*yes*'!"

I too was swept along on the tsunami of excitement. "Mr Honey," I informed him grandly. "Make an offer for three hundred and forty-five thousand pounds!"

I could hear Honey swabbing his groin with a fifty-pound note glugged in massage oil – the unctuous, parasitic bastard. "Excellent, Mr Williams. I'll be in touch as soon as."

I chucked the digital phone on to the table and it spun round several times before pointing to Dungeness Power Station. The pair of us laughed and shook hands.

"Congratulations, partner!" I said slapping Rambo's heavily muscled upper arm.

"Thanks, Matt! My first ever water!" Rambo enthused. "Something I've dreamed of since I was a boy!"

My brain was racing with all the implications of getting Hamworthy *Fisheries*' second water up and running. "All we need to do is put some fish in it! And a hundred other things!"

Hamworthy Fisheries. Plural. And for a *proper* reason. Fantastic!

We both beamed at each other, although behind the veneer of my smile I suddenly thought of Steffi and another job I would have to do sooner rather than later. It was next on the list. "When are we going to find The Carper?" I asked bringing us back to the harsher side of reality.

Rambo scrunched his brow in thought. "I think we need to put in an appearance at Hamworthy before we dive off there. See if everyone's behaving themselves."

"Thursday?" I ventured.

"Gives us a nice forty-eight hour session to check."

"Won't Pup think we're a bit lax leaving it so long?"

"Like I said, The Bait Baron's given him a week to think it through, especially since I told Pup to soften his intractability."

"The Bait Baron's in a generous mood. I didn't think that was his style."

"Pup's special, hence the flexibility. By the end of the week, we'll be on to the bastard."

"What if The Carper won't tell us what we want to know?"

Rambo gave me a what-on-earth-are-you-on look. "He'll tell us all right, boy! Don't you worry! I'll get it out of him one way or another!"

"Yeah, you do seem to have the knack," I commented, thinking of Carl and Pimply Paul.

Rambo folded up the map and stuffed it in the back pocket of his combats. "How come you're wearing them?" I asked. "Steffi let you off."

"She'd already gone out by the time I left this morning," Rambo answered casually, now taking the Glock out of his other pocket and casting a discerning eye over the piece.

I was tempted to ask where the other one was and how Steffi had been lately. I was keen to ascertain how she had been acting, knowing what I did since my sudden realisation at The Bowl. Wisely I kept my mouth shut on the subject and pursued another. "When are you going to Hamworthy?"

Rambo pocketed the Glock, apparently satisfied it was in good nick. "Now," he answered. "My gear's all in the van, boy." He looked me in the eye. "Are you coming as well?"

I moved my head to avoid his stare. "Not straightaway. I've got a couple of, um, errands to run. I'll see you out there later on today I expect," I scratched my ear rather self-consciously. What was it they said about people who scratched their ears when making statements? That they were lying? Not so much lying as hiding the truth. "I'm going to check through my finances as well and make sure I've got my share ready to transfer when we get the green light."

"Don't go and catch a seventy and claim Pulimov's Prize to put an extra twenty-five grand in your kitty!" Rambo joked. "In my capacity as Hamworthy's lieutenant, I'll be on you like a ton of bricks, owner or not!"

"I won't!" I said laughing and thought Rambo might end up on me like a ton of bricks for another reason, namely not telling him what I knew Steffi had been up to! As for publicising a seventy – definitely not!

Once Rambo had gone I steeled myself for what I was going to do. Fortunately, Sophie was out with Amy catching up with Melloney, offering her support for the torrid time she was having putting up with a mega-stressed, Wilton-less, Pup. This situation gave me time and space to think. Time and space to think over what Steffi had done behind Rambo's back. She had to be told and told to stop. I didn't want to see Rambo, my best buddy and prospective business partner, being taken advantage of. Sure, it was a delicate situation, interfering and poking my nose in, especially considering the subject matter, but even so, I thought I had a duty to my best friend. Or so I kept telling myself.

Unfortunately, there was the other side to it. The scenario I kept telling myself wouldn't happen, and yet somewhere brewing, brooding and kicking around in the back of my head, a small part of me ludicrously hoped it would. This was the alternative scenario I kept telling myself I would *never* give in to. Giving in was the side of me that had cost me dearly in the past and there was no going back to it. *No* going back. Not now I had wrestled my life back on to an even keel.

Despite the ludicrous, minority collection of brain cells' desire for the alternative scenario to occur, I was riddled with self-doubt at my ability to resist and not give in, which in turn caused massive unease. In short, I was www.confused.co.uk!

I mooched around the house sorting out my food and tackle for the session on Hamworthy without so much as looking at a bank statement. Sod it! I would get the money sorted later. As I packed my stuff on autopilot, the real thing I wanted to do niggled at me constantly. It itched, itched so badly I couldn't help but scratch. Solemnly, with a dollop of self-loathing, yet with a tingle of anticipation, I took the world's first pornographic carp fishing DVD from its secret hiding place and sat down and watched it. Despite the warnings to myself, I watched it, watched it intently all the way through, not even skipping to the money shots.

When it had finished, I headed off to Rambo's house knowing he wouldn't be there and hoping, by now, Steffi would.

When I arrived I parked my van on Rambo's driveway, thinking this was the very spot where I had met her for the first time when she had materialised out of Japp's Chrysler Voyager. Walking to the door I recalled my first conversation with her and how I'd had to tell her I wasn't living with Rambo because I was gay, but because I had split from Sophie. Moving on chronologically, I recalled glimpsing her in her bathrobe earlier this year and how I had imagined her going into porn star mode. I remembered talking to her on Rambo's phone when she had thought it was him – obviously – and how she had still told me she had 'nozzing' on. On that occasion the conversation had turned to her asking me if I'd had another psychic revelation and how I must tell her if I ever did. My brain thought back to my awakening in my bivvy, having been dreaming *my* version of the DVD, the one I had just revisited, and finally, on top of the spoil wall, how I had realised what she had done and why she had phoned Rambo in the first place. It was this act that had combined with chance to unveil her treachery.

Guilt can make people do funny things – and it was nothing to do with credit card spending.

I knocked on the door, not knowing if she was in or not. *Don't* be weak, I told myself as I waited. Don't let things slip back into how they had turned out in the past. I wasn't so stupid I couldn't see the dangers laying ahead, should they turn out to be as real as my denied wishful/scary thinking. I heard footsteps. She was in! My last thought before the door opened was to remind myself I *had* changed. *Forever*!

The door opened and a fully made-up Steffi stood behind it, the shock of blonde hair and piercing blue eyes *so* more stunning in daylight than on a TV screen – high definition or not. The eyes looked at me, cutting me in two. Something different from usual went on behind them. I could tell she had feared this moment, feared my 'seeing' what she had been up to – but it wasn't yet time for her to say so, not until she was absolutely sure.

"Hi, Matt. Rambo isn't here. He has gone fishing to Hamvorzzy," the heavily accented well-read, East German, ex-porn star told me.

God she was *so* sexy! Images tumbled in the hot dryer of my mind.

"I know," I replied. "It's *you* I wanted to see." Her eyes flickered again. It still wasn't time. She *still* couldn't be sure.

"In zat case you'd better come in."

I went through the door and followed Steffi into the lounge, unashamedly watching her pert arse as I did, images coursing and flashing through my head. Maybe watching the DVD hadn't been such a smart idea. The DVD player had a 'stop' button – my brain didn't!

"Sit down, Matt. Vould you like a cup of tea?"

"No, thanks."

I sat down in one of the large armchairs whilst Steffi sat on the settee opposite, leaning on its large padded arm, her feet folded up on the cushion so they nearly touched her arse.

"A beer, sen?"

I shook my head. There was no point beating about the bush any longer, only the manner of storming it had to be decided. I hoped she would fly out on her own. "You know why I'm here, don't you?" I asked levelly, although internally I was so out of kilter the bubble in my spirit level had disappeared out of view.

Steffi pouted. "Maybe."

"You were shit scared I would find out, weren't you?" Steffi didn't answer. "You shouldn't have asked. It was the spark. A self-fulfilling prophesy."

"Ser spark?"

"Phoning up to say you loved him in the first place. He said it was unlike you. That was your first mistake. Me answering the phone was just bad luck, but you compounded your mistake by asking me if I'd had any more revelations. Something clicked." Steffi sat in silence, her eyes locked on to mine. "It took a while to click," I explained. "I woke up dreaming about you in the middle of the night, went for a walk and then I knew, it suddenly came, and I knew."

"Vott vere you dreaming?" Steffi asked, her voice taking on a sultry tone.

Alarm bells frantically started clanging in my head. It had begun! She had spotted the chink in my armour! I had said too much by mentioning the dream. If she was determined to carry on with what she was doing, she would have to play her hand now! This was the moment she would try to blackmail me in return for my silence!

My whole life, my relationship with Sophie and Rambo teetered on a knife's edge. Give in, go back to old ways and I was doomed! Doomed!

"Just dreaming." A forward defensive prod of the bat. The next ball was a screaming bouncer designed to rip my head off.

"Vas I gudt?" Steffi asked huskily. I'd seen this act before and not on a DVD. It was where it had started.

For some absurd, suicidal reason I nodded.

Steffi languidly got up and walked over to my chair, put her knees either side of my legs and manoeuvred herself so she sat facing me, her arse resting on my lower thighs. My pulse kicked into overdrive. This was the situation I had dreaded and dreamed of. A familiar feeling strained my trousers. I wrestled for control of my body and the rest of my life. She wanted to carry on her game! She was determined!

Steffi ran her immaculately manicured fingers through my hair. "I've told Rambo I find vott you can do vitt your brain fascinating. Has he told you so?" Through my laboured, heavy breathing I managed to say the word 'yes'. "Vott haff I done, Matt?" Steffi asked, her hand now running down the side of my face. "Tell me. And then I'll tell you vott I'm going to do to you."

"With them?" I insanely inquired. "With *them* as well?" My throat was dry, my penis rampant – I lent into the abyss and stared at the black, awful nothingness.

We were nearing what I believe is termed 'the end game' in chess. Whether it would end up in a form of 'mate' seemed to hinge on how unhinged my state of mind became. I frantically leaned back from the dark abyss and crash-hammered six-inch nails into the thick marine ply I was trying to use to shutter it up.

"Vitt who? Who is sem?" She wanted to make doubly sure.

"With Hollywood's stunning looking, lap dancing, ex-international gymnasts, who were also bisexual nymphomaniacs," I gasped. "You kept the address from the time you met them in the pub when you tried to pump them about Hollywood, didn't you?" There was no repudiation. "You've been meeting them ever since and having sex with them behind Rambo's back, haven't you?"

"And you vant to play as vell, ja?" Steffi slid down off the chair, so she was kneeling on the floor and started to unbutton my jeans. "Sey'll do vott ever I ask. It can be our *big* secret!" she breathed sexily. "Vitt *sem* as vell!"

Steffi *and* Hollywood's stunning looking, lap dancing, ex-international gymnasts, who were also bisexual nymphomaniacs. In bed with me! At the same time! And all I had to do was say nothing!

Steffi had already unbuttoned my jeans and slipped the zipper down to the bottom when I felt her warm hand ease my dick out from the confines of my pants. I just *knew* she would do what Sophie had done to Hollywood.

The thought shattered the spell.

I stood up abruptly, pushed her gently out the way, groping at my pants and stuffing my desire out of sight. "No, Steffi! *No*!" I cried. "It's not that I don't want to, not really… but I *don't* want to! I *can't*! I can't go through it all again! Not with you and Rambo! *Please* just stop seeing them!" I pleaded. "Just stop! I won't tell him, I promise. If you promise to stop, I *won't* tell him."

Steffi looked in state of shock. Sexual rejection was hardly likely to have put in a regular appearance on her list of personal experiences. "I'm sorry," she said quietly.

"Why?" I asked. "You've got everything you want. Nice house, nice lifestyle, great partner? Think what you've got away from…" The words fell away from my mouth and fell in an impotent heap on to a four-bedroom, suburban house's lounge carpet. What was the point? All these dumb questions had been asked millions of times before. *I* had asked them of myself! The primordial beast wiped out all reason when it sunk its claws in you.

This time, however, it had been different! I had *ignored* it! I had succeeded where in the past I would have failed! I had denied temptation for the very first time! At long, bloody last I had stood the test! I felt proud.

"You know only too vell, vhy," Steffi said, her head bowed. "I'm sorry, Matt. I vill stop, I promise."

"Thanks," I said with feeling and I kissed her forehead as a man in control. I had grown up! The shock and elation were overwhelming.

"You're a gudt friend and Rambo is a gudt man. I von't ever see sem again," she affirmed as got off her knees. "Old vays are sometimes hard to stop," she explained.

"Would you really have let me in on a foursome?" I enquired as she saw me out the front door.

Steffi nodded. "Sinking twice, now?" she added cheekily.

"*Nope*," I said assuredly. "All right as an abstract concept, *not* as a reality!" I heard the recently matured Matt Williams confirm.

Steffi laughed and looked beautiful. Fleetingly I wondered what I had turned down – what a once-in-a-lifetime opportunity I had spurned. "See you later, Steffi."

"Bye, Matt."

No, I told myself as I climbed into my van. The baggage problems associated with becoming embroiled in Steffi's dirty little secret were horrendous – worse than Heathrow Terminal 5's opening day! I had done the right thing for once. I drove off to Hamworthy, hoping she had been telling me the truth, but more importantly, knowing I had done the right thing.

Chapter 14

The first two or three hours of my session on Hamworthy were ones spent with my fishing head rolling around in the back of my bivvy under the bedchair, along with the old chocolate bar wrappers, dried mud, dead foliage and abandoned, tragically lost boilie stops. Try as I might, I couldn't get to grips with carping and instead went harking back to what had happened earlier. When it had come down to the wire, Steffi had returned to type and tried to use sex as a weapon (that would make a good song title) in an attempt to maintain the status quo of, what I shall delicately call, her 'social life'. Sex had probably been the one constant in her whole life, the one thing that had worked, and when pressed into a corner by my accusation of her participating in a torrid, triple tango, she had tried to use it to barter her way out. And I, with a magnificence resembling a galloping unicorn filmed in hi-def, soft focus on a sunny day against a backdrop of snowy mountains, had survived the temptation – for once – and come out with my new reputation intact. Go, Matt Williams! Even if I do say so myself!

To be honest I felt quite empowered by my achievement and a fresh wave of confidence surged through my mindset. All I had to do now was enjoy my session on Hamworthy and then right the wrong which had wickedly waylaid the bait-tasting, bait-testing pet of Pup, Wilton, by returning the magnificent, mainstay moggie back to his boilie-bound base camp. All that was required was the capture of a few thirties or even a seventy followed by a quick trip to the MoD range to unearth The Carper; ascertain the whereabouts – by violence or otherwise – of The Bait Baron, give *him* a little visit and Bob's your proverbial! Home in time for tea and biscuits!

My mental high proved to be short-lived and overly optimistic.

Four hours into the session, during which I had barely managed to get my three baits out and get into the fishing, I fielded a call from Rambo asking if I was on site. I confirmed I was and he went on to ask if I had managed to get a handle on the financial implications of our joint purchase of the new water. I skated over the enquiry, fibbing I had everything organised. Rambo's latest question brought home other implications rather than solely financial ones. In a nutshell it meant I would have to hide my earlier confrontation with Steffi for the rest of my life. If she kept up her end of the bargain by blowing out the stunning looking, lap dancing, ex-international gymnasts, who were also bisexual nymphomaniacs I would have to keep mine. I have to say it did make me feel a tad uncomfortable – keeping a sizeable secret hidden from my best mate, one concerning his cheating live-in partner.

I had known this would be the case as soon as I had sussed what she had been up to, but now it had been confirmed, it was an issue I could have done without. Before today, Rambo and I had been through thick and thin with all cards facing upwards on the table, including my fling with Melina. And now they wouldn't be, couldn't be, because I had promised Steffi.

If Rambo's first money related question lead me to feel proportionately as uncomfortable as having been forced to wear cheap, itchy underwear, the second one was more akin to being drenched with a garden hose, having a bucket of coarse-grained sand poured down the front of your underpants and then made to run a half marathon into a stiff, cold, north-easterly headwind.

The gritty question asked was. "You know who's phoned, don't you?"

Like at any good (read 'crap') awards ceremony, I proffered my list of top three candidates in reverse order. "Carl?" I asked.

Rambo informed me, basically, it wasn't Carl, right!

"Grant?"

"Try again, boy."

"*Not* The Bait Baron?" I groaned.

"You're right, *not* The Bait Baron. 'Pup' was the correct answer," Rambo informed me. "Pup called me up a couple of minutes ago to say The Bait Baron had been on the phone five minutes earlier giving him serious grief," Rambo's voice grew concerned. "Apparently he's gone and moved the fucking goalposts and says he needs Pup to say yes to joining up soon or he's going to turn Wilton into a pair of cat skin moccasins!"

Shit! And I had *just* got set up! Not the most selfless thought ever, but you know how it is. "How long?" I demanded.

"To fit a size nine."

"I meant, how long before he guts the moggy?"

"I *know* what you meant!" Rambo barked down the phone. "Forty fucking eight hours!"

I gave my mobile a double take to make sure I had heard it correctly. "What's that mean, then?" I asked fearing the worst.

"What it means, boy, is we've got to get our arses down to the Lydd MoD range, find The Carper and then get to The Bait Baron sharpish!"

"End of session?" I whinged.

I felt I detected a hint of frustration in Rambo's voice indicating he felt similarly to me. "End of session! You'll have to wind'em in, boy," came the terse response.

I felt the clammy squeeze of pressure with the unexpected call of duty – some forty-eight hours before I had mentally settled for action – grip me tightly by the throat. I felt a hot flush wash over me. "I'll meet you back at the clubhouse as soon as," I reluctantly told Rambo. "You got the spare Glock with you?"

"No. Steffi's got it." Rambo's brain ticked over. "It might not be a bad idea to pick it up. We'll call in at my place on the way. I've got to get some other tools and gear we might need from out of the garage. We'll go in one vehicle, you can come in the van with me and we'll leave yours here."

It was one of my most disagreeable packing-up-from-a-session stints in ages. Since being a man of leisure and fishing on Hamworthy, aided and abetted by the exclusive, revolutionary, indented, dirty brown bottom bait boilie, the going-back-to-work-on-the-back-of-a-blank scenario had long been conscripted to ancient history. Now I was faced with being forced to pack in long before I wanted to the old frustrations came flooding back. In a way it emphasised what a fortunate bastard I was on a couple of crucial fronts and re-emphasised how million-to-one lucky I was to own Hamworthy and be fishing a Pup special. The fact The Bait Baron might jeopardise our source of boilies gave me good reason to clench my jaw and get on with it. Sadly, the elation of surviving Steffi's suggestion of sex had leaked out of my body quicker than a cheap flavour from a semolina/bird food mix boilie.

A grumpy Matt Williams sat next to a grim Rambo on the way up the mile-long farm track leading out of Hamworthy. As we turned on to the tarmac road I mentally remarked to myself that if he knew what Steffi had been up to, and what she had been prepared to do to prolong it, he would have been a bloody darn sight grimmer! What if I had succumbed and he had eventually found out? It didn't bear thinking about. He had let me off with Melina – Steffi, surely, would have been a different matter. Thank whatever deity – real, imagined or quantified as an object, lifestyle, material possession you wanted – I had done the right thing!

Mercifully Rambo let me sit in the van on the driveway whilst he nipped in to pick up the second shooter from Steffi, affording me the luxury of not having to suffer the anxiety of facing her.

Gloomily, as I was still on the downward spiral from earlier, I mused on the hideous notion of your wife/partner playing away with another woman. Hold on – other *women*! Although I doubted if it reflected poorly on Rambo's sexual prowess, Steffi had obviously missed the endless variety on tap generated by being involved in the adult entertainment world. A variety unavailable in a monogamous partnership with an ex-army, ex-mercenary, ex-gun running, camouflage clad (part-time) man mountain. Perhaps the least savoury part was she had never offered him the chance of a foursome like she had to me.

It was better he never knew.

Rambo flung open the van's door making me jump and, in utter disregard for every Health and Safety guideline issued, waved the Glock at me barrel first. For an instant I thought Steffi had told him a perverted version of the truth – one where I had forced myself upon her, telling her Rambo had said it was okay for her to put out for me because I had lent him half a dozen Korda flat pears – and he was going to shoot me.

"There you go, boy!" he said handing me the gun a more sensible handle first. "Seventeen slugs to go!" Rambo's tongue appeared briefly in his cheek. "But you knew that already, didn't you?"

I sort of laughed and carefully put the gun on my lap, pointing it away from my vital organs. I reminded myself, without meaning to, of the hideous exit wound on the would-be assassin's head. Ah, memories! We had some grim secrets between the pair of us – and now I had a little one all to myself. How sweet!

Rambo opened up the back of the van and chucked several huge holdalls and a rucksack into the rear. The jolt of the van's suspension hinted at weight. The back door slammed shut and Rambo jumped into the driver's seat.

"Let's hope Rick wasn't telling porkies," I said, wrestling my mind back to the job in hand, as Rambo sped off up the road. Rambo gave a brief twitch of the head to show he hoped so too. "Why do you think The Bait Baron's getting twitchy? Do you think Pimply Paul, Carl or Rick's blabbed about us."

This time Rambo gave me a full on, massive shoulder shrug. "Who knows? Perhaps The Carper's coming apart at the seams from all the stress of trying to haul out the mystery seventy! Perhaps he needs Pup's baits to help him so The Bait Baron can launch his new company on a wave of publicity. Twenty-five grand's worth of winning carp."

Not a bad shout, I thought. "I wonder what sort of bloke The Carper is?" I said. "Old school hardcore, got to be. He probably fishes three hundred and sixty-four nights a year on an Argos, tubular ratchet-framed, six black rubber bands for suspension bedchair, blanket as a bag, builder's sack of rubble as a pillow, all underneath a forty-five inch Nubroli that's been blown inside out six times, dressed in a tee shirt and shorts using no battery powered devices whatsoever! No torch, no radio, no phone, no digital camera and no alarms! I expect he's on speed to keep himself awake for twenty-four seven monkey climber observation."

"The mortar fire practise probably has a similar effect," Rambo pointed out. "Not unless he's already been blown up, in which case nothing'll wake him up!"

"Old school, fucking mental hardcore!" I stated. "I mean, there's poaching and there's poaching and then there's what this fucking nutter's up to! Ultimate poaching? Extreme poaching? *Paramount* poaching?" I shut up because I couldn't think of any more words and my perfect bound pocket thesaurus had disintegrated two days earlier.

Rambo, a man not prone to hyperbole (*hyper* poaching! That's a good one) muttered. "We'll soon find out, boy."

"Provided he's there and we can unearth him. He must be really well hidden to fish under the army's nose."

"I doubt he's sitting outside his bivvy in neon surf shorts, that's for certain, boy! He'll be well hidden, all right. Very well hidden." Rambo flicked me a glance across the gear stick. "If he *is* there, *I'll* find him," came the statement of fact.

I, for one, never doubted it for a minute. I went quiet and weighed the Glock in my hand, remembering what it felt like to have the power of an instrument of death at my disposal.

By the time we arrived at the small town of Lydd it was late afternoon. I had the Ordnance Survey map across my knees, the Glock now hidden in a pocket, and noted we had followed the B2075 from the A259, passing the tiny airport of Lydd minutes earlier. The whole district was certainly proving to be at the back of beyond, much as the map had indicated. Since leaving Ashford the countryside had turned flat and the further we headed into the marsh area the more quiet and deserted it had become. The local population looked tiny and predominantly involved in the agricultural and service industries, with, I assumed, a hefty seasonal summer boost to serve the sandy beaches not far from where we were.

The narrow road we were on, unnamed on the map, skirted the small conurbation of Lydd town centre to our right – blink and you would miss it – where a mixture of inexpensive housing lay close to the road's verge. A few derelict-looking farm buildings dotted the pancake landscape to our left. Surrounding them flocks of sheep mingled with fenced-off farmed fields, fields with horses and other areas of untouched wild ground. Driving further saw a couple of small, tired-looking local food outlets crop up, attempting to catch some of the summer trade spill-over from the nearby Camber Sands with its Pontins and caravan holiday camps. Looking into the far distance I could see the massive white blocks signifying Dungeness Power Station. A line of electric pylons, in pairs, stretching as far as the eye could see, carried the power station's output off to the National Grid.

I thought I could recall reading in a newspaper that its useful lifespan was nearly up. "I wouldn't fancy having to decommission that lot," I remarked, staring at the large, monolithic structures comprising the station. "I mean, what would they do with all the nuclear waste?"

"Dig a hole in the ground and bury it? Chuck it in the sea?" Rambo answered without looking and apparently not caring.

"There's no smoke, though! No CO2! No global warming! Good old eco-friendly nuclear power!"

(Save The Planet by using your personal consumer choice wisely. Is the product you are going to buy eco-friendly? Is its packaging both minimal, sustainable and recyclable? Does the company practise Fair Trade? Does the company offset its carbon footprint to the point of neutrality? Does the company grow the produce organically? Does the company recycle old jokes and ideas in its advertising to save the energy costs of writing new ones? And finally, is the product absolutely vital to your welfare and not a frivolous, luxury item marketed to appease your ego and to allow yourself to reflect in its gross mega-materialistic expensiveness in a manner designed to make you feel superior to people who can't afford it? If the answer is 'yes' to all these questions, then it's probably a product not worth buying.)

"Yeah, too right, boy! The only drawback is the babies that glow in the dark! No good to anyone unless you chop their fingers off and Sellotape them to your bobbins for isotopes!"

"You're a sick man, Rambo," I jokingly chastised.

As we followed the road to the range we passed a couple of army vehicles, one lorry and a jeep, driven by soldiers dressed exactly like Rambo. Secretly I doubted if any of them were tooled up with a couple of Glocks like we were. Knowing the army and their lack of resources, they were more likely kitted out with water pistols – empty ones. Summer in the UK, water shortage, massive utility bills, water pissing out of underground pipework everywhere – it all adds up when you piece it together. Joking aside, although the place wasn't exactly crawling with an army presence, it did bring it home how careful we would need to be working so close to the range. One careless mistake and we could lose the chance of finding The Carper for good.

Within another minute's worth of slow driving we came to our destination and the top end of the MoD range. This was evidently the main entrance, and a collection of differently constructed and generally poorly maintained buildings met my eye behind a mass of fencing and different access gates. All of the fences and gates were covered in MoD signs telling anyone interested enough to read them to keep out. Behind the warnings, asbestos sheet buildings mingled with what I presumed were red brick barracks. The barracks, although tired and lacklustre, were considerably newer in construction than the appalling asbestos sheet buildings – they reminded me of the crap farm buildings and outhouses we had seen earlier. In fact, the immediate effect of seeing the range was a similar threadbare feel to that of the surrounding civilian and agricultural dwellings. It was as if the two opposite walks of life had suffered the ravages of time and declined into a depressing, dilapidated downward spiral. On a more positive note, from the gates to the buildings, where the ground wasn't covered in concrete, short grass grew through what I could clearly see as predominantly shingle/sand/clay ground. This was gravel pit country!

I checked the map once again to make sure we were driving along the road bordering the range closest to where the pit was situated. This section of road meandered very close to the camp and I spotted various tiny training exercise areas designed to test the mobility and endurance of the troops. Beyond this section the road veered away from the camp and the space between it filled with a thin row of pine trees, the first sizeable trees I had seen for ages. It didn't last long and a sign, no more than three yards from my passenger window, warning of guard dog patrols indicated the road was now directly adjacent to the camp. And I do mean directly. All that lay between the road and the camp's perimeter fence was a yard's worth of long scruffy grass.

The perimeter fence was a basic wire mesh fence, posted by concrete uprights, with three lines of barbed wire running on top to a height of around seven foot. The standard warning signs we had seen at the camp's entrance were posted every hundred or so yards, but the impression was hardly one of Fort Knox. I reasoned it didn't really need to be so – who in their right mind would want to break in? Allegedly I knew of one person. Was he in his right mind?

We were down to a crawl now, both of us rubbernecking like crazy through the fence. We were now looking at the actual firing range part of the MoD site. Away from the narrow top end and its entrance, accommodation, reception and training areas, the firing range part was much more vast and more natural. A wasteland of mainly shingle predominated – normally natural and flat – occasionally pushed into shingle dunes by long departed bulldozers. A tiny snake of tarmac ran through the shingle. As we watched, a jeep drove along it – evidently on its way back to the top of the range – indicating another danger to being spotted and a cue for caution. Moving down the range, damaged houses sporadically appeared on the far side along with a walled-in area of seven or so buildings. This area had a high watchtower and either cameras or floodlights on tall columns.

"What the hell's that used for?" I asked. "And what's with the damaged houses?"

"House to house fighting, boy," Rambo answered. "The houses behind the wall are a mock-up for practising urban fighting techniques. They were built at the time of the conflict in Northern Ireland. The other houses are mortar and rifle targets, you can see the damage."

I nodded staring intently. "Not a good idea to kip in them, then?"

"No. Not a good idea."

I glanced to the other side of the road. Something had caught my eye and it was water! A swathe of farmland fanned out across the marsh on the other side of the road to the range and to the fore was a narrow gravel pit. A quick recce showed it to be devoid of anglers and any signs of swims. This was good news; we didn't want bloody carp anglers around when we were trying to break into the range! With no angler evidence on the water there really was no chance of being overlooked because the immediate area was totally devoid of dwellings. The only threat to puncturing the perimeter fence – short work with the correct tools – was passing traffic, both inside and outside the range. A facet I could see, as I had some experience in this type of thing having been embroiled with Rambo over the years, most readily negated by timing. Ruefully I booked myself in for a very early a.m. shift, one in the dark.

What I did recognise, even more fully than before, was that simply getting into the range was only the start of matters. From The Carper's point of view he'd had to surmount the logistical problems of carting enough gear for a how-long's-a-bit-of-string carping session into position and then fishing undetected under live fire for an unknown seventy. My mind boggled even more at what The Carper was allegedly attempting to achieve. Having clapped eyes on the place for myself it seemed even more incredible. No wonder they called him *The* Carper – all the rest of us were only mucking around with it! Severe, double strength, diamond-tipped hardcore! Respect where it was due, was due in skip loads if the myth became reality.

"This isn't going to be a picnic, is it?" I grumbled.

Rambo was scouring the range as he drove. "No," he answered distractedly. We carried on slowly down the tiny road for another hundred yards until Rambo pulled over. "I'm going to have a look through the glasses. I can see water."

Sure enough out through the van's window, past the perimeter fence and a half-mile away was the pit's closest margin. It was so obviously a gravel pit because the whole range now looked very similar to a huge shingle beach. Of the natural elements, pockets of yellow flowered gorse bushes dotted the shingle all over and around the water's edge a few squat trees had managed to grow – and that was it! There was nothing else! It was drum flat in some areas, undulating in others and several, huge, man-made shingle dunes reared out of the surrounding flats like a Hawaiian surfer's wave.

In truth the huge gravel pit wasn't *so* huge and although it's notoriously difficult to judge acreage the pair of us reckoned on somewhere between forty to fifty acres. Whatever, it was still head-banging big enough to try to catch *one* fish from it. Given the other obstacles I felt compelled to let out a low whistle in admiration of what The Carper was attempting

"Doesn't *exactly* look a runs water," was the only rather banal comment I could conjure.

Rambo gave me a look tinged with pity. "Looks fucking rock hard to me! *And they're not even firing* today!" Rambo got out, opened the van's sliding side door and stood on the floor pan, resting his arms on the roof and looked through his binoculars. I got out and went round to stand next to him. The binoculars moved across the range as he started to scan the water. "There's another pair in the blue holdall if you want them."

I found the pair in the smallest holdall amongst torches, radios and various hand tools. Quickly I was back out with Rambo and copying him. With everything miraculously up close through the very powerful, high quality lenses I could see sections of the far margin. Of the bits visible the water level appeared three to four foot below the level of the ground meaning the near margin remained, even when not obscured, a complete mystery.

"Anything?" I asked. I didn't really know what I was looking for regards telltale signs of a holed-up carper.

The low grunt indicated nothing of interest. Minutes ticked by. Rambo pulled away the glasses from his eyes and gave me a scrunched expression combined with a shake of the head. "He's too well hidden even if he's ensconced on the far side I can see. If he's tucked under this bank I'll never spot him." Rambo sucked his top lip. "I was hoping I could spot something to narrow down the search."

"But you can't?"

Rambo let out some air in the manner of it being a rather sore point. "No. I don't think it's even worth the effort of looking from the road on the other side, we won't see anything."

"So what does *that* mean?"

"It means we have to get in at night and walk the whole of the pit's edge to find where he's fishing."

Great, I thought, more nocturnal activity to add to my expanding repertoire. "How's he hiding his bloody rods?" I demanded, my annoyance manifesting itself in the tone of my voice. "What about casting? Baiting up? Getting food? How the fuck's he doing it?"

"He might chance it and do it very early morning when he hopes no one is around," Rambo explained. "Personally, I think he does it all at night. I think he's a good enough angler to fish as efficiently in the dark as in the light. He's dug in somewhere and somehow so he can fish undetected. As for hiding his rods... I'm not sure how he's doing that," Rambo admitted. "The only time he would *have* to come out during the day would be if he got a run."

"Food?" I reiterated.

"If we had enough time we could go up and down this perimeter fence, not necessarily on this side, maybe on the other side, and I bet we'd find an opening, or at least an opening made to look like all's intact. That's where I reckon someone drops off his food and water. One of The Bait Baron's top men, he's got to be a trusty to be so close to the truth, makes the drop at night, once or twice a week and then The Carper ferries it back to his den. It might even be The Bait Baron himself. Again, if we had more time, we could do a stake out."

"How the hell did he get established?" All I had was questions.

Rambo raised his eyebrows in respect. "With a lot of effort. Breaking in at night originally, digging out his hole over a few more nights, continually concealing it and opening it back up until it was ready to move in with his gear and start fishing." Rambo gave me a hard glare. "You've got to remember, boy, the bastard's digging in fucking shingle! Talk about instant backfill! He's had to shore it up with timber or it'd cave in. And then there's the water table! He can't go too low or his hole would fill up with water!"

"And this is after he's already put in hours and hours to fish spot and worked out the best place to fish! It's not as if he can move swims. He can't move on to fish, can he?"

Rambo nodded once. "Exactly! He must have spent days, possibly weeks, making sure he was going to set up in the right area."

"He can't have fish spotted at night," I pointed out.

Rambo shrugged. "Perhaps there are times, if you studied the place enough, you could get a few hours each morning or evening when no one else was around. Failing that, you'd have to sit up in the dark, listening for crashing fish or hope for a bright, moonlit night."

"Can *you* distinguish between a thirty crashing out and a seventy?" I asked, my mind reeling more than a lure fisherman's right hand. I was incredulous. "What flash of inspiration, *if* you can call it that, maybe 'masochism' is a better word, gave him the idea to look here in the first bloody place?"

"When we meet him you can ask him," Rambo replied with an air of finality. The time for verbal theorising was over.

"So, what's next?"

"A fish and chip supper on the beach, find somewhere to leave the van and prime ourselves for a night hunt."

"Cod or plaice?"

"You can have whatever you want, boy, seeing as you're buying!"

Chapter 15

Preparation for the night hunt went well initially – sitting in the warm, evening sun, propped against a wooden groyne watching the sea roll back and forth eating excellent fish and chips was never a particularly onerous task. Unfortunately, things took a distinct turn for the worse when an irate Sophie phoned to let me know that when she had gone to put on Amy's Tweenies DVD, a rather more graphical one had popped out of the machine.

Like an utter moron, and obviously in a state of high distraction, I had left the world's first porno carp fishing DVD in the machine. Not a smart move.

Not only did I have to fend off her indignant questioning, I had to do so without Rambo getting wind of what I had done. All her bluster about me falling into old ways, the inquisition into why I needed to watch such despicable material and her insecurity demanding to know why she alone wasn't sexually stimulating enough, became secondary when she asked which one was Steffi. I could see where this was heading and I really didn't want to go there.

"Oh, come on!" I answered.

"Have you got the hots for *her*, now? Is *she* next on your list of acquisitions? My God, Matthew, I thought we had managed to put this type of thing behind us!"

"It's not *that*!" I shouted into the phone, watching Rambo stuff a bunch of vinegar-soaked chips into his mouth from the corner of my eye. "Can we please discuss it later. I'll tell you later."

"Tell me *what*, later?"

"It's nothing to do with what you're thinking," I said, desperately trying to keep my voice level and composed. "Something's happened. There's a *reason*!" I blundered. Something *had* happened – Steffi had been a naughty girl – but it was still no reason for watching the DVD. I would have to think of some type of excuse later – although what it might be I hadn't a clue.

Thankfully, the first hint of her foot coming off the pedal made itself apparent. "And you'll tell me? Everything?"

"Of course." I hadn't promised Steffi I wouldn't tell Sophie, only Rambo.

"All right, Matt." She had calmed down a little now. "You wouldn't have wanted Amy to see it would you?"

"No, of course not. I'm sorry. It was stupid of me."

"What are you doing now?"

"Eating fish and chips with Rambo. Say 'hello', Rambo." I held the phone up to his mouth to verify I wasn't out with some floozy – a floozy named Steffi.

"Hi, Sophie. We're off on another adventure soon!"

"What's it this time?" she asked as I put the phone back to my ear.

"Helping Pup."

"Melloney says he's well stressed."

"Yeah. Hopefully he won't be when we get Wilton back."

"Is the adventure dangerous?" Sophie asked.

"She's asking if it's dangerous." I relayed to Rambo.

"Tell her only if we get blown up."

"Only if we get blown up," I told her.

"You *are* joking?"

"Sure. It's fine… I'd better get on, I'll say bye for now. See you later. Love you."

"Love you, too," she said. I think she still meant it.

"She asked if you were joking about getting blown up. Were you joking?" I said to Rambo as I stuffed my phone in my pocket.

"I always joke in the face of danger," Rambo replied, giving me a wink and a grin. "But you heard the girl in the chip shop. There's no set time for the range going live. Any time of day, any day."

"Except at night."

"So she said." Rambo resumed the attack on his chips. "What did Sophie have the hump over?"

"I forgot to put all the financial papers away, the ones I looked at this morning to check on my side of the money for Hamworthy *Fisheries*," I fibbed.

Rambo jerked his chin upwards in acknowledgement. "What have you got to tell her later?"

I stopped in mid mouth-cramming, a tiny Medusa head of chips held between thumb and index finger. It was very unlike Rambo to give me the third degree over my domestic arrangements. I cocked my hand to horizontal and used the back of it to wipe my nose. "It's…"

"I know where you were this morning, boy," Rambo stated, his voice level and uninflected. "Steffi told me."

I stuffed the chips into my mouth and over-chewed them to make sure I could swallow the greasy mouthful. "Oh," I said as casually as I could. "What did she say?"

Pulse rate up to one twenty and rising.

"She said you'd come round to visit her and made a pass at her. She said you'd been watching that DVD and wanted to play the Frans role with her."

You've probably seen novelty shop, joke eyeballs that pop out of a pair of fake glasses – the ones that boing up and down on a tiny, coiled spring? The ones that if you practise for a few minutes you can get to flick out and if you jerk your head backwards get them to ping straight back in again? Well that's what my eyes did – only on a couple of elasticised optic nerves.

She had winged it! Had to have! Her mind had invented a plausible – too fucking plausible for my liking – scenario to showpiece my philandering lust for her as a backup to me telling Rambo the truth about her. Who was the big man going to believe? The love and lust of his life, or his fishing buddy?

Not a word fell from my lips. Pulse rate, one forty.

Rambo suddenly stood up and whipped the Glock out of his pocket and pointed it straight at my head. There was that look on his face, the one from the old days, when he had fronted out Watt, flattened Spunker and snapped Rocky's arm to name but a few occasions. I saw the muscles bulge either side of his lantern jaw.

"I'm going to ask you some questions, boy," he said his voice harsh from tension. "*Don't* lie to me!"

I wanted to rush out my denial, to tell him the truth instantly – fuck whatever deal I had pledged to Steffi – but all I could do was quake! I stared at the tiny black hole, the one that could spit a 9mm trip to the cemetery.

"*Did* you go round and see her this morning?" Rambo snapped the words out. He held the Glock at arm's length, his huge hand gripping it tightly, the barrel rock solid and still aiming at my head.

"Yes, but…"

"Shut *up*, boy!" he barked.

"Did you watch the DVD first?"

Oh, shit! Trust him to be asking all the wrong questions. "Yes," I whimpered.

"Did Sophie find it and was that what she was phoning up about?"

Rambo's eyes were now doing some very funny things. His pupils were dilating like those of a cat before it pounces. My pulse rate appeared to have levelled out to flat line at one sixty. I wondered if it would soon flat line at zero.

"Yes."

Rambo's pupils pulsed as I realised – ironically – I might die even though, even *though*, I had done the right thing for once.

I prayed the next question would let me expand on my innocence.

"Did she get your cock out?"

At last indignation and a deep sense of unfairness pushed me out of my pathetic, passive state. "Oh, fuck *me*!" I blurted. "That's *not* fair! Ask the *right* fucking question!" I too staggered to my feet, fuelled by a rage I never knew existed inside me. As I did I waited for the thud of bullets ripping into my flesh. They never came. I yanked out my Glock, pointing it at Rambo's head. "Ask the *right* question!" I screamed.

"Do you think I *actually* loaded that thing with any bullets?" Rambo asked coolly. "Do you think I'd give you a loaded gun after she had just told me what had happened."

I turned my goggle-eyed stare from Rambo on to my Glock. I thought about it. "As a matter of fact I *do*!" I told him, returning my throbbing gaze back into his. "It feels the *right* weight! Like last time! When I saved *your life*!"

Christ knows what anyone – should anyone have been available – would have made of the pair of us. Standing there, on a beach, four-foot apart, discarded, not quite finished, traditional British takeaway at our feet, with two Glock 17s aimed at each other's canisters! Madness! Utter madness!

"In any case, we'll both find out, if you don't start asking the *right* questions!" I warned.

Rambo sniffed. His nostrils flaring like a bull ready to charge. "What's the 'right' question?"

"Ask me *why* she got my cock out! And why I got up and put it away!"

Rambo pulled the corners of his mouth down and considered my suggestion. "Okay, boy. What you just said."

I told Rambo the truth.

Rambo lowered the Glock, slung it on the beach and slumped back down against the groyne, picking up what was left of his fish and chip supper. "I knew something was up, boy," he told me as he emptied the crispy bits left at the bottom of his paper chip bag straight into his mouth. "The silly cow came back late a few nights when I was fishing. I wondered where she'd been."

I felt a bit stupid training my gun on a bloke sitting down polishing off chips, so I put it away and sat down next to him. "How do you know that?"

"CCTV camera on the drive. It's well hidden, much like The Carper! It records back to a video tape recorder." Rambo gave me an earnest look. "It wasn't put there for her, you understand, boy, more for any unsavoury types turning up from my chequered past."

I nodded, noticing I was suddenly feeling drained, now my heart had returned to somewhere near its normal going rate. "Right," I said not knowing what else to say.

"Were you tempted, Matt?" Rambo asked matter of factly.

I exhaled heavily. "It wasn't a lazy lob I had hiding in my pants," I admitted. "What bloke *wouldn't* be tempted? But I *didn't* succumb," I added proudly. "For lots of reasons."

Rambo wrapped his arm around me and scrunched me like an aluminium can. "You're a good mate, Matt, a good lad. I'm sorry I needed to test you under duress. It was the only way to find out for sure." Rambo gave me a grin. "I never really doubted you. Well, not much, anyway."

"So you were never going to shoot me?" I enquired, totally relieved to have been vindicated.

Rambo pooh-poohed my question. "I don't think we need to sit here wondering about who might have shot who in the head, do you? It's not important and it's over, the books relating to our life continue to be written… and the next chapter is the job we've got to do."

"What about Steffi?"

"Job to do," said Rambo pointing a finger rather than a gun. "No more, okay?" When Rambo was certain I wouldn't ask anymore silly, petty, unimportant, time-wasting questions appertaining to how close either of us were to splattering each other's brains out all over the beach, he continued. "We'll make our way back to the van, rest up, wait for nightfall, get kitted and break into the range and try and find The Carper."

"And then try and find The Bait Baron."

"Right! Focus on those two, not Steffi. You leave her to me!"

He *might* forgive her, I thought, provided he gets to go to the foursome. I knew I wouldn't have – the lying cow.

At six in the evening, as I sat frittering time away in the van, Grant phoned me. His posh voice was urgent and business-like. The foppish-haired reporter was not in the mood for chit-chat and I was reminded of his energetic wish to nail The Bait Baron and get his story on the front page. "Hi, Matt, Grant here. How are things?"

"Fine," I answered with little conviction. What the hell did he want?

"The article's put to bed. Good copy if I say so myself. The photographs look great as well. Oliver's done a top job. Make sure you pick up a copy, ya? It's as you wanted it, nothing else apart from the competition and the effect of Mr Pulimov's Prize."

"That's great. We'll definitely get hold of it this weekend," I replied, trying to sound enthusiastic.

"Any news on The Bait Baron from your end?"

"Enquiries on-going. Nothing concrete yet."

"I've been doing some digging my end, with the help of Carl," Grant told me.

"Oh," I said, as I am often prone to do.

"Ya. He's been interviewed by the police and it looks like there might be enough evidence to bring him to trial."

"He's still sticking to the line he torched the place under threat, but made sure he was seen to bring it all out in the open?"

"Ya! Absolutely!" came the public school educated voice.

"And you believe that, do you?" I sneered.

"Credit me with some intelligence, Matthew. I know it's garbage. Carl got caught. It's obvious. His lies are his way of trying to manoeuvre his arse off the line. From my point of view it makes sense for him to believe I accept his version of events."

I felt a cold chill run down my neck and I pictured Grant's bright, intelligent, dangerous eyes gleaming as he ran his hand through his washed and conditioned hair. "Yeah, of course. So what have you come up with?"

"Luckily, more than you," came the cold reply. Was Grant hinting he knew we were holding out on him, that we were being secretive and non-cooperative? That we had a couple of dozen skeletons hanging in a cupboard?

Nothing was forthcoming. "And?" I asked.

"You didn't tell me you ran a syndicate water for a living did you? Self-employed electrician, I think you'll find is what you said. Oh, yes, here it is, I've written it in my article."

Bollocks! Big style! This was leading exactly to the place I hadn't wanted. "I was one," I lamely replied.

"'Was', Matthew. Past tense."

"People get jealous, especially within carping circles," I hastily continued trying to develop a defence strategy off the cuff. "They think *they* should be the ones earning a living out of a hobby. I don't like to bandy the fact about, it only causes ill feeling." I hoped all this was sounding plausible. "It wasn't an intentional slur against you, I can assure you of that."

Grant's voice was calm, yet eerily detached. "I'm not saying it was."

"How did you find out?" I asked, trying to sound unconcerned.

"As I've already said, I've been doing a bit of digging. Carl, Tom Watt again, Paul, the oddly named Michael Kane, they mentioned other people and I've been on to them. And Pup, I went to Pup's house. It's been… enlightening."

"Anything regarding The Bait Baron?" I asked trying to push our conversation in a different direction.

"Yes," Grant answered slowly. "Look, I'm sure you're on to something in your own inimitable style, both you and Rambo, and the chances are you won't tell me what at this precise moment…"

"Something like that," I agreed.

"From what I can see so far, I'm waiting for some more specific details, I would take caution. Anecdotal evidence suggests The Bait Baron is a nasty piece of work. Very nasty."

"What makes you say that?"

There was a brief pause. "For a start, I haven't heard from Carl for over twenty-four hours. "I think he may have been abducted."

"You're joking!" I exclaimed.

"Be careful, Matthew Williams, owner of Hamworthy Fisheries, and tell Timothy Eugene Ramsbottom, or whatever he's calling himself nowadays, to watch out too!"

I heard the phone disconnect before I could ask anything else. My head span with the avalanche of new and implied information. I opened the van door and jumped out.

"Rambo!" I called, looking in panic for my soon-to-be business partner. He was fifty yards away looking into a drainage ditch, no doubt hoping to spot a fish or two. "Rambo!" I shouted even louder. I saw his head move and look in my direction.

"What?"

"The shit's hit the fan!"

Rambo jogged over. "What's happened?"

"The shit's hit the fan in so many places it's been flung all over *everything*!"

"Whoa! Calm down, boy!"

"Fucking Grant!" I started. "Been on my phone! He's fucking on to us! I swear! And he reckons Carl's been abducted!"

Rambo put both of his huge hands either side of my neck and pushed me back into the van's passenger seat. "Stay, boy!" he instructed as he shut the door and walked round the front of the van to take his place in the driver's seat. His door slammed shut. "Now! What's happened?"

I told him. His visage hardened and became more like the facial interpretation of a major thunderstorm as my recount ticked by. The last line Grant had spoken produced the lightening bolt. Rambo smashed his hands on the steering wheel – the van jolting such was the force – and then punched the dashboard, cracking the grey, injection-moulded plastic. "I'll fucking kill him!" Rambo raged. "And I'll fucking kill everyone else who opened their big mouths! I'm not letting some jumped up little twat ruin everything I've schemed and scammed so hard to make happen!" he animatedly declared. "I'll burn down his office! While he's still in it! Him and all his info! I'll destroy The Telegraph! Burn that down as well!" Rambo stopped his bender and looked me dead in the eye. "He won't do it, Matt," he said softly. "I won't let him! I'll do whatever it takes to stop him!"

If I was feeling shaken by the apparent infiltration of our collective dodgy past by a young investigative reporter, Rambo's unrealistic, eccentric, OTT re-action made me feel as if I had just stepped off a five-litre paint can, colour mixing machine. If Rambo was panicking and becoming slightly unglued, I reasoned, things must be even worse than I had thought! I tried to get a grip on it in my head and think it through logically.

"Hold on! Hold on!" I cried gesticulating with an upheld right hand. "What does he actually know?" I had Rambo's complete attention. I could tell because he stopped smashing his fists into things. "What does he *actually* know? And what is he hazarding a guess at?" I raised my eyebrows at Rambo. "Eh? I own Hamworthy Fisheries and your name might be a false one and Carl *might* have been abducted. Fuck, Carl!" We were firmly into the domain of every partnership for itself. "It's not much. Not when you calm down and think it through."

Rambo felt the stubble on his chin. It was a classic cartoon moment. He *was* Desperate Dan when he did it. "You're not wrong, boy. You might not be right, but you're not wrong."

Rambo seemed happier with this, even as I grappled with the true meaning of the words he had spoken. "You see?" I remarked. "It's not time to hit the panic button. Not yet!"

"Yet."

"I know," I conceded. "It's not a great state of affairs I admit." A hundred watt light bulb suddenly turned itself on over my head, although obviously, if I was serious about Saving The Planet I should have used an energy saving bulb in my allusion. "I'll tell you what I think. I think we need to concentrate on giving him The Bait Baron on a plate so he can get his front page article, with certain conditions, if you see what I'm getting at. In the end he didn't tell me anything concerning him. Not one single fact. Only 'he's-a-nasty-piece-of-work-so-be-careful'. How rubbish is that?"

Rambo nodded slowly and deeply to indicate his approval. "You're right, boy. One step at a time! Find The Carper, locate The Bait Baron and take it from there."

We both sat in silence. I stared out of the van's windscreen thinking all in all, it had been a pretty heavy day. Everything so far had been unforeseen – so much for the amazing psychic Matt Williams – and we still hadn't reached the big event! I glanced at my watch. At least another four hours until we would make our move. It was weird how we had been sucked into the situation we now found ourselves. How a mighty oak tree of a mess could grow from the small acorn of ridiculously allowing yourself to be talked into entering a baitboat versus casting competition!

"Steffi phoned while I was out of the van," Rambo unexpectedly offered. "Must have been around the time you were talking to Grant."

"Oh, yeah," I said not attempting to conceal the bile in my tone. "What'd she have to say?"

"Asked me if I'd confronted you with the truth. Her version of the truth."

"I hope you didn't tell her it was like Mastermind minus the chair, but with weapons!"

Rambo laughed. "No. I told her you told me your version."

"And?"

"She asked who I believed. I told her the CCTV camera never lies."

"I've got a thing about cameras and the lies they tell," I said. "Ever since we took that picture of Michael 'holding' Swansong when he was already dead."

"Swansong wasn't dead!" Rambo jibed.

"What did she have to say about being caught on the CCTV camera?"

"Cracked like a walnut and admitted the truth! Said she'd do anything by way of an apology to you. She said she panicked and what she did was… well, completely wrong. She's very sorry, Matt."

I thought Rambo had been going to say 'out of character', but had decided against it because it was patently 'in character'! "*Anything*?" I asked suggestively, pulling his leg

"That's right! Absolutely anything!" Rambo replied picking up on my nuance. "Unfortunately, I had to tell her the new, morally enhanced version of Matt Williams, as she is only too well aware, wasn't able to accept such gifts, whereas I, the morally bankrupt, Rambo, was! I told her you would settle for a personal, grovelling, verbal apology... but I wouldn't!"

"Oh, God! I saw this coming a *mile* off!" I ridiculed. "When's it happening?" I asked, even though I wasn't the slightest bit interested. No. I wasn't. Honestly.

"Soon!" said Rambo rubbing his hands together with glee. "They'll do it to keep in with her and she's got to do it to keep in with me! It's perfection." Rambo tried to look honest, only to end up looking like a second-hand car dealer or a Westminster politician asked to publicly declare their expense account. "I'm only doing it to get back at Hollywood even more!" he lied.

Something approaching jealousy stirred within my deepest darkest desires. "That could have been me!" I pointed out before I regained my composure. "Had I not been such a decent cove," I added in a pseudo posh voice.

Rambo pulled the gurning face of anguished doubt. "But would it have worked? You, the two stunning looking, lap dancing, ex-international gymnasts, who were also bisexual nymphomaniacs, Steffi… the abject horror of shitting on me and Sophie."

I expanded my chest cavity to its massive thirty-nine inch capacity. "Yeah, you're right. Not a bloody chance! I know what you're saying is true, but it doesn't stop a tiny bit of me thinking about it!"

"You've finally grown up, Matt," Rambo remarked. "You see, you're *only* thinking about it!"

I smiled. I had come to the same conclusion. "Aren't you a bit annoyed with her going behind your back? You know, with them, and then offering to go with me in order to try and hide it?"

Rambo tilted his head as if weighing up the thoughts in his brain. "I guess some leopards can never change their spots, boy." Rambo looked wistfully at the van's roof and spoke quietly, like he was talking to himself. "But they're *such* exquisite creatures!"

Chapter 16

The body armour vest fitted snugly. The notion I needed to wear one, less so. Underneath I wore combat fatigues, (Rambo knew my size and at least this set were without bullet holes) and on my head rested the crowning glory – a Kevlar helmet.

"Why take the chance?" Rambo had said.

"They're not going to be firing at night are they? The girl who works down the chip shop said so," I argued.

This was technically true, when I had plaiced our order, Rambo had chipped in with the dreaded sole-searching question – Did the range have live fire at night? The girl had replied, 'D'you want salt and vinegar?' And had then said 'No'.

On reminding him of this, Rambo had looked at me as if I had the IQ of an average white-skinned, comprehensive state school educated, sixteen-year-old male. (What's the current benchmark? Two GCSEs? One in Practical Nintendo and the other in Applied Classroom Disruption?)

"There have been enough surprises today, boy. We don't want to be underprepared for another. Besides," he said giving me a conspiratorial wink, "going in as a couple of squaddies might have other benefits."

"Like?"

"Fooling The Carper and anyone else who might see us."

"Pretending we're both proper soldiers?" I asked to see if I was reading it right.

"That's right, boy. I've an idea we can extract our info out of The Carper without resorting to more 'physical' methods by impersonating a couple of real soldiers. The same tactic might even get us out of a hole if things go badly wrong."

I didn't much like the notion of things going badly wrong, but I could see Rambo's impeccable logic. He was certainly right on all the surprises of late. There had been a bloody herd of them! On the plus side, Rambo was firing on all cylinders and I sensed, now he was over the initial Grant Gibbs rant, he was in the zone. He had told me over the years the only way to function when under stress was to compartmentalise. Lock away the individual threads of worry and focus on the immediate. Easier said than done, as I had found out with my previous endless video replays.

At the moment I was struggling to stop worrying, A) if Grant had cracked open our past, B) if Sophie would forgive me for watching the DVD, C) if our new partnership deal on Felix's water would go through safely, D) what the hell Rambo was going to do with three women in bed at once, and, E) about The Carper and The Bait Baron! I had to learn to prioritise – and fast.

By the time it was nearly midnight, I had heroically managed to haul 'E' up into the top half of the list – a play-off position, if you like. It was better than nothing. Rambo had cropped a hole in the fence mesh with a small set of bolt cutters and we were ready to go in, dressed in a manner wholly appropriate to our surroundings. As well as the dress code I had a Glock (safely stored inside a waterproof bag) and a torch. Rambo had the same plus a huge rucksack full of what he would only describe as 'goodies'. The van had been safely parked over a mile away, well off the road. The only thing left to do was get into the range and find out if The Carper was man or myth.

Rambo held the cut section of fencing away from the concrete upright and I crawled in. I was trespassing! Rambo eased himself past the mesh and stood alongside me. The warm summer south-westerly of the day had died down and a pleasant overcast night, with no hint of rain, had set out its stall for the hours of darkness.

And it *was* dark. The range was dead and black, which suited me fine, the road unlit and the farmlands and pit adjacent to it added not one single luminaire. Dark, windless, dry and silent – all fine circumstances for what we were about to embark upon. Until we started to walk!

The noise we both made seemed horrendous! The crunch of our shoes on the shingle cornered the silence, roughed it up a bit, stole its mobile phone and told it to stay put until it had gone.

"Hark at the bloody racket were making!" I hissed as we made our way in the direction of the pit. "I hope they're not using any guard dogs tonight, they'd hear us from miles away!"

"The terrain is the terrain, boy. Try and walk softly."

"Walk softly! It's all right for you with that anti-gravity pack on your back!"

"Hardly. Fifty kilos of gear." Rambo paused and pointed. "Look. There's the tarmac road."

Sure enough, only a matter of fifty or so yards in from the perimeter fence, lay the range's M25. A narrow ribbon of tarmac running through the shingle to allow access from the camp's main body of buildings and its entrance to the firing range area. We crossed it quickly as if being on it represented some kind of extra 'being out in the open threat'. The crunch under our shoes recommenced once it had been crossed.

Clearly I didn't hear the extra noise as early as Rambo. "Vehicle coming!" he said urgently. "Quick!"

Rambo darted behind a very conveniently placed gorse bush and I followed. We both dived on to the ground and turned to face the road. I could hear it *now*. 'Now' would have been far too late.

"Me and you, hiding under a bush again," I whispered sarcastically.

"Shut up!"

A camouflaged jeep, headlights on full beam, passed us by heading towards the bottom end of the range down by the coast.

"Single driver," Rambo stated.

"Good? Or bad?"

"Let's go," Rambo instructed without answering. "No torches."

We got up from our prone positions and headed off, deeper into the range and towards the pit. The shingle kept its level for a couple of hundred yards and then changed to the undulating terrain we had seen through the binoculars. A lifetime of night fishing meant I was reasonably adept at walking in the dark and I could keep up with Rambo without tripping up or barging into a gorse bush. The familiar signs of not being fit enough manifested themselves as we yomped through the energy sapping shingle, but apart from this, considering the magnitude of what I was personally attempting, I felt relatively fine.

The first shingle wave, a six foot one, proved to be a bit of a scramble to get over, especially as Rambo insisted we crawled over the top on our bellies to minimise a highpoint silhouette. As we topped the ridge Rambo told me to turn and go down the other side backwards. With us both facing back towards the way we had come, we saw ten camouflaged lorries follow the line of the tarmac road going the same way as the jeep.

"I don't like this," Rambo told me, instantly making me feel frightened. "I think we may have chosen a *bad* night!"

I said nothing, my stomach feeling suddenly hollow and sick. All my previous sensations of coping fled like bats out of a sinking hell. Damn the girl at the chip shop! She had said there were no night-time events on the range. And, if pushed, she would have probably said Elvis was working the next shift, I reprimanded myself!

"Do you think they'll be firing soon?" I asked anxiously.

"Let's hope they're setting up for an early morning start, boy," Rambo replied. "Once the sun's up and when we're hopefully out of here!"

We pressed on from the shingle wave and the terrain changed again to something we couldn't have possibly seen from the road. The landscape, although flat, had become dotted with mini-craters, some ten-foot wide and three to four foot deep. They weren't prolific, perhaps averaging one within every forty-yard diameter circle, but the first one nearly caught me out. My right leg went down much further than I had expected and in the darkness I stumbled and fell over. Rambo, who had been eating his carrots like a good boy, hadn't made the same mistake.

"Poorly aimed mortars," he informed me as I picked myself up. "I bet the far side of the range will be peppered."

Following in Rambo's footsteps this time, we pushed on to the near margin of the pit, which we estimated to lay less than three hundred yards away.

As we traversed this last section, the sickness of worry nestling in my gut became blended with the excitement of trapping The Carper in his lair. Where was he? I asked myself – *if* he was here at all. I wanted him to be. *Really* wanted him to be. I wanted him to be fishing, out of all the surreal venues you could think of, on a live

MoD range. Not only as a device to help get to The Bait Baron and rescue Wilton, but also to prove the pioneering spirit of carp fishing still existed.

The drive to surmount all of the obstacles needing to be overcome in order for The Carper to have the chance of sticking a bait under the nose of an unknown seventy were mind boggling. The 'at-any-cost' mentality, with its flagrant disregard to health, sanity and social life were gargantuan – the determination, the mindset and the tenacious willpower, awesome. If he existed, if he was here, *if* he could crack the hardest nut of all, he would definitely be *The* Carper – no questions asked. Forget Walker, Maddocks, MacDonald, Hutchinson, Yates – you put the names on the list – this was the hardest gig of all.

The hardest nut to crack – of course – being the *capture* of the unknown seventy.

Catch the unknown seventy and he would truly become the legend others had prematurely named him. Without putting the final piece of the jigsaw in its place, The Carper was simply another name on the list of valiant British failures. However gallant the attempt, a blank was always a blank and would forever pigeonhole his efforts into the hole marked 'folly'.

Naturally, us finding him could scupper his heroic plans – but I hoped not. If we found him I hoped we could dupe him into giving us what we needed and then we could leave him to fish on to the bitter end of failure or to the euphoria of success.

Either that or the smug bastard already had her sacked up and we would end up taking the bloody photos!

We reached the pit's edge.

As we had seen on the far side, the water level was four-foot down from the top of the ground. Rambo flashed a torch into the cutaway face, closer inspection showing the composition of pit to be a mixture of shingle of differing sizes, sand, silt and clay.

"Time to start searching, boy. And quickly! The dark won't be with us for long."

"Together?" I asked praying Rambo would say 'yes'.

"Yeah. I know it'll take longer, but to split up could be fatal… for you that is."

"I *am* the weakest link, and I know it," I ruefully admitted.

Rambo said nothing and moved off, following the edge of the pit up to our left, towards the camp end.

"Why this way?"

"If the fish follow a warm south-westerly that's the end The Carper will need to be fishing."

"Good thinking!" I said. At least Rambo was applying some logic in amongst the chaos.

We made our way slowly following the excavated edge, carefully checking it and the proper water margin for any signs of carping life. Fortunately, this was a relatively easy process as the excavated edge was walkable and unimpaired by any vegetation. The squat trees we had seen earlier were always rooted in the excavated face and presented no problems in terms of access. Had we been trying to repeat such an exercise on Hamworthy it would have been considerably more difficult. With its mass of greenery, trees, bankside growth and cover, more than half the margin was virtually inaccessible, certainly without a chainsaw and machete – here, on this bleak, barren pit it was the exact opposite.

In twenty minutes we had walked up what I considered to be half of one side. We had hit the pit midway up its closest margin and had moved more or less in a parallel with the road, now, as we followed a right-angled curve in the pit's shape, we were moving away from the road and even further into the range.

"This is where a south-westerly would push," informed Rambo. "This area's prime real estate."

"*If* the seventy's read the carp behaviour manual!" I replied.

We circumnavigated further. Nothing. On we pressed until we had reached the furthest limit of the pit from where we had illegally entered the range. The Carper remained as elusive as ever. On the way, the edge had turned through several ninety-degree changes of direction, first one way, then the other, then the same way again making a 'notch' shape in the pit's outline. The final turn had made a slender finger of water with the far margin and it was on this far corner we stood with nothing to show for our efforts.

Rambo stopped. "Well, that's blown my theory out of the water. He's not fishing into the prevailing wind."

"If the wind's in your face, you're looking in the wrong place," I said paraphrasing the old angling adage. "It'll be *really* great if it turns out he was thirty yards to our right from where we started!"

"I'd settle for it, boy," Rambo replied. "So long as we find him. I'd hate to think we were here on Rick's wild goose chase."

"Don't!" I said with feeling. "Being duped by a Watt family member would be too bloody much!"

"He *must* be fishing to a feature," Rambo hypothesised.

I looked down the vast expanse of slate coloured sheen stretched out before me in the night. I had never seen a more featureless place on earth.

Rambo, amazingly, by use of Delkim receiver box technology, caught my thoughts. "An underwater feature," he explained. "A bar, a plateau, a natural food source, something strong enough to make fishing to it the banker swim rather than going on the prevailing wind."

"Come on," I said tiredly. "Let's get on with it. I don't want to be here any longer than necessary."

With no alternative to the long painstaking game of walking the entire margin we started off once again. We were now walking the visible section of the pit's far margin – from the road by binoculars – which Rambo had scoured yesterday. With each crunching step I started to feel less inclined to believe there was a solitary, mad soul carping the venue. Perhaps The Carper was a myth perpetuated by the manipulative Bait Baron. A figure dreamt up to inspire and galvanise his minions, a tool by which he sought to control and influence the gullible and easily impressed. At least those dumb fuckers weren't out in the middle of the night, risking life and limb looking for him! And if they were dumb fuckers, what the hell did that make Rambo and I?

As we trudged on I began to notice a distinct lessening of the gloom. A quick look up revealed the reason why. The cloud cover had broken up and the moon, a waxing half-moon, was reflecting some of the sun's rays on to us.

"Look," said Rambo. "Over there."

I looked to my left and saw rows of inky, black shapes, the shapes of old tanks, jeeps and lorries – ghost vehicles for a ghost army – strewn over the range.

"Targets," Rambo told me. "Filled with sand."

As I tried to distinguish the targets by virtue of the moonlight, out the corner of my eye I caught a line of orange dots radiating from the bottom end of the range, snaking across the far corner of the pit and heading towards more distant inky shapes. The unmistakable sound of gunfire followed an instant later.

"Tracer bullets!" Rambo barked. "Quick! Down into the margin!"

I don't think I had ever moved so fast in my life. I literally dived down the four-foot drop to the water's edge, the impact of my leap jolting my face into the wet, sandy shingle. I wiped coarse grains from my lips and spat, righted my askew helmet and gawped at the spectacle.

Wave after wave of orange dots and lines flew across the bottom section of the pit, the section we hadn't yet walked. The whole show was strangely bewitching and I had to keep reminding myself each eerie dart of orange light was instant death.

"Machine gun tracers," Rambo told me. "Every one in four rounds is a tracer, except from the furthest gun, he's the lead gunner and all his rounds are tracers. The other two are using him as a marker. See! See how his tracers make more of a line than the others."

Hypnotised by the pretty, orange blurs of death, I could see what Rambo was getting at. One set of bullets was almost a long, orange snake as it dud-dud-dudded its arsenal of destruction out into the night, the other two lines were more punctuated.

"How come they seem to start off slow and then speed up?" I asked in confusion. And there was something else very strange. "They seem to be starting out over the water! Surely they haven't got guns afloat on platforms! That's not the kind of feature you were on about!"

"The slow fast effect is an optical illusion, a well-known one, for those on the receiving end of tracer fire," Rambo calmly answered. "The tracer bullets have a delay element so the enemy can't trace *you*! Tracers work both ways! The phosphorous or magnesium, the thing that gives them their glow, is set to start one to two hundred yards from the gun's barrel. That's why it looks as if they're firing from the water. In reality the guns are much further back... They're probably using a 7.62 GPMG," Rambo said to himself rather than to me.

"I wonder if The Carper is anywhere near that lot. He's probably returning fire with his catty telling them to keep the noise down!"

Fuck knows why I was joking. It was most likely a nervous response. And if my eyes were to be believed it was time to get even more so. "Shit! They're coming up closer!" I screamed.

Rambo had seen it as well. "You're not wrong, boy. Keep well down! Let's hope the fucking gunners are good and don't drop their aim too low!"

The orange snakes and dots wormed their way up the pit, getting closer and closer as the gunners angled their fire further up the pit.

Dud-dud-dud-dud-dud. Dud-dud-dud-dud-dud. Dud-dud-dud-dud-dud.
Dud-dud-dud-dud-dud. Dud-dud-dud-dud-dud. Dud-dud-dud-dud-dud.
Dud-dud-dud-dud-dud. Dud-dud-dud-dud-dud. Dud-dud-dud-dud-dud.

Rambo and I were flat on our bellies, lying in the very edge of the water. I felt its cold ingress soak up my right sleeve. This was horrendous! I cocked my head out from underneath my Kevlar helmet to see the orange flashes now virtually overhead, a distinctive whine accompanying each bright blur of colour. And then it stopped.

"Out of ammo," came the voice from the horizontal body next to me. "Hundred round disintegrating link belt! Don't fucking move a fucking muscle!"

"Oh!" I moaned. "And I was just going to take my helmet off and sit up on the bank and have a fag!"

Dud-dud-dud-dud-dud. Dud-dud-dud-dud-dud. Dud-dud-dud-dud-dud.
Dud-dud-dud-dud-dud. Dud-dud-dud-dud-dud. Dud-dud-dud-dud-dud.
Dud-dud-dud-dud-dud. Dud-dud-dud-dud-dud. Dud-dud-dud-dud-dud.

The barrage started again. Please, God, don't let me die! Please, God, don't let me die! Please, God, don't let me die! (He must hate me. I only ever recognise Him when I'm up to my neck in the shit!)

A deeper, whooshing whistle sound manifested itself out of the night.

"Mortar! Incoming!" Rambo cried.

It's all right for you, I callously thought. You've got the experience, what with giving me a running commentary on what might rip my guts out from their puny packaging in the next few seconds.

"Why the fuck didn't we walk round the other way?" I whimpered as a much heavier impact thudded into the ground somewhere too close for comfort. "We'd have covered this bit by now and been round the safe side!"

"Shut the fuck up!" Rambo ordered, who, on reflection, was possibly dealing with a few memory revisits he could have done without.

The next heavy thud was really close. A spray of shingle fell on top of us and splattered into the water. The ripples made the water soak up my sleeve a little more.

"Fucking hell! What the fucking hell are they aiming at? There's fuck all to aim at near here!" Although not particularly lucid, I felt I got the gist of my point across.

Rambo agreed. Stress wracked his voice. I *so* knew he was thinking he didn't want to die and miss out on a foursome! "Fuck knows! The mortar team are useless!

Crawl! Crawl! Let's go!"

We crawled like snakes down the margin, machine gun fire and mortar fire winging its way over our heads. But not by much. Another lousily aimed mortar round – don't they teach basic trigonometry in the army any more – smashed into the ground less than thirty yards away. It rained shingle, lumps of it dropping on to my back and legs. Fuck this, I thought. If I needed the experience I could go and see Saving Private Ryan again in Dolby 5.1 Surround Sound and chuck popcorn up in the air for a limited – and much safer – physical effect.

The fact of the matter was, I realised with blinding insight, without the cover of the four-foot drop to the water's edge, we would have been in disastrous trouble, deep shit, dire straits and Dickie's Meadow. As it was one more mortar round dropping a bit shorter and it would be curtains. Rambo, *if* he survived, would have to borrow The Carper's landing net to scoop my legs back. I presume you can get a thirty-four inside leg into a forty-two inch net.

The prospect of my legs floating in the margins made me panic and I started to crawl so fast I clambered on to the back of Rambo's legs.

"Calm down, boy! You don't need to hitch a ride!" he protested.

I was gone, mentally, and scrambled even faster. At one stage I was completely on top of Rambo's rucksack, crawling on him whilst he crawled along the ground. The sensation was that of a tardy airline passenger hurrying for a last gate call, walking along the moving belt walkway – only without the live crossfire.

I thought I heard Rambo say 'Fucking hell, boy!' as I pushed off from his helmet with my right foot – starting-block style – in an attempt to gain extra purchase in the sacred cause of trying to get away from everything faster. My arms, doubled up stumps with elbows acting like an amputee lizard's front feet, pumped in frantic alternation, my legs squirming manically behind, seeking grip on a non-grip surface. I *had* to get away. On and on I crawled until the outline of one of the squat trees dotted around the margin loomed into my letterbox slot of vision between the ground and my helmet rim. I tucked my head down, manoeuvred further out into the water, and without slowing, pressed on under the tangle of branches.

Cold water raced through my armour vest and fatigues as the water deepened. My face nose-dived and my right leg began to do a lame attempt at a breaststroke kick as the margin shelf dropped steeply away to a depth unknown – only my left leg stopped me from going under. I quickly grabbed branches with both hands to stop me sinking and pulled myself round, branch to branch, hand over hand, in a manner similar to what the squaddies – who were now engaged in the very personal act of trying to kill me – must have practised on the elevated ladder in the exercise area.

With a body nearly vertical and the cold water giving me the physical equivalent to a smack round the face, I looked out over the water as I heaved myself around the tree. The orange bullets flew over my right shoulder. I was getting there! I was getting under the fire. I dragged myself further forward with the pull of my right hand and my left foot re-engaged with something solid. I praised my lucky stars. A large branch was in my way, one running out at water level, one I would have to go under rather than over. I held my breath and dunked below the surface, pushing myself back up when I thought I was clear. I emerged back into air. I had judged it okay, only a few more skinny branches and I would be back at the foot of the excavation. I put my head down and bulldozed them out of the way, the sound and sensation of the branches scrapping against my helmet filling my mind. I was crawling once more, and soon was up on to the shingle and dry land.

I suddenly remembered Rambo.

I turned my head with difficulty to make out his helmet bobbing up on my side of the big branch. He was fine and the bullets, I noted, were well down the range, which was even finer. My panic attack subsided a fraction. The lack of overhead ammunition and the cold slap of total immersion in water had made me take stock. I stopped crawling and waited for my partner.

"Jesus, boy!" Rambo commented as he edged his large body alongside mine. "What came over you?"

"The fear of death."

"Always a nifty motivator," Rambo admitted.

A mortar exploded some way behind us. I had hardly finished grimacing when out in the pit I heard a crash.

I looked out into the water and saw a mass of ripples emanating from an epicentre a tad over a hundred yards away to the front of us and around eighty yards out from the bank.

"Christ! They're aiming even fucking shorter!" I blurted, whisking my head back to confront my crawling buddy as if it was his fault.

Rambo lowered his head from looking out into the pit and glared at me. "It *wasn't* a mortar!" he said slowly. "Much too big… or not big enough!"

"What?" I said not understanding.

"They're using contact fuses. When the mortar hits the deck that's what makes it explode. If one went into the water there's a good chance it wouldn't detonate, so, too big a splash. If it did go bang on hitting the water, or if it had enough impetus to detonate when it hit the bottom, the splash wasn't big enough."

I yanked my head around to look out into the pit. "So what the *hell* was it?"

Rambo's gaze had followed mine. "I can only think of one thing."

I was on message. We both looked down into the pit. Dud-dud-dud-dud-dud. Dud-dud-dud-dud-dud. Dud-dud-dud-dud-dud. Dud-dud-dud-dud-dud. Dud-dud-dud-dud-dud. Dud-dud-dud-dud-dud. The machine guns were off again. I ignored them and willed it to happen again, wanting to see what had made the crash more than anything I had ever wanted to see in my life – including several women (okay, a lot of women) with no clothes on. The deep thud of another mortar launching wafted over the pit, shortly followed by the thumping explosion of it landing.

Come on! Come *on*!

And then it happened.

In the soft moonlight, barely ten yards from the spot it had happened first time, a *mahoosive* carp, the biggest I had ever seen – and remember (how could you forget?) I've caught a sixty – surged out of the dark water. For a majestic split second its phenomenal flank hung in mid-air before she smacked back down into her watery home.

A leaping leviathan like no other!

I turned to Rambo, his eyes glinting like hard chips of granite. We had found the feature!

"I bet my bollocks another set of eyes has seen that!" I stated.

"Me too, boy!" said Rambo, his voice riddled with elation. "If he's half the angler I think he is, he's dug in just down there," Rambo stretched out a sodden arm pointing the way we were facing. "On the money and on the spot, only a hundred yards away!"

Chapter 17

Despite the discomfort of being wet through and of starting to feel cold, I was burning inside. The Seventy existed! And if The Seventy existed then so surely did The Carper! I wouldn't have to wait long to find out.

Rambo and I edged down the margin on our saturated bellies. Machine gun bullets flew over the top of the pit far behind us, mortar fire cascaded down to our rear, but fascination lay in front of us. He had to be there!

"The other side of the tree," Rambo whispered as we crawled in tandem. "I bet he's holed up the other side of the tree."

Now only fifty yards away stood the tree to which Rambo was referring. Rooted in both the margin and the almost vertical bank of the four-foot excavation, it was a similar tree to the one the pair of us had recently struggled through. However, by a quirk of nature this tree was much more robust, it had a greater number of branches and they were much heavier and more densely foliated. To plough through it looked nigh impossible, certainly without making a lot of noise – noise that may or may not be heard by a secret angler who may or may not have been dug in on its other side. It was more than we dare to shine a torch through the mass of wood to try and locate him because, despite the moon making an appearance, there was still insufficient light to confirm his existence.

Halted, we lay on our sides tucked up against the extremities of the tree's longest branches. I was at a loss as to how we should play our hand given the circumstances.

"What now?" I hissed at Rambo.

"It's perfect timing!" Rambo replied in a low voice. "Couldn't be better! He must have seen The Seventy crash! He's bound to be sitting up all night watching the water. He'll be thinking this is his *big* chance! We confront him now, he'll tell us *anything* if we offer the carrot to allow him to carry on fishing!"

I nodded vigorously, my helmet wobbling in time. Rambo's logic appeared impeccable – not unless The Carper was a Noddy and was fishing the other side and The Seventy was an habitual night-time crasher, the act meaning little in terms of catchability. I didn't believe either scenario.

"Yes!" I quietly concurred. "Good point." I shivered. I was starting to feel really cold, yet I was determined to see out the night's events to a successful conclusion. "How are we going to get to the bastard?"

"We'll have to go over the top," came the reply. "Or swim round."

"I don't want to get back into the drink. I'm frozen now," I admitted. "Not that I fancy sticking my noggin above the parapet very much."

Rambo dismissed my concerns. "We'll be fine. The fire's all up the other end. If we're quick we'll be round in seconds."

Rambo waited for my answer. "Over the top it is," I told him somewhat reluctantly.

"Good, boy! Get your Glock out of its waterproof bag and we'll go."

I did as instructed. Rambo took off his rucksack and hoisted it up on to the top of the higher ground, pushing it tight into the tree. He took out his Glock, waggled its barrel to indicate I should follow and he climbed up and over the excavated face. Cheerfully, to coincide with this action, a new burst of machine gun fire spat its way across the pit.

I saw Rambo's boots disappear. It was my turn. I stood up and pulled myself up on to the higher ground. What must it have been like to do this for real, I wondered? To go over the top into a barrage of hateful machine gun fire intended to kill you rather than to plug decrepit, sand-filled vehicles. All those young boys, some only seventeen years of age, slaughtered at the Somme and Passchendaele during WWI, on the beaches of Normandy and the Pacific Islands in WWII. It was a sobering thought. And, here tonight, we were still practising, I reminded myself, still practising to kill people. The setting for world conflict and the nature of the enemy had changed, but the smack of a bullet, when it came, would feel no different.

This last assumption was pure conjecture on my behalf – not having had the experience – and most definitely one *not* on my 'to do' list!

Shivering with cold and fear, but eager to trap The Carper, I clambered up and over the top. Once there, I crawled as fast as I could after Rambo. Rapidly the pair of us skirted around the tree, the haze of orange dots still darting up to the top end of the pit. I was a good four yards behind Rambo and I kept my distance, not wanting to repeat the piggyback charade of earlier. Rambo soon stopped abruptly and held out a flat hand on a straight arm stretched back towards me. My heart thumped a little harder, no mean feat considering the entry level at the time. Had he spotted him? Two flicks of Rambo's fingers indicated it was time for me to pull up alongside. I could barely contain my excitement and crawled at a pace, I believe, technically termed 'at the double'.

Rambo put his left index finger to his lips and then pointed, thrusting his digit at the ground a few feet further on. I narrowed my eyes and, thanks to the moonlight, saw the top of The Carper's lair. I shook my head in veneration.

There, under several branches radiating back from the water, was what I can only describe as a Realtree shingle groundsheet. Although obviously not made by Realtree, unless their new catalogue was going to have some *serious* surprises, there lay a bespoke shingle-pattern camouflage sheet made to the highest specification. Covered on three edges by real shingle to blur its outline, the sheet was approximately two yards square and incredibly realistic. It had been meticulously made and meticulously placed in position. When I'd had chance to absorb this, Rambo pointed something else out to me, its ingenuity as staggering as its deployment.

A large branch ran out from the tree along the line of the edge of excavation, exactly where the flat groundsheet turned down through something approximating ninety degrees to become the face of the four-foot drop. The branch's positioning hadn't happened via the course of nature. On closer inspection with a carefully shielded torch, the branch had been cut back at the tree's trunk, mitred and nailed so as to follow the line required. A square edged ground sheet, with some type of lintel supporting it underneath, turning downwards, wasn't a good look for someone intent on hiding. The branch, tight to the ground/groundsheet cunningly disguised the clean, unnatural, right-angled aberration.

Rambo signalled for us to move. We both crawled around the back of the groundsheet, giving it a wide berth, and eased ourselves back down the drop-off to finish sitting hunched on the margin's edge a few yards away from the lair. From this lower vantage point I could make out the turn of the groundsheet underneath the branch. From there it hung down to the margin's shelf, its two sides embedded in real shingle. A couple of lower branches run across The Carper's opening completing the illusion of undisturbed normality. I didn't doubt they too had been 'adjusted' to run at the optimum height and angle.

My brow furrowed – how did The Carper get in and out? In the gloom, by craning my neck, I searched for access clues and eventually spotted one. A Velcro seam ran down the middle of the vertical groundsheet, the pattern of shingle and sand – different to the horizontally flat pattern I had seen above – matched both halves perfectly with all the precision of wallpaper hung by a master decorator.

As the machine gun fire dud-dud-dud-dud-dudded across the pit, I took the chance to ask Rambo a few whispered questions. "Where the fuck are his rods? And how's he watching the water?" Rambo said nothing. "Do you think he's even *in* there?"

Rambo continued to ponder these important questions and, on not being able to answer them to his satisfaction, resorted to the only course of action he knew – *action*, action! "Get your gun and torch ready! We're going to storm his hole!" he hissed vehemently. Glock first, Rambo crawled up to the vertical groundsheet, paused, then tore at the Velcro strip, ripping the two halves asunder.

"All right! The game's up!" he shouted, pointing his gun into the black aperture caused by the divided groundsheet.

"Don't shoot! Don't shoot!" I heard an alarmed voice cry.

The Carper was at home, but apparently not expecting visitors!

Tantalisingly, *I* still couldn't see him. All I could make out was Rambo's arse poking out of a pair of shingle camouflage curtains now he had wriggled his upper body through The Carper's front door. The arse disappeared and seconds later Rambo's head popped back out into what little moonlight there was. "Well, are you coming in, private, or are you going to stay outside in the gunfire all night?"

Keen to get inside and see The Carper, yet thinking somewhere along the line the spatial dynamics didn't seem to add up – unless The Carper was fishing inside a

TARDIS – I accepted Rambo's invitation. Eager to glimpse the man behind the elaborate fishing hole and outrageous carping campaign, I burrowed my way in, my excitement similar to a six-year-old entering Santa's Grotto. At last I was going to set eyes on The Carper!

The scene greeting my eyes as our torches lit up the interior of The Carper's lair was even more staggering than the cunning deception I had beheld outside. Crawling through the Velcro opening I was dumbstruck by the bizarre scene before me.

The Carper was fishing in a TARDIS – of sorts!

I had immediately crawled over The Carper's landing net, lying as it was, poised for combat, directly the other side of the two camouflage flaps. To my left were The Carper's three rods; they were set on short banksticks combined with miniscule buzz bars topped out with Delkim receiver heads. The buzz bars were so narrow two of the reel arms had to be folded up into their 'packed away' position to fit on them – no 'wide load', albatross-style spacing for The Carper! Amazingly, the rod tips, angled down on a slight gradient, stopped just short of the shingle groundsheet opening and were almost touching the ground. Detailed inspection revealed the line running from them carefully hidden by a tiny covering of sand until, presumably, they safely entered into the pit's water. With the tips ending just short of the camouflage sheet opening it meant The Carper's three, twelve-foot, two-piece carbon rods stretched way back into the dugout. The tip section was under the flat part of the groundsheet – a headroom of around three and a half feet – whilst the butt section disappeared into a strutted and supported rear section with only two-foot six of headroom.

The two-foot six headroom section ran much wider than the front opening and went back even further than the distance required to accommodate the length of the rods. At its rear, behind the rod butts, was a bedchair with adapted cut-down legs, complete with pillow and bag. A rucksack, cooking apparatus, spare clothing and a pile of tinned food were stacked to the side of the pillow end. A void, currently occupied by Rambo, completed the 'L' shape design. Four by two struts supported inch-thick marine ply throughout the whole area not underneath the camouflaged sheet. Similar marine ply shuttered back the shingle and made the dugout's walls.

Wedged in between a couple of struts in the clear area to the right of the opening, lay Rambo. On the aforementioned bedchair, lying on his back, appearing to fiddle with a rosary bead necklace made up of 10mm fluoro pop-ups, was The Carper.

There was more room than I imagined there ever could have been from the outside, but 'more room' was a relative concept. I found it hard to imagine the time and effort and exactly how The Carper had excavated his underground bivvy bunker. Imagining the gritty – good pun – reality of fishing a long session within its confines proved even more daunting. The darkness, the claustrophobia, the isolation and the restriction of movement were bad enough, let alone having to put up with the frequent live fire, wondering if the next thud or whine was going to separate you from life itself! Whatever demon/obsession/compulsion drove The Carper to go to such lengths was, in its way, heroic. The shadowy figure of nervous energy lying on a cut-down bedchair, a sheet of marine ply inches from his nose, was some angler. No doubt.

"Been quite the little *mole*, hasn't he, private?" said Rambo shining his torch directly at The Carper's profile.

The picture in my mind was one of a rabbit getting caught, fluffy arse on a white line, by the halogen lights of a fast-moving, luxury car driven by a maniac. The Carper looked shit scared – his rosary bead fiddling becoming faster and more frenetic. It remained to be seen whether he was plain shit scared, or shit scared of losing the opportunity to bank The Seventy.

"You're not wrong, Sarge! Some den!" I replied keeping up the pretence we were genuine soldiers whilst shining my light on the marine ply with all the reverence of an architect inspecting a splendid cathedral ceiling.

"Now all we need to know, boy," Rambo asked threateningly, diverting all his attention on The Carper. "Is what the fuck you're doing here?"

I shone my torch on The Carper to add to the pressure. "I'm *fishing*!" he exclaimed. He stopped fiddling with the fluoro pop-up, rosary bead necklace (he had probably completed his five decades of Hail Bait Barons) and held out his hands. "Look at all this!" he said moving his hands around the confines of his hidey-hole in a gesture hinting we should take a look at the equipment surrounding us.

I thought he sounded desperate. *Very* desperate. The edge in his voice hinted at something much more than having been discovered. I concluded this must mean he was aware The Seventy had crashed out in front of him only minutes earlier. How he knew this golden nugget of carp fishing information remained a mystery.

"Of *course* you are!" Rambo sneered caustically.

The Carper struggled off his bedchair and approached me on his hands and knees.

"Easy, boy!" Rambo warned, levelling the Glock. "One iffy move and you're dead!"

Once he was up close and my torch could fully expose his features, I had my first decent look at the legend known as The Carper. I was convinced he was a man in his mid-thirties – a man in his mid-thirties who unfortunately happened to look as if he was in his late forties! Staring at the myth, who had recently become a real living, breathing man, I could see the reasons for the aura of premature aging, the most striking of which were his heavily bagged eyes and sagging eyelids. These four small bellies of skin gave the impression gravity had played an especially mean and long-winded hand on his visual perception organs. Both eye bags appeared heavily cross-hatched with a 6B pencil and the sagging lids above attempted to narrow and half close the haunted, brown eyes beneath them. To complete the look of premature aging, grey stubble smothered drawn, tired, line-etched, pasty cheeks. Framing the gaunt visage, greasy dark hair – so hideously untidy, uncut, unwashed, ungroomed, uncombed and unkempt I was momentarily reminded of Grant in a diametrically opposite recollection – hung lank to his collar. Grubby, stained clothing, two sizes too large for the body they enveloped, drooped from The Carper's frame making him a prime candidate for 'Mr Before' in an advertising campaign promoting male muscle development.

Chaffed and cracked lips parted. "I *am*! I'm *fishing*!" he implored directly to me. "Why wouldn't you believe me?"

"'Mole' has two meanings," I heard Rambo say with sinister inflection. "It's better if you play straight with us, boy. So… what Islamic fundamentalist faction is bankrolling you?"

"*What!*" The Carper turned away from me to face the ominous voice from the alcove. "Don't you understand? I'm fishing! Look at all my gear! What could I spy on stuck in here?"

"Bollocks! There's no fish in that pit! Not *one*!" Rambo derided.

"Oh, yes there *is*!" replied The Carper with rising tone certainty. "There's one. Just one. The *One*."

I had to stop myself blurting out 'We call it The Seventy!' "This isn't 'The Matrix', mate." I heard myself say instead. "This is serious."

"Look! Wait!" The Carper said in a voice bordering on hysterical. He turned round and scrabbled back to his rucksack and started to rummage in it. Rambo trained both his torch and his gun on his back. "Look at this! This'll prove what I'm saying!" The Carper crawled back and thrust a handful of glossy seven by fives at me. "They're all of me with fish I've caught over the years, going right back to when I was a teenager!"

I shone my light on the photos and skimmed through a muddled mess of non-chronologically ordered snaps of 'carp angler holding carp'. There were loads of good chunks in amongst them and it was obvious the set of prints constituted The Carper's entire photographic c.v. As with most of us, the more recent fish tended to be of better quality, although I doubted any of them meant more than the low double – probably a first – held by the The Carper when he was barely fourteen.

One of the photos had a fish looking to be easily over fifty – the nice, dark, ancient looking mirror had immediately caught my attention. A fifty, I thought dismissively. Big deal! I felt a sudden compulsion to tell him I had once caught a *sixty* before I quickly choked it down in order to maintain the charade of my impersonating a soldier. Getting to grips with my carping ego, I turned my attention to the angler holding the fish and perused him. The Carper looked much younger in the photo and I was curious to know when he had caught it. Casually I flicked it over to see if there was any info on the back. There was – the figures '56-12' and '16/5/2006' were written in the top left-hand corner in biro. No way! Was the image overleaf really him from only *two* years ago? I checked – it *was*! The shape of the nose, the mouth and the eyes – it was the same person! Jesus H Christ! Two years ago! The handsome, dashing, tanned man in the photo looked the best part of twenty years younger and two stone heavier than the pale, wizened wreck kneeling on all fours before me.

I passed it to Rambo. "Take a look for yourself, Sarge."

Rambo took a look and must have thought much the same as myself. However, he kept his inner feelings concealed.

"That's not you!" Rambo lied. "That's someone else. It's someone younger, better looking and heavier built," he remarked tossing the photos on to the ground with disdain. "All this is *bullshit*! Backup in case you get caught!" Rambo voice turned to stone. "Are you directly in touch with Bin Laden's group? Or, yeah, maybe I'm barking up the wrong tree here… are you working for the Chinese?"

A mortar thumped into the ground. It was the first one I had noticed since we had entered The Carper's lair.

On his knees literally and on his knees mentally, The Carper winced at the sound and went into defensive hyperdrive. "It *is* me and I *am* fishing for The One! It's a huge great carp! A mirror that weighs over seventy pounds! If you two had been looking out into the pit half an hour earlier you'd have seen it jump out of the water! Right out in front of where we are!" The Carper's mouth had a build up of white froth in the corners as he frantically tried to convince us.

"How did you see it, stuck in here?" I asked. I really was rather interested.

"Wide-angle lens binoculars," The Carper replied. "I had them specially made. There are two hinged cut-outs set at the correct spacing in the left-hand flap. I saw *you* as well. That's when I went back to my bedchair. I prayed you wouldn't see the entrance…" The Carper's voice lapsed into despondency as I swivelled my head round to find the two keyhole type flaps covering two circular cut-outs in the vertical groundsheet. So that's how he watched the water!

Another mortar thumped in even closer than before.

The Carper instinctively flinched and put his hands up to protect his face. "That's *me* in all the pictures!" he proclaimed once he realised he hadn't been blown to kingdom come, his spirit of defiance and obsession flooding back to recharge his defences. "I might have aged a bit and lost weight since I caught the fifty. So would you if you'd been fishing this place for five fucking months! Bombs! Bullets! The constant fear of being found out! No sunlight! Junk food! Shitting in a bucket! I can't even walk about! I only get to stand up for a few hours at night. Is it any wonder I've gone downhill physically!" The Carper speedily wiped his mouth with the back of his hand. "Don't you *understand*? This is my chance! *Tonight*! I know she's feeding and she's out there right now over the top of my baits! The Carper began relating the cost of getting within shouting distance of an unknown seventy. "Five month's solid fishing without a bite! Stuck in this dungeon! A year's worth of preparation before that! Finding this place, forever watching the water in hope and then after months and months of time, seeing her! Seeing The One! And then setting out to try and catch her." Again The Carper waved his arms around. "Digging out all of this, getting it all set up! The effort! This has been my *life*! Been my life to try and achieve the capture of a lifetime." The Carper's eyes widened. "She's the biggest carp in the UK, but above all else, you wouldn't understand this, you see, she's *unknown*! Un-

fucking-known! All the other big fish have got names, have been caught by lots of different people, had their pictures splashed all over the magazines!" The Carper stopped. "*Not* this beauty! She ticks *every* box."

"It's got a name. The One. You called it that earlier!" said Rambo.

"Named by me and no one else because hardly anyone else knows! There's a *mighty* difference!" The Carper answered. He was into it now, trying to convey the epic nature of his struggle. "The other thing is, I've been using a new bait this last week," he suddenly revealed. "I *know* it's going to do the business!" The Carper started to fiddle with his fluoro rosary beads. "I'm *so* close! I'm *begging* you! *Don't* stop me now!" The Carper instinctively reached out and laid one hand on my leg. "You're all wet!" he said, puzzlement clouding his face for an instant before he was back on track. "Let me stay and catch her! *Please* let me stay and catch her! Then you can chuck me off. Arrest me! Do what you have to do. But *please* give me some more time!"

"What sort of bait?" Rambo asked. "And how did you get it?"

"I use things called 'boilies'," The Carper keenly explained, mistaking Rambo's interest as a sign of an opening. "Round balls of special flavoured carp food. I'll show you my new ones." The Carper went back to the stash of stuff near his bedchair and dug out a bag of the boilies. He gave one to Rambo and one to me. I looked down in bewilderment at our exclusive, revolutionary, indented, dirty brown bottom bait boilie, which instantly became our non-exclusive, revolutionary, indented, dirty brown bottom bait boilie.

"How did you get it? How do you get your supplies, your food and water?" Rambo managed to ask in a remarkably controlled tone.

"At night. At midnight, always at midnight. A friend brings me my supplies up to the fence by the road, the road that runs round that side of the range." The Carper jerked a thumb towards the road opposite to the side Rambo and I had used. "I've cut the fence by a big warning sign, but faked it to look untouched. I sneak out and meet him and cart it all back."

"What friend?" Rambo asked. He was like a dog with a favourite bone now.

"Not so much a friend," The Carper admitted. "More of a sponsor."

"A sponsor?" said Rambo gnawing on the end of a human thighbone.

Dud-dud-dud-dud-dud. Dud-dud-dud-dud-dud. Dud-dud-dud-dud-dud.
Dud-dud-dud-dud-dud. Dud-dud-dud-dud-dud. Dud-dud-dud-dud-dud.
Dud-dud-dud-dud-dud. Dud-dud-dud-dud-dud. Dud-dud-dud-dud-dud.

The machine gun fire seemed louder and I thought I heard the whine of the bullets again. The Carper blinked at every dud. No wonder his eyelids had gone all saggy, all the blinking on live fire exercises had stretched the skin and he was blinking so hard he had compressed the skin underneath creating bags in the style of Mr Gladstone!

"He makes the baits, I use them and he gives me a financial package. It's not a bad package... until you work out the hourly rate, then it looks a bit crap," The

Carper admitted. "I am putting in a one hundred and sixty-eight hour week, you know." The Carper shrugged. "The truth is, I'd do it for nothing. I *love* it! They, other anglers, call me 'The Carper', you know. If I can catch this fish on his baits we're both made for life. The angling press, *all* the press, will lap it up!" The Carper told us, his animation kicking in quicker than a Disney Studio cartoonist. I didn't miss the reference to the impact of Pulimov's Prize – someone was keeping him abreast of recent developments in the outside world! "I'll be carp fishing's first media superstar! My own show, my own column, my own tackle consultancy deal! I'll be like David Beckham! I'll be a real carping celebrity when the world knows what I did to catch a fish."

"And your friend?" asked Rambo.

"He'll be able to say the biggest ever carp caught in this country was hooked on his baits!"

"He made these ones?" I asked trying to pull The Carper back into a world I wanted to know about.

The Carper shook his head. "Not personally. You don't have a dog and bark. He's the man behind the company, though. He's the brains who…"

The Carper was cut short by his middle rod giving out a couple of bleeps, the noise coming from the receiver in his shirt's top pocket.

We all knelt/lay transfixed.

"What was that?" I had to ask, feeling a right numpty.

"A *liner*! A *fucking* liner!" screamed The Carper. "That's the first bleep my alarms have made in five months! I've been checking the batteries by tweaking the line through them every two hours just in case!" The Carper grabbed my leg again, its soggy nature not registering on one of his brain cells. "The One has knocked into my line because she's feeding on my baits!" he gabbled, the excitement frothing from him more violently than the bubbles from an uncorked jeroboam of champagne strapped to the back of an industrial road breaker. "Near to the one with my hook in it! There's *every* chance she'll pick it up soon!"

Rambo pushed his Glock's barrel into The Carper's temple attempting to control his monumental high. "His name," Rambo growled trying to refocus The Carper's mind.

"He calls himself The Bait Baron," The Carper distractedly replied, his attention heaped on his indicators and the cool end of Rambo's gun in monumentally disproportional measures. Well, he was 'The Carper', and what was a gun aimed at the head compared to the possibility of a pick-up from an unknown seventy?

Rambo tried again. "What's his *real* name?"

The Carper slewed his head around so the barrel now rested dead centre of his forehead. "He doesn't like people knowing his real name. I promised not to tell *anyone* his name. If I told you his real name, I'd be in deep shit."

Rambo pushed the gun hard into The Carper's head forcing it backwards. "Believe me, boy, you're in the deepest shit you could *ever* imagine! If you don't tell me his name, you'll wish you'd died yesterday!"

Dud-dud-dud-dud-dud. Dud-dud-dud-dud-dud. Dud-dud-dud-dud-dud.

Deeeee-deee-deee-deee-deee! Deeeee-deee-deee-deee-deee! Deeeee-deee-deee-deee-deee!

The shock of the run nearly sent me leaping out through the shingle camouflage groundsheet ceiling making a Matt Williams-in-army-fatigues-complete-with-helmet-and-Glock-handgun shaped hole in the process. Holy *fucking* Christ! The One had picked up one of our, Pup's – apparently any Tom, Dick or Harry's – boilies!

The Carper went to hit the run only to be restrained by Rambo's huge hand that had locked around his throat with all the tenacity of a mastiff suffering from trismus. The Carper frantically pointed at a pogoing hanger indicating fish on! Rambo's head moved the other way indicating 'no fucking way!'

"No!" Rambo howled. "His *name*! Or I'll cut the fucking line!"

Instinctively I looked at the line speeding out from the middle rod, now jagging above the sand, a tiny pile of misplaced particles to either side.

Dud-dud-dud-dud-dud. Dud-dud-dud-dud-dud. Dud-dud-dud-dud-dud.

Deeeee-deee-deee-deee-deee! Deeeee-deee-deee-deee-deee! Deeeee-deee-deee-deee-deee!

Seminal moment time.

The Carper's brain wrestled with the difficult ideology of staying true to one's word and hitting the run caused by an unknown, uncaught, twenty-five grand winning, carp-superstar-making, seventy pound mirror.

"John McFie!" he said instantly.

Satisfied, Rambo released him. The Carper plucked up his middle rod, clicked its reel arm into place, snapped shut the baitrunner spool conversion and disappeared out the shingle camouflage flap and into what was left of the night.

Rambo and I rushed to the opening. The very first hint of dawn had lifted the darkness much more than the earlier moonlight could have ever hoped and the pair of us could clearly make out The Carper's rod hooping over in an impossible arc.

"He's fucking hooked it!" I said to Rambo, a massive smile on my face. We'd given him a rough time earlier and I was hoping he was going to slot the last piece of his jigsaw puzzle into its place.

"But will he land it?" came the sober reply.

I watched The Carper shuffle down to our left making an angle away from the tree to apply side-strain to counteract The One/The Seventy's movement to the right. I knew how The Carper was feeling. The mixture of an incredible rush of mega-octane euphoria induced by the take combined with the dreaded, dark, paranoid fear of the train wreck disaster of loosing it – times God knows what factor. Whatever rush any angler had ever received during a take, surely The Carper, by virtue of what he had put himself through to get it in the first place, was feeling an elevated version of it. Ditto the dreaded prospect of a hook pull, or even worse, if it was humanly possible to tack the adjective 'worse' to such an horrendous loss, a snapped line.

"He's a class act," I said smacking Rambo's doom laden ball back with interest to his backhand, deep on the baseline. "Maybe the classiest ever. He'll land it. Rigs. Line. Hook. All spot on. He won't make a mistake."

"I didn't mean that," Rambo replied looking the other way.

Dud-dud-dud-dud-dud. Dud-dud-dud-dud-dud. Dud-dud-dud-dud-dud. Dud-dud-dud-dud-dud. Dud-dud-dud-dud-dud. Dud-dud-dud-dud-dud. Dud-dud-dud-dud-dud. Dud-dud-dud-dud-dud. Dud-dud-dud-dud-dud.

And with it the screeching and whining.

The orange dots, dashes and lines were back. The gunfire had shifted back down from the top of the range. The useless mortar crew dropped another one way short and it exploded perhaps only fifty yards behind us. I lifted my head up from my prone position, lying half in and half out of the camouflage flaps, and saw the orange tracers up in the sky.

Suddenly, one line of bullets dropped.

Thwack-thwack-thwack-thwack-thwack. Thwack-thwack-thwack-thwack-thwack. Thwack-thwack-thwack-thwack-thwack.

A storm of projectiles exploded through the tree sending branches and chunks of wood everywhere.

Thwack-thwack-thwack-thwack-thwack. Thwack-thwack-thwack-thwack-thwack. Thwack-thwack-thwack-thwack-thwack.

A split second later another burst ripped along the bank and as I buried my face into the gravel, I felt the vibration of a loose camouflage sheet being yanked and jerked, this way and that, by a peppering of machine gun bullets.

The Carper was ten yards further down the bank. I doubt he ever noticed the orange tracers until it was too late. He was consumed with something far more important than his own safety. The line of fire from the wayward gun hit him across the midriff as it strafed down the bank. His body hinged dramatically forward as pulverised wads of flesh and bone flew out from his back – punched out in great big, gory gobs by the large machine gun rounds. In slow-mo The Carper's whole upper body grotesquely rotated about a static pelvis due to the pull of The Seventy on the still gripped rod. Whether this was due to a normal death contraction or The Carper managing to hang on to his rod for longer than he could cling on to life, I shall never know. Nauseatingly, I saw intestines slop from his gutted body as his upper half pivoted on the remaining physical connection to his pelvis and legs before finally nose-diving into the margin water. His legs, hanging on by a bloody thread of gristle and skin toppled down a second later.

The Carper had been cut in half by the machine gun fire. It carried on the same trajectory for ten more yards and then stopped. The night-time exercise was over.

In an instant, Rambo was up on his feet, rushing down to The Carper whilst I remained frozen solid with horror. In a haze of massive, uncomprehending shock, I watched Rambo dive into the pit's water a few yards ahead of the The Carper's severed torso. In an instant Rambo stood up, simultaneously lifting The Carper's rod up into the air. It started to bend.

He turned to me, his face hard with concentration, tiny rivulets of water running down his cheeks. "I've got it, boy!" he shouted in triumph. "It's still on! Get the fucking net!"

Chapter 18

"Come on! Come *on*! Get the net!"

Rambo's words eventually permeated the fog enveloping my brain and nagged me into a response. I got up, left my Glock on the ground, grabbed the net and walked dazed and confused (for so long it's not true; wanted to throw up, because of the view; lots of words floating around in my head; soul of The Carper above now he's dead.) to where Rambo was playing an unknown, uncaught seventy on the rod belonging to a dead carping legend recently sliced in half by machine gun fire. How many times had *that* sentence ever been written?

"Oh, God," I moaned as I reached Rambo's side. "The poor bastard." I was violently and copiously sick.

The dreadful head exit wound of Rambo's would-be assassin and the delightfully hilarious propeller-driven removal of Hollywood's face hadn't prepared me for the stomach churning sight of the remains of The Carper. Two isolated legs, reminding me of the bottom half of a Legoman figure, lay angled across the margins. In a pile next to them, a good percentage of The Carper's internal organs sat on the sand like a macabre, beached jellyfish. I was no biologist, but I recognised the coiled large and small intestines, part of a kidney, his stomach, liver and bladder. Connected by a slither of flesh, thankfully face down, at a different angle to the legs, was his torso and head, arms haywire to either side. If I had dared to finger the mound of internal organs I would have found them still warm and sticky. A cold morning would have seen them steaming. I retched again.

"Nasty little mess," Rambo commented, kindly hinting my projectile vomiting wasn't an OTT reaction. "Shit! It's off again!"

Rambo's, sorry The *Carper's* – let's get this right – The *ex*-Carper's clutch clicked off again as The Seventy, unaccustomed as it was to having a hook in its mouth, tore off down the pit with all the indignant rage of a drunken lout going off on one after being refused entrance to a trendy nightclub. As Rambo battled The Seventy, I was left with nothing more to do than prop up my weakened body with the landing net handle, spit the remnants of my regurgitated fish and chip supper into the margins, ponder on the temporary nature of mortality and the morality of our present actions. My body made an involuntary shudder – my wet clothing pleaded not guilty and I judged the case against it be dismissed. The side effects of physical sickness were strongly reminiscent of how I had felt after the ghost had completely overwhelmed my emotions on my first Hamworthy overnighter. I'd had the heebie-jeebies and cold collywobbles on that night as well!

Other memories returned and prompted me into asking a question. "You know this is the second time you've done this, don't you?"

Rambo turned and looked at me. "What? Landed a carp on a dead man's rod?"

I ignored the temptation to try and think up a sea shanty starting with the first line; Seventy pound carp on a dead man's rod, Yo-ho-ho and a bottle of flavour enhancer and merely nodded. "I don't think we'll take a photograph this time," I said dourly.

Rambo gave a concurring head movement, his eyes fixed out on to the water. "Yeah. He's not exactly photogenic, is he? He wasn't looking too smart when he was alive, now he's…"

"Have you ever seen anything like it before?" I asked quietly, cutting Rambo off. I didn't feel happy him talking in such a manner – especially not in front of what was left of The Carper.

"Yes," Rambo answered with what I regarded was an air of finality indicating the close of the topic. Surprisingly he added more. "The first time was awful. It was my first proper combat mission and the first time I'd lost a colleague… Come to Rambo, my beauty." During his explanation, Rambo had managed to turn The Seventy and was putting stripped line back on to the spool. "Nice rods," he commented, flashing me a quick glance.

I had to say what I was thinking. "Don't you think this is a bit wrong? Shouldn't we be *doing* something?"

"I am. I'm trying to land The Seventy," came the honest reply.

"I didn't mean that. I meant doing something about The Carper."

"You can *try* and put him back together if you like, there's a brick trowel in my rucksack along with a first aid kit." Rambo turned his head backwards at the gory mess behind him. "I can assure you, boy, you won't have any luck."

"I didn't mean that," I said, a little put out by Rambo's flippancy. "I was just thinking…"

Rambo forcefully interrupted. "*Learn* to stop thinking for once!" he advised. "He's *dead*, Matt. There's *nothing* we can do. We can't change history, not unless you've got a time machine in your back pocket."

"It got wet and stopped working," I replied, duly put in my place.

Time – uninterrupted and still very much in a linear mode – passed by.

"Fucking *hell*!" I suddenly exclaimed with such alarm even Rambo flinched. "What if The Carper becomes a ghost? We know it can happen! What if he's a wronged spirit, trapped in between our world and the next? What if *he* comes back! What if he's watching you right now! What if he visits me in the future and says he *didn't* like you touching his rods!"

In the light of a new day, a look of fleeting terror washed over Rambo's face. Rambo defended himself vehemently. "Shut the fuck up, Matt! You're giving me the willies! I'm only trying to do the right thing here! I'm positive he wouldn't want us to leave The Seventy to get tethered up and die as well, aren't you?"

I nodded my head vigorously. He wouldn't have wanted that, Rambo was quite correct. "You're right," I commented, resisting the temptation to turn and see if a ghostly, all-in-one-piece The Carper was hovering above his mound of guts.

"Thank you." Rambo appeared pleased to have my condonation. "Look, boy," he began in a soft voice. "Let's land the fish, hopefully before we get spotted, and after we'll sort out what to do next."

"Okay," I said. "Agreed." Typically my brain moved on to new areas of worry. "You're not going to go round saying you've caught a seventy, are you? Not when it's on someone else's rods!"

Rambo glared at me as if I was a door-to-door salesman interrupting a favourite TV show. "I know that's not on, boy! I *have* read the fucking carping etiquette rulebook, you know! I'm not *that* desperate!"

"Not even for twenty-five grand?"

Rambo was highly indignant. "*No*! Of course not! This is a fish welfare issue."

Cringing at my own crassness, I looked at Rambo via rolled up eyeballs from a suitably penitent, bowed head. "Sorry."

I lifted my eyebrows even further – probing for one last time – and gave the big man a grin.

Rambo saw this, flicked his head back out to where The Seventy had boiled on the surface and flicked it straight back. "All *right*! *And* I wanted to know what it felt like to play in a seventy! I admit it! I'm human and I'm a carp angler… and not necessarily in that order!"

I allowed myself another grin before deciding this was an inappropriate action under the circumstances. "That's a fair enough deal." I said "Doing the right thing and getting a little payback at the same time. His rod would have been over the other side if it had been left to me."

Rambo proceeded to gain a few more precious feet of line. "We've still got the next steps of our plan to formulate before we can go," Rambo reminded me. "The Carper was only a pathfinder to The Bait Baron, remember? And if our boilie's hanging from this fish's mouth we've another puzzle to solve."

The pair of us lapsed quickly into silence, mainly because the huge fish had broken the surface ten yards out. I stopped using the net as a prop and placed its mesh into the water – water tinged red with the blood of The Carper. I forced myself to look forwards, concentrate on my job as Rambo's gillie and not to look back at the source of the colouration. The rather odd human fascination with death and injury goaded me to go take another gawp at The Carper's guts, similar to how I had viewed the desperately unlucky Eduardo's awful leg breaking tackle on YouTube. My spine became immersed in liquid nitrogen at the prospect of revisiting the morbidly fascinating/frightening sight. I fought the compulsion, told myself ghosts were an *exceptionally* rare phenomenon, and focused on my tiny role in capturing The Seventy.

And then on the enormous one already played by The Carper.

The Carper had risked everything in the highest of all poaching stakes. He had gambled spectacularly and, horrifyingly, had lost – the roulette wheel coming up zero fifty times on the trot when either red or black would have won on any single occasion – and ended up paying the ultimate price when on the very brink of winning the jackpot. He *could* stake claim to being 'The Carper' as far as I was concerned and I surmised if his story became common knowledge, as often is the case in death, his legend would grow even larger because of it. I wondered exactly who he was and what family, friends and acquaintances would shortly have the most unexpected of bad news knock on their doors. *If* he had any left. The obsessive road, as I was so acutely aware, pretty soon turns into a very lonely one.

Back in the real world, outside the machinations of my meandering brain, Rambo was having a spot of difficulty.

"Jesus! She's powerful!" he exploded in a voice steeped with deference.

The Seventy had got her head back down and was motoring up the margin towards the tree by The Carper's lair – the rod in Rambo's hands looking as if it might snap at any moment, unless the line pinged before it!

"Don't *lose* it, for God's sake! Not after all *this*!" I screeched with feeling.

My tone wasn't exactly conducive to calming the furrowed brow of my soon-to-be business partner.

Zzzzzzzzzzz! Zzzzzzzzzzzz! Zzzzzzzzzzzzzzzzzzzzzzzz! Line pulled off the clutch and even the mighty Rambo was forced to tuck the rod's butt into his six-pack. The fish was absolutely mental! All that time in solitary confinement, no wonder!

"The clutch is as tight as I dare!" Rambo said in the style of Scotty caning The Enterprise for more warp speed.

Completely enveloped in the imagery, I thought I heard, 'I cannae stop it, Captain!' emanate from Rambo's mouth as The Seventy ploughed under the tree with the most bullet marks on the whole pit and snag itself.

"*Fuck*! She's snagged!" Rambo roared. "Quick! Go and get my rucksack."

Rambo barks – I jump. It's the way things are.

Dropping the net, I ran back to the tree, up the four-foot excavation and hauled the heavy rucksack out from the branches. By the time I had staggered back, Rambo was up to the tree trying his hand, very gingerly, at extracting The Seventy from the snag.

"It's no good, boy. The line's caught round an underwater root. I can feel it grating," Rambo told me, returning the rod tip to above water. Frustration radiated from his body language. "Bollocks! I *couldn't* stop it! It was like trying to halt a bloody train!" he said shaking his head in wonderment at the raw power displayed by The Seventy. The wonderment, having ousted the frustration, proved to have little staying power and soon drifted into pragmatism coupled with a dash of initial sentiment. "We *can't* let The Carper down! Not after he did so much spadework! We've *got* to land her!" Rambo insisted, paying homage to The Carper's incredible preliminaries. Rambo wiped a swift tongue over his top lip. "You'll just have to go in for it and free the line."

I did feel like saying to Rambo, seeing as he was the instigator of trying to bank

The Seventy, that he might quite like to get in the drink himself and let me do the dry stuff – even if I was already wet. But I didn't.

"Chop chop, boy! Daylight's already here! Open up the rucksack! Inside are flippers, a mask and a snorkel! Get them on and get down to that fish!"

Rambo's urgent words put paid to any hopes of role reversal and spurred me into action. This is for The Carper, I told myself – landing The Seventy would be our way of honouring his memory and making sure the act of him being cut in half by machine gun fire and having his guts slop out all over the sand wouldn't have been in vain. Somewhere in my head a sarcastic voice said, 'Yeah, right,' but I ignored it and delved into Rambo's giant jamboree bag of 'things-you-might-need-when-visiting-a-poacher-on-a-live-MoD-range'. I hauled out the required items by shoving the flame-thrower, grappling irons and small, tactical thermo-nuclear device to one side.

After yanking off my shoes to facilitate putting on the flippers, I took off my Kevlar helmet, donned the mask and snorkel and waded out into the pit. Jacques Costeau, eat your heart out – although I doubt he ever jumped in from the deck of Calypso wearing camouflage fatigues and a flak jacket. The cold water found its way to my skin for the second time in the day. Seeing as it still wasn't breakfast time this constituted a personal record. I edged over to where Rambo's line (let's stick with it being his, seeing as he had effectively commandeered The Carper's tackle, it's much easier) entered the water and grabbed it loosely with my hand. Carefully I started to follow the line down to where I hoped The Seventy would still be attached to the end. Pretty soon I was right under the tangle of branches, the ones ironically we had earlier deemed too difficult to circumnavigate by water. The water level was now up to the top of my shoulders, so I dunked my mask into the water to have a peer into the world of The Seventy. There wasn't much to see.

I popped my head back up and spoke to Rambo with the ridiculous nasal inflection of a man wearing a diving mask. "Cand we come back when id's a bid brighder?"

"Course we fucking can't! Follow the line and dive down deep enough to see where she is. And don't spook it! And don't knock it off, either!"

"Do you wand to do id? You'll be much bedder dan me," I answered, fearing I was going to be responsible for all The Carper's hard work and premature death ending in a downer blank to end all downer blanks.

Dear diary. Rambo lost an unknown, uncaught seventy from a secret pit today. I inadvertently bumped it off with my left flipper after going in for it because it'd got snagged. I felt awful... but not as awful as the angler who'd had the original take! He'd got machine-gunned to death...!

"Get on with it, boy! You'll be fine," came the reply.

"If I yank dwice, cud me some slack!" I shouted.

I sucked in a big gulp of air down the snorkel and carefully duck-dived into the water, flicking the flippers to push me down as I followed the line. Deeper and deeper I went, the extra pressure pushing the mask hard against my face and making my ears hurt. The depth was much greater than I had imagined as the vagaries of gravel extraction had by chance created a drop of what I estimated to be at least twenty feet. Near to the bottom the line ran under a stray root from the tree, one jutting out into the water. I grabbed the root with my other hand and held on tight to stop my natural buoyancy taking me back up. On the other side of the root, just sitting there, still hooked, no more than a yard away, was The Seventy. I looked at her and I swear she looked back at me.

To say I was the definitive expert and highly accustomed to viewing fish of large sizes would be an overstatement. Naturally, I had seen plenty on the bank, including the sixty I had caught from Hamworthy Fisheries, the finest carp fishery etc., but to view this monster, this leviathan, this lump, this kipper, this whacker, this – let's be frank about it – fucking great carp at such close quarters in its natural environment, was mind blowing and unlike anything I had previously encountered. The massive flank, barely visible in the gloom, looked like a wall of carp. I thought I could make out big pectoral fins, twitching in irritation at the strange sensation of being attached to 'something', and a massive rear tail fin wafting gently – for the moment – with its gearstick in neutral.

I felt an odd desire to want to swim with her, to follow her around the pit all day, when the bright sun was up and I could see her properly. I felt the need to bond with the beauty, perhaps even mind-meld with her if I could, so I could know the story of her life and how she had become the biggest, most beautiful fish in all of England. I wanted to do it in tranquillity, under no stress, underwater – under the bullets!

This ideological eulogising was all well and good, until my lungs ran a point of order up my spinal column into my brain, the general drift being, 'We're bursting! Get us some fresh air and be bloody quick about it!'

I yanked the line twice. Rambo eased some off the clutch and I carefully, trying to pull out from the clutch rather than pull at The Seventy, guided the line under the root. With a kick of my flippers and with the very last bit of oxygen left in my lungs – I decided there and then not to drop the day job I didn't have to become a sponge diver – I pushed out into the pit effectively leading The Seventy away from the snag.

At the point of feeling I was going to drown, or piss myself, or both, I released the line and struck out for the surface. Swallowing hard, trying desperately to keep what little air I had inside me, the pain in my chest welling to the point of being excruciating, I begged the surface to come down rapidly. After what appeared to be an age I broke out of the world of liquid, ripped out the snorkel and mercifully gasped in air. As I trod water, recovering from what felt like an attempt to swim the entire pit underwater, I also looked back towards the bank. I saw Rambo pick up the net as the water close to him erupted into a frothing frenzy. I watched fixated – fixated mainly with getting my breath back and reducing my banging heart to under a pulse rate of one twenty – as Rambo struggled to contain the beast I had given him a second chance to land. After a couple of minutes I saw the net move out and up.

"Yes! *Yes!*" came the cry across the water.

The emphatic conclusion had, at long last, arrived. Timothy Eugene Ramsbottom had banked The Seventy, on the back of The Carper's groundwork, ably assisted by 10m Underwater Bronze Badge Holder, Matt Williams.

Weakly, so weakly (to crack the old joke) it was fortnightly, I swam to the shore. Once within my depth I stood up only to fall over, tripping over the ungainly flippers on wobbly legs. I was gone, physically shot to bits, although admittedly, in a rather less severe version of the problem experienced by The Carper. Rambo, good old Rambo, waded in and helped me up. He squeezed me tightly around my shoulders in a one-armed bear hug, almost lifting me off my flippers as he dragged me back to dry land.

"Well *done*, Matt!" he gushed. I thought for a mad instant he was actually going to kiss me. "Brilliant stuff! You need to see her! *What* a fish!"

Rambo had found The Carper's unhooking mat as I had been swimming back and had placed it on the gravel by the entrance to his lair. Soon our prize was on it, enmeshed, as fish tend to be, by the landing net. Our non-exclusive, revolutionary, indented, dirty brown bottom bait boilie, hung from a size 4 Mugga hook firmly embedded in The Seventy's bottom lip. Rambo carefully removed it, checking out The Carper's rig as he did. We both ogled it with disbelief.

"Oh, my, God!" I said in the style of any American TV show you could care to mention.

Rambo held it up in front of both our sets of eyes. Eight inches of it rotated from the swivel by the lead – imagine a clichéd hypnotist putting his client 'under' and you have the picture.

"Jesus!" Rambo said simply.

"How many times have you read there would never be a rig revolution equal to that of the Maddocks/Middleton hair rig?" I asked in a faraway voice.

Rambo, his large lantern jaw hanging down to his belt buckle eventually answered. "Loads."

"They were wrong," I stated, looking at the most incredible piece of rig thinking I had ever seen in an angling context. "You see how the hair's…"

"Yeah."

"And the way the hook…"

"I know."

"But the *really* clever bit, is how it all…"

The Seventy flapped on the mat – she wasn't used to not being the centre of attention – and redirected our thoughts. Rambo lifted the huge fish up as I pulled away the net and put her back down.

"Oh, my, God!" I said in the style of any American TV show you could care to mention.

"Jesus!" Rambo said simply.

The mirror of all mirrors lay before us. Mirror, mirror on the mat, you are the fairest – simple as that!

I ran my fingers down the vast expanse of The Seventy's side. I would have been no more fascinated if it had belonged to an alien recently pulled from a crashed flying saucer. Shear size in any animal is always eye-catching and impressive, when it's combined with aesthetic proportion – the organic equivalent in build-quality to a Teutonic luxury car and the flair of an Italian motorbike – you have before you the royal flush. The beast of beasts – the carp of all carp!

I could see why The Carper had been driven to the lengths he had to try and catch her. He must have spotted her at some stage of his campaign, in clear water, at close range and had been summoned, in a visual counterpart, like a sailor to a siren, only to end washed up on the shore, holed by machine gun bullets rather than by rocks.

Every scale, every hue, every fin, every line and every detail was one of perfection. A 'David' of a carp – only with a bigger penis – sculpted by the maestro Michelangelo and given the gift of life.

It was getting brighter by the minute. Sadly, we didn't have the time she warranted. "Weigh her and put her back?" I suggested. "We have to see if The Carper called her size correctly."

Rambo dragged his eyes away from The Seventy and locked them on to mine. "If we do, we'll *never* see her again." There was real sadness in his voice.

I knew what he was thinking. "The first fish for our new water?"

Rambo lifted his eyebrows. "We could, *could*, sack her and come back for her."

"What? Forget about getting a Section 30?" I said smiling. "How naughty!"

"Find the scales and the sling. We must go soon," he replied delaying a decision.

It may seem strange to think we had to weigh her – to find the number of the beast, so to speak – but we did. It's deeply ingrained in all us anglers. I quickly found the required implements, once I had taken the flippers off, and whisked them back to Rambo. For all we knew we were in some squaddie's binocular lens this very second. Rambo hurriedly wetted the sling, zeroed it in and placed The Seventy within it. Smoothly, Rambo hoisted The Seventy up off the deck, his powerful arms barely transmitting a shake to the scale's dial needle.

"Seventy-eight pounds... six," I said flabbergasted. "*Now* what?"

"Your call, boy" said Rambo painstakingly lowering the monster to the mat.

I gave it a moment's consideration. "Let's take the memory of her to our graves," I said. "She's The Carper's, no one else's, not even ours."

Rambo gave me a look of defiance, one that burnt out in an instant. "You're right, Matt, one hundred per cent right. The risk of moving her is too great... and it would be wrong, *very* wrong."

In silence the pair of us stood in the margins. A small bird started to sing a warning. Rambo picked up the weigh sling and moved it into a couple of feet of water. There, he unwrapped The Seventy, which, by autumn, would be The Eighty. We both took a long last look. Remember her, remember her, *remember* her, I told myself in a mantra attempting to conjure up a photographic memory.

"Ready?" Rambo asked.

"As I'll ever be."

Rambo released The Seventy. She swam vigorously back into her lonely home, leaving me thinking I would never have believed it if I hadn't seen it with my own eyes. It was an emotional moment. The Carper had come within a whisker of making the greatest carp capture of all time – one with the enormity, gravitas and yet, paradoxically, sheer impudence to knock Walker, Yates, Jackson, whoever, off their pedestal and crunch them one notch down the all-time list. Instead of glory The Carper had been ripped apart, his life cruelly taken from him at the very moment his carping star had risen to within moments of its zenith. The only question mark over his greatness was whether The Carper could have landed The Seventy by himself. I knew he would have.

"Now what?" I asked yet again, my eyes misty from moisture, salty moisture.

Rambo had been staring at the water, at the point of lost contact with The Seventy, immersed in his own thoughts and his own world. A nigh audible click went off in Rambo's head and he snapped out of it. "Put everything away as you found it! It's imperative we find The Carper's mobile. Make sure you pick up your Glock and pack all my gear into my rucksack while I try and disguise we've been here! And get our fucking boilies as well!"

"You take the rig!" I reminded him, as I commenced my work. "Cut it off and chuck that rod back out under the tree and leave it near to his body, it'll look like he got snapped off."

"I'm on it," Rambo replied.

Misty sentimentalism was out – harsh reality was back in vogue.

In ten minutes we were ready to leave and had achieved all that was necessary. Rambo pulled the rucksack on to his back. "I haven't had time to do it properly," he told me earnestly, referring to his 'wipe down'. "I'm hoping anyone finding The Carper's remains and lair will be so shocked they'll mess up any tell-tale signs of our presence before they even begin to think of third parties."

"They'll know he was killed by range fire, won't they?"

"Definitely." Rambo pulled his lips over gritted teeth. "Knowing the military they might even try to keep it under wraps." The lips relaxed into a smile. "They will if Prince Harry was on one of the guns at the time, getting a bit of practise in for a tour of duty in Afghanistan!"

A release of air indicated my disdain. "He wouldn't go *there*!"

"He might," Rambo countered. "To buck the royal lounge lizard, bit-of-a-pisshead image. A few months out there before the cover breaks, whisk him home with a few sound bite quotes of gallantry and what a great 'normal' bloke he is and all of a sudden he's zero to hero!"

"The great British public would never buy it," I protested. "It's too contrived."

Rambo laughed. "Come on, let's get moving."

We started to move off, tracing our route back, keeping low and as inconspicuous as possible. Before departing I had one last look at The Carper's insides and his outside. "What do you think went wrong for them to shoot so low?"

"Him, singular. It was only one gun… Who can say? It happened. The consequences are there to see, boy." Rambo faced me as we walked quickly to our escape. "Unfortunately it was million-to-one bad luck to get the run at the exact moment the bullets were right in the precise spot to hit him! The poor bastard."

I went quiet for a few minutes. "Do you think he'd have landed it on his own?" I eventually asked. "You probably wouldn't have."

Rambo's answer was without ego. "Yeah. He'd have done it! He was The Carper!"

"Do you think he'd have got the run without our non-exclusive, revolutionary, indented, dirty brown bottom bait boilie? Even on his super-trick rig?"

"Ahh!" said Rambo. "Now you're asking."

"So?"

"You know, I don't think he would have," Rambo reflected. "Or at least, not so quickly. He would have had to put more time in. Our non-exclusive, revolutionary, indented, dirty brown bottom bait boilie contributed to killing him."

"I agree," I confessed. "Although I'm not too sure a bag of boilies would ever go down as an accessory to murder! Having said that, it kind of answers the point why The Bait Baron wants Pup in. Bait is still a big part of the equation."

"Maybe Pup's already in, and we've been wasting our time," submitted Rambo.

"He's sure got some explaining to do," I said my voice hardening.

"I think you'd better take a look on The Carper's phone, boy, and pray The Bait Baron's number is on it. If it isn't, we've definitely wasted our time."

I pulled it out of my pocket. Rambo had given me the phone after he had eventually found it in The Carper's pocket. To be honest, I doubted I could have ever brought myself to take it out, but it was all in a day – and night's – work for the big man. I went into the menu screen on The Carper's Nokia 6300 phone, selected 'Contacts' and then 'Names'. An alphabetical list appeared. Sadly, proving my earlier theory correct, there were precious few names on it. "Pup's not on there, but JMF *is*!" I declared.

"Excellent!" said Rambo. "Send him a text. It's time to try and catch another big fish! You know what to send."

I carefully checked The Carper's texting style from previous 'Sent items' messages and punched in; 'Caught the 1. G8 fish. Come usual time 2nite for photos. Bat v low so turning off for emergency.'

"Okay?" I said holding the small screen out for subeditor Rambo to see.

"That should get The Bait Baron running."

I pressed the 'Send' button – a nice tight cast to a lily pad. I was bound to get a bite.

Chapter 19

The morning after the machine-gunning of The Carper the night before. I was lying on the beach in my shorts, roasting in the hot sun, propped up on one elbow, reading Grant's Weekend Telegraph piece, whilst my army fatigues dried nicely over a wooden groyne. I was warm at last. Rambo, in a similar state of undress, in between scaring the seagulls with his biceps, was on the phone to Pup. The matter of how our non-exclusive, revolutionary, indented, dirty brown bottom bait boilie had managed to find its way to The Carper and what information Pup had spewed to Grant concerning the pair of us, were the thorny subject matters. Both topics were as hot as a south facing, black pebble on a beach in southern England at midday in summer. Good old global warming.

(Save The Planet by donating money to as many eco-friendly/charitable organisations as possible. By doing so, you can allow its executive staff to concentrate on nagging and whining at everyone without the worrying distraction of having to get a proper job that pays 50k+ a year.)

"So it was *nothing* to do with you?" I heard a sceptical Rambo ask. "Possibly," Rambo said after a period of time. "Just leave it to us," he advised after another. "No more threats from The Bait Baron? …Good. We'll let you know as soon as it's done." Conversation over.

"Well? What's the news? Has he sold out? You know, to The Bait Baron *or* Grant Gibbs," I caustically demanded.

Rambo had already made his mind up. "He says not and I believe him. Pup's never let us down before. He's not as loose with his mouth as *some* people I could mention." Rambo looked at me at this juncture and I swear one of his biceps scowled. "He reckons someone must have managed to nick a kilo of bait when we were at The Bowl and he swears he didn't mention Hamworthy to Grant any time at all."

"I don't know when they would have nicked the bait," I said huffily. "I think *one* of us would have noticed."

"We'll find out tonight."

I sat up and felt a cooling breeze waft around my head, one not capable of touching me when I was in the lee of the groyne. "I ought to phone Grant. Now we've got a name. Get him to start chasing his front page story rather than chasing our murky past."

Rambo's face darkened at the mention of Grant's name. As it did, the sun fleetingly went behind a tiny cloud. It was a poignant moment. "Okay, boy. Might be useful to see if he can turn anything up his end. See what the opposition's all about. Just be careful what you say to the twat."

"Shall I mention The Carper?"

Rambo gave me one of his looks. "What do you think?"

"Fine. No mention of The Carper," I answered suitably admonished.

I recalled the night's surreal events – they were never far from my consciousness, although I was relatively pleased with how I was dealing with it – and squeamishly evoked The Carper's innards. Talk about having someone's guts for garters – I had seen enough to lace up a pair of espadrilles, make a belt, a set of braces and still have enough for a washing line long enough to hang out the Chelsea first team squad's match day kit. (A ridiculous analogy – I couldn't imagine they ever wore a match day kit more than once, so why wash it?)

"Do you think anyone's found him yet?"

"I'm not sure, boy, but I hope not."

"Why's that?"

"The bloody place will be crawling, that's why!" It was a mild rebuke, Rambo was used to my sporadic stupidity. "If the body has been found there'll be increased security with extra patrols to make sure no one else attempts to do the same thing, plus they'll try to find out where and how he got into the range in the first place." Rambo's face flexed into a wry smile. "It might seem like bolting the stable door after the horse has fled, it *is* like bolting the stable door after the horse has fled, but that's the way authorities work. After nine eleven… increase in security. After the failed London bombings… increase in security. It's a traditional knee-jerk reaction, one that *has* to be complied with."

As ever Rambo was making sense. Ideally we wanted our little rendezvous with The Bait Baron to be a on a strict invitation only basis. We didn't need the British Army gatecrashing our secret tryst, barging in, knocking over the furniture, raiding the fridge, stealing DVDs and pissing in the wardrobes.

"I'd better phone our pet journalist." I rapped The Telegraph with the back of my hand. "At least the article's good and he's stuck to his word. It only relates to The Bowl and the Pulimov's Prize effect," I said trying to convince myself Grant could be trusted.

Rambo grimaced, unimpressed. "Pet? Huh, what sort? Poisonous snake?" Rambo didn't like Grant, I could tell. "Give him the name and see what happens," he continued. "Personally, I wouldn't trust that bastard as far as I could chuck him!"

Rather than point out I expected Rambo to be able to chuck Grant a considerable distance given his physical prowess – especially if he started from a good vantage point, say the edge of the Grand Canyon – I called Grant.

The now familiar educated voice answered on the third ring. "Grant Gibbs, speaking."

"Hi, Grant, Matt Williams here. We've got a name for you," I said getting straight to the point. This needed to be a single subject matter phone call.

"The Bait Baron?" Grant asked eagerly.

"Yep," I cockily confirmed, trying to mask my ingrained worries.

"How?"

"You don't need to know. Sources, shall we say," I stated trying to front him out. There was a pause. "Ya, fine. I can live with that."

Again I felt a deep unease dealing with Grant and speculating how much he really knew about the pair of us, who he had been talking to and what exactly he had found out. "You ready?" I asked.

"I'm *very* ready, Matthew."

I was briefly tempted to put some kind of retainer on the info, telling Grant if I gave him the name he should stop poking around in our past. I stopped myself, reasoning it would be a clear indication of something ludicrously loathsome lurking in the locker labelled 'Matt & Rambo'. Equally, I could have warned him Rambo had threatened to burn down his office while he was still in it *and* destroy The Telegraph with fire as well, but on the whole, it too seemed a poor idea. An Internet campaign urging people to buy The Times might have been a wiser option to take down the newspaper as an entity, but it was hardly Rambo's style and lacked immediacy.

"John McFie," were the three syllables to leave my lips – I neglected to mention we were meeting him tonight, all things being equal and the army permitting. "Ring any bells?"

"No. Mc as in M small C and capital F, I, E? John with an H?"

"I bet you were top at spelling," I lamely cracked.

"Leave it with me and I'll get back to you."

And he was gone.

"Not so much as a 'thank you'," I reported to Rambo.

"He's got his bone, let the cunt go play with it," Rambo growled.

Rambo *definitely* didn't like Grant, I really could tell!

"Let's go and get some fish and chips," I said. "I'm starving having regurgitated the last lot. And it'll give us a chance to bollock the girl who works there for giving us a bum steer on her 'no fire at night', spiel!"

Rambo sighed. "You've no idea have you, boy? No idea, whatsoever!"

The rest of the day was spent killing time, waiting for the night's big event. There's only so much lazing around you can do, without rods in the water, and only so much worrying about what leads a junior reporter on a national newspaper has on your dodgy past before you start to get fidgety. By mid-afternoon Rambo was bristling with energy despite the previous late night. He made the call for us to take a drive around the MoD range to check out army activity levels and to find the spot where The Carper used to receive his supplies. The location where, hopefully, we would meet The Bait Baron, AKA John McFie, on the stroke of midnight.

On driving around the range it appeared the rub of the green was still going our way regarding the army, mercifully, conspicuous by its absence. The concluding inference to this discovery being The Carper had remained undiscovered and was beginning to either rot in the hot sun or get eaten by indeterminate wildlife – or both. Nice.

Very few military vehicles were around and on the 'far side' road as we called it, the one where The Bait Baron had periodically met The Carper, normal civilian traffic was equally light. The reason why The Carper had chose the far side, as opposed to the road we had picked, despite it being a much longer haul to the pit's perimeter was now evident. The far road wasn't the road holidaymakers would use to get to the most popular piece of coastline, the Pontins camp and caravan parks and therefore was usually devoid of traffic. Consequently, we had little aggravation in stopping at every large warning sign to surreptitiously check for fence tampering. On the fourth stop we found the concealed opening, much as we had predicted, middle for diddle regards the location of the pit.

I felt mildly relieved another small obstacle had been overcome. Unfortunately, the horror and surreal nature of last night's experience was beginning to seep into my very soul and edged out my earlier thoughts of how well I was dealing with it. Maybe it was due to revisiting the area and knowing less than a mile away from where we stood, flies, birds, even the odd fox, were possibly crawling all over the remains of The Carper. I worried a flock of seagulls would be an obvious calling card to a gruesome event – one as awful as the haircuts of the members of the band with the same name!

It was odd really, you would have thought I would have started to get used to it by now – another grotesque chapter in the bizarre lifetime of experiences belonging to the carp angler, Matt Williams. My carp fishing life was some story. Even in my most self-effacing mood, I had to admit to it being an incredible yarn!

"Penny for them, boy?" Rambo asked as we drove away in his van, operation 'MoD pit portal' successful.

"It's fifty pence now, what with inflation," I said trying to lift the gloom in my head with poor humour.

"You're thinking about The Carper's rig aren't you? Combining our non-exclusive, revolutionary, indented, dirty brown bottom bait boilie with his revolutionary, super-trick rig, like he did?" Rambo guessed – incorrectly as it happened.

"My fishing head's not on. I'm thinking of everything else bar that, actually."

"It's your penchant, boy, no doubt."

"What are we going to do tonight providing The Bait Baron turns up and he hasn't smelt a rat?" I asked, pushing my thoughts into the future rather than resting them in the past.

Rambo drummed a quick tune on the steering wheel with his thumbs before answering. "I was thinking along the lines of grabbing him, shoving a Glock at his head and getting him to take us back to where Wilton's being kept. Once there, we take the moggy, tell The Bait Baron to keep out of our lives or else I'll beat him into a pulp and we deliver the world's finest bait tester, safe and sound, all whiskers present and correct, back to Pup. Game over! We get on with our lives and start work on my lifetime dream, our new water! And with a brilliant new rig to add to our armoury!"

"You and your sophisticated, psychological approach."

Rambo fixed me with his hard eyes. "Got a better idea?"

I hadn't. All I had was consternation. "This McFie character, sounds like a kind of antivirus software manufacturer, admittedly… what if he isn't the type to be intimidated?"

"What! By *me* with a gun! Come on, boy!" Rambo scoffed.

"Point taken, but he must be a nasty bastard. Even Grant warned us…"

"Grant!" Rambo spat the word out like a vegetarian tucking into the wrong hamburger at a cater-for-all-choices barbecue. "What the fuck does he know?"

As it turned out, when he phoned two hours later, quite a bit.

"John McFie." Grant informed me, "A man with, how shall I put it? A colourful history."

"Hold on, Grant, let me put the phone to loudspeaker so Rambo can hear." Surprisingly, for a relative Luddite, I achieved this within an acceptable timeframe, i.e. no one died of boredom, and held the phone out in front of the pair of us. "Okay. Go on."

Grant continued, his posh voice sounding oddly distorted through the phone's tiny speaker. "Born in 1963, Grammar School educated from working class stock, his father was a bricklayer, mother, a factory worker. He entered employment at eighteen as a trainee manager at a branch of a large supermarket chain. He was employed there for ten years, when, having reached the position of branch manager he was dismissed for selling supermarket goods to the black market. However, he was never criminally convicted for this offence due to the scale of the deception."

"Too small?" I enquired.

"No. Too large."

I looked at Rambo, who looked back at me. The pair of us looked at the phone. On cue it laughed. "Ya! Let me explain. This guy had lorry loads of goods going all over the country supplying his network of black market crooks. The drivers were all getting backhanders and McFie was doctoring the paperwork to cover it up. We're not talking a few bags of sprouts and the odd box of cornflakes here. Tens of thousands of pounds' worth of goods were going missing, an unsustainable haemorrhaging of profits eventually pointing the finger of culpability at McFie's store. This took nearly a *year* to come to light, so lax and disjointed were the accounting procedures, and more to the point, so *embarrassing*. McFie was dismissed, the loss of his job his only punishment, the supermarket chain electing to keep the matter a purely internal affair to avoid the public spectacle of their ineptitude becoming evident during the proceedings of a court case."

"Do you reckon he knew he would eventually get caught and had chanced his arm on them reacting exactly as they did?" I asked.

"Ya, almost certainly. With the money McFie made, most likely secretly stashed away in a fake account, he delved into counterfeit videos, DVDs and importing fake designer labelled clothing… and got caught. A four-year jail term and with all his stock destroyed saw him return to a sojourn selling cut and shut cars before moving on to publishing illegal magazines aimed at the outer fringes of pornographic taste. A police bust with a custodial sentence finished the business and left McFie scratching out a living at the lower end of market stall retailing upon his release into society. This downward spiral coincided with his first conviction for violence, apparently he stabbed a rival stall holder in the eye with a fake plastic Power Ranger in a dispute over a petty cash transaction."

"Go! Go! Power Rangers!" I commented.

Grant ran a hand through his hair – I didn't have to see it. "The bottom's still a little way off. The new century saw our subject try to muscle in on the lucrative drug scene starting off as a small-time pusher, before successfully overthrowing the local drugs baron and becoming the proverbial big fish in a very small pond. With the aid of additional muscle and a vicious line in violent punishment, McFie's little empire grew, until he unwisely tried to expand and encroached into the next neighbourhood. McFie got knocked back, his arse resoundingly kicked by serious organised crime. His mini-empire collapsed, all of his thugs moved on, and he was left to start from scratch once again."

"So then he tried similar tactics within the gentile world of carp fishing baits," I said.

"As you almost correctly say, he then tried similar tactics within the *not* so gentile world of carp fishing baits," Grant repeated.

"I wonder what gave him the idea?" I asked whilst silently speculating at the stressed 'not' in Grant's last sentence.

"You don't need me to spell it out, the parallels are obvious," Grant stated.

"I like it when people do, just to make it crystal clear," I admitted.

Grant ignored me. "On the whole a very interesting story reflecting the versatility of small-time crime and human nature, specifically, how many people will co-opt into transgression if you happen to be peddling their 'type' of drug… in this case carp baits!" A tiny sigh emitted from my mobile. "I *was* hoping there might be some major league tie-in with the Russian Mafia operating in the UK and Pulimov promoting carp fishing to highlight the sport as a payback for past favours, but you can't have it all. McFie's morphed into an exceptionally violent chancer over the years, but no more. The story's not strong enough or big enough to be a stand-alone front page item, but it could sit nicely in a piece covering wider crime issues. In addition to its central theme, there's a certain pantomime, comic element within it, what with the cat kidnapping and the very involvement of angling. That makes it more interesting than usual."

I wasn't sure how to take the information in Grant's monologue, whether it was good, bad or indifferent.

"When are you going to pull the rug from under him?"

"Soon, when all the loose ends are tied up. There's no panic now," Grant answered casually, his usual intensity apparently spent. "I'll put a word into the editor explaining what I've got and take it from there."

"How did you find out all the history on McFie so quickly?"

"You don't need to know. Sources, shall we say," Grant answered, mimicking what I had said to him earlier. "Are you going to try and get the cat back without going to the relevant authorities?"

"We might."

"It's your style, I guess," Grant commented. "That just leaves us to address the one matter we spoke of earlier. You owe me, Matthew."

I gave Rambo a nervous look. "What's that?" I gingerly asked.

"Your story! The one in your draw! The one you wrote concerning Watt and the blowing up of his bivvy."

I was getting to like this conversation less and less, what with the snide comments and innuendo. "Oh, right, yeah, the story," I mumbled, tripping over the words.

"What else is there?" Grant said easily. "I want to read it. You promised me if I gave you the inside track on The Bait Baron you'd let me read it."

I went to Rambo for advice and received a play-along-with-him gesture. "Sure, you can read it. I guess that was the whole point," I answered, my voice sounding unsure in my own ears.

"Good. Mail it to me. Have you got a pen and paper handy?"

I rummaged around on Rambo's dashboard shelf, found a pen and wrote the address Grant gave me on to the back of an old tackle catalogue.

"You send your manuscript off to me ASAP. Ya?"

"Will do, Grant."

"And let me know what happens with you and McFie. And tell me if you find out anything about Carl. I'm worried."

"Sure."

"Ah! He's worried about Carl. Like fuck he is!" Rambo derided once the journalist had hung up. A look of gravity clouded Rambo's face. "You're not going to send him your banged up, bivvy-based blockbuster, boy."

"Not if I can help it!" I replied zealously.

"It was a statement, not a question, Matt."

Rambo was calling me the dreaded, 'Matt'. When he occasionally dropped it into our conversation it was invariably synonymous with a serious theme. I shook a very worried head and began spraying my thoughts out into the van. "Do *you* think he's on to us? What has he got? How *much* has he got?" I blustered. "I mean, what the hell is the prick up to? I can't get my head around the way he's coming at things, not now McFie hasn't turned out to be a Vodka-swigging, sharp-suited, Godfather from Leningrad!" I flung my hands up in despair. "Why the bloody hell did we ever get involved in that stupid baitboat versus casting comp?"

Rambo's brow furrowed. "I wish I knew," Rambo eyed me earnestly. "That's an answer to *all* your questions!" he turned his gaze out of the van's window. "I'll say this, boy, Grant's got his agenda and if a by-product of it includes dropping us in the shit, he'll have no qualm in doing so. None whatsoever."

"Maybe you *will* have to kill him and destroy all his info!" I suggested.

And I meant it. I really did! We were too far down a wonderful, leafy road with two waters nestling on either side to let a ladder climbing, ultra ambitious young journalist with floppy, conditioned hair ruin it.

Rambo's demeanour seemed to lighten at my thought. "Yeah! Maybe I *will* have to kill him!" he agreed, as if it was the first time he had considered the idea as a genuine possibility rather than a pleasant threat.

I emphasised the point further. "If he does know more about our past, our horrible, nasty past, I wouldn't like it at all, because our future, the one I'm sitting here thinking about, the one involving lots of great fishing with our great bait and The Carper's, God rest his landing net, super-trick rig on two fantastic waters, could be gone. Me!" I put my thumb to my chest, "You!" I pointed a finger at Rambo. "*Both* of us," I flickered an agitated hand, "*could* lose the fucking lot!"

Rambo's flint-like eyes locked on to mine like a pair of rutting stag's antlers. "You wouldn't like it anywhere *near* as much as *I* wouldn't like it. And when I *really* don't like something, it normally stops breathing."

The thought of Grant Gibbs getting terminated was the most reassuring thought I'd had all day. Suddenly, with realisation and a hint of irony, I realised how sage Grant's comment had been. He was correct; it *was* easy for men like John McFie to get sucked into using escalating forms of violence to procure their desired ends. (Copy and paste the words 'Rambo and I' at the correct juncture in the sentence above.) People did get sucked into committing foul deeds when it involved their 'type' of drug. True enough, I had already taken a man's life, but this time it was different – the first time had purely been an act of responsive self-defence to halt aggression aimed against the pair of us.

On giving it second thoughts – it was *exactly* the same this time!

Chapter 20

"Here he comes, the fucker! Watch out, he might be armed with a Power Ranger!" Rambo whispered.

The pair of us were lying in the dark on the opposite side of the road to the MoD range, directly adjacent to the hole in its fence, dressed in sun-dried army fatigues, our Glocks ready to hand. I was pumped – if Grant had happened to wander by I would have put seventeen bullets straight into his head without even thinking twice! I had done it before, so I didn't see any reason why I couldn't do it again. Rambo was even more pumped than me – think overinflated monster truck tyres – and ready for anything the Bait Baron could throw at us. And that included violently wielded kids' TV merchandising spin-offs.

It was ten to midnight and the slowing set of front headlights meant The Bait Baron was early, obviously unable to contain the excitement of The Carper coming up trumps regards The Seventy/The One on one of his – read 'our' – baits. Twenty-five grand, thank you very much, and a kick up the arse for his fledgling bait empire so strong it might have been supplied by a mule genetically modified with nanotechnology to recreate the punch of a 32-megajoule Electro-Magnetic Laboratory Rail Gun.

I watched the Jaguar – *the* car for the criminally minded according to ancient TV cop shows – coast past us for two hundred yards before the stop lights burned a brighter red than the rear ones. All red lights were soon extinguished and in the pitch black I heard a door shut with a precise clunk – one guaranteed to make a Jaguar factory worker's chest swell with pride. The Bait Baron was on his way, summoned by a terrifically tantalising, tumultuous, top trump text from The Carper's mobile phone!

A mobile phone no longer in my possession.

Two hours earlier Rambo had decided to run the gauntlet and go back into the MoD range to replace The Carper's mobile into the back pocket of his somewhat isolated trousers. It was a risk he had deemed vital to take. With the carefully cleaned phone back in The Carper's possession there was no direct link to say we had ever visited him. The Carper was certainly incapable of telling anyone. In cold, rational retrospect it had been a big mistake and an unbelievable oversight to have taken it in the first place. Perhaps we had still been wonder-struck by The Seventy.

At least the second trip had given Rambo the opportunity to double-check his earlier clean up, albeit in the dark, and double-check everything else, not least as to whether The Carper's remains had been found. Fortunately for us, they had not.

The only discrepancy left, as far as we could figure, was the timing of the text message I had sent not coinciding exactly with The Carper's time of death. Rambo and I had reckoned on the gap being in the order of approximately fifty minutes – the time taken to land and release The Seventy plus the arduous aftermath admin. We hadn't dared turn the phone back on again to pinpoint the timing of the text message, partly as the exact gap was irrelevant, but mainly because this would have registered the phone as being in use at an even later hour. We doubted the missing fifty minutes would be a significant gap regarding a post mortem investigation, should The Carper, or what was left of him – Rambo had noticed signs of him being eaten by wildlife – ever receive one. No coroner, however diligent, would be able to precisely authenticate the exact time of death. The significant discrepancy rested with the end of the night-time firing, the cause of death – presumably the British Army wasn't so shambolic as to not have a record of this – and the sending of the text message.

"Maybe they'll think he sent the text message as he was dying. It'd confirm his complete enslavement to carp fishing. No last message to a lover or family, just, 'I've caught the biggun'!" I had commented, tongue slightly in cheek.

Rambo had replied with sarcasm. "Fifty minutes *after* he's been cut in half by machine gun fire *and* he still manages to turn the phone off and slip it into his back pocket!"

My top lip had twitched and a tiny bit of false indignation had been present in my words. "He hung on to the rod for a while after he got hit."

"Not *quite* the same thing, boy. I don't want to pick holes," Rambo had stated dryly, "but for a start, his arms wouldn't have been long enough to *reach* his back pocket!"

And we had both laughed. How callous was that? One man's getting machine-gunned in half is another man's sick humour.

When all was said and done there was nothing more we could do. The discrepancy would have to sit there, waiting for someone clever enough to suss it out. As long as we were out of the equation and there was nothing physically tangible to put us in it, we hoped it would never become an issue.

The line we were going to take with The Bait Baron was one of complete ignorance regards The Carper – apart from the one fact we were aware of his existence and knew he was fishing the venue. The fact The Bait Baron wasn't a Vodka-swigging, sharp-suited, Godfather from Leningrad, but was a small-time, violent crook with a list of convictions as long as an extendable landing net handle/supermarket till receipt for purloined black market goods was a double edged sword. Good in the respect McFie wasn't the head of a serious organised crime outfit even Rambo might struggle to contain, bad in the respect of it leaving Grant with no front page story. The dreaded prospect being we might eventually fill it with an in-depth article embracing every foul, fiendish, filthy, fraudulent facet of an astonishingly amazing angling anecdote.

Rambo had decided, and I had fully agreed (like it mattered), we weren't on an altruistic crusade intent on cleaning up the bait industry and eradicating the likes of

McFie from its high profile, 'pro-carper' endorsed, 'this one's the bollocks', 'nine fifties in forty minutes' mega-hype style. All we wanted to achieve was to get Wilton back and re-establish our non-exclusive, revolutionary, indented, dirty brown bottom bait boilie as our exclusive, revolutionary, indented, dirty brown bottom bait boilie. That was *all*! The remit went no further. As far as we were concerned, McFie could carry on doing whatever he liked as long as it didn't interfere with us. Call us uncaring, shallow, selfish, self-absorbed, self-first, self-last and anything else self again, should you wish. We simply didn't care – Grant was perceived as the more likely threat, not McFie, although how much McFie would need convincing of this remained to be seen.

The Bait Baron's footsteps became audible as he walked hurriedly up to the cut section of fencing. I saw the dark silhouette glance at an arm. It's five to, mate, I thought, and waited for Rambo's lead.

Rambo led. "Hello, McFie!" he menaced, standing up from his prone position and walking briskly across the small road, headtorch illuminating a stunned Bait Baron. "We'd like a word."

I quickly joined my mate and prospective business partner and scuttled to his side to fulfil the royal 'we'. In the dual headtorch LED lights I saw an expensive camera case slung over McFie's shoulder – not that he would need it.

McFie – he didn't look much like a Bait Baron to me now I had clapped eyes on him, he wasn't wearing a baseball cap/beanie hat with his corporate logo on it for a start – seemed to regain his composure from the initial shock and soon managed to put his 'hard man' shields up. I mentally belittled him. What was it with blokes like him and Carl and all the OTT macho posturing? Or was I merely jealous due to the unarguable fact I was incapable of pulling it off?

In the LED light I quickly sized him up. I knew he was mid-forties and he looked fit for it, of solid build, six-foot tall with short, dark hair, slightly receding at the front. My cerebral cortex grinned – if it came down to a ruck, he would be no match for Rambo. End of.

"What about?" The Bait Baron demanded. The voice was level, low and gruff. Even before he had changed vocation to the wrong side of legality, I could imagine it berating the late-night, shelf-filling, minimum-wage-earning staff.

"You've got something of ours. Something belonging to a *friend* of ours," Rambo answered, his voice sounding Hollywood film pitch perfect for the portrayal of the ruthless, psycho, killing machine character.

With the headtorch lights shining directly at him, McFie couldn't make out who we were. "You tell, Ian, Chardonnay's with me because she loves me!" McFie cried, jabbing out a pointed finger in a theatrical stab in the dark – which was exactly what it was.

Rambo's response was cool. "We're not interested in your fucking love life, you cretin. We want the cat back!"

There was a slight, but appreciable pause. McFie took stock. "Are you two the carp anglers? The friends of Pup? Matt and Rambo? The ones who gave Paul and Carl a pasting and won The Bowl comp?"

Rambo magnanimously said, "That's us!" even though my involvement in the 'pasting' of Paul and Carl had been purely as an entertained observer, although, clearly my angling skills were a great contribution to our glorious win at The Bowl.

"Did one of those two bastards tell you about this place?" McFie angrily snapped.

"Relax, McFie, they didn't know," Rambo dismissively answered.

Unfortunately, McFie's brain was starting to get sidetracked – unfortunately for him, given Rambo's highly charged state. "How did you know I was coming here? Tonight? At this time?"

"Look, McFie," Rambo replied, lying with irritation. "We know The Carper's fishing the pit for a huge, uncaught seventy and we found the hole in the fence. It wasn't *that* difficult. We've just been sitting it out waiting for a run. We're used to it. And here you are, we've got one! ...We *want* the cat back!" the threat was back in Rambo's voice.

McFie was in a state of confused conflict, torn as he was between the knowledge he had a gusher of a leak from high up within his band of cronies and the rising desire to photograph the ultimate carp-bait-advert capture. "*I* want Pup's baits!" he stridently declared, only too well aware our nicked kilo of non-exclusive, revolutionary, indented, dirty brown bottom bait boilie becoming available to The Carper had coincided with his success. "And if hanging on to that dumb bastard's cat is the way to get him on board, then *no* way!"

In the dark, I raised my eyebrows thinking, firstly, rather strangely, that no one in the world would ever know I had, and secondly, that McFie's actions were akin to agitating a hungry tiger by flicking it in the eye with your penis.

The tiger had had enough and unsheathed its claws. "Listen, you fucking idiot," Rambo rumbled from the back of his throat, pointing the Glock point blank at McFie's head. "I'm not wasting my time listening to you ramble on, boy! I don't think you understand who or what you're dealing with. We don't give a fuck about you, your bait company and your methods. We want the cat back and we don't want to ever see or hear from you again. Comprehend?"

I raised my Glock and pointed it at McFie's head. A strange thrill coursed through my body, the power of the gun mobilising my adrenalin. "Just do it, McFie!" I shouted, my finger perilously close to pulling the trigger. "Just do what we tell you and save us all the hassle!"

The small arsenal focused McFie's mind. I saw his eyes wildly take in the gleam of the headtorch lights on the two barrels. He might be a self-proclaimed Bait Baron with a cute line in beatings, arson attacks and intimidation, but shooters were a step too far for him. No wonder the serious drug dealers had kicked his butt! In the moment I realised that if McFie wished to carry on his life in crime, he would have to consider an escalation in tactical violence and consider getting himself 'tooled up' to avoid a third experience of being put in a pathetic, powerless position. The facts were incontestable – even to pass yourself off as a reasonably unscrupulous, intimidating and scary Bait Baron you needed to be armed! Especially if you happened to cross Rambo's path! The muppet had had one chance to learn this lesson earlier in his career and had singularly failed!

And so the world turns and gets more dangerous every day – knives for primary school children, anyone?

"But he's caught it!" McFie limply squeaked. "He's caught the fucking seventy! The Carper's *caught* the fucking seventy! I'm going to photograph it!" McFie gestured with the camera case. "You can come with me and see it! Don't you want to see it?" The last question was almost a plea.

"No." Rambo was adamant.

"But it's a *seventy*! Caught on one of my baits! This'll put both me and The Carper in the big time!"

Rambo gave a slow shake of the head. "I said 'no'."

"I'll take you on as consultants," the Bait Baron gabbled, changing tack and becoming ever more drastic by the second. "Fuck The Carper! We'll go over there, blow him out, and I'll photograph *you* holding the fish! We'll go halves on the Pulimov twenty-five grand prize! What do you say?"

It was all too much for Rambo and the pent up energy fuelled by concerns over Grant, Pup, Wilton and our non-exclusive, revolutionary, indented, dirty brown bottom bait boilie sheared the bolt holding back a sledgehammer left. The punch, performing a very representative impression of a horizontal piledriver, (see Carl's nose earlier) slammed straight into McFie's face. McFie fell to earth like an eight-ounce lead on an open bail arm from an up-ended, thirteen-foot rod tip.

We both looked down at the tangle constituting the unconscious figure. "Bugger!" Rambo exclaimed, his Dalek-like light now shining at mine. "Too hard, boy!"

I laughed. "You certainly are, mate!" I gave Rambo a playful poke in the chest. "Here, I hope you were going to split your cut of the Pulimov's Prize fifty-fifty with me."

Rambo chuckled. "Have I *ever* left you out?"

We dragged McFie down to his Jag, frisked him for his car keys, opened the car up, shoved him in the back and waited for him to come round. When he did, I was firmly ensconced in the driver's seat and Rambo was alongside McFie, his Glock aimed at The Bait Baron's bonce.

"I'll take that as a 'no' shall I?" McFie asked, his brain still rooted at the point of his last question.

Rambo ignored it. "Which way to Wilton, arsehole?"

"Head for Hastings," said the groggy, resigned, ex-supermarket manager. "He's safe in an industrial unit on the outskirts of the town."

"He'd better be, or you'll be the one making me a pair of moccasins, out of your own skin!" Rambo warned.

"My cheek bone's broken," McFie whined. "I'm in agony."

Rambo's reply was blunt. "If you've hurt *one* hair on that cat's body, you'll look back on the state you're in now and pray to God you could feel so good again!"

I started up the Jag's engine, giggling to myself. It was great being around Rambo, watching him in action, The Terminator with Tackle. He was indestructible, well almost – the one time he had slipped up, I had been there to save him. What a team!

The journey to Hastings took less than forty minutes and had been conducted in silence until we had required directions. A pained McFie guided us to his small warehouse, the end unit of a row of half a dozen or so identical buildings.

"Is anyone else in here?" Rambo asked as a befuddled McFie fiddled with a large set of keys, trying to find the right one to unlock the reception door. "Because if there is, and if they try anything, just remember you're the one with the gun in the spine!"

McFie never answered. I looked on from the side, leaning against the metal roll up door that gave access to the warehouse part of the building, waiting impatiently for him to open up. At last, after a couple of incorrect choices, the lock was turned with the correct key. We entered into a small corridor where McFie pushed a four-digit code into a beeping alarm system keypad. The beeping stopped.

"Shut the door, Matt, and be ready!" Rambo told me and then in a harsh voice instructed McFie to get the lights on.

A fluorescent tube flickered into life. After the couple of seconds it took my eyes to adjust to the brightness, I gawped in disgust at McFie. He was doing a passable physical impression of Joseph Merrick, the right side of his face swollen well beyond normal proportions, not by Proteus syndrome, but by Rambo's recent left-hander.

"I shouldn't let Chardonnay see you looking like that," I warned him pulling a face. "Or she'll run back to Ian quicker than a margin hooked wildie!"

I doubted McFie fully understood the angling analogy, although he did tenderly touch the side of his ballooning cheek with trembling fingertips. What the hell did I care? I was the one with the gun and, even better, the one who was on Rambo's side!

Rambo moved us on. "The *cat*."

McFie took us along the corridor, up a flight of stairs, where, at the top, was an unlocked door. With his gun rammed in McFie's back, Rambo shoved him through the door, using him as a shield against the unknown, ordering him to get the lights on pronto. McFie pawed the light switch and a typical small company office became bathed in light. What wasn't typical was the sight in the far corner. My jaw did its customary drop-back – heavily weighted hanger/spring return arm – and my eyes popped out, not so much on stalks, more runner bean canes.

"Well, I, never!" I said fully flabbergasted.

"Fuck me!" said Rambo, a huge grin creeping across his face. "What a reception committee!"

I drank in the scene. The reception committee comprised three living entities of which one was a dead cert, unless McFie had a death wish, the second, logical, yet incriminatingly unlikely, and the third, a complete stunner – in more ways than one!

McFie, dully eyeing the personnel with a hangdog, 'the-game's-up' expression plastered over the one moveable side of his face, said nothing. He had known we would eventually meet the unlikely triumvirate from the very second he had regained consciousness. I doubted this knowledge had helped to prepare him to make the actual moment any more comfortable now it had occurred.

Wilton, curled up on a blanket within a caged, wicker cat basket, looked safe and well. The tabby cat's eyes were closed in sleep and he seemed oblivious to the drama unfolding around him – much like he had when Pup had first let me see him. Instinctively I touched my ear where the cat had mauled me after taking exception to my pumping it on the contents of our non-exclusive, revolutionary, indented, dirty brown bottom bait boilie. Despite our chequered relationship (with a *cat*, I ask you) I breathed a sigh of relief at Wilton's not-turned-into-cat-skin-moccasins status. The safe condition of Pup's ace bait tester meant we were nearing, thankfully, the end of a long road – a road, admittedly, leading right back to where we had started. In truth, we weren't advancing anywhere by returning Wilton to Pup, all we would achieve was parity and the right to set foot back in square one.

The square one appertaining to bait that is. Sadly there was the chance Grant might never allow us a square one setting for our overall lives – and nor might the other two complicating components of the reception committee.

On the cheap, nylon carpet, bound, blindfolded and gagged, looking like a bondage website refusenik lay, Carl – unmistakeable due to his shaven head. The sight of his jewellery on bound hands caused me to fleetingly wonder if McFie had kept him captive due to the rising price of gold, forced ever upwards by investors looking for a 'safe haven' in the current economic recession, rather than the consequences of Carl's testimony at the upcoming arson trial.

No.

It was clear why Carl was being kept captive. Why he was lying here on the office floor, instead of being stashed out in the warehouse with the boilies, *was* a mystery. I dismissed the notion the poor fucker couldn't be moved because he was too heavy, due to the gold, like a downed knight of old dressed in armour, and settled on the theory of McFie nailing him to the industrial thickness, chipboard floor with a handful of rusty cut nails in order to taunt him with the sounds of passionate sex. Passionate sex between – if not for our intervention – the returning, ultimate-bait-advert-carp-safely-photographed-on-camera, owner-of-the-boilie-company-on-which-she-fell, McFie, and the final, scandalous member of the reception committee.

Melloney, youngest sister of the Witches of Eastwick, dressed only in stylishly seductive, red lingerie, a pile of hastily shed clothing near her feet, sat on a pseudo black leather computer chair. It was more than obvious why she was here, but her body language and the look on her face told of the recent evaporation of all sexual thoughts – thoughts dashed from her head the minute she had become belatedly aware McFie had company. And what company! If any two people – and I could confidently stake this claim to include all *dead* people from throughout all history – were capable of knocking every last scintilla of lust from her, it was Rambo and I. That and the fact, McFie, her prospective lover for the night, looked like The Elephant Man! Not a great appearance for revving up the hanky-panky lustometer past the red line.

Inwardly grinning, I wondered if Melloney knew about Chardonnay – a no-brainer, of course. Still, I guess any self-respecting Bait Baron needed at least *two* women on the go at any one time!

Rambo strode to the middle of the room, slapping the Glock's barrel into the palm of his hand and theatrically spun full circle. "Well, well, well. What *have* we here?" he asked as he scanned the five sentient creatures, crap office furniture, computer and peripherals in his presence. "Anyone care to explain, or shall I have a guess?"

I was minded of the situation being the culmination to any Hercule Poirot film, where the whole cast are assembled by the dapper, chocolate-gobbling, clandestine-Eddie-Merckx-worshipping, Justine-Henin-stalking Belgian to have their recent labyrinthian movements unpicked in revealing flashbacks, culminating in the most unlikely candidate being declared the murderer – via time travel with a length of black iron heating pipe taken from room 206. 'That is why, Mademoiselle, you saw *two* simultaneous versions of this man and why your radiator was cold on the last day of your stay!'

There were no immediate takers to Rambo's question so he turned his withering gaze on to Melloney. I have to admit she did look very sexy, what with her curvaceous, bootylicious body barely being concealed by her bright red underwear – underwear that stood out so vividly against the pseudo black leather chair. As I regarded her, a whole host of memories came flooding back, as they must have for Rambo, especially seeing as he'd had carnal knowledge of her – a loving knee-trembler around the back of Hamworthy's functional wooden clubhouse during the inaugural *charadee* fish-in.

Once a Witch of Eastwick, always a Witch of Eastwick, I told myself. The three sisters and sexual mayhem were still inextricably entwined – as all three of them were with their disastrously dominant promiscuity gene. I was so glad I had matured enough to put all such nonsense behind me. No, I had! Really! I wasn't looking at her *that* much, nor in *that* way that much.

Rambo's comments were cutting. "The Agent Provocateur outfit's not a good one for cat sitting, Melloney," he informed her. "Wilton's claws will click up on the crotch of those knickers… if they've got any." Melloney's head lowered to the floor and she crossed her legs. "So how long have you been screwing McFie? Banging the brains out of The Bait Baron! I suppose Pup is out fishing tonight, or more likely up to his elbows in fifty kilos of bait mix?"

Melloney's mouth stayed shut – not a scenario likely to have happened had McFie's night-time excursion gone to plan. With a shake of his head, Rambo turned his attention to the body on the floor and undid Carl's gag and blindfolds.

"Peek-a-boo!" he said in a high voice as the blindfold fell from Carl's eyes. "It's Rambo!" Rambo continued untying Carl's limbs until the shaven-headed one was able to struggle to his feet and stiffly dust himself off. As Carl tried to restore his dignity I surveyed his head. One eye was swollen shut, strangely bulging like a frog's and his head was completely smothered in lots of small, round bruises coloured various shades of blue, green, black and red combined with a multitude of cuts. He looked a right mess and had obviously taken a hell of a beating of some kind – and that was ignoring the earlier efforts Rambo had inflicted upon him.

Rambo was unsympathetic to Carl's painful suffering. "Tch! You're losing your touch, Carl. What's a tough guy like you doing allowing himself to get kidnapped, trussed up and smacked about?"

Carl tried to stick up for himself. "Basically, *four* of them, right! Jumped me at home, right! They brought me here."

"What the hell have they been doing to you?" Rambo asked, squinting at Carl's plethora of bruises and cuts.

"Basically, they hung me up in the warehouse, right, and he," Carl glared at McFie with his one good eye, "fired boilies at me with a catty from point blank."

"What size?"

"Twenty-mil."

Rambo winced. "Nasty."

"And they were air-dried!" Carl added.

"Just at your head, Carl?" I asked, trying to picture the inhuman detail of firing a twenty-mil rock hard readymade – I can't imagine they would have used a decent food bait – from a fully stretched catty at one yard's range into someone's head.

"And my goolies," Carl answered dolefully. "My nutsack's the size of a melon."

Not wishing to stretch my imagination into that domain I walked over to Carl. "Let's have a look at your eye. Did one hit it?"

Carl grunted. "Think so."

I gently teased back Carl's upper and lower left eyelids and winced in horror. Instead of an eyeball, a blind, twenty-mil semolina-special stared back at me. "Oh, fuck me!" I cried. "Your fucking eyeball's been squashed behind a fucking boilie!"

"I thought it hurt, right!"

"Fucking right!" I agreed. "Jesus, Carl, you *need* to see a doctor!" I suggested, resisting the childish temptation to grab a marker pen off the desk and draw a temporary iris on to the semolina-special's surface.

"Not yet, right?" Carl limped over to the corner and picked up a 28mm Jumbo Cobra aluminium throwing stick from behind a desk "He was beating me with this as well, right! When I was tied up on the floor."

I had often imagined violence and an aluminium throwing stick being partners in crime – I had been correct!

Rambo was on to Carl's drift. "Don't worry, I've softened him up for you. He's all yours, Carl. We're out of here. Do what you want." Rambo scooped up Wilton's basket, the cat's eyes opening for the first time with the sudden jolt. "Get your clothes, Melloney!" he shouted. "We're going!"

Melloney jumped from the chair and started to pick up her jeans and step into them, apparently more than happy to leave the dead-in-the-water McFie to his hideous fate. Ah, the fickle nature of transitory lust. What a cow!

Rambo stopped her, his face contorted with anger. "I didn't say put them *on*, did I!" he roared. "You're going to show Pup *exactly* how you were waiting for him! Get down the stairs and get into the Jag. Matt! You take her."

"Come on, Melloney," I said softly. "Let's go."

The pair of us pushed past McFie, who, I think it would be fair to say, was bricking it. As I held the door open for Melloney, I looked back to see the latterly boilie-bombarded – bonce and bollocks – stick-battered and one-eyed, Carl, tapping the lethal looking, black powder-coated implement on to the floor a few paces behind the basket-carrying Rambo.

Rambo squared up to McFie and spoke. "*If* you survive tonight, McFie, I never want to hear or see from you again. Understand, boy? *Never*!" And with that advice clearly imparted, Rambo's knee whisked up into McFie's groin with a sickening crunch. McFie promptly repeated his falling down act. Over Rambo's shoulder, Carl, his face wearing a hate distorted grin, moved in to exact his revenge.

"It's a good feeling, Carl!" I shouted. "Believe me, I know!"

For a second, Carl's face clouded with the confusion of my message – it soon passed. By the time all three of us were down the stairs I could hear the muffled thumps and cries of a former Bait Baron getting worked over by a disgruntled former employee with a large bore aluminium throwing stick.

"The violence was all very genre-specific, wasn't it?" I asked, as I cranked the Jag into life. "Do you think Carl could actually manage to kill him with that stick?"

"Yeah," Rambo answered casually from the rear seat. "Provided he can sort out his depth perception."

"And the body?" I was always curious about dead body disposal, having partaken in one.

"He can spod the body out into a lake," Rambo suggested.

"Christ," I remarked as we pulled out of the industrial estate. "That'll take some doing!"

"You didn't see the industrial mincing and blending machines in the warehouse," Rambo replied. It was hard to tell whether he was joking or otherwise.

The Bait Baron's *very* personal spod mix – might be a new edge. Get on it now! Limited supplies only!

Chapter 21

"If you can sign here, Mr Williams, alongside the cross, and you there, Mr Ramsbottom, directly below, the water is yours!"

The slender, clean, nail-perfect finger on the never-seen-a-screwdriver-in-its-life hand belonging to Mr Honey pointed to the appropriate spots. Rambo and I scrawled our monikers across the legal document lovingly prepared – at a horrendous amount per hour, plus VAT, plus contingency fund for something nice for the wife/fit young secretary – by the aforementioned solicitor and Felix's water changed ownership to us. It was a fantastic moment. I shook Rambo's hand and had mine scrunched in return.

"Hamworthy *Fisheries*! The name's right, at last. Congratulations partner!" I enthused.

Rambo gave me one of his playful slaps nearly sending me sailing across Mr Honey's highly polished, antique oak desk and into the large aspidistra behind it. "Too right, boy! Brilliant!" Rambo's chest swelled with pride to quadruple-X size. "My own water. At last! Fantastic!"

"Excellent, gentlemen! Business concluded." Mr Honey stood up from his leather chair, keen to move us along before an expensive item got damaged, and offered out his hand. Compared to Rambo's, his grip felt as limp as the last section of mainline wafting in the breeze after a crack off and as clammy as the Brazilian Rain Forest – you know, the one that won't exist in forty minutes time if you, personally, don't do *something* right now. "If I may be of assistance in any way in the future, please don't hesitate to call." Mr Honey then foolishly shook hands with Rambo, who gave him a real car-crusher of a grip by way of minor recompense for the monstrous bill he would soon be sending the pair of us.

With that very marginal victory over the purveyors of legal advice tucked into our belts, we departed the oak panelled offices of Honey, Honey, Splenda and Sucre of Maidstone – *fully licensed and accredited bandits in all aspects of Law; hideous one-sided terms and conditions apply*. Once outside in the summer sunshine the initial euphoric high faded slightly as I considered the financial consequences of writing my name a few minutes earlier. I swatted them away like a pesky fly. What the hell! It would be all right – so long as a load of members didn't bail out and ask for their 1st deposits back! And who in their right mind would bail out of Hamworthy? I was as safe as houses, but obviously *not* those ones built on UK flood plains or part of the US – pun intended – sub-prime market.

"Cup of tea, boy?" Rambo asked. "Before we head back?"

"Yeah. Why not."

We walked further down the street and Rambo nipped into a newsagent to get a paper. He chose The Times, obviously feeling intellectual – or trying to look it – whilst at the same time making a personal statement in not boosting a certain other broadsheet's sales. A little way further down the street we found a small café and went inside. Rambo insisted I sat at a table making the acquisition of drinks his shout.

"Okay, partner," I said sitting down. "I'll have a Swiss bun as well, seeing as you're buying!"

Rambo rolled his eyes and joined the lengthy queue as I sat and thought, as I am prone to do, when time is on my hands. It had been a week since the night we had left McFie to his beating at the hands of Carl and had driven home to Pup's house in the Jag with both his cat and his woman – forgive my political incorrectness – on the rear seat. On the way back, under intense scrutiny from Rambo, Melloney had confessed to the nature and level of her involvement with McFie. It had been an interesting insight into the workings of her mind – one unfortunately not conducive to liking her.

She had explained that McFie's constant haranguing of Pup to join forces with him, *before* the snatching of Wilton, had lead to Melloney often answering Pup's phone when he was either too busy or too stressed to do so himself. As a consequence a 'dialogue', as she had put it – 'blatant flirting' I would have called it – had grown between them and Melloney had started to become intrigued with the gruff-voiced, self-proclaimed Bait Baron. So intrigued, in fact, that she had arranged a clandestine meeting with him and, on having met him, had opted for the sex-on-the-first-date option – in the opulent interior of the Jag. Melloney admitted she had become Bait Baron besotted and so desperately wanted to keep on having sex with him that at a later secret tryst, she herself had suggested the kidnapping of Wilton. She had hoped this would force Pup into a partnership with The Bait Baron, the desired outcome being a legitimate reason for McFie to be around her on a day-to-day basis – thus making him available for sex on tap. It was she who had explained the moggy's magic bait testing credentials to McFie whilst she rode him on the Jag's front seat. During that pre-orgasmic moment I suspected a smug McFie thought he had so many boats coming in he must have been convinced he was Dover Harbour during peak season!

The blame for Wilton's abduction lay squarely at Melloney's door – *not* mine and my loose-mouthed chat with Pimply Paul! A point I had indignantly pointed out to the forlorn boiliemeister once we had delivered cat and slag – there really is no other word – to his residential boilie factory.

Pup had been delighted to see Wilton again. Not so, Melloney, especially once Rambo had informed him of the night's details and he had set eyes on her outfit – or lack of it. Melloney admitted full and utter culpability, answering the final puzzle when she had revealed it was she who had nicked a kilo of our non-exclusive, revolutionary, indented, dirty brown bottom bait boilie and passed it on to The Bait

Baron who had in turn passed it on to The Carper.

"How *could* you?" Pup had demanded. "After all we've rolled together!"

"Mate, if she can have an affair with you when you were married to her sister, pretty easily," I had commented.

"And a one night stand with *him*," Melloney had said nodding at Rambo.

This had opened a can of worms, which had exploded and wriggled around Pup and Rambo until I had managed to calm them both down.

Melloney had exploded into laughter, her breasts threatening to escape from the flimsy brassiere as her bootylicious body convulsed. We had all looked and she knew it. "You men," she cackled. "You're all right about it when it's coming *your* way, but as soon as it goes someone else's, you can't handle it!" At this point I had unwisely smiled at the truth she was speaking. "I don't know what you're grinning at, Matthew," she had misconstrued. "You were just as infatuated as these two, it just happened to be *Melina* you went with when she was *Rambo's* girlfriend! You're all hypocrites, the lot of you!"

The smile had been wiped off in an instant at her misunderstanding. "I've changed!" I had protested. "I was smiling because, unfortunately, you're right! Right about us all!" I had admitted. "But I have changed! I really have!"

Melloney had licked her red lipstick and fixed me with her gleaming eyes. "Of *course* you have!"

The tone of her voice had grated. "You didn't have to sell our bait *and* Wilton down the river! And whatever you say about us, *none* of us would have done that!" I had shouted, scrambling to the moral high ground. "True, we might have taken the sex, but that would have been all!"

I had been quite pleased with my argument. At least it had shut her up and stopped her questioning the new Mark I Monogamous Matt Williams.

"I think you'd better go, Melloney. I can't trust you with my recipes. Thank God I only ever let you mix up half the ingredients and not all of them," Pup had said.

"If you'd really loved and trusted me you'd have let me mix up all of them," Melloney had retorted.

"Call it a type of pre-nuptial agreement, even if we never were married," Pup had answered. "Now go. And never darken my rolling tables again."

"You'll never get another woman to put up with the smell!" Melloney had bitched as she had turned to go. She had swung back in an instant and stomped back to Pup – no mean feat seeing as she was barefoot. "You're knob," she had stated. "Isn't as wide as your twenty-four-mil foreign pop-up specials. I measured it with your micrometer when you were blindfolded and tied up. I thought you might like to know."

"*You* might like to know, McFie has been two-timing you with some woman called Chardonnay," I had said. "When we jumped him, he initially thought we were mates of her old partner."

"Liar!"

I had given her an exaggerated shrug of my shoulders. "I'm not making it up, Melloney. Go and ask him if you like, but hurry, Carl might kill him before you get the chance!"

And then she had gone. Gone for good.

Pup had been philosophical. "Oh, well. It was a crack while it lasted. There'll be others." I was pretty sure I had stopped my lips silently mouthing the words 'I doubt it'. "I'm pleased she's gone! I'm glad! At least I've got fishing to replace her, thanks to you two." Pup had taken Wilton out of the wicker basket and lifted him out. "And I've got you back, Wilton. That's the best bit!" The tabby cat had started to purr loudly as Pup petted him. "Thanks for getting him back," Pup had said facing us in turn. "I'm sorry I blamed you."

"No worries, Pup, glad I could help,"

"I told you we would!" Rambo had said.

Any animosity between us had gone – our friendship remained afloat despite the rough sea. Square one, regards to bait, had been achieved.

On another positive note, once I had explained what had been going on, Sophie had forgiven me for my DVD moment. Her acceptance might have been something to do with Melloney and Steffi's behaviour making the pair of us look and feel good. We had matured beyond all that sort of nonsense and could now regard it with the contempt it deserved! We had, after all, been there and done it – in the *past*!

"There you go, partner," Rambo said plonking a tea and Swiss bun in front of me. He hadn't mentioned how he and Steffi were getting on or anything concerning the foursome. I hadn't broached the subject – my dislike of my best mate and now business partner's woman was not a subject I was fond of discussing.

"Cheers, partner," I said pouring a couple of tiny containers of milk into the conker brown tea.

I watched the tea lighten from the bottom of the cup as the milk billowed into the vessel. Oddly fascinated, I stared ever more intently and got sucked into a different world. The world of water and a body sinking slowly down through it. Down and down the body went, silently corkscrewing ever deeper – a body wrapped tightly by hundreds of yards of heavy diameter monofilament line and weighted by an old car engine. I saw the grotesque, lifeless face as it went down – down, down, deeper and down.

"The status quo's changed," I said looking up from my tea in astonishment. "The Bait Baron's *dead*! Carl's killed him and buried him at sea!"

"What?" Rambo blurted as he sat on his chair.

I leaned closer to my new business partner "A vision! I've just had a vision! In the tea," I told Rambo's left ear in disbelief.

Rambo's eyes gleamed brightly. Both excitement and worry were etched all over his face. "It's about time! You haven't had one for ages! Anything else?" he asked urgently.

I shook my head to clear its muzziness. I suddenly felt weak and drained – they came when they came and there was *no* controlling them. A cold shiver ran over me. I'd had a few over the years, yet the concept of it was still no less earth-shattering, no easier to comprehend and no easier to accept. I quickly sipped the steaming hot tea. "No. Nothing else," I shuddered.

Rambo let out a low whistle. "I have to say, partner, that's a nasty surprise."

"I might be wrong."

"You've *never* been wrong when it comes to this sort of stuff! I wouldn't *be* here if you were wrong!" Rambo eulogised, attacking his jam doughnut and licking the sugar from his lips.

"Have you ever tried to eat one of them without doing that?" I enquired, Rambo's brow scrunching in lack of understanding. "Without licking your lips."

"Good, God, boy! Doesn't your magpie mind *ever* sit still?" I smiled a very silly little smile. "As I was saying," Rambo said seriously. "A nasty, unexpected surprise."

"I know Carl wasn't capable of turning a blind eye to his beating, but are you saying you didn't think he had it in him to kill?"

Rambo's first statement was tongue in cheek. "I think it's pretty safe to say Carl will be turning a blind eye to *everything* after that boilie hit him!" Rambo swigged his tea, washing the doughnut down. "To be honest, no. I didn't think he could kill him. He might be trying to push the tough guy image, but he's no killer. At least I *thought* he was no killer." Rambo stared out of the window, his eyes unfocused. "It's the witness aspect of it that bothers me, Matt. There's us at the scene, there's Melloney who knows what went on, plus all the other cronies working for the bait firm will be left wondering where the hell the boss has gone." Rambo's voice fell to a disturbed hush. "And we're *badly* implicated this time. It's not like when Michael murdered that woman. He would *never* have been found out if her ghost hadn't found you."

I nodded grimly. "Don't you ever worry about the would-be assassin's associates?" I asked seeing as we were discussing old times.

"It's in the back of my mind all the time, hence the CCTV," Rambo admitted before flicking his eyes crotchward. "It's also why I'm risking a mandatory five-year prison sentence carrying the Glock!" Rambo noted the look of concern on my face. "Don't fret. No one knows it was you who pulled the trigger, apart from me. If they come, they'll be looking for me, not for you."

"Do you ever get the feeling we're entangling ourselves in an ever expanding and intricate web?" I asked, a horrible, suffocating cloud rolling over my shoulder.

Rambo sniffed deeply, his nostrils flaring. "Sometimes. It is starting to get beyond what we could possibly hope to control, especially now stupid Carl has done this. I was only trying to put the frighteners on McFie when I said to him, '*if* you survive'. All the stuff in the car was to try and wind Melloney up! It was all a bit of a joke. I never in a million years thought Carl would go that far!"

"Maybe he did it to impress you, because he thought you'd expect him to do it."

"Possibly," Rambo conceded. "I'm kicking myself at the thought of it."

"What if it all comes out into the open and Grant finds out!" I whined.

Rambo puffed his cheeks in something approaching despair. I had never seen him so flat. "I can't see how it won't come out. Let's hope Carl has a cunning plan to get away with it *and* can keep it under wraps for good."

I scoffed at Rambo's suggestion. "Carl! Cunning plan! You *must* be joking! He's got less cunning about him than the weight he used to sink McFie's body!" The Swiss bun was rapidly turning to ashes in my mouth. "We should be on a high having got our new water, yet all I can see is big trouble brewing!" I quietly, but vociferously complained – we were in the public domain after all.

"Just relax, boy," Rambo suggested, at last getting a grip on himself. "Let's look on the positives. As you've said no one knows *that* much, not even Grant, and *we* didn't kill McFie."

"No! We just roughed him up and delivered him to Carl so *he* could kill him!" This was awful! My brain rattled out all the permutations of what we had done, what other people had done, how much of it might become common knowledge, how much Grant could rake out into the open – and gave up. The overall conclusion, however, wasn't in dispute. "We're on a fucking knife edge, here!" I proclaimed. "Our story's on the verge of coming out! It's bloody disastrous! It's global fucking meltdown!"

Rambo, adding to my disconcertion, nodded his agreement. "Drink up! Let's go to our new water! We can have a walk round and a think. We can discuss things better in private."

We left the café and strode quickly in silence to the street where Rambo's van was parked. My head reeled at all the possibilities as we dodged the aimless, meandering, window-shopping pedestrians on the busy streets. Once in the van and on our way I flicked through Rambo's newspaper to try and steady my nerves by taking my mind off all my perceived problems. It didn't work.

"Oh fuck! They've found The Carper!" I cried.

Rambo pulled the van over as soon as he could – we had gone about four hundred yards! We both stared at the headline a few pages in from the front. 'Angler in horrific death on MoD range', it stated, a panoramic photo of the range beneath it.

"Read it out," Rambo instructed.

"Okay," I said, my heart banging on my chest like a police hit squad on the front door of a drug den. "'Police forensic experts were called to an MoD live fire range after a body was discovered within its boundaries. The remains were found close to the large lake within the range along with a substantial amount of fishing tackle. Brigadier Simon Watson-Smythe, the commanding officer of the Lydd MoD range, told how the body had been discovered yesterday during a daytime exercise. The, as yet, unnamed angler had constructed a hidden den in what is a heavily restricted area, and is believed to have been fishing undetected, prior to the incident, for some considerable time. First indications report the angler was killed by heavy machine gun fire from a recent night-time exercise. Brigadier Watson-Smythe said in a press release, 'The unfortunate death of this man highlights the very dangerous nature of live fire MoD ranges. Trespass on MoD grounds is inherently dangerous and illegal. Therefore, I would like to take this opportunity to stress to the public in general, the need for absolute compliance with all warning signs and not to cross any perimeter fencing. It appears the individual in question went to great lengths to conceal himself and was actively fishing on the lake for considerable amounts of time. Sadly, the folly of his actions, and their terrible consequences, have only come to light now it is too late.' The Brigadier also told of the implementation of increased security measures around the Lydd range and of the need for a complete review of all security measures on all MoD ranges. Later developments, in an attempt to help identify the man in question, saw police contacting local angling clubs, requesting any additional information from their members to further aid with enquiries'."

"Huh! What did I tell you?" Rambo sneered. "Horse in the lower field, slam the stable door shut! Notice they didn't say 'the night-time exercise a week earlier'! Wouldn't look too clever would it? An obliterated body under their noses for all that time!"

"Is this good or bad?" I asked. I was so confused I had no idea.

"It was inevitable, boy. *If* they decided not to cover it up. Someone high up decided they didn't need to, probably because they, the army, are completely blameless. Anyone reading that would think, what an idiot!"

"Or what a hardcore hero."

Rambo tilted his head. "Without knowing the full story of The Seventy, my money would be on idiot. I'd say it was good because it looks like they see it as a straightforward accident, albeit self-inflicted. Its bad because it's more meat for Grant to get his teeth into."

My body sagged in the van's passenger seat. "Who would we have to kill to be totally safe?" I asked.

Rambo laughed. "Grant, Carl, Melloney, Pup, Wilton, all The Bait Baron's crew, The Eye, all the would-be assassin's crew…"

"Realistically."

"The first three would put a pretty good lid on it, boy, but you're talking about so many imponderables, we might not need to…"

My mobile rang. I looked at the display screen. "Private number," I informed Rambo. "Hello."

The voice I had been dreading spoke. "Ya! Hi, Matt. Grant Gibbs. Have you read the news on The Carper… or did you know before?"

Always niggling away. "We've only just read it in the paper."

"Ya, sure!" Grant's voice sounded as if he was unconvinced. "Matt. Your book," he went on. "I still haven't received it. I don't know whether you've sent it or not got round to it, just remember, we had an agreement."

"What if I've changed my mind?" I said trying to control the anger rising up inside me. "What you gave us on The Bait Baron hasn't really helped."

"How is The Bait Baron? Have you heard from Carl? And what about the cat?" the unflustered, educated voice enquired, its mocking tone rising with each question.

"Nothing yet," I stonewalled.

"Matthew, Matthew, why are you being *so* difficult?"

"Probably because I don't trust you and don't know what game you're playing. I can't figure why you're so interested in us," I said. The time for bluffing seemed over. Grant wasn't going to let go. Confrontation was inevitable.

"Stories! Ya! I like good stories," the educated voice informed me casually. "I think, no, I *know*, Matthew, you have a good story and you're trying to hide it from me. I don't know *why* you're hiding it or what you're afraid of."

"I'm the shy retiring type," I said through course-grain gritted teeth.

"Matthew, tell me how Michael Brown died in such odd circumstances and why he left you, of all people, a syndicate freshman, the Hamworthy Fisheries estate." A rush of whistling wind howled through my brain – the obligatory tumbleweed came soon after. "We need to talk, Matthew, that's all. If I'm right about you and Rambo, and I'm convinced I am, we might be able to do something together that will be of benefit to both of us."

I put my hand across the phone's speaker and spoke to Rambo, relaying Grant's words.

Rambo's face did the black clouds of thunder thing. "Tell him we'll meet him at the new water. Tell him to come alone."